MY SECRET LIFE
BOOKS SEVEN & EIGHT

This edition published 1996 by
Wordsworth Editions Limited
Cumberland House, Crib Street
Ware, Hertfordshire SG12 9ET

ISBN 1 85326 627 2

Printed and bound in Great Britain by
Mackays of Chatham plc, Chatham, Kent

CONTENTS

CHAPTER I

Gertrude's history continued. — Lusts roused. — The sister's confidences. — The wounded Captain. — Gertrude's nursing. — Antonio's greed. — Margaretta's moral views. — The Captain's lust. — The price of the watch. — Gertrude reckless. — The Captain's exhibition. — Success by the bedside. — Margaretta with child. — Gertrude and Captain at Paris. — Her disappointment. — Her love for me. — Our secret meetings. — The Captain's sodomitic wishes. — They separate. — She marries. — His death. — Her fine qualities. — Of my treachery.

Next day the battle of Solferino was fought. Every hotel and house in the town was filled with the wounded French, most of the Austrians were taken elsewhere. Every body was compelled to help the wounded. — Gertrude, a strong, big woman, was glad to get an employment at the largest hotel, in which most of the French officers wounded were placed. — Her future pseudo husband with a wounded leg was among them; and it fell to her lot to attend to him in some degree when his soldier servant was not there.

So as to make room for worse cases (the hospital headquarters were in the hotel), the Captain, like others, was moved to a private house. He had money, he liked her attention to him, and for money she went to attend him there. One day, when better, he threw his arms round her, kissed her, and said he wished she was his wife. Soon after he let his clothes be so disarranged that she saw his cock standing stiff as he lay, and either was, or shammed being, asleep. — She looked at his cock attentively and felt a liking for him. The cock evoked her lust, and she went to her room and frigged herself.

Both sisters never mentioned to any person the shagging the soldiers had given them, but it had a very stimulating effect on both. — Margaretta, it seems, had never referred to Gertrude's escapade with her lover at Strasbourg, nor talked about marriage pleasures, nor seemingly, as I made out in my many conversations with Gertrude, done or said anything to make Gertrude long for a cock to be put up her. She wanted evidently to stop sexual aspirations, to keep her steady, and get her married as soon as possible. — Gertrude told me that she herself was late in her monthlies coming on, and had no great longings for a male, and had not frigged herself till seventeen or eighteen years old. — She had spent with her lover at Strasbourg, and she pined after him, but it was for him rather than for fucking.

An Italian was at this time paying attentions to Gertrude, of what are called an honorable sort. But she never thought of his fucking her, and no man had laid hands on her ankles even, still less touched her quim, since her Strasbourg lover, till the soldiers did. — That shock to her nervous system set her and her sister eternally talking about fucking. The very night of the affair, tho half dead with fright and fatigue, the excitement and irritation of her cunt and brain was such that she frigged herself.

There was such difficulty in getting accommodations in the overcrowded town, which they could pay for, that the whole family slept on the floor in one room. Her brain would not let her sleep, fucking was on her brain. The old man and children alone slept soundly, she laid as if asleep, in hopes Antonio would stroke her sister. — Margaretta had told her that she also felt need to be fucked again. — Antonio had been out all next day to see about his affairs, the two women talked about fucking all day, and about the soldiers' pricks and spunk. They compared their experiences, and at last frigged themselves before each other. — Margaretta told Gertrude what sort of prick Antonio had, and how often he fucked, and Gertrude told Margaretta, how *her* lover first got into her. There was at last complete confidences about sexual matters between them. — Lewedness had taken possession of them, and it's not to be wondered at.

The next night all huddled together, Margaretta let Antonio shag her. — She knew Gertrude close by was feigning to sleep, for the two women had so arranged it between themselves. — Antonio had hesitated for fear Gertrude should awake. — "Hush — no" — he said. But his wife, his cock in her hand, roused it up till he eased it in her. — Gertrude frigged herself — Margaretta imagined to herself a soldier doing it to her whilst Antonio operated. Gertrude's masturbations were accompanied by similar thoughts, about the many cocks which had plugged her cunt. — Working and attending to the wounded, then separated the two much after that night, but they talked of the soldiers whenever they met. Some time after, Margaretta was ashamed of having let Gertrude know about her husband's fuckings. — Gertrude ceased to frig herself much, but now looked on men with different eyes, and desired to have one at her cunt, instead of her fingers. She wished she was married, for Margaretta had disclosed everything, even to the size and look of her husband's cock — the reserve which Margaretta formerly had maintained on such topics, for fear of encouraging lewedness in her sister, was gone for ever.

The sight of the Captain's doodle stimulated Gertrude's want of a male. — Soon he kissed her again, she kissed him, and a circumstance brought things to a crisis about two months after the battle. The Captain could then move about with crutches in his room, but could not get his trowsers on.

Antonio's house, barns, and stores were burnt, and he was nearly ruined, like hundreds of other peasant farmers. He had some money, but was not spending it. The Austrian officers had promised to pay for the things they had taken, and there was compensation to come — but they could not be realizable till the end of the war. — He and his wife worked in all sorts of ways to get money. His object was to get back to his farm, and make the place habitable again. A good opportunity then offered, but money was needed, and then her sister reminded Gertrude of her watch, chain, and money. — She agreed to sell it and lend the proceeds privately to Margaretta, but how to sell it was the difficulty. They went to a Jew, who offered something ridiculously small, and told them he knew that they had stolen it, and would tell the police. — "Ask the Captain to sell it — or buy it of you" — said Margaretta. "He is fond of you."

Another difficulty arose. What would Antonio think about Gertrude having the money? — "Say the Captain gave it you for nursing him," said Margaretta. — "No," said Gertrude, — "Antonio will think I've been letting him do it to me." — "What if he does?" — said the other. — Now she had never told her husband that her sister Gertrude had been poked by her lover at Strasbourg, and sent quietly to them on account of *that*; having a fear perhaps that, if he knew it, he might fancy a poke in the same hole himself. — Gertrude refused, but the sister became so pressing, said how kind they had been to *her*, what a help it would be to them *all* if Antonio could only get back and pay for roofing their cottage (the walls were standing) and they could start again, that she prevailed on Gertrude to try to sell it to him.

Gertrude asked the Captain if he would sell the things for her. — "Mon Dieu," said he, "they are worth 1500 francs." — She was staggered — thinking them not worth a quarter of the money. — The Jew had offered her 100 francs. — Who gave it her? — Her lover before he joined his regiment. — The Captain at once said she was lying. — "He must have been a gentleman, and well off then, for there are armorial bearings on it — and the watch is of German make — why the watch alone would have bought your lover off the conscription." — She stuck to it that it was all true. — "La, la, la, I see it. — Your lover kept you and gave you it — now wasn't you his mistress?" — in vain she denied it. — "You come and live with me," said he. — "We'll go to Paris, and be so happy" — and then he began to talk baudy — which he had never done before.

She in tears and agitation went to her sister and told her all. — Said the sister, who did not seem now to care about anything so long as they got the money to enable them to go back to the farm, — "Why not? you can't do better." — "Then I shan't marry Pietro." — "Well, he's only a little farmer — and you'll have as much money in a week with the Captain as Pietro will give you in a year." — Gertrude revolted at this advice, the sisters had a row, and parted, Margaretta finishing by saying that Pietro could not marry till his father died, which might be years hence, and that if Gertrude liked to wait years for her fucking, she might — and more fool she.

But it was such a fortune to them just then, those 1500 francs or even half that sum, that her sister was at her about it soon again nearly every day. — Once she said she would tell her husband if she did not get the money. — Then Gertrude said she would tell *him* all about the soldiers having tailed his wife. But it never was told him, they were both too wise for that.

She determined not to accept the Captain's offer, and for a week resisted. The leg of the Captain got better, and he was incessantly worrying her to be his mistress. He would take her thro Italy and give her no end of pleasures. At last he said, if she would sleep with him one night only he would give her half his estimate of the value, and the other half for a second night. — She resented it with affectation of modesty, but the offer upset her very much. — The offer of sleeping with her made her long for the male, she told me frankly.

There had been another wounded officer in the house. The mistress with an old servant attended to him, and in fact all three helped both of the two wounded men. — There was only opportunity of a brief kind for the Captain to tail Gertrude in the day, for the House Lady was, or affected to be, prudish, and said that Gertrude might not to be assisting the Captain alone, and was constantly in the room with her. The other officer then left, sufficiently cured. — The mistress' husband was out all day, and their one servant was also out one day — the Captain was moving about the room with crutches, but had no trowsers on, and a great dressing gown covered him.

Gertrude was with him, and he renewed his offer of money. — She had a lewedness on her that day, she supposed, her cunt was yearning for copulation, and his talk put the soldiers into her head. He caught hold of her as she passed him, — he was sitting at the edge of the bed — and kissed her, held her tight, and talked downright baudiness. She boxed his ears, and then he talked worse. His crutches slipped down on to the floor as he tried to get his hand up her clothes. — She struggled, but was frightened to make a noise, as he touched her cunt. (Ah, those male fingers, how few women can say nay when they have rubbed the clitoris for a minute.) He opened his dressing gown and pulled up her clothes, his cock was stiff, but he could not achieve his end, for he could not move excepting on to the bed without assistance. — She was dying for a fuck, but got away from him. — Then he sat at the edge of the bed, holding his cock, began to cry, asked her to pity him, and said he would buy the watch and chain at once if she would. — She refused still, but helped him on to the bed. When there, he got his arms tightly round her, and pulled her up on to it. (She did not need much pulling for she wanted it badly) then freely she opened her thighs and let him fuck her. — I'll bet there was lots of spunk on her thighs when she got off that bed.

Thus she tasted cock again, was twenty-one years of age, big, healthy, and needed fucking, and she laughed when she told me that as soon as he had finished she went down stairs, saw the landlady as a blind, and then quickly went back to him, and when he begged her to go to him, she went without demur. He fucked her that and the following day as much as he could, and less than she wanted. She helped him with his wounded leg on to her. "I didn't care," — she said — "I was longing for him to begin again as soon as he'd finished, tho I didn't tell him sò, but made him beg and pray me a little." — Then the old servant with whom Gertrude worked was away one night, and Gertrude went to the Captain's room and slept with him, risking the landlady catching her. It was her first, full, naked, flesh pleasure. — He kept his promise and gave her 1000 francs, and afterwards 500 francs more, which sum he actually sold the things for. She didn't tell her sister what had taken place till the Captain was well enough to move off. Then she lent her brother-in-law the money, saying that her intended husband had given it to her.

Margaretta then, in excess of gratitude, told her in confidence that she was in family way by one of the soldiers. That she felt sure of it at the time, from some sensations *she* experienced when she spent with him. — She had denied before that she had had pleasure. It was not fancy, and that night she was anxious to get Antonio to do it to her, so that when the child came there might be no doubt about parentage. (— An old dodge this, I have had women who pláyed that game.) — "If ever you tell your husband anything about me and the soldiers, I'll tell him the child not his," — said Gertrude — Margaretta said she should not be such a fool. Soon after Gertrude and the Captain left.

She was happy enough with him, tho disappointed that he had not married her, till he took to drinking. He always insisted that she had had a rich lover who gave her the watch, or that she had stolen it. — That he said once or twice when they had words. — One night, in bed, they had had friends and were jolly and randy, she was fool enough, under a pledge of secrecy, to tell him the facts about the soldiers. It astonished him, and he always was for a time talking about it to her. — Then, when drunk, she was sure he had told one at least of their friends. They had had frequent rows about it, and she had threatened him that if ever he told it to a man and she knew it, that she would let *that* man have her. — That occurred a few months before I knew them. — She had asked him if he had told *me*. He denied it, but confessed he had told that he had heard of a woman having been ravished by soldiers. — That was nothing, he said, in war. — The French soldiers often did it. He had heard of cases where they had both fucked, and buggered as well, a mother, and a whole family of girls before their mother's eyes. — It was fair in war, some thought.

This history, not a word of which I disbelieve, was not of course told me in the consecutive way I have narrated it — I never knew a woman who would or could tell straight off, intelligibly, all about her first fucking, or any fucking affair. First the broad facts were told me, then the little incidents as I questioned her from time to time. It was first told me on the Sunday, when I stayed the two days and nights in his absence, and we lay naked in each other's arms, kissing and feeling and fucking, and talking over this story, till I knew it by heart. Many a time after, when we met, I questioned her and stirred up our lust by talking over the incidents.

Afterwards, she told me about her first poking by her lover (an ordinary commonplace affair) and all her feelings and thoughts about copulation. — She would tell me what passed thro her mind when I was poking her, for she was frank and open, and I soon reasoned her out of the idea of there being any shame or disgrace in our voluptuous pleasures, or in talking about them, or disclosing frankly what we thought, however lascivious it might be. — I came to the conclusion that she had not been a woman of ardent temperament until she was about twenty — I think I have known that to be the case with some women of high susceptibility, who only became voluptuous when full grown, and their passions were fully evoked by the male. — But women are so cunning, so taught early to hide all their thoughts and feelings about sexual affairs, that I may have been wrong in the opinion I formed. They are so damned cunning about their cunts, and their prick hunger — are women.

My liaison lasted with her many months, during which time I was tolerably faithful to her when at Paris. — Not when away, for I had Amelia German and others. The difficulty of getting at her gave a zest to my pleasures. I could not often call when he was out, for it might have got to his ears through the concierge. The difficulty with her servant was more easily got over, for I arranged to go to her when the servant was out, but the concierge, who watched every one who went in the house, might at any time have told the Captain that I was a frequent visitor. To have attempted to tip him might have put him on the scent. — I was living at a hotel, and she used to come to my room in the day time, — stop an hour, get her cunt basted, and go. — When I thought it would be remarked — I moved to another floor and part of the hotel, on pretext of not liking the room — and so had a different set of servants.

Then I changed my hotel to avoid suspicion, and at length took lodgings where they were not particular. There we used to go to bed and enjoy ourselves fully, two or three times a week. — I liked her embraces very much and used to love looking at her cunt, which was remarkably small and pretty and had the crisp close, curly hair on it I so much admire — her breasts were large but wonderfully firm, and sucking her nipples would make her randy in no time. — She could make herself lewed by pressing or playing with her own nipples — she once told me. — We are many of us strange in our ways of rousing our lusts, and I used to lay kissing and sucking them, and rubbing my hand open flat over the whole of her cunt with my finger just up it — pressing and rubbing hard the clitoris with the palm. Then she would tell me anything, everything, answer every question of detail of her military fucking I could suggest, and bring to her mind incidents she had not mentioned.

She grew fond of me and begged me to keep her. She had never much liked her man. — The money, her sister's advice, and her own lust, she admitted, had made her let him have her. — Tho he was very kind, she didn't like his habits, and his drunkenness made him at times a beast. When he was drunk, he used to fart all night to an extent that disgusted her, and she used to leave the bed and lay on the sofa. — He would not marry her, which he had solemnly promised to do — and he now wanted to sodomize her — which she resisted. — Of course I had only her word for this — I wanted to go back to England and could not keep her. — We had a scene. — She did not upbraid me, nor say anything offensive — she only wept bitterly at her loving me without return. — Then she said she would keep with him, if I would only go and see her once a month. — That was impossible. — Then she declared she would go home to her parents.

I went to England, and soon longed for her so that in a month I went back, and for a fortnight or so we had a jolly time. She wrote to me on my return to England as she had promised. — From her, and from him afterwards, I learned the result. She left him. He behaved very handsomely to her for a Frenchman, and she went home to her father. — Two or three years after that she married, or so he told me. — His drunkenness ended in his losing his appointment, but he was a man of some property, went to live near his relatives at Chalons, and I lost sight of him.

To omit nothing. — She told me that her sister's child had blue eyes and light hair — As Antonio, *his* family, and Margaretta and *her* family, were all dark eyed and haired, this caused astonishment. — Only the two sisters knew that it was German sperm which had caused that. — Antonio prospered, but Gertrude could not get the money back she had lent him. — She wrote by my advice to her sister, saying she would, unless she were paid, tell how the child came to have blue eyes. That brought a return threat, — but it also brought some of the money and promise of the remainder. — Gertrude whose monthlies were, I think, regular, and who never had an ailment of any sort, did not get in the family way by any of the pricks she had up her, including mine.

So ended my acquaintance with one of the most charming women I ever had. — One beautiful when dressed and beautiful in bed, with a lovely cunt, and who was a lovely fuckster. — She was a careful manager, a good cook, fond of her home, and had every quality a woman needs to make a home happy. — I doubt most women's words on fucking subjects, for when a woman has had two or three men — a fresh bit of meat up her cunt, put in on the sly, and with or without the chance of a present, is a treat few can refuse themselves. — A knowledge that another prick has rubbed up her lends an additional charm to and fills a woman's impressible mind with voluptuous images and sensuous delight and adds to the pleasure when the regular legitimate prick is working its way. I firmly believed that I knew of every male Gertrude had had up to that time.

There was one drawback, — I never could bear to be shaking hands with him, when I knew I was tailing his woman behind his back, it was treachery. I felt it then, and do so still. I have not always felt so in similar cases (why in some and not in others I know not. This is a plain narrative of facts, not a psychological analysis.)

CHAPTER II

At Aldershot. — The postage stamp. — The Major's mistress. — The Railway carriage. — Carnal hints. — Carnal practice. — A pretty foot. — At the garters. — Head near tail. — A seductive priapus. — Upon the floor. — Upon the seat. — After dinner. — The Major's tool. — The lady's vulva. — A screaming gamahuche. — Good bye. — Madeline the milliner. — My amatory career. — The sexual law. — The Crystal Palace. — After the dinner. — A brooch and garters. — A thigh recipient. — Overflowing testicles.

In the month of **** I had been at Aldershot to visit a friend. He came back with me to the railway station and left me there, the train to London had not arrived. — When it did, and just as I was about to enter a carriage, a tall, dark-eyed, handsome, and elegantly dressed young woman came up in haste and asked for a postage stamp of the guard. He said he could not get one, there was no time to go to the station master. The train was a quarter of an hour behind time. "Oh! do, pray, it's most important," said she. — "I'll put it in the box Ma'am without a stamp." — "Oh-no." — At the instant I pulled out my pocket book and took out a stamp. "Here's one, give me the letter." She handed it to me, and I put on the stamp. "Wait, guard, a second only," — and I rushed to the station master who just then appeared, and gave it him, turned back, saw the lady looking anxiously out of a first class carriage, jumped in to it with her, winking at the guard, who locked the door, and almost before I was seated, the train went off. It was an express to Waterloo.

The lady said she was deeply indebted to me and explained, as if in apology, why it was so important the letter should go off that night. Of course we got into conversation, and confidence begat confidence. — She had been to see Major **** of the ***** regiment by arrangement, and on arriving there found he had gone away. A telegram had sent him off to his mother who was dangerously ill — "Here is his letter," said she, and I read it. It was in very affectionate terms, and signed — "John."

Then I found out, tho she did not admit it in those words, that the Major kept her — I am too old a bird to believe all a woman tells me, but her tale seemed probable. Not that she volunteered much, but in talking it all came out; and I in return let her know something about myself, and the reason of my being at the camp.

Gradually I ascertained that she had not seen the Major for a fortnight. His regiment had moved from ***** to Aldershot recently, and whilst arranging for moving, it was useless for her to have visited him. He liked all to be quiet when she went there, he objected to his brother officers knowing too much about her, and he did not know where his quarters for a night would be, and so it was impossible for him to get to town to her. — All was I knew quite in the order of things, when a regiment was changing quarters. It taught me at the same time that this fine young creature, who didn't look more than three and twenty, must have been without a prick for a fortnight, unless she had had one that did not belong to the Major; and therefore must want that article badly, unless she had frigged herself vigorously or been licked by her maid, if she had a faithful fanatic at such amusements. — But I did not reason with myself much on the detail. — A fortnight without a lover, was enough to make me know she then must want a poke. I came to that conclusion before I had been in the carriage ten minutes.

The sensual fire which always seems smoldering in my balls then began to burn brightly. I had sat opposite to her, looking at her; now I moved to her side, saying that I didn't like the wind in my face. Leaning on the arm which divided the seats, our faces were now closer together, and our breaths mingled. She had turned towards me, as I had towards her. But there was no desire in her eyes. — They were a dark pair, bright, but quiet looking. — I noticed that she was thin, had but slight signs of breasts and not much of backside. — Those two exquisite parts of a woman that I love to see full and round, and feel solid and smooth. She didn't seem my sort at all in form, but her face was lovely. Then I noticed that her foot looked thin and narrow, tho not very small, and was in a natty boot, and she had a little hand. Altogether she seemed a sweet and pleasing variety of the sex, and as I thought of her part by part, my cock swelled slightly.

"You miss the Major — you expected a husband and must remain a widow," — said I, delicately feeling my way — "I wanted to see him of course." — "Of course, and it's hard to be disappointed as you meant to stop all night." — "Yes, and had brought my things, but only to stop two days," — and she pointed to a small valise, which had been put on the netting above us. — "It's only a change, for he expected to come back to London with me." — "To where?" said I. — Smiling, she replied, "To our house." — "Let me go to the house with you, he won't be there." — "Oh, I dare not, what a proposal." — But I saw a voluptuous smile in her face. "Let's make this a house" — I was getting warmer and warmer. — "What a house," said she, turning her eyes away, and I saw she understood me. — "A railway carriage isn't much like a house." — "Or a bed, but I've used one as both before now." She laughed heartily. — (Neither sleeping cars, nor any convenience for night travelling then existed on any railway in England.)

She turned the conversation to theatres, but soon I got it to the amatory tone again — asked what she'd do sleeping alone, and got the usual evasive replies which a woman knows how to give when she doesn't want you to see that she understands you. But all my questions and suggestions were to the bed and male society, for I know the subject heats a cunt that has been once fucked. — I played with her hand and buttoned her glove. — She let me do all that. — Then risking it, as lewed intentions made me bolder, "You must give me a kiss for my postage stamp." — "No thank you, not for a penny." — "You'd have given me fifty sooner than have lost the post." — "That I would," and she laughed. — "Then I'll have them now," and putting my hand round her, I pulled her to me and kissed her half a dozen times; there was but little difficulty in doing it. — "Now you kiss one of the fifty." — "No thank you." — Then I asked her to dine with me. As she wasn't expected home, there would be no dinner there. — No, but she should get some tea and make it do.

I got as close to her as the arm between the seats (a fixture) allowed. — My leg met hers, and she didn't move it away. Carelessly I laid my hand on her knee, and, pinching up a bit of the silk dress, admired it. — A minute after. — "You garter below knee," I said, determined to see how far I could go, for three quarters of an hour would take us to London, and there was no time to lose. — "That I don't, I garter above knee, how rude you are." — "My God! I feel rude, and can scarcely sit still," — and, again taking the seat opposite to her, praised her foot and boot, and asked who her bootmaker was. — "I shan't tell you." — "Well, let me look at your foot, it's a slim and pretty one." — Up she put it on the seat by the side of me. — I felt it, pinched the ankle, and as she didn't flinch, rapidly ran my hand up to her knee, felt the garter, and just the flesh beyond, before she put her foot down.

She was angry, I was taking a mean advantage — I apologized, I could not help it. — "Your beauty has put me in such a state of desire that I'm in actual pain for want of you — how smooth your flesh is — and you do, I find, garter above knee" — and much more. To all she made no reply, but kept first looking out of the window, then at me, and so on.

Again I asked her to dine with me — would she give me her address. — "I won't, I dare not. — It would do you no good, and it might do me harm."

There was something in her manner which for the moment kept me at a distance from her. — But soon I went on quietly again, talking of the officers in camp who had their mistresses there, and told of one who made such a noise when with his lady, — "Embracing her in bed, you know," — (I perceived that she knew well what I meant) that several heard him outside the hut, and chaffed him about it at mess. — Something of that sort had been told me, and I exaggerated it, and at intervals I felt my ballocks outside my trowsers, looking her in the face, till she turned her head to the window and smiled at my remarks. I knew that she guessed the condition of my pego, that some of her smile was at that, and felt sure that lust was stirred in her. Now every second she looked at me, and then out of the window, then at me again, and I saw in her eyes voluptuous wants.

Then I seated myself again by her side. I soon clutched her to me and kissed her and said I was madly in love with her. — "It's your fault — my God, what a state you've put me in! — Show me your lovely foot again." — Coquettishly she put one foot on the opposite seat, I stooped, and had my hands on her thighs in a second. She crossed them catching my hand between them, but it was embedded in the hair. — I had not only broken ice but gone clean thro it, and went on trying to force my hand further. "My darling, let me feel your cunt, only for a minute, let me feel it, just feel it, and I'll take away my hand."

"You shan't, I'll get out at the next station — Oho — ho — you — shan't" — she cried as I threw myself on my knees, lifted her petticoats, and got my face on her thighs. Tho she resisted, my lust now unbridled made me strong. — Violently I got her thighs apart, my head between them, my nose on her motte, my lips near her clitoris. I could not get my mouth lower, but smelt the stimulating smell of a nice cunt that was yearning for a fuck — I am sure that the cuntal aroma in the sweetest women, intensifies, gets ranker even, when want of the male is on her. I cried, "I can smell your cunt, it's delicious, open your thighs, let me kiss it, do, love." I tried to pull her forward, but did not succeed, but I kept my head on her thighs and motte for some minutes, feeling round her buttocks, talking lewedness under her petticoats, till she ceased striving against me.

My head still where it was, I pulled out my prick, and rubbed it hard against her calf. "What am I rubbing against your leg? — Oh, let me have you." — "Get up, get up now — don't be foolish — Oh! if the guard should come. — I'll call out for the guard."

Up I got recklessly lewed, and sat down; my prick standing up stiff in front of her. Her eyes were humid and she stared hard at me. — "Oh, take care, here we are at the station." The train just then slackened pace, and seemed as if going to stop. "Oh! how you frightened me, suppose it had stopped. — What should I have done? — how foolish you are." — "I'll put it bye if you'll feel it, — feel it," said I. — Taking her gloved hand, I put it round it. How smooth the kid felt to my sensitive rammer.

Soon her glove was off and she was feeling it with her naked hand; whilst my fingers were rubbing between the lips of her cunt, and how moist it was— I pulled her to me and kissed her. "Let me have you, let us fuck, love." — "I won't, how can you talk so, we can't here. — Now leave me alone. — Oho — don't — do leave off. — We shall be seen." — We whisked past a station. "Oh, if my husband knew, I should be ruined for life. — Oh — I *will* dine with you then, and you *shall* after dinner. — I can't take you home, I daren't tell you where I live. — Oh! — I *will* after dinner — oh — now," — and her backside and thighs moved with that uneasy yet voluptuous movement, that restless, wriggling of belly, buttocks, and cunt that a woman can't help giving when a man is frigging her and the luscious sensation of complete lewedness, and the want of fucking, are coursing through her body.

I thought she might give me the slip at the station, and my chance would be lost. — I saw victory before me now and frigged on. — "We'll fuck now, love, all's safe here." I rose up standing before her, my prick almost touching her face, as she sat with her eyes fixed on it, whilst I begged her. — "I won't, — I can't lie down on the floor." — "Take off your bonnet then and sit where you are." She did. — I put cushion after cushion on the floor, to bring myself to a convenient height, then, kneeling down, I opened her thighs, threw up her petticoats, and, gently pulling her forward till her cunt was well away from the edge of the seat, and she was leaning back, I inserted my prick. Altho the angle at which it stood, and that of her cunt was not quite favorable, it glided up deliciously and plugged her to my balls. — Then, putting my arms under her thighs, I fucked her. — We looked in each other's faces till our eyes closed in the swooning pleasure of the crisis, my prick gushed out its sperm, her cunt tightened, gripped, and liquefied, in the blissful spasms of spending, and mingling our sexual juices.

Recovering ourselves, she gave no signs of desire to uncouple. Looking speechless in each other's face (How I longed to know what she was thinking of), we held together. She was thin, but neither skinny nor bony; her backside not being great nor her cunt fat lipped; it was well on to me and kept my prick wonderfully up her, spite of the movement of the train. (Some thin women, I have since noticed, can.) In the lovely warmth and embrocating moisture of her cunt, I lingered long; but at last withdrew my softened priapus from the Paphian temple. Putting my hand under it as I did so to receive it, a little flood of spendings rolled out after my prick left her. Telling her to be quiet, I got out my pocket handkerchief and put it to her cunt, which she wiped with it. Then I wiped my hand. "Ah, it's nasty," — said she. — "Nonsense, my love, neither prick nor cunt nor spunk are nasty at any time." — Then we sat and talked. — "It was awfully quickly over." — "It was — where is my bonnet?"

"That's the consequences of asking for a postage stamp," said she. — "Lucky for me," I replied — We then talked about the Major ****. "Oh don't mention him, poor fellow, he'd shoot me and himself too, if he knew what we have done. — I've never before been unfaithful." — "But he won't, my dear. — Let me feel it." — "No, don't, it's so wet still," — but I did, and was feeling it, and she my prick, and just then the train went slower and then stopped. — We thought we were at a station, but something had gone wrong with one of the carriages. Then a carriage was detached, the passengers distributed in other carriages, and the train moved off again. The guard had locked our door.

Whilst waiting, she stood looking out of the window, I sitting felt her bum, and by the time the train moved off, was game for another fuck. — She refused. — I insisted, pulled her up from her seat, and getting her to kneel upon the seat diagonally, with her backside towards me, I fucked her standing, and never enjoyed a cunt more. — "Oh! if Major **** knew," said she again. — "But he never will, my love, for you've no tongue in your cunt, and it can't speak." — "Well, I never did hear such a beast." — "You compliment me," — I went on talking baudy, and she burst out laughing.

When we arrived at Waterloo, she wanted to leave me. There was no dinner for her, for she was not expected home, so I drove to K***s, got a private room, and ordered dinner. — We washed hands and face, and prick and cunt got their share of soap and water. — Then: "Now I will, it's of no use your struggling, you shan't leave this room till I've seen it" — and I did.

I saw her slim but well shaped thighs, and a small looking, rather pouting, but thin lipped cunt between them. It had not much hair of a nut brown color. — Clitoris and nymphæ were scarcely visible. — It was not a lovely cunt, tho no fault could be found with it, but it was a novelty, and again I stiffened, put my prick up, gave a dozen or two shoves, but not feeling impetuous desire, withdrew it. — The bed room was only given us to wash in, and we could not have it afterwards, so we got thro dinner as quickly as we could and drove off to a house. When we got there she was a little groggy.

At dinner she refused wine, saying that a little got into her head. — I thought it sham, pressed her, and filled her glass. — The champagne was good, and this was the result. — "Oh I've drank too much, how shall I get home?" — "No you mustn't — I won't tell you where, — I dare not." She scarcely seemed to lose her wits, tho staggering, and I couldn't get out of her either where she lived or her name. She laid on the bed at once, let me undress her, and said she was sleepy. "I'll fuck you first." — "Yes, fuck me." — It was the first lewed word she'd uttered. — But a whim seized me. "No, I'll gamahuche you." — "What's that." — "Lick your cunt, may I." "The Major does it more than anything" (laughing.) "Doesn't he fuck you?" — "Sometimes" — I pushed my enquiries about his sexual tastes.

I am always curious about other men now — "Has he a big prick?" — "I don't know, I think it's little," and she laughed. "Where do you live?" — "Shan't tell you, ain't you going to do it?" — "I'll gamahuche you." — "No, don't, it makes me scream." — "Scream?" — "Yes," she said thickly — "it hurts me as well." — Nonsense I thought. — Bringing her to the side of the bed, I wiped her cunt with a towel and began the libidinous exercise. It must have been because there was scarcely a vestige of clitoris or nymphae which made me, for never have I yet seen a vulva so devoid of those appendages. When the lips were opened, nothing was to be seen but the red lining and the vagina.

I found the excitable spot just above the little bone, and licked away gently. She soon felt my tongue, tho I thought she was nearly asleep. "Oh don't! — oh put it in me." — I went on furiously, — "Oh! — I'm coming — leave off — he — ha — hi" she yelled. "It hurts — hi — I'm spending" — and she clutched my hair till I thought she'd scalp me. Ceasing, all was quiet for a minute. — I recommenced. She was a shorter time in spending, and I never heard such screeches given by a woman in her pleasure. — "Oh — hi — her — hi — hi — ha — oh, I can't bear it!" — She half raised herself, and then fell back, spending and exhausted. — "If you do it any more, I shall have a fit. I'm obliged to stop *him* sometimes, I've had fits through his doing it."

I was still between her legs, squatting on my heels, when she said she should have a fit. But that, and her screeching, tho it irritated me, seemed at the same time to stimulate me to continue.

— I felt as if I must have been giving her intense pleasure, and that delighted me. I threw her legs over my shoulders again, grasping them tightly, buried my mouth in her cunt and recommenced gamahuching. — "Oh don't — I'll have a fit" — grasping my head, she tried to raise herself up, but fell back again as I tilted her thighs with my shoulders, spluttering out, my mouth half buried in her cunt. — "Spend, spend, love, — spend." — On my tongue went, as rapidly as tongue could move. — Her bum shook, her belly heaved and jerked. — "Oh — leave — off — oh — my God — I am coming. — Oh — Ahrr — oho" — she screamed till the room rang, and just as her pleasure spasm ceased and her backside lay tranquil — a servant knocked at the door and wanted to know what was the matter.

The sexual excitement then seemed to have sobered her, and a strong cup of tea I had brought revived her. I laid her on the bed again by my side, and heard all about the strangely exciting effect of gamahuching on her. I came to the conclusion that tickling her clitoris with his tongue, was the Major's principal amusement and that he preferred it to fucking. — No doubt also from her description, his cock was a very small one. But as she sobered, she got less free in her revelations. — She had, however, declared that the Major two or three times had gamahuched her, till she had had some sort of fit — I never heard anything of the sort before, in any woman.

I stroked her twice more before leaving and really enjoyed her very much. Her cunt was deep and elastic, and such is the effect of novelty on me that I thought its thin externals gave it a great charm and added to my pleasure. — Certainly I laid unusually long up her after spending. Her cunt seemed to fit round my prick afterwards like a glove, and I put it in her and the sperm as well, till I withdrew. But her thighs and belly made it not such a luxurious bed to lie on after fucking as a stout, large thighed woman with a soft belly does.

(Tho I never heard a woman screech so loudly and painfully when being gamahuched, I have known more than one scream in a subdued but half maddened tone, but a tone of delight, when she spent, and several ejaculate the baudiest words and thoughts as erotic images rose up in their brain. — I myself cry out now in similar manner, when a charming creature draws the sperm out of me into her mouth. It is pleasure, to utter lewed words as my sperm issues.)

After the second fuck she was anxious to go, she had no latch key and began to wonder if *they* would be out, and up to tricks in her absence, as they didn't expect her home; but I couldn't learn who *they* were. — "No." She became as close as wax. "Give me some silver, I'm unnerved — now don't you follow me." — I gave it her and nothing more, and off she went. She made me no promise of seeing me again. — No. If even she might like it, she wouldn't, it would ruin her prospects. — If ever I saw her in camp. "If you're a gentleman you won't notice me. — I'm sure you wouldn't like to ruin a poor woman." — I was in camp several times afterwards, but forgot both the name of the Major, his regiment, and branch of service, so made no enquiries. — She named a place for me to write to, and gave me a name. I did write but never had a reply. She gave me a day's delicious amusement. — I have had many such, but without such curious incidents.

Some weeks before this affair with the postage stamp lady, I began a flirtation with a pretty creature named Madeleine S***h, without meaning anything but to have the pleasure of talking to and being with her. — It ended in a liaison, very short and very sweet, and there was a voluptuous incident in it occurring to myself, and not of an every day kind — I have in the after talk of dinners, and in the salacious disclosures of men in club smoking rooms, heard of similar physical crises occurring to men, and once, if not twice, recollect similar things having occurred to me. — Perhaps under sexual excitement they have occurred to many men in strong health. But I approach middle age, so the incident rather surprised me, tho it was gratifying as evidence of my sexual vigor and strength.

Sometimes I wonder at the amatory course I have run — and whether these temporary connections with women, these liaisons of lust, are forced upon me by circumstances, or whether I am instinctively seeking them? Whether it is the women who bring them about — or my self? — Which is it? — I cannot answer. — I know certainly *when* I seek them, *when* I am cunt hunting, as I term it. — But so many women (not courtesans) have fallen to my embraces (and in this narrative I have only told of my amours of a special character), as it seems to me by pure force of opportunity and circumstances, pure chance as it were; unless those seeking to form them were the women. Does a thirsty cunt and a hard scrotum set men and women together, without either of them intending or thinking about coition, until lust steals on, and strengthens, and modesty gradually vanishes, till the barriers of conventionality are broken by one or both, and they bend under the spell of concupiscence till they fuck?—Is it not the law of animal life that the male and female shall blindly and instinctively seek each other for copulation? Is it not in the great scheme of creation that they should? If so, why should they be blamed for satisfying this imperious want, this universal law, this blind necessity of fucking? Why should man frame laws, legal and social, for hindering man and woman from coupling, blending, and satisfying their love or lust whenever they like?—Love and lust are terms identical in meaning, synonymous; tho often the former is called pure, the latter foul. It is the priest who determines that. But again I ask myself, was it mine, or the women's *fault,* or rather by whose *virtue,* that we fell into each other's arms and copulated?—and whose fault or virtue was it, that Madeline and I came sexually together for a brief while?

A few days after I had had the postage stamp lady, I went to the Crystal Palace (then a fashionable lounge on certain days, it not having been opened many years), expecting to meet a nice creature, a dress maker, who was about twenty years old.—She had worked at my house for years previously when quite a girl, but was now well grown and womanly for her years.—I had often noticed her years before, and one day gave her a sly kiss, and half a crown on some pretext.—I lost sight of her when I gave up that home as a freed man, and then met her by chance one evening a year or so after. I found she was still a milliner, and seemed as modest as one might desire, took her, spite of her reluctance, to have a glass of wine, and, giving her my arm, walked some part to her way home with her. It was in the suburbs, and in the dark I gave her a kiss, which she liked, then tried to feel her unsuccessfully; tho I got a touch on her thigh and made her cry, gave her a sovereign, and a kiss which I made her return, and never saw her again till recently, two years *after* my unsuccessful attempt at groping her. Now she seemed to me quite gay and frolicsome, she was an under forewoman at Mrs. ***** a dressmaker, and had she said, a sweetheart. She was a very handsome creature, with soft grey eyes and lovely auburn hair. — I got it into my head that she, like most milliners, fucked on the sly, a little for love and a little for silk dresses. She told me when I met her, which I did three days after my visit to Aldershot, she was going on Saturday to the Crystal Palace. I said I should do the same. She remarked that she knew that I could do as I liked now. — Her name as already said was Madeline S***h.

To my annoyance, I found she was with a friend, a milliner, who looked to me as frisky, as if two pricks would suit her better than one. Getting hold of Miss S***h, I told her I was so vexed, for I wanted her to dine with. She was sorry, but her friend's young man would meet them at four o'clock. — Then said I, "Well miss them, and you come out and dine with me." That she agreed to, I went off, found a quiet sort of half restaurant, half tavern (houses of that class were just then springing up there), ordered dinner in a private room, paid half down at once, and went back to the Palace.

It all came off as arranged, and at about five o'clock, when some music was over, which she wanted to stay for — we left quietly and had dinner. She eat and drank well, and seemed as frisky as a grasshopper. — I'd not hinted at anything. Beyond the convenience of the sofa in the room, and my hoping it would bear the weight of two restless people, I had said nothing concupiscent in its tone, tho I was longing for her during dinner. For since the unknown postage stamp lady, I had kept myself from women. — The cloth removed, the waiter gone, I brought her to the window to look out, put my arm round her waist, kissed her, and said I thought she ought to kiss me for the dinner. — After a very little sham she did, and we kissed each other quite amorously. Then I sat her down on the sofa where I meant now to experiment on her virtue, and pulling the table a little nearer, and pouring out wine, began.

As I usually do, I first told suggestive stories, then smutty ones, but without baudy words. She laughed at them all. — "Oh, my! — He *was* up to his tricks." — "Oh what a shameful story!" and so on. — She didn't blush, but got excited, and I thought all was right. Ever and anon I kissed her. She wouldn't tell her sweetheart, she said, for she had one who was going to marry her. Then

I began about her garters, asked if her lover had ever put them on for her. What next should I imagine. "Of course not." — Why should she refuse him? I asked. — "It wouldn't be proper." — "That's not the reason." "What is it then?" — "You fear he'd put his hand higher up between your thighs?" — "Oh, you blackguard, to talk like that." — She tossed her head. — "And feel your cunt, Madeline?" I continued — she gave me a smack on my head. — "If you talk like that I'll go." What a lot of women have said they would smack my head, and some have, but not very hard.

"What's the harm, my darling, even if your lover did, and what's the harm of calling it *that* if I say your *thing*, you know it means the same." — "Oh, you blackguard!" — I went on in the same strain and pinched and tickled her till she screeched. "Oh, you blackguard, leave off." — "The waiter will be coming in if you make such a noise," said I, getting up and bolting the door. — "Well, don't you do that to me." "I can't help it, I'm madly in love with you." — For a time we were quieter, then I pulled her back on the sofa and began spooning. "You know your lovers' been in bed with you." — That he hadn't, she shouldn't be such a fool. — "Let me." — "What?" — My arm was round her waist, my lips close to hers, my hand on her lap. I grabbed at her clothes just above her notch. She must have felt the clutch on her motte, and I said, "Fuck you," and kissed her with mad lust on me.

She slapped my head hard now and threatened to go, but didn't rise. — "Did I hurt you?" — "Don't do it again, or talk like that, or I'll never speak to you again." — Again we kissed, I gave her more wine, and spilt some over her dress. — "You've ruined my dress," said she anxiously. — "Never mind love, tell me what it cost, I'll pay for another," — and I took out my purse. — "You were always kind, but perhaps I'll get it out." — "Well here's a sovereign to clean it" — she wouldn't take the money.

Some years before I had bought a lot of pretty, small priced brooches. — Most had been given away to servants and other women, and even to favorite doxies. I had put one in my pocket now, and also had brought two pairs of beautiful garters with me.

Ah, what a repetition — how many times has nearly the same occurred — I seem to have been rehearsing it half my life, but thus it occurred now. "Now isn't that a pretty brooch?" — "Oh, it is." — "I'm going to give that to a lady friend." — "Oh!" said she in such a tone that I saw at once it had crossed her mind that I was going to give it to *her.* — "And a pair of these garters as well, on one condition." — I produced them. — "What's that." — "That she'll let me put them on." — "Will she?" — "I think so, I did so once before, and she's a nice little lady." — "Not much of a lady." — "She is tho, and married." — "She ought to be ashamed of herself then." — "Pough! my dear, who'll know but she and I? The last pair I put on her legs as she laid on the bed, and then I got on to the bed with her, and then." — There I stopped. — "*You — are — a — regular scamp,* I've been told so," said Madeline, blushing. — "Why my dear?" — "For tempting a poor woman so." — "Nonsense, my love, *she* tempted *me,* but which pair would you like?" — "This pair." — Then I said I'd give them her if she'd let me put them on. — She refused.

I chaffed her. "You tie yours up with string don't you?" — "Wouldn't you like to know." — "Yes, and to feel." Saying which, I made the attempt, didn't succeed, and got another slap on my head. — She rose up, saying she wouldn't stop any longer, but after a little consideration sat down again.

On I talked in the same strain — all she replied from time to time was, "Oh, you scamp." But I thought she looked as if the talk was affecting her sensually, and she let me kiss her easily, after every time that she called me that name. — At length, by constantly asking her, the bait took. She selected a pair, and, with just the same precautions that other women have taken, one after another the garters were put on. — As I fastened the last, I put my mouth down, and kissed the little bit of thigh which was just clear above the stocking. — The sniff of the warm flesh exalted my randiness, lust then overpowered me, and pulling her back on the sofa, kissing her rapturously all the time, I got one hand up her clothes, and just felt the thighs and the hair of her mount. — She repulsed me instantly with a loud cry. — "Let me fuck you, my love. I'm dying for you." — "Oh, you blackguard, get away." — "Look what a state you've put me in," and out I pulled my glowing rod, which pulsated as if going at once to discharge the semen which lay in my balls.

Up she got, leaving me sitting on the sofa, with my pulsating, crimson tipped, cunt-rammer out. "You mistake me altogether if you asked me here to behave like that. — I'll go at once." — She meant it. — No. She'd go back to the Palace by herself. It had been arranged that we were to find her friend there, and all go to town together. She said a lot more, all the time standing close by me, and looking every instant at my nodding engine — looking spite of herself I expect. I got her round the waist, and swearing I would go no further, got her sitting again on the sofa, and hid my prick in my trowsers. — She was upset. The sight of a good sized, stiff prick always upsets a young woman whether she has been fucked or not, and stirs up lewed sensations in her.

She didn't know exactly where to go to find her friend, or I believe she would have gone off without me — I now saw I shouldn't succeed in having her, and that she was wide awake. She had a sweetheart who was going to marry her, and wouldn't run the risk of getting with kid, I thought. I also felt sure she'd been poked. I've had a dozen young milliners, and only one was a virgin, and altho this woman lived with her parents and seemed respectable, I know that the more women living as she was are fucked out of doors, the more careful for a time they are to hide their games from their parents and employers. — Disappointed for the minute, I ceased.

It was getting dusk, she was anxious to go, I more and more anxious to have her. My prick would not subside, but threatened to spend in my trowsers. — It was on the Monday that I had had the postage stamp lady, and since then had been keeping myself chaste, with the pleasurable hope of deluging Madeline's cunt with rich spermatic juices. — Again I grasped and kissed her. "There is the brooch, I'll give it you, but am awfully disappointed, for I do so long for you, and no one would know but you and I." — "Don't be foolish, don't be a beast."—"Oh, let me then just feel your flesh, by the eternal God, if you'll let me feel your thigh, only half way above your knee — I'll be content, I'll go no further." — "You beast, let me get up," and she made a half attempt to rise. — Was lewedness subduing her? — It was a miserable small sofa, with scarcely room for one person to lie down, she was reclining sideways, I holding her so that one of her feet was on the ground, the other nearly so, and she contemplating the brooch most of the time, was seemingly delighted with it.

I have often wondered since if it was the brooch which absorbed her thoughts and made her careless, or gratitude for it, which made her half indulge me for the moment. Or did she feel a sensuous pleasure in my attempt, secure in the knowledge that she could repel my hand when she listed? Was she lewed at that moment and therefore yielding? — What a pity that some visible sign of lewedness is not in a woman; that she hasn't something which will rise up and stiffen as a prick does. — A man has always that sign of his lustful state, and a woman need be in no doubt about it.

She went on looking at the brooch, pinning it on her breast, then taking it out to look at it, whilst I went on kissing, coaxing, pinching her thighs outside, and attempting slight liberties. "No, I won't." — "Only one thigh — a little bit of the flesh only this side. Now do." — Holding her round the waist, I hitched up that side of her clothes, and got my hand on to her thigh just above the garter. — With both hands she stopped me. — "There now — you've done it, now leave me alone. — I'm foolish to let you. — Now don't. — Oh, what are you about?" and she dropped the brooch.

Rapidly I pulled away the only button which kept my prick within my trowsers, and out it stood rampant; raised her clothes on that side, put one hand under the thigh, with force hoisted it a little up, and turned more towards her, with the intention of letting my prick touch her flesh. I had neither hope nor idea of getting into her. — The thought alone of my prick touching her flesh filled me with voluptuous delight. — I pushed my prick wildly, now holding the thigh still more exposed with both hands, and pressing my body to it. — My prick spite of her struggles touched her. — She cried out loudly. "Leave off — oh you scamp, don't." — I heeded not, heated by the contact, I went on. — A spasm of delight shot through my prick, and an ungovernable movement of my buttocks shoved it to and fro. — Its tip rubbed against the tiny bit of naked thigh, pulsated violently, and before I knew if I could control it, or she free herself from me, shot out a torrent of hot, thick sperm on to her thigh. It ran down to one of my hands, whilst I sighed out. — "My God — I'm spending — it's on your — thigh." — Then I sank, half fainting with pleasure, upon her shoulder.

"Don't — what are you doing — let me get up" — was all I heard, and by that time she had pulled down her clothes, covering up sperm and all, and I had fallen back on the sofa holding my prick. — The whole affair, from the time I got hold of her thigh, had not occupied the time it takes me to write a dozen of these lines.

CHAPTER III

*Madeline's lover Richard. — Mrs. B**t*n's mischief. — Complaisance in cab and house. — Bertha the fruitress. — Male chaffing. — An erotic vision in the shop. — Is she virtuous? — Madeline again. — A ruptured membrane. — Mutual fucking sensations. — Inheritance of a marbly rump. — A woman's virgin spend. — Absent at Paris. — Madeline's lover is reconciled. — Onanistic emissions. — French letters and cunt sponges. — The influences leading women to copulate. — Madeline's intentions and admissions.*

She rose, picked up the brooch, put it on the table, and put on her bonnet silently and hastily. I arose feeling ashamed, enclosed my still swollen machine, and said I was so sorry for what I had done, I couldn't help it, that it was her fault. — She made no reply beyond, — "I'll never dine or speak with you again, you're a blackguard." — "If you'd only let me." — "You're a scamp." — I chattered on, she begged me to be quick, "I'd go without you but I can't find the place, what will Mrs. B**t*n (her milliner friend) think about my being late?" — I didn't want to injure her, so rapidly paid my bill, and we got to the rendezvous late, but not too late. — There was Mrs. B**t*n alone, her male friend had gone. — She approached Madeline and said, "Richard's been here and has gone off nearly mad. — I couldn't say you were not here, so told him you'd gone with a lady friend, etc., etc." — Madeline began to cry, saying to me, — "You've made plenty of mischief for me," — and turned sulky. The two held a long conversation apart, Mrs. B**t*n seemed excited. — Madeline cried, till, with a rush for the train, we got seats.

It was then a long way across London, from the station to the neighbourhood where Madeline lived — I got into the cab with them — Madeline sulked all the way — I knew where she lived, and she insisted on being set down at the end of the street. Only her companion alighted with her — I bid them good bye, hoping her young man wouldn't be angry long. — Madeline said it was a misfortune for her my meeting her at the Palace — and we parted.

I had heard from Madeline that her friend the milliner lived in the heart of London, not far from another workshop, and knowing she would have to get there, put my cab away from the end of the street, and on foot waited myself in sight of Madeline's house — I had noticed in the cab Mrs. B**t*n's glances, which were curious, and as much as to say, "I know what you've been up to together." She seemed also I think a little lewed — I had heard she was a widow. She was about thirty, and a smallish, thinnish, matured, well shaped looking little woman. — Really feeling anxious about Madeline, and hoping not to have done her any injury, I waited to catch Mrs. B**t*n to make enquiries.

It had taken a long time to get from the Palace to **** (done in exactly half the time now, owing to railways.) It was about half past nine when Mrs. B**t*n appeared, and was astonished to see me. Would she take a seat in my cab, and I would drive her home. —She accepted at once. — In a minute afterwards. "What have you two been up to together?" said she inquisitively, and laughing suggestively.

"Nothing." I had known Madeline a girl and liked her looks, met her by accident at the Palace, and, going myself to have some food, offered her some. Nothing more. — "Was that all?" We had been a long time. — "I wish it hadn't been all, for I'd give twenty pounds to have her."

"Hush," said Mrs. B**t*n putting her hand right over my mouth. — "I don't believe you" — but I repeated it, said she was a lovely creature, but I wouldn't on any account harm her, and directly I got to **** St. and sat Mrs. B**t*n down, I'd go to the Argyle and get a woman for the night.

"You're a nice boy. — I've heard of you before, you'd better go home *now*." "No," said I, "I'll have a woman first." In five minutes after I was kissing Mrs. B**t*n, in another five minutes was feeling her cunt, ten minutes afterwards was in a baudy house, and five minutes after that, a dose of sperm had been administered to the red lipped, hair encircled, moist, warm, aromatic organ, which she, like other women, had lying between her thighs, bum hole, and navel. — As quickly as possible afterwards, she had another dose. — Neither of us undressed, for Mrs. B**t*n, tho evidently liking prick exercise in her, and altho a widow, also lived with a friend and got home at early hours.

In the interval between the fucks she told me all about Madeline. — She believed her virtuous, and didn't believe she'd been fucked. I made her say those words. It is a great pleasure to me to make a woman who is not gay speak baudily. — A young man, of her own condition in life, meant to marry her. He had come to the Crystal Palace to meet her, having heard by chance that she was going there. — Mrs. B**t*n's male friend incautiously said she had gone to dine with a gentleman, and the sweetheart in a rage went off, swearing he'd have nothing to do with her any more, and would blow his own brains out. Mrs. B. had told Madeline that she had told Richard it was with a lady she had left. That was to calm her — I have since fancied Mrs. B. was not a true friend.

I met Mrs. B. two days afterwards and fucked her. She took a little present this time. Madeline had heard nothing of her sweetheart, and thought she had lost him, so did Mrs. B. — I fancy from her silence that Madeline had said nothing about garters and brooch, or my spending over her thigh, she had said that I behaved as a perfect gentleman. "Well, I shan't meet her again at the Crystal Palace or elsewhere," I observed, but I tried to catch Madeline on her road to and from her work, and failed. I expected that she and her swain had made it up, and that she avoided me. I didn't go near Mrs. B**t*n, and almost forgot all about the affair, for I was, and had for a month or two previously, been on the cunt-hunt, and now was on the trail rather smartly, which put Madeline out of my mind, and I had given up all hopes of getting her. — Dinner, wine, baudy talk, and trying to grope her, the sight of my prick, my spending on her thigh had all failed. — No, most likely she's been fucked, but sees the chance of marriage, and will run no further risks; so ran my thoughts, and in my heart I did not blame her.

[The narrative now goes back a little. — The liaison with Madeline has been told hitherto consecutively — (a custom usually observed in this history of my secret life). But one with a girl named Bertha, commenced whilst I was courting Madeline, — the amusement with the postage stamp lady already told of — and a Paphian ball yet to be told of, also took place whilst my amours with Bertha and Madeline were going on, and I find it difficult to arrange the narrative in my usual manner, so much were all these amours intermixed and also mixed in the manuscript.]

A few months before I met Madeline, I had been a good deal into the city speculating. — Buying something one day at a very little fruiterer's shop — I noticed a pretty girl who served there. — She was shortish, sturdy, dark haired, and dark eyed, and had a look and manner superior to shop women generally. I thought her twenty but she was not eighteen. I shall call her Bertha.

The mistress had two shops and was usually at the other and Bertha alone at this one. The customers seemed almost exclusively well to do city men, and usually bought their goods after midday. They chaffed her at times broadly, which she didn't seem to mind, and at times returned. — A look in her eye made me think she was amorous, women can't help feeling lewed, and how they manage to look perfectly modest with clipping, perspiring cunts, puzzles me. — At length I found myself going often to the shop, and then chaffing her like the others. — Then I noticed some of the men say "Keep the change, I can't bear coppers" — so to ingratiate myself I did the same. One day I snatched a kiss which she didn't seem to mind at all, and giving her a sovereign for some goods, and a half sovereign being among the change, I pushed it to her and told her to keep it. — She eyed me fixedly and curiously for a few seconds, and then refused it. "Oh, dear no, that's too much," said she, pushing it away. — On saying that I should take it out in kisses, — "That you won't." She would not take it, and a few days after being in the shop, which happened to have a quick succession of customers, the following occurred to me. — One of the strangest, and most complete, yet almost unconscious efforts of erotic fancy I ever had. It more resembled an erotic dream.

Without any sexual desires as far as I know, and certainly without any sexual intentions, I sat looking at her pretty face, and particularly at her mouth, which was unusually small, and with little handsome fat lips; lips which make me want to kiss them whenever I see them. — After awhile looking — I wondered if her cunt had thick lips. — I know the idea of their being fat on account of those of her mouth being so was absurd; and that a small mouth does not imply a small cunt, nor thick lips above, mean thick lips below; but there is no accounting for the association of ideas, however absurd they may be. Then I felt suddenly a desire to see her cunt and to fuck it, and sat thinking about its size, its hair, and its looks, whilst I talked to her and looked in her eyes, and at her mouth. Then my cock tingled with lust, then swelled, then stood erect and hard for an instant, and just then she turned to some one who came in, to serve him.

Whilst she did so I shut my eyes, violent lewedness seized me, and I fancied my sperm was spurting into her — I had all the pleasure of imagination, without the physical reality. — I saw a lovely little fat lipped cunt, with a little bush around it, and fancied I saw the voluptuous pleasure in her eyes as my prick gradually entered. — Ah! what exquisite joint sensation of mind and body, experienced as the glans is first pressed by the cunt and feels its road. — No doubt the female experiences similar thoughts as her cunt feels the distention by the smooth prick tip, and she knows it will search it to its innermost depths.

Said I to her, "I've been dreaming awake about you, whilst you were serving those people." — "What was your dream?" — "It would make you blush if I told you." — "Then don't tell it." — Then I began wondering if she were virgin or not, and half thought not, for I saw a young man attempting to kiss her as I entered the shop soon after, and thought it improbable that a mere shop girl, serving well dressed men and gentlemen both young and old, could have so long kept her cunt to herself, under the temptations which I fancied she must be subject to there. I began to long for her, tho I was fucking ****** about that time, and varying her pleasures with Paphians both English and French, and a big German woman as well, tho I soon had done with *her*.

I came to the conclusion at last that she was no more virtuous than she should be, and that I might as well be one of the happy ones. Yet I didn't approach the subject till one day, seeing another fellow kiss her, I said, "Hulloh, Miss Bertha, I'll tell Mrs. C*h*n." — The same young man I had talked with one or two days before was eating strawberries and laughed with me. "We all kiss you, don't we Bertha?" said he. — "No, don't you tell stories about me to that gentleman, I let some of you, and Mrs. C*h*n knows it,

I shouldn't be here long if I made a fuss about every thing that's said to me. Miss *** was turned off because she did, and *you* lost her her place." Then she turned to a customer who entered. — I remarked to the man that I supposed she was pretty intimate with some fellow. "I expect so, and plenty have tried." Then, nodding to me, he left.

Directly afterwards she told me not to believe what that man said, he was a nuisance and was always annoying her, but was such a good customer that she didn't like to offend him. — "He wants to get to bed with you, Bertha." — "He's like a good many more then, but they'll be disappointed," — said she, looking me in the face and not all abashed. — "Don't disappoint *me* or I'll hang myself." — "The sooner you do it the better." — This coolness astonished me. I didn't think about what a hardening moral process incessant amatory chaff is; how soon a young maiden learns to return it, and how pleasant veiled allusions to marriage, to the pleasure in having company in bed, and other indirect allusions to fucking, are, — how they keep the mind and body in a slight state of voluptuousness, particularly pleasing to a woman, who feels, among other things, complimented by the allusions being made to her; for a woman always feels pleased at a man's desiring to possess her.

Then I was sitting on a little stool in the shop one day, and she told me a lot about the business and herself. — She lived with an aunt, and nightly went home by herself. Their business was generally over by eight o'clock, sometimes they kept open till ten, if the weather was bad for keeping fruit. — "Come and sup with me, and say you've been late at shop." — "No thank you, I know what you mean by that."

Another day I took her the last of my Neapolitan brooches. — She was delighted. Soon after she had to stand upon a stool to reach something down, and I risked putting my hand up her petticoats. "That's not fair," said she angrily, getting down. — "I didn't expect that of *you*." — "I'm mad for you, dying for you, I'll not leave you alone till I've had you." — "I've heard that said many times." — "Good bye, I shan't come again." — "Why." — "Because you won't let me." — "Good bye, don't be foolish, I should be sorry if you don't come, you talk nicer than most of those who come here, but I know all your little games. — There's a middle-aged man comes here, who's had the impudence to offer to keep me, and give me five hundred a year; and I've seen his wife and his children here with him — a blackguard."

Thought I, she's a little out of the common, but if she's not been already fucked, she will be soon. I went there less often, then was away from town. — When I returned she wondered why I hadn't been. — "Because you won't come and dine with me." — "It will be no good to you if I do" — again I put my hands on to her ankles, and she seemed less angry — I did it another day, but couldn't get to her garters, she was too quick for me.

"If any one comes in and catches you trying that on, you'll lose me my place; kissing doesn't matter, but improper things do." — "Come to dinner with me then." — "Oh! you do so plague me. I will some day, but it will be no use to you, mind." — There the matter rested, for, having lost money, I ceased speculating, and did not go to my stock brokers, and amused myself by tailing my doxies.

Again I went, and, chatting with a man in the shop whom I knew a little of, he said that he thought Bertha up to snuff, and that Mr. ***** had had her. She seemed very pleased to see me, and I, being very bold and hot that day, got my hand up her clothes on to her thighs, at which she was excessively angry and declared that if I ever made such an attempt again, she would neither speak to me, nor serve me, and would tell the shop owner — "and I will never dine with you." — Off I went and didn't see her for some time.

A few days afterwards, I met in the street Madeline (I cannot make up my mind whether she threw herself in my way or not). We talked, and she began to cry. She had never seen her young man since. — He had written to say he had done with her, and it was all my fault, she said. I couldn't admit that. It was an unfortunate accident, nothing more. — She never would meet me or any one else again, but it ended that day in her agreeing to dine with me the day following, to talk over what was to be done.

At the ***** hotel, I took a bed room and sitting room, leading out of each other, and took a small trunk there; feeling sure that she had been poked, and was coming to poke, and that the hotel would be more comfortable than a baudy house.

She was punctual, had a good appetite, and, tho crying at

intervals when I mentioned her Richard, was in good spirits.— She was still dressmaking at Mrs. ****'s, but being out of sorts through the loss of her young man, had been fit for nothing; and her mistress had told her she must improve or go. Madeline seemed to me in a reckless frame of mind about that, said she must do what she could. If she must leave, she must; she couldn't help what her parents said, and so on. Hers was the sort of Devil-may-care manner which I have seen in women of her class who are tired of their work and position, and who want pleasure.—In fact as a main cause of that, and perhaps unconscious of it, want fucking; and are half disposed to get a prick up them at any risk.—Her coming to meet me again after what had taken place between us led me to think she might be in that state, and from her answers to, and sometimes evasions of, my questions, I came to the conclusion that Richard had been up the red inlet to her body, which she had between her thighs like other women.

Dinner over, we sat on the sofa and I began kissing her.— She was so far complaisant. Talking about Richard, she had heard he was now, "Sweet upon another young woman," and, altho she then whimpered, said she didn't care much. I found that it was the loss of a husband, and one who was so respectable, that she fretted about, more than the individual. I began to doubt then if she'd had Richard up her, and joked her about her not getting a bedfellow so soon as she'd expected, offered myself instead, talked about matrimony, on the absurdity of a man and woman who liked each other not doing before marriage all that nature prompted them to do, and how they lost pleasure, which they couldn't take too young. She sipped wine and got amative in manner, I held her to me, and our kisses were many.—"That's enough," said she, as if it had just occurred to her that she was giving way too much.

My prick now got on the ramp, and I resolved either to get her or let her go. Tho I'd promised her never to refer to what had taken place at the previous dinner, I asked her if she'd washed her thigh since, and if she looked at her chemise after it.—She coloured up and rose to go, I pulled her down, said I'd forgotten my promise and couldn't help it.—I'd like to do it again to her, or if she'd let me, do something better.—Women are so cunning, you never can make them, until they have long had a man, confess their lust; but

I've no doubt that, with this talk, Madeline's cunt was beginning to sweat inside. The half bashful way she looked at me, and the ridiculous resistance to my kissing which she now offered for a second or two, made me feel sure that she wanted fucking at that minute, and was struggling against it. — Women can control their passions to a certain point, and then they droop, and yield helplessly all at once, I have found.

She really was angry once, yet returned each of my kisses. "Have you the garters on?" — "Yes." — "Let me see them" — and I made the attempt. — "No, no, you shan't," and she struggled, but I got my hand on her thigh.

She got it away, but in another minute her head was over my shoulder, I was kissing now her ear, now her cheek, and whispering baudiness. — I had reduced her to silence, whilst speaking of my sperm on her thigh when it ought to have been in her cunt, and she have had pleasure as well as me, whilst my prick discharged it. — "Let me feel your thighs. — Do — if you don't I'll do that again." — "Oh don't," said she in a half whisper. — "Well, let me see your garters, I will," and, letting go her waist, I pulled up her clothes, saw garters and thigh, and, stooping, kissed the flesh before she could prevent me. She gave a slight cry, but next moment I was clasping her round her waist, again her head was on my shoulder, my fingers on her cunt, and I was whispering about carnal love into her ear, and titillating her clitoris.

[How commonplace it all seems as I write this afresh now. — To how many women have I done as nearly as possible the same, and how many under similar circumstances have behaved like Madeline? It can't be varied. — A woman's a woman, a cunt's a cunt, everywhere. Voluptuous sensations are common to all, lewedness makes the man attack, and the woman yield. All the world over it's the same, and ever will be. — Yet each woman who is fresh to me in copulating preliminaries gives as much pleasure to me as if she was the first I had. I feel as if I never had such sensual felicity before as at that moment, and was still to have with her.

Does the woman mean to let the man have her when she meets him, or from the moment he touches her cunt, or when, or at all, or does she unconsciously acquiesce, and gradually yield, as sensations overcome all sense but that of carnal voluptuousness? — Do visions of his prick entering the hitherto sacred precincts of her cunt pass through her brain as he gently masturbates her? Few women can answer this themselves, I find.]

Absorbed in feeling her cunt, and the delight of giving the sweet creature pleasure, wondering if I dare put my finger lower down and try the passage, I titillated her in silence. All was silent now, excepting the gentle smacking of my kisses on her upturned cheek and lips. — I frigged gently between tightly closed thighs, till in that charming way a woman has, when she feels the premonitory thrills of the coming spend, and doesn't like to show her pleasure; she moved her face up from my shoulder with a start. — "Oho! aha! leave off now. — You shan't"; and, with a jut back of her haunches, she removed my finger for a second. I instantly recommenced, frigged quicker, still quicker, harder. Now I ceased kissing her. "Spend darling, spend, love," I said, looking into her face, which was again on my shoulder. — Her eyes were closed, her mouth slightly open, rapid breathing and quick sighs of pleasure came from her. — Ah, that quiver of the thighs and belly, that tremulous shiver in her bosom, I knew it well, and the squeeze of the thighs on my hand, — tight for a second — then the convulsive opening of them, again the tight closing, and then the languid opening of the fleshy columns. — I knew it well, for I have frigged scores of the angels, and knew that Madeline had spent.

Whilst her thighs in voluptuous languor lay loosely, I slipped my hand between them and grasped her whole cunt, and my fingers lay between the lips. She started up and pushed my hand away. On it as I withdrew it, were the copious evidences of her pleasure. — "You've spent, love. — I've frigged you. — Ah! if my prick had been in you, how much more pleasure you'd have had. Come to the other room, let us — come." She sat looking at me full. What was she thinking of? Again I cuddled, kissed and fondled her, again my hand touched her clitoris. She was passive, my fingers moved over all the moistened surface, and then her thighs closed again. — "Come with me, come." — Gently and uninterruptedly I frigged on, murmuring "Come, love," till with a sudden rousing, she pushed away my hand, gasping out slowly and hesitatingly, "No — I — can't."

"Feel my prick then," and I put her hand round it. She was now sighing, her head again fell on my shoulder with eyes closed, my prick in her hand, when I recommenced frigging. — "Oh leave off. I can't." — "Come to the bed, or my spunk will go all over you again. — Oh, how wet your cunt is. — My love, let's go, or I shall spend." — She was almost insensible to every thing but lust and didn't reply. I rose, seized her hands, and gently pulled her up. — "Come." "No." — But gradually and easily I led her into the bed chamber — She wouldn't get on the bed. — "I won't let you now." — "What nonsense, then I'll leave you — get on love, and I'll only frig you." — On she got.

I got on the bed unbuttoning as I did so. There was no light excepting what came through the sitting room door. For a moment I frigged her, gradually pressing her on to her back, then slowly mounted her. — "I'll do it so. — I'll spend over your thigh so, and frig you after, be quiet dear." — She knew what I was going to do, tho she feared it. — My legs pressed her thighs apart, I lodged my prick and gave a gentle push, to my astonishment, it did not enter. With a little wriggle she murmured "Oh, don't!" — Then she is virgin! — Oh, the delight as I grasped her buttocks for a forcible thrust, had her firmly in hand, guided my prick low down (I know the point of entry well) and lunged, — "Oho — oha" — lunge — "oho" — lunge. "Oh, don't" — I felt that never-to-be-forgotten sensation which a hymen when splitting up gives a prick, the tightening round it, then the loosening, and the next instant the shaft was up to its roots in her cunt.

That was a short business, but not a quick fuck, for I had fucked the night before. — I enjoyed both the sensation and the idea of the virgin cunt which I had ruptured, but fucked slowly till nature urged me on faster, and spent as her cunt tightened and her murmurs of pleasure reached my ear, as I lay with my head over her shoulder. Coming to myself I felt the stem of my prick yet up her, and sanguinary proof I found. "You've never been fucked before," said I. — "What?" — said she astonished.

[Some men, and some women say that females don't spend at the fuck which destroys their virginity; generally they do not, but I have had several who did, and can swear to it.]

I locked the bedroom door, which I had not done before, lighted candles, wiped her cunt myself with a towel, and inspected her jagged slit. — She objected, and I almost used force. — "What nonsense, to the man who's just fucked you." — Then she seemed faint. — We came into the sitting room, I gave her wine, and she sat with my handkerchief against her quim, for she bled unusually. — In an hour we fucked again, and soon after she went away still bleeding. She wanted to get home early; I stopped all night at the hotel.

Next night she could not meet me, the next she did. I could not get to the same hotel again, but knew of three where they shut their eyes. — At one I hired a sitting and bedroom. The dinner was not so good, but was wholesome, the wine excellent. — A charming tête-à-tête meal we had, and a comfortable bed there was to go to afterwards. "We are going to get into bed presently Madeline." — "Oh, no." — "Oh, yes you are," — and so it was. What a fuss she made, but at length, in chemise only and I in shirt, I forced her up on the bed, and, throwing up her chemise as fast as she pushed it down, and insisting on my right, I had her thighs wide apart, and gloated on her private charms, and kissed and smelt them (for I liked the smell of her cunt) till my impatient prick would let me look no longer. Then into bed I got, and pushing up chemise and shirt to our necks, covered her sweet fair body with mine.

I recollect nothing in my life more exquisite, than the minute when my prick glided up Madeline's cunt the second time that night, with a slow movement which it pleased me to make. Going up it inch by inch, resting between each stroke, watching her face, hearing the slight cry of pain which her lacerated and still sore cunt forced from her, whilst voluptuous sensations higher up in her cunt coming at the same time, issued in a lovely murmur. A murmur expressing mainly the pleasure that fucking was giving her. Her irritated, heated, spunk-filled vagina was longing to relieve itself by a discharge of its lubricating mucous to meet my spermatic injection, and thrilled her with burning lust. I lay a minute, letting her enjoy the complete distension of her cunt, that pretty little cunt, tight, stretched and gorged with my prick, which never was larger or stiffer. Then I thrust hard, banging its red tip against the portals of her womb, which made her jerk her bum back but stimulated her to a crisis of pleasure. — All this time I was wondering at my luck at having her a virgin, and my stupidity at having thought she was not. Thus I lay in her arms, clasping and kissing, and thinking with that rapid evolution of lascivious thoughts which go thro my brain as my prick is in a cunt.

After our second fuck, as recovering from our elysium of lasciviousness I lay tranquilly between her smooth legs, and restlessly began feeling her satiny flesh from hips to thighs, and lower, I became conscious of much hardness of the lower part of haunch and backside; and still later on when we had exhausted ourselves in each other's arms, and she had washed and was preparing to put on her clothes, I felt her all about those fleshy parts, and looked at and kissed the fair globes, and found that her bum had an unusual hardness, a hardness far beyond what would be called solid, but was even marbly in its solidity; such as I have felt perhaps in half a dozen women, but not more.

She was conscious of it. It was solid when a girl, and in rising womanhood, sleeping with other young women, her hard bum had been noticed. — I suppose they felt each other, and why not? — I have always hitherto found that substantial flesh, in the arses of stronger, coarser-built women. In this slighter and more delicate town-built woman it was an agreeable novelty. She had told that in a moment of jocosity, her mother had once told her that she also had one of the hardest bums, and that if she put a walnut on a wooden chair and sat with naked bum upon it, she could crack it. — This I suppose was figurative, but possibly may be true. So Madeline inherited her mother's solid buttocks. I am not sure that such hard flesh there is beautiful. A slighter solidity, and more elasticity, is preferable to the feel, I think. It is pleasanter to clutch an elastic rather than an inelastic arse, when fucking.

She was a beautifully made creature; slim, with fine bones delicately covered, and had a most exquisite foot in size and shape. Her cunt was small both in look and feel and had but little hair on it. — In her armpits there was scarcely a hair visible. I don't recollect before seeing a woman of her age without hair there, tho I have seen some with very little. I never saw a more ragged jagged edged split than my prick had made in her hymen. She told me that, before fucking, she couldn't quite insert the tip of her little finger, in the orifice thro which her courses drained off. She had a fair sized clitoris and trifling inner lips, and that is all about her cunt.

She could not get out next night, but on that following she met me again. — We dined as before and took our pleasures directly afterwards. — What a difference in her manner! In the cab I felt her cunt and did what I liked, there was no fuss about the groping, and by the time I reached the hotel, we had felt each other till I was stiff, and she was moist and lewed. — How charming at dinner to set opposite to the pretty creature, knowing what was to follow, that there was no part of her fair body which I had not seen, that she knew the size of my prick, from its normal state of quiescence to its utmost and active rigidity. Such thoughts passed through *my* mind, and similar ones no doubt passed through *hers*, tho, with the hypocrisy so common among women, she denied it when I asked her.

She could not stop out till eleven o'clock anymore, for her parents became inquisitive. But a woman who wants fucking will risk anything to get it. So she afterwards left her business early on some excuse, and we went to a brothel, and I had her almost nightly for week or two. Often it was only one fuck she could wait for. I waited impatiently for her every night, so fresh and nice was she, so intensely did she enjoy me, and I her, in teaching her postures and the art of love in all its ways and shapes. Then I again got her to dinner at a hotel, and in bed began talking about her future, and Richard's name came up.

Said she: "It's of no use now if Richard came after me again, for he'd find out that I've done it, and I couldn't marry him." I told her that half the men had never had a virgin, or had had only one in a state of tremendous excitement, and with a little skill that she could deceive him. — He'd gone off and had left his place, and she had quarrelled with her milliner friend, Mrs. B**t*n whom she heard had told Richard that she (Madeline) had gone to dine with a regular swell (myself) who had met her by appointment at the Palace. Richard had written her that. — Mrs. B**t*n was jealous of her, for Richard was a fine man. Then Madeline got spooney on me and hinted at my keeping her. I was going over to Paris (which I did, to see for the last time the French lady whose ravishment I have told of). She burst into tears and hoped she wasn't in the family way. — I told her that in such an event, and she couldn't get her courses on, that I would provide for her (and would have done). But she now had taken to fucking, so that I feared in my heart that, when away, she would get another prick in lieu of mine. Cautioning her against that, I went to Paris.

I was gone nearly three weeks, on my return wrote her to meet me, and she did. — At first she would not go to a house with me. — When in one, I sat down on a chair, and, clasping her naked backside with both hands, pulling her towards me, and asking her if she wasn't longing for a fuck, and how many times she'd frigged herself in my absence, she, standing up, still with bonnet on, said she couldn't let me do it any more. — No, it was not her poorliness and she was not, thank God! in the family way, and didn't want to be, for Richard had come back to her, and would marry her in a year.

I was pleased, but it made me want to fuck her more than ever. — "Well, take your bonnet off." — "For a little time, but I won't let you." — A kiss and cuddle on the ample sofa, followed. — "Let's feel each other a bit, and stop, I *will* look at it first. — Oh! what a lovely little cunt!" — and I kissed it again and again. — Then I felt her, and she felt me, our tongues met, distilling their liquids, and we were both sighing with the languid pleasure our hands gave us. "I shall spend in your hand." — "No, don't." — "In your cunt then." — "Oh, no. — I'm coming Walter," — for she knew my name — I left off, not meaning her to come. The gentle wriggling of her backside and belly ceased, her thighs were quiet, we relinquished each other's genitals and looked lewdly at each other, she with petticoats half up her thighs, I with prick vertical. — "Let's do it, and I'll pull it out when my spunk's coming." — "Be sure you do, if I get in the family way you know I'm done for." — She got on the bed as nimbly as she could, for her cunt was craving for a stretch, was hot and moist with desire for the male.

The pause let our juices subside, but soon the pleasurable friction of prick and cunt roused them again. — "I'm coming love, are you?" "Aha — yes — aha — don't do it in me. — Aha." — "No — aha." — "I'm spend — ing!" — At the crisis we both forgot. She clasped me to her, her cunt constricted and held my prick with that peculiar, grinding grip which a cunt gives when spending, whilst my prick, with short wriggling thrusts, shot out my spunk into its proper place.

"Get out and wash quickly," said I, ere pleasure was well over or my prick done spending. Getting off with her, I put down the basin, poured out the water, and soon saw the pearly lumpy, stringy sperm, which ought to have been still comforting her cunt, at the bottom of the basin. She looking as I did, rubbing her cunt with a towel, and hoping it was all out. — "That's the stuff which comes out of a man's thing?" — "You've seen it before?" — "Never." — "More was on your thigh five weeks ago." — "But it was all on my chemise when I looked." She took up the basin, and looked curiously at my semen. — "I hope it's all out, you didn't keep your promise." — "I couldn't, your cunt gripped my prick into you so. — You should have jerked my prick out when you found I was spending." — Madeline had certainly not had then enough experience to know to a second when a man is going to spend; I dare say she does by this time.

We talked, with passions appeased. "No, not again" — but frigging recommenced and altered her mind. — I called out for the servant and told her to bring a French letter, a bit of sponge, and a piece of thread. — All were brought, and the maid laughed. I gave Madeline the experience of a prick covered with sheep's gut, but neither of us liked it. So I pulled it off, and we fucked till consummation approached, and then put it on. We did the same with the sponge. I tied it by the thread, and pushed it up her cunt a little way, she further, and my prick pushed it right up — and so we fucked on to the pleasurable discharge. When I drew out the sponge holding my sperm, and she had washed her cunt out again, we agreed that our pleasure was much destroyed, both by the gut and the absorbent zoophyte — Madeline learnt something that night. I wonder if she has applied that knowledge since.

Fucking creates such a tie between man and woman, that, altho she said she wouldn't ever meet me again, added, "I'd better not, had I?" and altho I agreed not to ask her, yet I did a few days after by letter. — She came and was on heat — I knew it by her looks and manner, and told her she was lewed. She laughed and, colouring up said she did feel as if she'd like me. — This time, not wishing to injure her, I took a nice little round sponge, and my sperm spat into that absorbent, but we half fucked before I put it up. I got her to dine that night, and we were both in fine condition. Her parents were told there was late work (the usual milliner's excuse) and I gave her a sound ballocking. Her poorliness she expected on every hour, and such was the state of lewedness which our heated genitals got into that, at the last fuck, we did without sponge, for I couldn't that time spend with the sponge in her. — When my pleasure was coming on, and my glans touched the sponge, so intensely sensitive was I that it stopped me spending. — When I did, I pulled my prick out nearly to the tip and spent thus, she washed directly and took no harm.

That night we parted for good, and I made her take ten pounds — I was to see her again some time afterwards as it happened.

I incline to think, now that a few years have passed since this intrigue, that Madeline came to the second dinner with me, intending to let me have her. — Her little struggles and resistance may either have been shams or timidity at the last moment, when I was getting to victory. Was it annoyance at the loss of her lover, a desire for a change of life, a speculation of becoming my mistress, or even my wife — or lust? — Lust does not influence women usually so much before they lose their virginity as it does men (unless so hot cunted as but few are). It influences women more afterwards, when they know the delights of a cunt plugged by a prick. Curiosity is powerful with them, and numbers fall under a mistaken notion of their own powers of resistance. "I did not mean to let him do it, tho I didn't mind his larking or feeling me," said Maria ***** once to me. Many have said the same when I have closely questioned them. — That's it. — The idea of feeling and being felt by the man, the sensuous delight increased because forbidden, — of having a little baudy chaff about sleeping together, and so on, is permissible. — Even the hurried feel, the glance askant at the stiff prick, is charming, and all very well. But they don't reckon the consequence of the chance of his getting his fingers on to their clitorises and their not being able to get them away. — A five minutes' good frig, whilst a woman is kissed, and lewed suggestions whispered by the man, settle most women. That is my experience. Half ready to spend, lewed images in their mind, curiosity at work, they almost helplessly let the man do his will. — "Open thighs — enter prick — exit hymen. — All is over, my love. Swab up the blood stained sperm from your cunt, and prepare for the next ramming. You are a woman now, in for a penny in for a pound. The gates of pleasure are opened, let the promenaders walk in."

Indeed that was the sum of Madeline's confession to me when we talked about the affair. She didn't think I'd dare to try to do what I did. "Why did you come again?" — "I don't know really, I wanted to come and didn't want, I like dining with you. I wondered what you'd do." — "You didn't think I'd be quiet and respectful." — "No — I don't know really, but thought you might put your hands up my clothes, that I really did." — "And show you my prick?" "Well, I did." — "Now you were lewed and came to be fucked." — "That I declare before Heaven I didn't, for I'd made up my mind if you did what you did before that I'd run out of the house." She didn't know her own strength of resistance, and they are nearly all alike. Nature has made them so. — Prick is potential. — Altho a woman cares less about seeing or feeling a prick than a man does a cunt, (for females have seen pricks all their lives, it's incidental to their sex as nurse, and they see them from their infancy), yet a stiff stander shown at the moment when the fingers have raised lust thro the clitoris, is an invincible persuader. "Open sesame," and the female opens. — It is her destiny.

CHAPTER IV

*Notable courtesans. — My amorous sexual habits and care. — A Paphian's ball. — Mixed female aromas. — Liz M***d*n at B****t*n S****e. — Nelly ****, and Captain Blank. — The Captain's caprice. — Four in the dark. — In the Captain's leavings. — Three in a bed. — The next day and night. — Amorous tricks. — The Paphian bedfellows described. — Bertha visited. — The Glover's shop at Paris. — Dinner with Bertha. — At the Argyle. — In the cab. — An unfortunate maid of all work. — Bertha dines with me again. — Vanquished. — A story broken off.*

In the intervals of poking Madeline, I of course had many gay women. I changed my women often and had settled to no one of them as a regular, since Amelia German disappeared. I longed for one woman whom I could like better than the others, and go to when tired of strangers, but had no intention of keeping to one alone. — Fidelity to one woman, I am convinced now, is impossible from me.

Having had my game with cheap women, I went to the opposite extreme and had the dearest. Those who said, "I never take less than a fiver," and were not satisfied with that, caught me. I had half a dozen well known courtesans. Baby J***s*n was one. — A dark, fine built woman of about thirty, called Kate H*m**t*n, tho not the ancient baudy house keeper, was another. — Sk*t**s took a fancy to me, but her foul tongue shocked me. I had a thin and lovely lady with exquisite eyes, since married to one of the rich ones of the land (and still alive and living in a square, and who shall be therefore nameless.)

I slept out more than at home for a couple of months, and then found my man also slept out, reckoning upon my absence. —

This change of women was lovely, the variety in cunt, and style of fucking, an endless pleasure both to mind and body. — I rested from my amours at intervals, never took cock stimulants, but revived myself by repose alone, when my doodle and body gave signs of fatigue; but, excepting at intervals of fierce rutting, I did not overtax my body. — Two spends a night were usually my exercise, unless the lady longed for more (and they often times did with me), and then I fucked till my sperm ran thin and short, and I rested longer afterwards.

These swell Paphians gave dances among their set, hiring rooms for the purpose, making the balls strictly private to avoid interference of the police, and not fly in the face of the Law. A dance of that sort was given by a woman whom I knew. She hired well known rooms in G***t P***l**d St for the purpose. There were men and women together, about eighty of us. The men paid for the suppers, and each paid also for a lady, and the pay was such that it left a margin, which enabled the hostess to pay for the rooms and band. — The men were all in evening clothes, the women beautifully dressed, and décolleté, and were such an exquisite set of young creatures as I have never yet seen elsewhere. — No introductions were needed, any man asked any woman to dance, altho, to avoid jealousy, that needed some discretion; and the women did not hesitate to ask men to dance with them. Every thing in fact was free and easy, but not immodest, until after supper, when it got more than free and easy.

Then the dancing became romping, and concupiscence asserted itself. I expect there was not a prick in the room which was not swollen and whitening with lust, nor a cunt which was not moist with randiness. — As I danced with one women, the aroma from her naked bosom and armpits quite enervated me. — I swear that, struggling up through her clothes and mixing with her other exhalations, was a smell of cunt in lust. I felt almost a voluptuous faintness come over me as I inhaled it, and told her of it. "Don't you like it?" said she, holding me tightly as we twirled round in a waltz. Suggestive talk was now the order of the night, baudy words escaped, the men kissed the women's shoulders as they waltzed, one or two couples danced polkas with their bellies jogging against each other, suggestive of fucking. — Then a fair lady quarrelled with a man, and broke out, — "I'm buggered if I let you fuck me to night." — Whereupon the lights were lowered and the party broke up, for fear the ball would degenerate into a riot. The patroness was wise.

About half past three in the morning, I went home with Lizzie M***d*n to her house in B****t*n Square. A house she had to herself, for she was a swell, and partially kept by *****, who thought, I believe, that he kept her entirely. — A lady of easy virtue, a friend of hers, who lived some long distance off and who was going home with a Captain **** she offered a bedroom to for the night, for the Captain was compelled to be at parade at **** Barracks early in the morning. We went home in separate conveyances, I in Lizzie's brougham. I had of course seen the other woman in the room, and the Captain also, but neither knew him or the woman, or who had come there for the night. — It was only on the road home that Lizzie told me what she had done.

Lizzie was a sweet, dark haired creature of about three and twenty. She had a short neck which rose out of most exquisite shoulders and breasts, had a pretty fat cunt, small waist, and big backside. A peculiar feature in her was the thickness of her head hair, as well as her eye brows, which were dark, and the broadest and thickest I ever saw in a woman. The same may be said of her armpits and cunt, tho in both places the hair was not long. Her cunt felt like a brush. She was a lewed devil, and on one or two occasions when I had slept with her before, fucked me well out before the morning. She undressed quickly, as did I, and kept saying, "My God how I want a fuck," and — "I wonder if Nellie **** and the Captain have fucked yet. — He's got a stunning prick, she says." — Talking and laughing thus baudily, she got on the bed, and I standing by the side was kissing her cunt, with her thighs wide open, and with my prick as stiff as need be, when knock knock. — "Lizzie, I want to speak to you."

Out got Lizzie, went for a minute outside the door, and came in laughing loudly as was the other woman. "Captain Blank wants to fuck me. — Come in, Nellie," and in came a pretty little creature about nineteen years old, with her chemise dropping off her shoulders and showing lovely breasts, and laughing like mad. We were all three indeed elevated enough. — "He be damned, that he shant," said I. — "Oh — do let me go, he says he'll give me five quid." — I said that I would leave the house at once if she did, but getting softened, and desiring to please her, and the idea making me still more lewed, said I would fuck her first and then she might go, and I showed my stiff prick to the women. — Nellie laughed. — "No, no, he wants her directly, and before she's had you or not at all." — "Then he won't." — Lizzie was vexed. "You have Nellie while I'm with him, you'll let him Nellie?" — Nellie would, and for a second I felt as if I would comply — but, "No, he'll keep you all night, and I'll see him damned first. — Let him fuck you in here and I'll see him." — Both women roared with laughter at the suggestion, which was a mere chance one, and which I didn't for a minute think would be agreed to.

"Go and tell him, Nellie," said Lizzie hastily. She did — I heard her and the man thro the open door, laughing, till she returned. — He would if the room was quite dark. — Then sprang up in me a lewed desire which had lain dormant some time, to see and feel a man fucking, to feel his standard. — But I didn't wish to be seen or known, so the idea of his fucking in the dark pleased me. "The room shall be quite dark, so that we can't see each other, but I'll feel his prick first." — Out went the girl with the message. He must have been standing at the open door of his room, for as he had the message delivered, he shouted with laughter, like a bull. — "Yes — yes" — I heard him say, and Nellie came back to tell us, and then went to fetch the Captain.

"Fuck Nellie whilst he fucks me," said Lizzie, as if she enjoyed the idea. — "There's no room." — "Yes if you get on the top of her." — I refused, being engrossed with the idea of feeling his big prick. My blood was boiling with that desire, and impatiently I got into bed — Lizzie seemed thoughtful on a sudden, went to the door and shouted to Nellie to come back, and then, "Tell him I want my five quid first." — Nellie went and in few minutes brought the gold. During her absence I felt Lizzie's cunt. — "Tell him to come in, and you put out the light, Nell." "You must be quite naked, and he will be so as well," he said. — Up sat Liz, and drew off her chemise — I threw off my shirt and cuddled her. — She felt my prick. — "Don't now, wait for him." Nellie then put out the gas, we were in total darkness, and she went off to fetch Captain Blank.

In a second, led in in the dark by Nellie, he was at the bed side. He was screwed, but knew what he was about, for he scarcely spoke, and then in a feigned, whispering voice.—He instantly put his hand to Liz' cunt, and met mine there. I removed it quickly, and stretching across her naked belly, felt for his prick and grasped it. It seemed big, and was as stiff as a horn. How I longed to see it. In a second he was between Lizzie's thighs, kneeling, then dropped down on her, and at once I felt the jog of her thighs and the oscillation of his rump, as he rammed up her like a steam engine.

Nellie just then in the dark came round to my side and said, "Let us do it"—and laid hold of my prick.—But I said, "No,"—for the couple fucking engrossed me. I felt him all over, then knelt up, and putting my hand between his thighs and under his balls, felt his prick as it moved up and down, I squeezed his balls gently and felt delighted. I don't believe that he even knew that in his pleasure, which seemed to absorb him directly, his prick was in her.

Both indeed were too wrought up in lewedness for their pleasure to last long, or let me long enjoy my libidinous amusement and curiosity. He soon sobbed out, "Cunt—fuck,"—and she,—"Oh—fuck me—spunk in me—oh—you beast—aha,"—all came jerking out of her mouth, mixing with his lewed ejaculations and murmurs. Then the gentle wriggles of his arse, as I felt them in the dark, told me all was over, whilst I still held his balls, and her naked thigh laid motionless against my knees.

Then I cried, with lustful desire which seized me suddenly.—"Come Nellie, get on the bed, let's fuck."—"Shan't then—come along Jack."—Without a word, Jack got off and left the room with her, leaving me and Liz together.—Disappointed of Nelly.—"Liz—wash dear, and let me fuck you."—"Oh—I'm so sleepy I can't get out.—Fuck me, it's all right."—Saying that, she laid hold of me with one hand, pulled me to her and with the other laid hold of my rigid prick.—"Oh! its as big as his, fuck me."—"Did you spend with him."—"Yes, and want it again. Do it."—"I shan't—wash."—"I won't, it's cold, and I'll frig you if you don't."—Nearly wild with lewedness, the next instant I was fucking in Jack's sperm, and few seconds afterwards we were both asleep. She had spent with delight, her pleasure, from her ejaculations, I believe were increased by thinking about the state of her cunt. I thought of my prick being where Jack's had just been, and not about his sperm being in her.

I awakened soon I think, she was snoring. Awakening her, we fucked again. Then I fell into the deep slumber which follows late hours, dancing, a good supper, plenty of wine, and fucking, that healthiest of exercises and sleep givers.

It was quite dark when we were awakened by heavy footsteps and loud voices; no servant was up. — "Who is that?" — shouted Lizzie. — "The Captain's obliged to get to parade, I'm letting him out." — The footsteps went down stairs, the street door banged, and then into our bedroom came Nellie in the dark. — Lizzie asked what the Captain had given her, and "Did he do you much?" — "No, he was screwed, and went to sleep directly he got into bed, after he'd had you. He only did me once, just before he left." — "Come into bed," said Lizzie. I joined in the request, and all three were soon in bed together, I in the middle.

I put out my hands and felt both cunts at once. — What a charming sensation to feel the palms of my hand full of crisp hair, and my middle fingers rubbing over two soft clitorises. — Nellie was fresh to me. — "I'll fuck Nellie." — Said Liz, — "Fuck away." — Nellie declined, resenting my previous refusal. "Don't be a fool Nell, let him, and let us go to sleep." — Nellie opened her thighs, and the next minute we were fucking. — Her cunt felt moist as I pushed up her. — "Did you wash?" — "I hadn't time, he only did me the minute before he went down stairs." Twice I'd fucked after the Captain, and this time in innocence. The Captain's sperm and mine had mixed in both their cunts. Then Lizzie turned her rump to me, my belly was to her rump, and Nellie's belly to mine, and in a minute we were all in oblivion. It was a cold night, and the warmth of the two beauties was deliciously soothing.

It was some hours afterwards and day light before I awakened. The women were asleep. Turning on to my back I felt Nellie's quim which roused her, and that awakened Liz. — "Get out and wash, both of you," said I. — "Why?" — "I've been beast enough to fuck you both after Captain Blank." — "What of that, it's not the first time you've fucked after a man, tho perhaps without knowing it," said Liz — We discoursed on the subject. Little Nellie, who had not been long out, listened whilst Liz, who with her six years' experience, told a tale of three men once having had her one after the other, and each time she had only given her cunt a dry rub with the towel, and neither man discovered that sperm was still in her cunt when they fucked her. "It makes me lewed when I think of it," said Liz grabbing my prick. — Nellie felt it as well, and for a minute we were silent. — Both women wanted fucking, Liz got out and pissed, Nelly followed suit, and I pissed after them.

We lighted gas, and both washed their cunts. We got into bed again, and I looked at both their carnal man traps. Then I fucked Nellie, feeling Liz's cunt at the same time. She frigged herself. Then we got up and had breakfast.

The night's fun pleased me. Liz wanted her little friend to go away, but I offered a dinner and to stop the next night. Nellie went to her home and came back. I took them both to dine, and we afterwards passed the evening at Liz's, playing cards and drinking champagne. They were both swell women. I made lascivious suggestions to them, which they were very indignant about seemingly. — It's the sham way with some of the upper class courtesans. — But a woman's a woman, most of them like lasciviousness and delight in a baudy novelty. Before the evening was over, they'd both pissed over my hand, I'd frigged Liz, and she had frigged Nellie. We went to bed together, and I fucked both before I slept. In the middle of the night I fucked Liz. When I awakened again, Nell I found had gone to the other room. I went to her there. She said she couldn't sleep three in the bed, for every movement awakened her. I fucked her, fell asleep, and was awakened in the morning by Liz, who had sought me. She was very ill tempered about my behaviour, and jealous, but got over it when I fucked her again. It was a very pleasant two nights and a very expensive one.

I several times had Liz afterwards, and we always talked about Captain Blank's letch, his big prick, and my poking twice in his sperm. — Liz said she liked the second fuck with her cunt full of it, but begged me not to tell any of the harlots whom we both knew. — I told her about Gertrude, who had been fucked by the soldiers twelve times. It was then quite fresh in my mind, for I had not long parted with Gertrude for ever. — Liz professed to believe it, after saying for a long time that she did not, but I doubt whether she really to the last did believe me quite. Gay women tell such lies themselves that they distrust others largely. She used to say that I made up the story to excite her, and it had that effect certainly. "Put it into me," — was soon said, whenever we talked about Gertrude.

Tho Captain Blank was at the ball, and of course I must have seen him, yet I did not know him from others, and tho he had been in the same room with me, and I'd felt his prick, I could not the next minute have picked him out from other men. Liz M***d*n was as said a fine, fattish made woman, with a handsome fat and full lipped cunt. I think she'd had a child, and her nymphæ were perhaps too large. She was up to every lascivious trick when she got lewed, and until then assumed dignity and modesty. — When she'd had a drop, she talked baudiness like a book. I don't think she liked women, tho I'd been told she did by other women.

Nellie **** [in her interest I don't give her initials, for I hear she is alive and a respectable married woman] was shortish, plump, and with small but beautiful breasts. She was rather knock-kneed — her cunt was pretty and had but little hair on it.

On the second night, I amused myself with putting my stiff prick first into one and then into the other woman, to see which cunt was the tightest. — I didn't thrust, but inserted it and let it feel its way about when up them. Nellie was certainly the tightest, and I told Liz so whilst my prick was in her. I was beginning to feel much pleasure just at that moment, and going to withdraw, so as to give my libation to Nellie's cunt, when Liz grasped me tightly to her, twisted her legs round mine, and squeezing her cunt up to me, gripped my prick tightly with it and fetched me. "Now you may fuck Nellie," said she, and turned her bum towards me. — Women who give themselves up to sexual pleasure have infinitely more enjoyment of life for a time than virtuous women have.

Again I went to my stock brokers, and called on Bertha, who was at first much pleased to see me, then of a sudden was cool. Had I been out of town. "Yes, to Paris." — "Nice games you have been up to there, I expect." (All women think Paris a sink of debauchery.) — "Not many, but I've had my hand up a shop woman's petticoats." — "I don't believe you — where?" said Bertha anxiously. "At a glovers, in a little room at the back of the shop. She fitted on my gloves, I was sitting down, she standing up, and I put my hands up them. both back and front." — "I don't believe you." — "It's true." — "She's a beast," — said Bertha angrily, and turned her back to me.

Now this happened to be a fact, and I gave the young woman three francs, and the next day bought another pair to get the same amusement. — If she got as much from each man whose gloves she fitted on in the course of the day, she made a good income. — Taken with a letch for her, at night I fucked the damsel at an accommodation house, but finding her a common place, so-so in shape, large, and ugly cunted and a somewhat faded and fucked out sort of bitch, tho she had a pleasing face, I never had her again. But I couldn't make Bertha believe what I told her. She thought that my tale about the feeling (I didn't tell her about my entry up the woman) was a narrative invented to induce her to let me do the same with her. I heard that afterwards.

As I was going, "When are you coming to dine with me?" — I said jokingly, not meaning it as an invitation, for I had given up all idea of getting her. — "Whenever you ask me if I can get away," she replied. Amazed, I named day after day till one suited. Off I went rejoicing, and wondering who she'd dined with before; feeling now sure that she'd had the male persuader in her vitals, and that she had some sweetheart whom she met at times.

The day came. I went to the city to see if there was any obstacle. She would be there. — "And mind, — I've told you what you ask me for, and it's no use" — were her last words as I went off. I took a bed and sitting rooms for the night, at ***** hotel, where I've had many a dinner with women before, and at seven o'clock we were at table.

I had kept myself chaste since the dinner had been arranged, and my prick was in very stalwart state, yet I felt uncertain about Bertha's compliance. Her manner was so unusual, her freedom of talk, the way she let men kiss and chaff her, had told me she knew quite well what I wanted, but mightn't let me have it. — Indeed she did and said all with an air of freedom, and yet modesty, unlike any other woman I have met in such condition. She eat well, but with an air as if thinking of something else all the while. When I began talking suggestively she remarked, — "Ah! I expected you to go on like that" — for a time this quite disconcerted me.

Dinner over, we sat on the sofa. I began warm talk, she told me to be quiet, and wouldn't hear it, and got up to go whenever I attempted a liberty. She listened to and questioned me on my stories about women when not told in free language, but got angry at plain words. Then all at once she asked me to take her to the Argyle rooms, she'd never been there, wanted much to see what it was like, and how the gay women behaved. — I told her she might meet there men who knew her, and what would they think of her. She produced a thick veil, and said she had both bonnet and mantle that no one had seen. I refused. — "You say you love me, and won't do that simple thing." — "Let me feel your legs just to your knees then." — She wouldn't. — At length I took her to the Argyle. She had evidently come to dine with me with no other object.

She sat for nearly an hour closely veiled, and scarcely uttering a word — Women looked at her as did men, but I think no one recognized her. A couple of lovely harlots whom I knew talked to me. — When was I going to sleep with her again? one asked. — The other wondered where I'd been. — "I'm engaged to night." — "Oh I didn't see," — said she, moving off, and looking at my companion, who then said she must go home — I would see her home. — Well she didn't object, she wasn't ashamed of her home, and in a four wheeled cab we went off.

In the cab, she got talkative about gay women. What money did they get? was it agreed, before men went home with them? and so on. "You know two, it seems, and how many more." — "Twenty perhaps." — "Story." — "I do, and have slept with every one of them." — In the dark, and as she couldn't escape me, I let go the bridle of my tongue, said I'd fucked them, described their cunts and other charms. To which she remarked. "You don't get me in a cab with you again. — No, I don't dine with you again," — but said not a word more. Then my lust roused me fiercely, I tried to feel her, and got my hand half way up her thigh, but no further. — There, stout resistance and tears stopped me. We dismissed the cab at the end of the street. I saw her nearly to her house, but at her request, as her brother might come out or be going home, I left her there. I took the number of her house and watched her enter it.

That district of London was but little known to me, but I knew that five or ten shillings there, would go as far with women as a sovereign or two further west: and that all the fine handsome women of London are not within a mile of Charing Cross, and also knew that the West End whores mostly come from the east, when

London born. Lewed to my marrow, and disappointed, I found my way to the main road, saw plenty of convenient creatures in simple attire, and offered a shilling to one to feel her cunt in a bye street, which she amazed me by refusing. "No, not for two shillings." She wouldn't be felt in the streets at all, give her five shillings and I might have her. Yet hundreds of women's cunts I have felt for a shilling and in the best parts of London. Further on I found one or two who were more complacent. A third woman I took into a public house to look at her, giving her a glass of liquor. It was to see her face. She was ugly and worn out, and I left her there. All was done in twenty minutes from the time I left Bertha at her house.

Then, perhaps because the woman had refused my fingerings in the street, I took a fancy to have her, went back, and there she was, standing at exactly the same spot. — "Yes" — she'd her own room, there was a house close by with a good room for two shillings if I preferred it, it was best to go there. I went to *her* room, and found it neat, clean, and comfortable. She undressed when I asked her without speaking, whilst I sat looking at her. Her linen was clean and neat and she was a well formed young woman of three or four and twenty, dark haired, and with but slight hair on her cunt. — In five minutes her cunt was a pond of sperm, which I had hoped to put into Bertha. She washed it, and I began talking. She didn't like being felt in the streets she said, she hadn't cheek, she should have it in time, the women said. — "Then you haven't been gay long." — "A month ago I was in service." — She didn't like gay life, she didn't seem to get on at all, and should try to get into service again.

She had half dressed when I said I should like to do it again. "I hope you'll give me a little more, then." — I doubled the fee. — "There it is, my dear — now let me look at your cunt." In my impatience for her pleasure, I had before scarcely seen it. After inspection, I laid down by her side, fingering it and talking. She was in a service at ****, about two miles off, She gave name and place with seeming exactitude. The son of her mistress did it to her first, and only two months ago, she didn't know how she came to let him, he was always after her, trying to feel her and showing his thing.

One day, his mother being out, she let him have her. She

supposed she liked him and perhaps she wanted it, or something, for somehow it was all over before she knew what she was about. She was astonished at herself. She was the only servant, and he the only child. This all seems very natural to me now, for some of the women I have had the first of yielded, I believe, without intention. — Liking, kindness, and lewedness at the moment, made them yield to me.

Then she couldn't keep him away from her. When at home, (he had some occupation out), he was always at her, and she was frightened when he and his mother were both at home. She was foolish enough to let him go to her bed at night, and the mother caught them there together and fast asleep. — Out she was turned next morning without a character. The son came to see her now, and gave her all he could, she believed, but he was only nineteen, and his mother half kept him. "Don't make a noise please, I'm the only woman in the house. I knew them before I came, and they let me the room as a servant out of place, I didn't go on the streets till I'd spent all my money. — They know now what I do, but won't turn me out as long as no one comes to me in the day, and I don't bring men home if I can help." It was a little tradesman's shop with three or four rooms over. This accounted for the room looking so different from the ordinary harlot's chamber, with its ragged, disorderly furniture, and trumpery ornaments.

The story interested me, it seemed quite likely, and was like a page out my own history in my youth. How I then managed to get into our servants has sometimes astonished me. "The fact is *you* wanted fucking and let him." — Then, as I had twiddled her cunt about, I began to want to enter it, and had made her also want it as well, for she handled my prick and in a whisper, "Do it to me." — "Do you want it?" — "Yes." — Next minute our backsides were in motion, and we spent together. — "I've a good mind to sleep with you" — "I wish you could, but they won't have it here." — Then I departed.

There was something about this woman that so pleased me that I wrote to her, naming the time, and went to her place two days afterwards. She met me outside the house. She had told me her name, which I found also was written in big letters inside the lid of her box. She'd had one man if lucky each night, she told me, not more, "But I scarcely get enough to live." Yes, she spent with them — "Thinking about it makes you want to do it, but I wish I were dead." — "Let's get into bed together." — "If you like, but the sheets are not very clean, tho nobody's been in them but myself, and I wash myself all over every day." We stripped, and I fucked her three times. She was getting thin, she thought, thro fretting, but she was in very nice condition. She enjoyed my prick, which added to my pleasure, and I heard a lot more of her history, of her misery the first night she was turned out, and so on. I told her I should know by a careful look at her cunt if she'd been fucked longer than two months. "Two months and a fortnight ago I was a virgin, you may look as long as you like."

I did, and am quite sure she hadn't been fucked long. I've had I can't say exactly how many virgins, tho I've written an account of all of them, but think a dozen and more, and have seen all their cunts after their defloration and some of them before. Certainly this woman's cunt looked as if it had been not long split, for the jagged edges were quite visible. I wished her to go home to her relatives, and gave her three pounds to go with. She said she would, and I think she did. I advised her to write from her home for a situation, and say she had never been in London.

I didn't go near Bertha for some days, feeling annoyed, and then took a fancy to watch her home from the shop, expecting she would go elsewhere; but for two nights she went straight and quickly home. Then I called at the shop again. "Oh," said she, "I thought you were lost." — Determined to tell her I had been with women, I began. — "I don't want to hear about your doings, tell them to some one else." — I had a long conversation, in which I reminded her (people coming and interrupting frequently) of what I'd said, and done in the cab; to all of which she objected. — "You only came to dinner to get me to take you to the Argyle." — "What of that? I knew what *you* wanted me to dine for."

I left irritated with the young woman, yet with a stronger desire to have her than before, and a half belief that I was wrong in my estimate of her virtue. — That belief became much strengthened by going to the other shop, seeing the mistress there, speaking slightingly of Bertha's virtue, and getting a smart reply, that there wasn't a more virtuous, respectable girl in London, and that all her family were. "Aye — ye may talk, and chaff, but that's all the fun you'll get out of Bertha."

I lived my usual life for a week, then went to Bertha's shop, and two nights after she again dined with me. Now I made all sorts of extravagant promises to induce her to sleep with me. I no longer minced the matter. — After what I had done and said previously in the cab, no modesty was needed. She took scarcely any notice of what I said — seemed not to hear it, sat reflecting, and then all at once, stroking my face with her hand, begged me to take her to the Argyle again, she would go away if I did not. — Immensely against my will, I took her there. She sat as before with veil down, completely hiding her features for a full hour, quite taciturn. Then suddenly she turned to me and with a shudder. "Let us go away — I've a horrible presentiment that one day I shall become one of these women," and she almost dragged me out of the building.

"Come and have another glass of wine, you need not get back for an hour or more." "Very well," said she in a voice almost inaudible. — At a tavern she gulped down a glass quickly. — Outside I said, "Come with me, have pity on me, I love you so," and with her arm in mine I led her in the direction of a baudy house. "That's not the way home," said she, stopping. — I hailed a cab, determined to risk everything. I saw the girl liked me, and began, as I thought, to like her more than I cared to own to myself — or was it mere lust? Telling where to drive to, I put my arms round her the instant the cab moved and got my fingers on her slit; for an instant she struggled, and then was silent whilst I titillated her clitoris and besought her to let me have her, in the salacious words which come naturally to me when so placed, and I suppose to most men, when lust is powerful in them.

[She was a girl of great self possession, none ever knew better what she was about. In after years she shewed this under difficult circumstances, and that she was a true honest woman. — Lustful she was not, and the only reason I can assign for what followed is that she had an affection for me, and believed the promises I made her under the influence of lust, of a strong desire to have her, and no great belief in her virtue: promises I did not, could not, keep, and was punished for it.]

I stopped the cab at the end of the street, and, taking my arm, she walked quietly with me to the house, From the time I commenced frigging her to the time when the room door closed, she never uttered a word. — Now she looked round the room, then despairingly at me and said, "It's a Brothel, I shall come to be one of those women." — It was said in a quiet tone, as if she had made up her mind to courses which would ensure her being one. [She never was.]

Without a word she gave herself up to me. She only winced when I put my hands up her clothes, and when I put one down her bosom, but she never spoke. Delighted, excited yet staggered with her submission, I uttered words of love and desire. "Let me take off your frock." — She did, but never spoke. She hesitated when I said, "Get on the bed now, love," but she got on tranquilly, like one doing penance and absorbed in thought. I had but loosened my trowsers, and thrown off my coat, fearing some sudden interruption, and as she got on the bed I did. Kissing her, I put my hand upon her cunt and tried to have a look at it. Then she sighed. "Ohoo — no — no, don't." Then instantly I threw my body on to hers, her thighs opened easily to me, and the next minute I was shedding my testicular emulsion into her. She lay quiet, with eyes closed and head turned on one side on the pillow. — My prick seemed to be stopped for a second by a barrier as I thrust at first, and then went up her rapidly, and as I came to my senses after my sexual paroxysm, my first idea was that she'd been fucked before.

As my prick came out, and I moved away, she lay with eyes closed and motionless, but with one hand pushed her clothes down over her cunt, and to all my endearments and questions and talk made no reply. I felt her cunt and looked at my hand, but no signs of bleeding was mixed with my semen. Almost directly I mounted her and fucked again, watching her now, waiting for her signs of pleasure. She shewed none till, just as my prick stiffened to the full and a premonitary throb of pleasure shot through it, I felt her cunt tightening round it. A few sharp, almost inaudible sighs escaped her, and she spent just as my spermatic emission wetted her cunt again.

I felt round my prick stem when its stiffness was subsiding, and dragging out the sperm with it, I covered her cunt with my hand, and withdrew it coated with our mixed mucous, but there were no sanguinary evidences of virginity.

She rose as quickly as I did, and began putting on her bonnet in haste. — "Wash, dear." — "I must get home as fast as I can." — "But wash first." She never looked me in the face, as I placed a basin by the side of the bed and turned away, respecting her modesty. In five minutes we were in a cab on the way home. She would scarcely speak, but she let me feel her cunt now, that cunt of which I had never seen but the mount, and for an instant only, as I moved from off her belly. She wouldn't say if she would meet me again or not, and was determinedly taciturn, even when we parted.

Next day I went to the shop. She had written to say she was ill, the shopkeeper told me so, and she was away for a week. I went every day to see if she had returned, tho I did not go into the shop to ascertain that. At length I saw her. She was as collected as ever; indeed, I never saw any sign of agitation in her at any time, or afterwards at critical periods. She at once agreed to dine with me, and when she did, I saw afterwards all her charms. Curiously I looked at her cunt, there was no hesitation in her letting me see it, and I couldn't make out from its look whether she was virgin a week before or not, and it was two or three months before I ventured to suggest that a prick had entered her before mine. — I never was quite quite sure whether one had or not, but think not.

[Here I break off purposely. I have given her a name not even phonetically resembling her own, and have avoided giving such description of her as would lead to identification. For the same reason I burn the rest of my narrative relating to her. The liaison so began, was fruitful in events which both regret, and the consequences of which affect me still. She is still living.]

CHAPTER V

A hairless cunted Moslem. — A shaven cunted Greek. — Three apprentice girls in a cab. — Alone with Winifred. — A sovereign bribe. — Cab riding. — The stationer's shop. — Sister Lydia. — The Gentleman lodger. — Piety against a wall. — Winifred on the watch. — The couple detected. — Sisterly arrangements. — The help of a book. — Winifred at a baudy house. — Verification of her sex. — Hands crossing, fingers active. — Lydia's advice. — Winifred consents. — A commonplace termination. — Utility of a medical title.

I was again in the East of Europe, and, going down the Danube, reached Constantinople. — Outside my hôtel there were two or three hangers-on loafers, in semi-oriental dress, who, when I and other visitors appeared, accosted us, offering their services to find men or women for us, or to show us about the city. The city was in fact their first offer. It was only when a little away from the hôtel and from other travellers that the suggestions about copulation came out. I had been talking with a gentleman at my hotel, who had been staying in the city for many months and had heard from him that all Turkish women removed the hair from their cunts, so when one of these *soi-disant* guides asked me if I would like "a lady without hair on it" — for the fellow spoke not bad English, — I consented to go with him.

He led me down hill into a tortuous narrow lane, about going into which, had it been in a Western city of Europe, I should have hesitated to accompany a stranger. — But here all the ways were crooked, and it was broad daylight. Knocking with a stick at a door in a wall of a house without a window in it, and giving a slight but peculiar howl, the door opened, a female appeared, and, accosting him whilst looking at me, closed the door which she had opened and beckoned me to follow her. My guide squatted on a mat, and without a word or taking any further notice of me, began to smoke a cigar which looked as if he had manufactured it himself. Useful as I have found pimps, often as I have used them, I never could bear the animals to await me at a female's house, but dismissed them, either paying them then or letting them know (and they knew well enough) where they could find me for their pay. But in this strange city of a Moslem race — where I did not understand a word of the language and where people disappear mysteriously, I felt rather glad than otherwise that he was waiting for me. — What does a man of that class think about when he knows he has led a man to a house where he may get a woman, I wonder?

The woman led me across a small dusty yard, in which stood one tree growing seemingly out of sand, up a flight of stairs to a room with two doors in it, one at which we entered, the other opposite to it. There she stopped, smiled, nodded, and held out her hand. — I understood *Backsheesh* and dropped a small coin into it. She looked discontented and I added another. Then, smilingly, she opened the opposite door, looked in, went in, and, turning round, beckoned to me. I went in, the door closed behind me, and I found myself in the presence of a dark eyed lady smoking a chibouque, with something like lemonade in a glass beside her on a small stool, whilst she lay on a long sort of divan about a foot above the floor.

Then began dumb play. Knowing she was a courtesan (though the guide had most volubly whilst going along with him said she was nothing of the kind), I didn't shilly-shally long. Thrusting my hands up between baggy trowsers as I sat down by her feet, I tried to feel her cunt, but felt nothing but linen. She laughed and held out her hand. I pointed to the door at which I had entered. She clapped her hands and in came the female who had of course been expecting it. They talked, I didn't understand a word of it, but saw it was about money, and it ended, after much gesticulation on all sides, in my paying about four times as much as I was told by my guide was the gay-woman's fee, and which I had already paid to the door woman. I knew I was being done, but had expected that, and it didn't even annoy me.

Then the lady, the financial part of the business being arranged, gradually divested herself of all but her chemise, and I saw a plump, indeed a fattish female, whom I should have guessed thirty in London or Paris, with a face painted in all ways, but who really was handsome, and who, without more ado, opened a pair of fat white thighs, and disclosed her split or slit.

Cunt it was, but a slit in white flesh it really looked, for not a vestige of hair was visible. She had but a small clitoris [perhaps she'd had it cut off, I have since heard that such things are done in the East] and very small nymphæ. — The cunt lips puffed out and I thought, on carefully looking, that I saw signs of stubbly hair, but could feel none. The cunt looked in fact like a long cut in a lump of dough, with a little red line indicating the parting. Pulling the lips wide apart, the red lining showed handsomely, and for a minute or two I amused myself with looking at it and feeling it. She was complaisant.

Then she investigated me, and said "Take off" — she evidently had had Englishmen, and suggested my taking off my trowsers, which I readily did. She felt and squeezed my prick, in the knowing manner of a harlot who looks out for ailments there. I knealt between her legs and shook my stiff stander in her face, and the next moment it was up her. There was something stimulating in the idea of having that hairless cunt. I put my fingers down and felt the smooth puffy lips which enclosed my prick, and soon left my mucilage in her vagina, to delight and soothe it.

She retired, and returned with a fresh washed cunt, pointed to an iron basin on a stool for my purification, and there I washed before her. Then in dumb play, and by a few words of English and much gesticulation, and the greater part of the time looking at and feeling her cunt, I passed away sufficient time to get another rise in my prick. The hairless slit received it, emptied it, rejected it in a slobbered state of exhaustion and unfitness for further sexual work, and after washing I left, escorted by my pimp — who wanted to know how I liked the lady.

I told my hotel acquaintance frankly all about it. — I've an impression he had had the woman himself, tho he didn't say so. She was an Armenian, he had heard, and not a Moslem woman, that Moslem women were not to be had. — That didn't matter to me, it was a hairless cunt, and I expect a Moslem woman, if this were not one, would have looked and fucked the same.

Afterwards, one night near the Bosphorus, I had an Italian woman, and a Greek also in the same room, both with cunts nearly as black as coal. Talking with the Italian and telling her what I had done with the hairless cunted woman, she said she would fetch one also. I fucked both her and the Greek, and a day or two after went to the same house in the day time, and in about an hour the Italian brought me quite a young woman without any hair on her cunt. I looked her carefully over from arsehole to navel, but not a hair could I see on her privates, tho I could feel a roughness.

I fucked her whilst the Italian, laying on the bed, showed me baudily her horsehaired sperm sucker, and I came to the conclusion that a hairy cunt in woman is much handsomer and more voluptuously enticing than a hairless one. It is different in a young girl, tho even in a tender lass I think I like to see a slight hair on her motte. — But the tender pink of the split-lining, becomes the hairless pad in which it lies, in the youngsters up to fourteen years of age.

[This adventure with the smooth hairless cunted ones, preceded my liaison with Madeline and Bertha. The narrative, by error in arranging the papers, has been placed after them.]

[Then chance threw in my way a young lass, it was my last piece of such luck before a great change took place in my social life.]

About five o'clock one evening in September I was walking along one of the main roads of the suburbs when heavy rain suddenly set in. Tho I had an umbrella, I turned under an archway at the entrance to a builder's yard. Standing there were three girls neither apparently older than sixteen, they were all neatly tho poorly dressed and looked like the daughters of small tradesmen. They all turned out to be apprentices to a dressmaker (not work women yet) and received a mere trifle (nine pence a day) as an encouragement, which was to be gradually increased as they grew older and could be more useful. This was told me by one of them later on.

They had no umbrellas. Standing there, I talked with them and asked how they expected to get home. — They seemed pleased with the notice of a gentleman, and answered cheerfully. The rain continued, and as I talked I began to think of the lasses' cunts, especially of one of them who was very pretty. They told me the way they were going home, and just then an empty four wheeled cab passed. Luckily I hailed it in time, and offered the girls if they liked to get in to drive them part of their way, as I happened to be going in their direction. Seemingly with much pleasure they accepted, and we all four get into the cab together.

Directly the cab moved off I began joking. Had they sweethearts? I was sure they had. — Impossible for such nice girls not to have them; they got kissed of a night in the dark, I was sure, didn't their sweethearts tickle them and try to feel their garters, and so on? The girls were delighted with the chaff and talked at once. — "No — no — Bessie has" — "And so has she." — "He's felt your garters, you told me so." — "No — no" — "Mother won't let me out of a night." — "Mine does sometimes, to go to aunt." — "I get out if father's out," — So their tongues gabbled on. — "Now you've all been kissed haven't you? — tell the truth and I'll give you each six pence." — With shuffling and hesitation they did. — "Winifred has" — "So have you." — "Oh, you story." — "I saw Bob do it." — Each got six pence, (tho I hadn't enough of that small coin). "Now, give me a kiss for the ride, and I'll give each a shilling." They demurred till the prettiest, who looked the boldest, let me take one, gave me a return, and then the rest did. I made each stand up before me to give the kiss, and pulled her to me between my legs, my hand round her bum which I pressed hard whilst I held her, tho not so as to scare her; longing when I did it to have my hands on the naked flesh.

I went on joking, approaching smuttiness, and had just offered them a shilling each to feel their garters, when one cried out. — "Oh, it's past our street, stop the cab please, sir." — I offered to drive down the street. "Oh, no, father might see us" — the little sluts were cunning already. The rain had come to a drizzle, and there was no help for it but to let them out. The two stood up together facing the cab door as the cabman opened it, and as they prepared to step out I put my hand in front and gave a gentle push up against one of their notches, and pinched the other's bum. — One looked up slily at me but without a word.

Winifred, who looked the oldest, was also about to alight, but she had said she lived further off to the right, so I stopped her.— "No, you can get out further on." — "I'd rather get out with them, it doesn't rain much." — I closed the door, the two girls walked away, the cabman drove off. — "I much want to go to ****," said I, "and then I'm coming back, drive with me there, and I'll set you down on my return." She refused, but the cab went on, the rain recommenced, she acquiesced, and sat quietly by my side, a little anxious seemingly. — For a moment I reflected, but my cock, erecting itself unasked, urged me on. I let the cabman drive on much further than I wanted to go, then, coming back, called where I had intended, Winifred sitting in the cab all the time. I did not stop at the house five minutes and then told the cabman to drive a long way round.

I kissed her, praised her beauty (she was the prettiest of the lot), and as she liked the praise and the kisses, offered a shilling to see her garters. That alarmed her and she wanted to get out. — "Oh, what a long way you're taking me." — I pacified her; on went the cab, I asked her to meet me another day, and at last. — "Now don't be alarmed, you have only to say no and you shan't. I'll give you a sovereign to let me feel your thighs." — I'd expected her to be scared, and even to desire to get out of the cab. To my delight all she said was, "You dirty man, I shan't." — I pitched the sovereign down on the seat in front of us, and begged and coaxed her. "Just to feel your thighs." A little time after, "Just to feel if there's any hair there, and you shall feel me, don't be alarmed, I won't do it if you so dislike it, but feel me." She began really to cry, it was no sham, but it soon ceased. "There, take up the sovereign, whether you let me or not it's yours." This was interlarded with her refusals, angry at first, but getting less and less vehement. At length, when it was getting dusk, she felt my prick, and soon after my fingers just felt her little notch. Soon it was quite dark. What would her mother think of her being so late. "Oh, where are you taking me?" — Soon I set her down near her house, with a promise from her to meet me next day if she could.

"You won't tell those two will you?" — were the last words Winifred said. — "Is it likely I should be so foolish? be sure *you* don't tell the girls or any one else, what we've done, and be sure you never tell any one." I gave her the sovereign, and she gave me her home address and that of her place of work. I wrote them down somehow in the cab, which I made move on to a gas lamp. Her mother kept a stationer's shop she said, and she had a sister named Lydia. — "What shall I tell mother about being so late?" she kept asking. — "Say the rain, my dear." I never knew what she did say, but girl, or woman, or crone, they always have an excuse ready, especially if it be to hide or help fucking. *That,* it seems to me stimulates the female brain to craftiness in lying, in a marvellous degree.

Five minutes after she left me, I drove to her house. It was easily found, and was in a poorish street, but seemed quite respectable. Stationery and many trumpery things were sold there. — The mother was in the shop, and also her sister whom she told me of the following day, and I came away, wondering if the girl would keep her word and meet me for another drive, at what she thought of my stiff prick, whether she'd ever seen a prick in that state before, and what the other two girls thought of my talk about their garters.

I wondered more than anything at my success in getting a young girl, after an hour and a half's acquaintance, to feel me and let her belly be felt. — In truth my fingers barely touched the top of the notch where it splits up from the belly. She didn't seem of the same class as the little boxmakers whom I had a few years ago.

Next day, and half an hour earlier than the day before, as arranged, I waited near to the workshop of Miss Winifred (her companions called her "Winny"). She is the only female with that Christian cognomen I ever yet have known in amatory affairs. — I had doubts whether she would show up, for it was only a minute or two before she left the cab that I felt her belly and forced her hand on to my prick. She was scared, and there was so much hesitation and anxiety in her manner, when she promised to meet me again. — I had suggested her leaving earlier, so as to get away from her fellow apprentices, who usually walked part of the way homewards with her. She was a little late, but appeared just as I had given her up and got into the cab as quickly as she could, evidently to avoid being seen. She was cunning enough for that. — What was really Winifred's object in thus meeting me a stranger? It must have been the desire again to finger, and be fingered on the organs of concupiscence, again to feel my fingers on her motte, again to feel, and perhaps now to see, that rigid male engine, about which no doubt she had heard and talked with her young friends, but may have never seen a full sized one. — It was dark when I had my persuader out in the cab, and if she saw it, it was only when a street lamp flashed on it.

"I must really get home by seven," said she, and telling me why. — "Oh, I don't want to go towards the bridge, I shan't get home in time, I won't go that way." — I was driving in the direction of a convenient house, but fearful of spoiling my chance, stopped the cab, and on her naming a road, told the cabman to drive that way. I was longing for it to get dark, but unfortunately it was a bright evening. On we went, till, passing a pastrycook's, I asked her if she'd have something. — Yes, she'd like a jelly so, she'd only once or twice tasted it in her life.

I made her sit in the cab, thinking her youth and dress, contrasted with mine, might cause remark, and crammed her with jelly, then took her cherry brandy, thinking that might warm her up. Then on we drove, I talking amorously and kissing her every minute. The cherry brandy opened her mouth, and she volunteered much about herself, I had only to ask a question and she spoke for five minutes, not that she was in the least degree tight. — I encouraged the loquacity, feeling sure I should get no liberties till dusk, I never had such a garrulous lass, and all about herself and family. — This is some of what she told me.

Her father had been a clerk, her mother kept the stationer's shop since his death, which took place about four years previously. Since then they had mainly depended upon the shop for their living. — They let the two rooms above to a single gentleman, who had lodged there for two years. Her sister Lydia had been to service, but now minded the shop with her mother. They two kept the house, and did most of the work themselves, but a strong char-woman came daily to do rough jobs. — Lydia waited on the gentleman, who was not much at home in the day. He was middle-aged, very religious, and anxious for Lydia to go to prayer meetings with him, but the mother objected. She however went with him sometimes on the sly. Lydia and her mother had had words about that. Mother says Lydia's had trouble enough, and doesn't want her to get into any more. — She (Winifred) used to take him his breakfast things sometimes before she was apprenticed, now she went away to work too early.

She was allowed now nine pence a day, soon they would give her a shilling because she was getting useful. — "But it's hard work, and I can't bear sitting sewing all day long. — I'd like something else but don't know what." — She had a bag with her in which I found she took her dinner, and the dressmaker gave her her tea, and she had her supper when she got home. Hungry and tired she was when she did get home. She hated sitting in the shop parlour or the kitchen, she liked serving in the shop, but was glad when her mother let her go to her aunt's, or to chapel. — They were very pious chapel people, seemingly.

With that fine perception in all sexual matters which I know I have, I caught at her remarks about her sister having got into trouble, — Something whispered to me — "Cunt" — Trouble to her mother? — "Cunt." — "What was your sister's trouble?" — I asked.

Winifred saw with the cunning of a female that she had said too much, her loquacity ceased, and she began to evade and equivocate. — She didn't know what, but had heard her mother say so — but it was all right now — and so on. — "You're fibbing, my little darling, you do know. — Perhaps she's had a foolish lover, who foolishly got her a baby, when he needn't, they might have had all their pleasure without *that*." — "Oh — oh — what a thing to say. — I don't know I'm sure — I don't know what you mean."

It was just the time for telling her what I meant, for it was getting dark, the lamps were lighted, and I could only clearly see her pretty face for the moment as we passed them. — So I told her what I thought of Lydia, and in voluptuous words, and for the first time said "cunt, prick, fuck," that trinity of words which conveys all, expresses all — I had never said them on the night before, but had used suggestive words, as my thing — your belly, and so on — simple words which nevertheless set the brain thinking, and the body lusting, yet do not scare. — At every baudy sentence, at every suggestion, she now only said. "Ho — ho," and at last burst into screaming laughter. It was a peal of laughter, amused, timid, almost hysterical, and then suddenly ceasing. — "I don't know what you mean, or anything about it, only what mother says — let me get home."

"I'll ask Lydia and tell *you* what *she* says," said I with coolness. At that she laughed again, but as I saw she was determined to know nothing, I changed my tone. — "Let's look at your boots, you want another pair, put your foot on the seat." — "Oh, they're shabby, I've got a better pair for Sundays" — and apparently diverted from what we had been talking about, she began to talk again and put one foot upon the seat, looking at it tho she couldn't see it plainly. At once I rapidly ran my hand up her clothes and got it between her thighs, just as she closed them tightly on it.

But it was too late, my forefinger was a little in the notch, I could feel the soft pad, the division, and a nubbly little clitoris. — She moved, wriggled, jumped up, sat down again, but somehow I managed to keep my finger there and move it slightly, pulling her to me with the other hand, kissing her and talking baudy. Spite of her. — "No — no — I won't." — I still felt the cunt. How delicious to feel that young virgin cunt, that soft pad above that little button of gristle — made for man's fingers to rub, to irritate. How voluptuous to *her* to have my fingers on it, and to know and think of what I wanted. Yet with a bounce she got away and sat opposite to me. "I'll never ride with you again," she said.

"Yes, my darling you will, and I shall give you pleasure, and you me, now come this side, I've done, and you shall feel me." — "Shan't — I won't." — But persuaded she did, for my erotic philosophy told. — "Why shouldn't we — who will know but we? — every girl does it but doesn't tell." — Sexual want, and voluptuous feelings pervading, settled it; and in five minutes in absolute silence, she was sitting with her little hand round my standing prober, and I was feeling the full little pad at the bottom of her belly, on which I could just feel the slight hair of puberty. She was just over sixteen years of age.

As we approached her street — "I wonder if mother's out, she sometimes takes a walk about this time on Wednesdays," said Winifred, anxiously relinquishing my prick and looking out of the cab. She got out at the end of her street, I dismissed the cab, and at a distance following her, saw her enter the shop and, going up to it, saw through the window Lydia as I supposed (it was). Staring at the good looking young woman, I wondered again what her trouble had been; and again said to myself, "Cunt's had some thing to do with it." — Winifred's street led out of a broad highway with but little traffic, it was the least frequented large highway so near the bridges in London [it is nearly the same now spite of buildings and population]. The footpaths were very wide with a strip of paving along them. — Some big gardens enclosed by high walls were there at places, and the rest of the houses fronting the road were oldish middle class and with very long gardens in front. A dull quiet road it was. I sauntered along it, in a madly lewed state thro feeling her little motte and having had my tool handled by her, and wishing for relief, looked out for a whore. — But it was just the hour when few of the professional fuckstresses were about, or indeed any one else. — At length a tallish girl but who didn't look more than sixteen came sauntering along. "Come and give me a kiss, Mary," said I, — chancing my reception.

She stopped and talked, and I found she was either gay or half gay, and after satisfying myself about her face under a gas-lamp, we went down a darkish lane or passage and against a high wall with trees overhanging it, felt her gap, and she my poker. Said she. — "I work at bonnets. — No I don't know a house near here, I live close by, but there's a nice house at about ten minutes walk." — Mutual handling of our privates went on during our talk, till I could wait no longer, and fucked the damsel as she stood against the wall, gave her half a crown, and departed, leaving her trying to piss. I like to see a woman squatting for that. — "You can't piddle, my dear," she laughed. — "I just did it before I left home, but I shall in a minute."

I could not go to meet Winifred for one or two days, and when I was at the appointed place she did not appear, nor for two days after. Thinking my chance lost, and not wishing to compromise the girl, I ceased going there, but the saucy chattering blue eyed lass, dwelt in my mind, my prick stiffened when I thought of her little hand having been round it, and of the little clitoris I had barely felt and not seen. So again I went near the workshop a little earlier, and waited inside a cab on the opposite side of the road. — At the usual hour out she came with the other two lasses.

I drove well ahead, alighted, told the cabman to follow me at a distance, and then walking straight back, met the three girls point blank. All looked confused tho they smiled, and they edged away from me. I nodded familiarly and passed on, as if I never meant again to speak to them, but noticed Winifred's face colour up, and that her eyes looked saucily at me. — Then I felt dreadfully in love with her and lusted furiously. When nearly out of sight, I got into the cab, and, telling the cabman what to do, followed at foot pace.

Just where the two girls had got out of the cab before, they turned off. Winifred crossed the road, and stood for a minute looking back. The fast little wench, I guessed, was wondering if I was about. I had reached her by then, stepped out of the cab, asked her to have a ride, was at first refused, and then she got in, saying she could only ride for half an hour. Was it in anticipation of a present?

The girl was anxious. I told her how I had seen her sister, and how a girl not older than she had let me feel her quim in **** Lane, but didn't tell I'd fucked her. — "They call it the dark walk," said Winifred, much interested. I began to think she knew a lot, but so do all girls sixteen years old in her class of life — It ended in her saying she'd meet me in an hour if she could get out. — If her mother was out she was sure she could, if at home she might refuse. "But your sister?" She didn't care about her, if she told of *her*, she'd tell of her *sister*. If she did not meet me, she'd leave earlier next day and have a ride with me. I dined off a chop at a poor dining place and at the hour named was at the spot, but Winifred never appeared.

Next day she got into the cab with me, near to work place, and again we had a long ride, jelly, cakes, and cherry brandy. — Again she felt my prick, and I a little bit more of her cunt, but she resisted furiously my fingers getting proper feel of it. In the day light now, I asked if she'd like to see my cock. No she didn't want — but, when stiff, I put my hat over it, lifted up the hat when no vehicles were passing, and the lass looked at it and laughed. — "You've seen one before, Winny." — "That I haven't," said she energetically. — We drove up and down the same road (I wonder what cabby thought) and talked. I felt her all about, but she resisted more than she had done before, and said she wouldn't ride with me again if I went on "at such games."

The jelly and cherries set her chattering. She hadn't spent any of the sovereign, and she was sick of work, she'd go to service or something else, she did not care what, her mother kept her so strict. She'd like to mind the shop with her mother, Lydia wanted to leave, but her mother wouldn't let her. — At last I heard that Lydia had stopped out all night when in service, and been dismissed. — Winifred didn't know where she'd been. "Yes you do." Well, she wasn't going to say if she did. — I concluded that Lydia had been fucked, and that Winifred knew it.

Then I resolved to try harder to get the girl, thinking from what had already taken place between us, from her voluptuous glances, from a wriggling, half lewed manner of moving and giggling, that she was of ardent temperament, and that her lower maw had craving for distension, and to have its hunger assuaged by the emollient liquid which a prick alone can give. "Pshaw, some man will get her soon, she is sure to get fucked — I may as well have her as another" — said I to myself, and tried to induce her to go to a house with me, but was unsuccessful. — I knew none in her neighbourhood for it was strange to me, and my brothels were two miles off. When we parted, she'd promised to meet me again.

Winifred's place of work was close to a road with good traffic, and that night I walked about it till I saw a well dressed doxy, and with her went to a nice quiet baudy house, which I never should have found out by myself, and as before on similar occasions, I emptied my testicles into her. I had intended doing nothing of the sort, but couldn't resist just looking at her calves, then feeling her thighs, then having a look at the red center cleft, and then I wanted to see her posteriors, and after feeling her about and saying that that was all. — "What a funny man you are, ain't you going to do anything, haven't you got a prick?" "Shall I frig you?" said the lady — A few minutes after, my poker was poking in her glowing sheath, and my semen shooting out from my balls into it. — I may add here that, many times in my life, I have found out the nearest accommodation houses by asking gay women to take me to them.

When I next met Winifred she was in a hurry to get home, but promised to meet me the next night at eight o'clock. She was to go to an aunt's, would stop there a short time only, meet me afterwards, and then we could walk. Winifred was tall and looked much older than "sixteen and a quarter," which she said she was, so walking arm in arm with me would not be noticeable — I think she was proud of walking with me. — We met, I told her I loved her, and in the dark talked unadulterated baudiness.—Said she, —"Not that way, Lydia's gone to meeting with our lodger, and may come that way home; Mother thinks he'll marry her and lets her go with him to prayer meetings now. Mother's alone in the house." Such was nearly the conclusion of our conversation in our walk, during which, I had kissed her in the street every five minutes at favourable opportunities, and tried to feel her but unsuccessfully. The little jade was either cunning or frightened.

We walked in another direction and came to a part where the high road was very wide, and where I had met the young fuckstress a week before. I wanted Winifred to go up the lane, and let me there feel her little cleft, but she resolutely refused. We stood for a minute or two talking, and I persuading, on the opposite side of the road to the lane, the mouth of which in the darkness we could scarcely see, for there was, I think, no lamp in it. As we stood, Winifred said with a start and almost in a whisper. "Oh!—there's Lydia—let's get away.—Oh! if she sees me."—"Are you sure?"—"Yes, and it's our lodger too."—Then in the darkness I just discerned a couple on the opposite side, who turned up the lane and were lost to view.

"Oh, let's go."—"No wait and see them come out to make sure you're right."—"What shall I say if Lydia sees *me* with *you*?"—"She won't say anything if she knows you've seen *her* go up there with the *lodger*." Winifred giggled.

I knew full well they'd be quick about their business, and get home as fast as they could, he with empty balls, and she with overflowing cunt.—So I led Winifred in the opposite direction and stopped just in view of the mouth of the lane. Soon the couple appeared, walking quickly. "Yes, it's our lodger, I know his walk."—"He's fucked your sister."—The girl made no reply.—We followed, keeping the couple barely in sight till we saw them enter the house, and then we parted with a kiss. "He's fucked Lydia," were my last words. The girl was silent. What was the riggish little wench thinking of?

At this time I was chasing Bertha, and had just lost Madeline. Sponge and sheep gut had been given up, for I could not bear them, and Madeline, frightened to do without them, being so anxious about getting in the family way and losing her Richard.—So the liaison languished and then ceased as told, but just then it prevented my hunting Winifred daily. Moreover, the cunning little slut was capricious, and at times even would now not cab with me, but some days after the spy on the pious couple, she met me.

She was bursting to tell me and began as soon as seated in the cab. She hadn't told her sister, but had watched her. That morning her sister had gone out for something. — Winifred hadn't been to her dress making. The lodger rang, and her mother sent her to answer "and what do you think?" "What?" "Oh, I shan't tell you" and she burst out laughing. With a little pressing she did. "I opened the parlour door, he wasn't there but was in the bed room, the door wide open; he turned round and — Ha — Ha — He — He — I won't tell you." — "Nonsense, do." — "He turned round and showed it me. — He — He — he thought it was Lydia, I'm sure, for he turned round again and put it away and then round again, and said, 'Tell your mother to cook me an egg.' Oho He — He — He."

Then I heard that when she took up the egg and breakfast, the pious lodger told her that he didn't know any one was in the room when he had turned round, begged her not to tell her sister or mother, and gave her half a crown. "But I'm sure he thought it was Lydia," said the cunning little slut. "Was it stiff?" She nodded.

I told her that no doubt they went to prayer meeting as an excuse, and that they then always fucked together. — Then I besought Winifred to come and chat with me at a house close by, but nothing would induce her, nor during two, three rides after would she do more than feel me, and let me just feel the top of her notch, so I grew tired of it. I had given her but a trifle more money, but had stuffed her each time with pastry, jelly, and brandy cherries.

"I'm going out of town, and shan't see you any more, if you won't come to a house with me, good bye." — "Very well," said she, but seemed rather astonished. — Then it occurred to me all of a sudden, and I wonder it hadn't occurred to me before. — "I shouldn't hurt you, you are so handsome that I wanted to look at you naked. — Doctors know how to get pleasure and give pleasure to girls, without doing them injury." — "You a doctor? why didn't you say so before?" — "Why should I?" — The girl began to think and agreed to meet me the next afternoon, but I got no further with her that day. I hadn't quite lost my time, for it was much pleasure riding about with her, and feeling her little naked bum and thighs, but I resolved to stay away.

In a fortnight I went again, waited two afternoons, saw work-women coming out without her, and then boldly went to the shop at dusk and brought something, being served by the mother, whom I found to be a very handsome woman, certainly not more than forty years old. Whilst serving, Winifred came in and seemed petrified when she saw me. I had fancied she was at home and had quite prepared for it, so pointed to some little article in the window that I wished to buy, and whilst the mother was getting it out, put into the girl's hand a slip of paper, on which I had requested her to meet me next day, as I'd something important to tell her.

She met me and was full of news. — She'd not been well, and had kept at home — had watched her sister, seen the lodger put his hands up her clothes, told her sister of it, had not told her mother. — A gentleman was now courting her mother, she thought, and the two now often walked out of an evening together, leaving the girls to mind the shop. — Lydia then went out with the lodger once or twice after the mother had gone, leaving Winifred alone, but not for long. They always walked in the direction of the dark lane she had noticed. — Lydia said it didn't matter if the lodger had felt her garters, for he'd marry her, Winifred told her she'd seen the attempt and then told of his showing his cock, and having seen them together go up **** passage. Lydia slapped her, she slapped Lydia, and they had a lively row. Winifred said she'd tell her mother, but at length consented not to do so.

That day I took a baudy book filled with pictures with me, shewed Winifred some of it in the cab, and lent it her. I told her also that I'd give her five pounds if she'd come to a house with me and strip. One or two days after, I heard that Lydia had caught Winifred with the book, and then they both read it together. — Winifred told her that one of the dressmakers had lent it her. Winifred still wouldn't go to a house with me, but she sat on my knee in the cab, and I titillated her little clitoris a long while, she wriggled and sighed but did not, I think, spend.

As after all these cab rides I didn't get further than a feel of her cunt top, I grew tired of the affair. It was one of the most singular I have had. — Here was a girl only a few months over sixteen, whose eyes and manners shewed she was lewed but who wouldn't answer any questions about fucking, yet would feel my cock, and allow the top of her split to be felt, but was cunning, and sufficient mistress of herself to go no further. The longer I live the more wonderful the ways of women in their lusts, and the greater variety in their manners there seems to be.

Intending to cease my chase of her, I begged her to bring me back the book, which she did one or two days after, when she'd resumed going to work. We looked over the pictures together in the cab, and I explained the postures to her. She said nothing, but she chuckled. — I begged her to come to a house with me. — "I'm frightened." Again I said that a doctor would never get a girl into trouble. — "I'm so frightened" — was all I could get out of her, even after she'd filled her belly with pastry and cherry brandy, and tho she kissed me now in quite a winning manner, as if she liked kissing, and I was her lover.

I went to B****t*n for a fortnight and amused myself there by fucking women on the sea shore. Several times I laid down on the beach with them, and altho it was hardish, it is a clean bed, and the women know the best places. What a lot of fucking goes on there when the night is dark. — "Come here, let's go to the beach — go ahead, I'll follow." When there, it was: — "Here's the money, don't let me if you have any fear of yourself." Then we were but one body for a few minutes, and then separated forever. — I took no ailment, and really as I only had the women when under the sudden impulse of a violent lust and great want of fucking, I enjoyed their cunts as much as those of swell Cyprians.

But I had a hankering after Winifred, returned to town, and, not seeing her in the shop, waited at her work place, and got her into a cab again. She was fuller of news than ever, and seemed delighted to see me. She had never expected to see me again, she said. — "And you won't unless you come to a house with me." — "I'm frightened, but Lydia says I'm a fool," said she, almost breathless.

I was astonished. I'd made up my mind that day to be brutal, to force my finger between her cunt lips, and break her hymen with my finger if she were virgin. — Now I deferred that intention, for luck in the fortnight had brought me nearer to my hopes.—It was now darkish at half past five, when we entered the cab.

She told me her mother walked out with a gentleman nearly every night, leaving the two girls together. Winifred wouldn't now be in the house by herself often, but would mind the shop if Lydia wanted to talk to the lodger. The cunning little lass had, I found, an object. By going to the staircase through the door in the shop parlour, and listening, she could hear talking on the first floor. One evening Lydia went to her bed room; all was so quiet that Winifred locked the shop door, went quickly up stairs and opened the sitting room door.—No one was there—opened the bedroom door leading out of the sitting room, and there on the bed was Lydia, with her legs up in the air and the lodger just finishing his fuck.—Next minute, with a screech, Lydia pushed him off and got on to the floor; he did the same, buttoning up his trowsers. Winifred told the tale very neatly, by help of a few questions from me; she was dying to tell me, but only did so fully when I asked this and that.

She left the room, Lydia followed, begging and praying her sister not to tell her mother. They slept in the same room, confidence begat confidence, and in a few nights Winifred let out that it was a gentleman who had lent her the book, and had offered her five pounds. Lydia said she was a fool not to accept it. I saw that the elder sister in a scrape herself, wanted to get the younger into similar pickle, in order to shut her mouth. Sisters do that.

Winifred was delighted to tell. "Did you see your sister's naked thighs?"—"Only one—he, he, he," she giggled. "Had he his hand under her bum?"—"Yes—he—he—he."—"What was he doing?"—"I don't know—he—he."—"Was his bum moving backwards and forwards?"—"Yes and quick, He, he—he."—"What were they doing then?"—"Oh, I don't know."—"You story, your sister told you and you knew before."—"Oh! he, he, he." And so the tale was told [it has afforded me many times since much amusement to think of the half artless yet cunning way in which the girl told the tale in the cab, whilst sitting on my knee, my finger trying to insinuate itself between her tightly crossed thighs.]

The sister had done for me what perhaps I might not have succeeded in by myself. Their talk, as I found afterwards, was constantly about fucking after that memorable evening, and I expect that heated Winifred's cunt pretty well. A few days after, Winifred told me that her mother was going to be married again, and thought the girls had better go to service, as her intended couldn't keep them. She also told me that they couldn't pay their rent, and at times could scarcely get enough to eat. They had meat only every other day, but they kept up appearances. Lydia said she shouldn't go to service again, she'd make the lodger marry her, but Winifred must. The family was evidently breaking up.

Then Winifred agreed to have dinner with me. She got a half holiday from her work, risking her mother's finding it out. — I got a room at a well known French restaurant, and at two o'clock in the afternoon, there we were at table.

How that girl ate and drank! she'd never tasted anything in her life, she said, so delicious, at last she hiccuped, and I could see by her eyes and manner that she was hot with lust, under the beneficent effect of a well filled belly. We talked over her sister's affair, what we had done in the cab, and what I wanted to do with her. It was — "He — he — he — ah!" every minute. Then. — "You won't hurt me if I do, will you now?" At about half past three we were in a house together.

There the first thing she said was, "Oh I'm so full and so sleepy, let me lie down." — "My love, you shall but take off your things." — A little soft persuasion and she was soon in her chemise. — "Did you ever see a man naked." — "No, — he, — he, — and don't want." — "Yes you do." — Stripping to my shirt, I pulled it up to my arm pits, and with prick in the randiest glory, went up to her as she sat on the sofa, and made her handle and kiss it. — She was not loath. — "Come to the bed dear." — "What are you going to do?" "To give you such pleasure. — I must see and kiss that dear little cunt, it will give you such pleasure, now I will, it's no use your struggling." — After a few minutes of voluptuous persuasion, she was lying at the side of the bed with legs wide open, and I on my knees gloating on her virgin treasure.

She was tall and well formed, but quite thin. It was the thinness of a growing girl and not of weakness. Her cunt had fullish lips, with the slightest quantity of light brown hair half way down them, joining that on the motte, which was not half an inch long, and lay flat on one of the loveliest looking mounts I ever saw.

There was no more hair on it than would cover half a crown. A delicate pale coral stripe, a little wider at the top, defined the cleft, the coral dying out delicately into the downy fringe and white flesh on the puffy outer cunt lips — With both hands I separated them, saw a small clitoris, little thin nymphæ, and the broad oval expanse of coral vulva looking exquisite. There lay the pink road to the lower part of the cleft, looking darker and darker, as it sloped inwards to the mouth of the warm elastic tube, which was to give her and me such exquisite delight. The aperture seemed barred to a prick at its entrance, all but a little perforation, up which a small finger could alone have been passed, without injury to the firm yet soft, and semi-flexible red membrane.

The smell of the cunt rose into my nostrils, my brain seemed to whirl with voluptuousness as I kissed, and kissed, and glued my lips to it. — I put my hands under her little buttocks, held her closely to me, and began to lick her clitoris with libidinous delight.

How grateful I am to my Creator that he has thus far made me better and wiser than the beasts of the field, to whom the heavenly delights of gamahuching and minetting are unknown. — It is in such delicious, voluptuous pastimes that man is superior to other animals on the globe. To lick such a lovely cunt and give delight to its possessor is a sign of the divinity which lives, whilst I live, within me. It justifies my hope of a heaven, when I have such a taste of paradise on earth as gamahuching and fucking gives me. [This reflection made at this period I give just as then written.]

"Oh! what are you doing?" — "Be still, dear, and you'll have heavenly pleasure." — I spluttered out, licking between each word, holding her now round her thighs tightly, so that no movement of her haunches could dislodge my mouth from her cunt. — Now my tongue sought the hymenial membrane, then tried to enter the little orifice, now it covered the whole surface of her vulva, filling my mouth almost with it, then it settled on the little red button, that enticing little knob to tongue and finger, where the greatest pleasure in gamahuching seems to be concentrated. I licked fast then slow, then gradually ceased, my tongue being fatigued by long exercise. She laid motionless, silent, and enjoying the sensual treat.

I looked at the field of my lingual exercise, holding the lips wide apart, seeing it all from motte to bumhole, and with prick well nigh bursting, then went on gamahuching. — She had ceased speaking or moving, but now and then a clip of her thighs told me of voluptuous thrills. — On went my tongue, quicker and quicker as it got tired, longing for her crisis. — "Aha" — A slight quiver of the thighs, an almost imperceptible fucking jog of the belly, a shudder of pleasure. — "Aha — h, h, har — harrrre," in a soft, sweet, moaning voice, and all was still. Winifred had spent.

I rose quickly, saw her cunt wetted with my saliva, and pearly moisture running from her hymen, whilst she still with eyes closed lay in the lassitude of her pleasure. Raising one thigh, I lodged my prick in her cunt gently, and with the other hand then grasping the other thigh, I bent over her and thrust. — "Oh. What are you doing? — oh, don't — Ohoo, you're hurting me — Ahar." — The posture was not good for a defloration, for my prick was upright, her cunt horizontal, but nature teaches, instinct guides aright in its great scheme of procreation. As she moved, tighter and tighter I grasped her, bending over her till my naked belly met her naked belly (for chemise and shirt in the twinkling of an eye I had thrown up) and pressed and covered it. — Holding her thighs tightly, I thrust, and thrust violently, my prick a horn with the merest flexibility — I had lodged it well, and her wriggles never dislodged it. — "Aha — don't now — aha — you said you wouldn't." — The creeping pleasure came on of my sperm leaving my balls where it lay like a load at its roots, till it rushed forward from some internal agency. Furious with lust, the whole strength of my loins, thighs, and backside, gathered together in compound force, and I lunged as if I would split her belly. I felt the tight clip of her hymen round my glans as it entered, and with one more thrust my prick plunged up her till it struck against her womb portals. With a softened shriek, and a gasp she then was still, and my prick, now with scarcely a thrust — its movements but short wriggles as the sensitive tip naturally sought her cunt's depths — shot gobbet after gobbet of thick spunk into her vagina, and I sank over her, holding her to me, kissing her pretty little mouth as the last throes of pleasure died away, and left me lifeless with tremulous knees, but still holding her backside to me, still covering her body with mine and pressing my prick still up her, to soften and shrink, in the spermy bath it had made for itself.

Thus we were copulated long in silence, not a word said by either, till full consciousness came. Then seizing a towel which I had put on the bed to wipe my mouth with, when gamahuching, but which I'd never used, I thrust it under her bum, ready to receive the overflow of our lust. — Shrinking gradually, out came my prick, drawing with it blood streaked sperm. I squeezed the napkin round my prick, then thrusting it between her thighs, sat down on a neighbouring chair. She raised herself, sat on the edge of the bed, chemise above her knees, napkin still between her thighs, and began to cry and sob. It was no sham.

I can't bear to see a female cry, and specially a woman whom I have fucked. I had triumphed after two months' strategy and had the highest pleasure in her virgin body, and it grieved me to see her cry. From her boldness and friskiness hitherto, I had not expected it, so set to work to soothe and comfort her.

It was long before she was comforted. I have had virgins look ashamed after they had been pierced, and cry a wee bit, but never one cry like this one. There she sat, sobbing, rubbing her eyes, taking no heed of her cunt or the napkin, till. "My darling Winny, let me look at your dear little cunt." Pushing her gently back on the bed again, without her resisting, she seemed almost as if my inspection was gratifying and a relief. I opened her thighs, took away the linen, and a sight of sanguinary semen it was. I wiped her cunt, looked at it, which she let me do quite placidly, and then sat her, with naked bum on my thigh, and at length comforted her successfully. Then, with warm water and a moist towel, carefully I wiped the outer surface of her quim.

As she rose to let me do so, blood and sperm were left on my thigh from her little lacerated cleft. — That sight stiffened me at once. — I was in prime condition, having kept myself from women for three or four days in anticipation of this treat.

She knows now what fucking is, and luckily for her, early in life. She will have ten years more pleasure than had she waited till twenty-six before she'd been penetrated by a penis. — A girl can't begin too soon, a boy had better wait longer perhaps, tho he won't. At sixteen his generators don't accumulate sperm rapidly or well. — But a girl suffers less loss of animal power from fucking, her juicy contribution in the exercise being slight, and not so exhausting.

The explosion of tears and sobs ceased. It was only caused by the shock to her nervous system. Fear, pleasure, pain, and the lewedness caused by the prick in her, upset her. She got better, talked frankly about her sensations, about her own and sister's poking, as if she was already a judge of such performances, and might criticise the manner of doing it, and the propriety as well. — I made a good fire, as it was now coldish weather. She sat with naked bum on my naked thigh, and whilst respecting her deflorated slit which was sore. I delicately titillated her nascent clitoris, whilst fucking, in all varieties, was what we talked about; till, what with the heat which I have noticed follows, and quickly affects lewedly a deflorated quim, after the prick has split it up, and my performance on her clitoris, she was ready to allow me my pleasure again in about an hour.

"No, it really won't hurt you again, I swear it will all be pleasure," I said, as she sat on my knee by the fire. I had twiddled her quim for nearly an hour, got her to feel my pego, to admit that the gamahuche had given her pleasure, that she'd frigged herself for fully a year, that her sister frigged herself as well. Then I sat her down on a chair, and made her, whilst I stood, feel and inspect my red tipped erection. — "It's a wonder it don't hurt more," she said with a "He — he — he." — Gently to the bed I led her, looked at her little quim which had changed from coral to an angry red at its orifice, and in another minute she was on her back, and my prick by gentle pressure was engulfed in it. — How deliciously smooth and tight the sheath was. How I now pushed and poked in it slowly and cautiously, feeling its way about in it and as it were sounding its depth. Then I lay for a minute in baudy tranquillity up her. — "Does it hurt you now, love?" — "No, not now." "Doesn't it feel nice in you." "Aha" — I pushed and poked, her cunt seemed to grow tighter and tighter, the sperm in it (for she had not washed it out) grew thicker and more adhesive. — Quicker and quicker go my to's and fro's within its grip. Baudy, voluptuous questions she only replied to by, — "Oh don't — aha — aha." — Her cunt clipped, and seemed to frictionize my glans with greed for my sperm, her belly grew into mine, and out throbbed my spunk into her.

In an hour more I fucked her again to her pleasure, her bleeding had ceased, she washed her cunt, and again I looked at the ravages I had made — again on my knees I gamahuched till she spent. Then in a cab I saw her nearly home, giving her jelly and a little cherry brandy on the way at a pastrycook's. Then we separated. — Never had I a more delicious afternoon. My voluptuous recollections lasted me all night. — I wondered what her thoughts were. Whether she felt her quim often, how far she put her finger up, whether she wanted fucking again, and if she'd told her sister. I had forgotten the five pounds and so had she.

I suggested her meeting me again, and she was anxious to do so. What a fascinator a prick is when once tasted. But what would the mistress say about the half holiday, and suppose she told her mother? — Luckily, work seemed to be slack; when away half a day she only got half a day's pay, which then suited the dressmaker — Winifred would have met me next day, but I couldn't. The day after that we dined as before, and the bagnio received us. Winifred shewed a strong liking for food and cherry brandy, got excited, not in the least muzzy or muddled, but elevated, spiritualized. It was clear to me that the effect of liquor on her was strongly salacious. Her bright blue and sharp eyes got sharper and clearer, there was nervous energy in her, she undressed rapidly, sat on my thigh, and laid hold of my prick almost without my suggestion. — When it stiffened she said, "Oh!" — not in an enticing manner, but as if surprised, as if it had evoked suddenly lewedness, and she stared, I recollect, right in my eyes, as if my prick astonished her. — A minute afterwards I was on the bed with her, a look at the pretty coral-faced cunt — a kiss, a sniff on it, and we were fucking.

[This girl, I find, became to me a study. She no doubt was strictly virtuous till I had her, but the poke evoked her nature, which was sharply erotic, without any soft, loving qualities. I never knew much of her subsequent career, but guess it was that of a lustful one, who cared about fucking rather that the man who did it.]

It was a most voluptuous afternoon, and delightful to give her full pleasure. — She spent each time with me like the most full blooded woman. "Tell me, dear, when you're going to spend, when your pleasure comes on." — Yes, she would. — As we fucked, "Oh,

I'm a going to do it," she sighed. I like to make women of whom I have had the first, tell me when the full tide of pleasure is on. They mostly enjoy it without a word, but if they tell they each use different expressions.

That dinner and afternoon was followed by a few others at intervals. — I could not entirely keep to her, for there was a woman whose society I could not quite avoid, tho I wished to do so when I had got this lass to poke and instruct. But I had such pleasure with her that I postponed all other meetings with women that I could, so that I could enjoy it, within the juicy folds of Winifred's pretty, pouting, downy edged, coral lipped, slit. I was strong, wanted a woman daily, and after two or three days' abstinence, sebaceous exudation in three or four hours, when anticipating my sexual treat, would cover my prick tip till it looked nearly white, instead of a fiery carmine. — It delighted me to put it in that white state into her unctuous little cunt. Then, after our first pleasure, it delighted me to watch the pearly viscosity meander from her cunt towards her arsehole, whilst kneeling between her legs, which I held up by the ankles high, but wide apart, so that I might see the channel which the pearly, lubricious stream took. She used to lay with eyes fixed on me, passive to all I did; indeed I believe, silently delighting in it. — Never have I found a young wench more ready to learn obscenity. All delicacy soon left her, and delight in lascivious fun seemed part of her nature. She shewed that at our first cab ride. Yet she had never been brought up in the promiscuity of the poor, nor mixed, I found, with loose companions. She was by nature hot cunted, and I expect in after life was blazing with sexual passion, but I never knew.

I gave her the five pounds, and found she'd not yet spent the one pound. Like other girls placed similarly whom I have known, large sums (to them) embarrassed them, not knowing how to spend it without being found out.

The half holidays soon led to remarks from the dressmaker. — I had then to content myself with an hour's society with her in the afternoon, and took her to the bagnio near her place of work. That was the easier now, because it was dark or nearly so when she left, tho even that was difficult, owing to the young lasses with whom she'd been accustomed to walk partly home. But no lies, trickery or risks, stand in the way of a gluttonous cunt. I had her every other day for an hour or more, and fucked her then twice regularly. Again she got one day a half holiday, we went to the other house, and after dinner fucked in bed start naked, to her delight. — She told me, every time we met, all about the goings on of her family. — Lydia was regularly fucked by the lodger. — The mother noticed nothing and seemed engrossed with her own love affairs — Winifred had told Lydia that she'd let me have her — Lydia approved and wanted to meet and see me, but I at once refused anything of the sort — Winifred had given Lydia her money to keep for her. — She had also looked at Winifred's cunt, and shown Winifred her own. How I should have liked to have seen them at that, and heard their talk. Both girls had frigged themselves together side by side as they lay in the same bed. I heard all this and lots more.

Two or three days afterwards, I heard that the pious lodger, catching Winifred in the house alone somewhere, had again shown her his stiff cock and had winked at her. — She had not told Lydia of it for fear of consequences — I have a suspicion that Lydia had told the lodger of Winifred's slip, but I never knew — I went out of town for a fortnight, came back after Christmas, and, not seeing the girl near the workshop on two afternoons, went to the shop and walked past it, till I saw her with her mother. Then I stood close to the window and near to the light, till the girl noticed me, as I saw by the expression of her face. I went away, next day waited near the workshop, and saw the girl loitering about. — In five minutes we were in the house together.

To my annoyance, she had her courses on but I nevertheless poked her. She'd a lot to tell me. — One morning the lodger left after paying everything properly, and next day Lydia also disappeared, her clothes it seems had all been taken away by the lodger. She had joined him and wrote a letter to the mother to say they were going to be married, but no address was given. — The mother was in much grief about it, but she was also going to be married directly, to leave the shop, and go to the native town of her husband, where it seems he had a business. They now would take Winifred with them, unless she'd like to go to service. — What was she to do, she asked me?

She had given very voluptuous amusement to me for quite three months off and on. I liked coition with her, her cunt was an unusually tight one, and there was a peculiar, soft, clinging, adhesiveness in her vagina, a gummy mucosity is the only term I can use to describe it, which was most delicious to my prick, and I think I have noticed something like that in the cunts of girls of about her age. But if she stopped in town in service, I could rarely expect to have her, and feared also from her lustful temperament that she'd soon go wrong, if she had no one to control her. So I advised her to go with her mother. She tossed her head at the advice and didn't like it, expecting to remain near me. At another meeting, she said she should stay in London, that the dressmaker had offered to take and keep her, but her mother objected. Winifred didn't much mind that. Wasn't I glad she asked. — I said very glad.

But I wasn't very glad, for I didn't wish the girl to come to harm, felt sure she'd get out from time to time alone, and with her temperament most certainly get another prick or two, and then turn gay. I told her so. Two or three days after she showed me a letter from Lydia, asking her to go to *her,* for she was very happy, and the lodger would keep them both (she wasn't yet married). On no account was the address to be given to the mother. — I gave her that day another five pounds to help her in case of need, and she said she wouldn't be fool enough to lend it to her sister this time.

I have much narrative written about Winifred, but it of much the same nature. Looking thro it, I find the only things worth noticing are that she got so salacious that one day, unasked, she took my prick in her mouth, saying with a laugh that it was what they were doing in the picture ****. The action stopped there, but it was a sign of a warm temperament. She also said that gamahuching was very nice, but I never did it to her but once after the day of the slaughter of her virginity. — The mother married, Winifred was at the wedding, the stationer's shop was let, the goods sold, and Winifred went to the country with her mother. I was glad when she was gone. I heard from her one or two months after. She was discontented and going to live with her sister who, said she, was married. I wondered if she was, and whether the pious husband who had shagged Lydia before he could legally do so would show his cock again to Winifred. I sent her five pounds to help her to go with. She wrote to thank me, and I thought I had heard the last of her, but I met her again four years afterwards by chance. She never knew my real name and address, and I always wrote in a feigned hand.

CHAPTER VI

Change in social conditions. — Fifteen months' fidelity. — Virtuous struggles with self. — Fornication resumed. — Lucubrations on sexualities. — Recurrent lusts. — Copulative power. — Knowledge of the art of love. — Girls surprized. — Influence over women. — Age guessed by pudenda. — Novel lusts. — Female humbugging. — Men deceived. — Impetuous stroking. — Camille revisited. — Promiscuity. — Clapped. — On lubricity in cunts. — My ways with Cyprians. — Notes on temporary connections.

[With Winifred terminated my four years of freedom. I fell in love and was changed, yet my amorous frailty clung to me. — I loved deeply, truly, shall love to my dying hour, and, spite of my infidelity, would at any time have slain any one of my paramours rather than have give *her* pain. — Why with this feeling I sought the Cyprians, demireps, sluts, and strumpets, which I have done, I cannot explain, nor the frame of mind which led me into lascivious vagaries and aberrations, fancies and caprices, yet to be told of. From time to time, I have already given my views on the sexual relations of man and woman, and of the uses which they may be permitted naturally, if not legitimately, to make of their own bodies. — From those views, coupled with my practice yet to be narrated, I might now "in my sear and yellow leaf," form some opinion of my own nature, which seems contradictory enough even to myself. But I make no attempt to theorize on my idiosyncracy, or to analyze my character. This is a history of my private life which deals with facts alone, and not with conjectures.]

[Again it must be stated that all paragraphs enclosed with brackets thus [   ] have been written since the manuscript of my life was finished, and have been added at this revision, when the narrative is put into form, revised, and much of the manuscript destroyed.]

I cannot tell the exact time that some of the following paragraphs were written, they are fragmentary lucubrations. Some were mixed up apparently with portions of my narrative a little later on, and some were not, but they possess evidence of having been all written during my period of chastity, and within a year or two after my chastity ceased, and no doubt all of them were written at this time of my life. All are evidence of my mental condition on sexual matters at that particular period, as I well even now recollect. They were not in many cases attached to particular pages of the manuscript, and some are without date, but I should have no difficulty in assigning their places closely, if it were worth the trouble to do so.

It is a full quarter of a century since my prick first entered a woman's cunt. — A great change has now taken place in my social condition, and full fifteen months passed away during which I have been chaste — I do not find a single note or memorandum about illicit amours as they are called. — Indeed can swear that I never had any, and that all my sexual worship was given to one woman. Never before or since have I been so faithful, but *she* is worthy of it. — Then a change ensued. How well I recollect when I lapsed into my former habits of sensuality, spite of my struggles with myself to avoid doing so.

[This change in social life, left me with a limited purse for free loves — I had generally not the money to enable me to have the high-priced strumpets of former days, tho at times I was seduced into such extravagances. — Excepting at intervals, the demand upon my time and my tool elsewhere prevented my engaging in liaisons requiring time to accomplish or continue them. — But I had varied, fantastic, and the erotic frolics of mature age, as well as the normal amorous amusement of a sensuous man. The administrators to my pleasure were content with their gains, relatively small tho they were, and also were often content with *me*, for I had not lost the natural faculty (not art, for I never really cultivated the art of attaching soiled doves, and (sub-rosa) frisky lasses, as well as other females to me; and making them the most complaisant of partners in my pleasures, and even my voluptuous extravagances and caprices.]

For fifteen months, I have been contented with one woman; I love her devotedly, I would die to make her happy. — Yet such is my sensuous temperament, such my love of women, that much as I strive against it I find it impossible to keep faithful to her, to keep to her alone.

I have wept over this weakness, have punished myself in fines, giving heavily to charities the money which would have paid for other women. I have frigged myself to avoid having a woman whose beauty has tempted my lust. I have, when on the point of accosting a lovely frail one, jumped into a cab and frigged myself right off, tho unavoidably thinking of the charms I had not seen. I have avoided A*g**e and C**m***e, and any other place to which whores resort, for fear of being tempted. I have fucked at home with fury and repetition, so that no sperm should be left, to rise my prick to stiffness when away from home; fucked indeed till advised by my doctor that it was as bad for her as for me.

All is useless. The desire for change seems invincible. The idea of seeing the petticoats lifted of some untasted beauty, the disclosure of neat ankles, swelling calves, the garters round white thighs, the smooth belly, and the cunt glowing in its crisp hirsute setting, framed in the smooth white flesh of belly, thighs, and bum globes, fill me with unconquerable wants. — I sicken with desire, pine for unseen, unknown cunts. — My life is almost unbearable from unsatisfied lust. It is constantly on me, depresses me, and I must yield.

I have yielded — Alas — Alas — I am whoring as of old — the charm is broken — my lascivious career recommenced. — Alas — Alas — I ought to feel disgraced. — But what maddening voluptuousness the variety gives me.

Tho I again indulge my voluptuousness with women in whose society I find the greatest charm of life, not only from their possessing the sexual organ which is the foundation of love for *them,* as the male sexual organ is of their love for *us*, but for their faces, form, and beauty, manner, blandishments, and kindness, which are the female attributes. But I must abstain henceforth from those delicious intrigues, which, for so many years, have helped to occupy my mind and to lighten the great trouble of my life. It would be impossible to intrigue, to go cunt hunting as I have done. That involves never giving up a chance, watching for and seizing every opportunity, and giving up all other occupations needful to attain the end — possession of the woman. This now I cannot do, without chance of being found out, and perhaps thus sacrificing the happiness of one for whom I would sacrifice my life.

I must content myself with the pleasures which courtesans can give me. Luckily, courtesans in their ranks have every class of physical beauty to gratify the taste, together with a libidinosity, the idea of which seems more and more to please me. — Luckily also there are those to be found among them willing enough to gratify every taste of mine, — tastes which by experience have now been enlarged in their variety, — tastes to which in my earlier life I was a stranger — tastes which may be aberrations, and of which I have only heard. Thus I see before me endless salacious enjoyments. These are the burning words which express the desires and actions of love. — Love, lust, letchery, lewed, licencious, lubricious, impudicity, salacity, obscenity, ribaldry, smuttiness, baudiness, concupiscence, carnality, fornication, lasciviousness, sensuality, meretriciousness, voluptuousness, lickerishness, ruttish, riggish, stupration and harlotry, all words found in the dictionary, and all of which I suppose may be classed under the term erotic. All are ridiculously used as opprobrious terms, instead of terms of praise and worship, for they are after all, only the charming expressions of the wants, tastes, desires, and concomitants, of the use of the prick and cunt, and for giving to each sex pleasure in some way. The terms should therefore be all gathered together under the word Love, of which they are but the expressions, the signs, and the consequence, and love and lust are almost synonymous.

[It is a quarter of a century since this was written and I have acted in the belief of the truth of them.]

I am forty-two years old: an age when nature should moderate my ardours. — It may have done so, yet I can scarcely find any difference in my physical force, whilst my power of imagination in all things sexual has increased. — This imagination adds infinitely to the charm of coition and makes the woman lovelier than ever to me. — I am in full health and vigor, and am told good looking, more so than formerly, tho I can see no difference in myself. — All agree that I do not look my age. I can fuck once nightly as regularly as clockwork, oftentimes twice, and feel none the worse for the double action. Frequently, even that makes me feed and sleep better, and feel more refreshed and stimulated next morning. — With a fresh woman I can fuck thrice within the hour, but with that have finished my amour for a time. — But so it was with me years ago. [With a little abstinence, and a lovely woman with a fresh cunt, I have many times done my fifth between night and morning.]

I can perhaps for a time control my lustful impetuosity better than I could, which may be a sign of relaxation of strength. Yet at times I have such a strong, hot, fit of passion at the sight of a woman, that nothing restrains me till I've had her, if she can be had. Neither cost (whether I can afford it or not) nor risk deters me. — It seems to me that I then have the same determined aggressiveness which, overcoming a constitutional timidity frequently felt by me with women, tho I have not often told of it, has given me hitherto such success in my amours, — and even with harlots. — Success often times unexpected. My temerity in the attack, so crowned with victory, often times astonished me when my passion has been cooled in the darling's arms, and I have had time to think over what has passed.

Certainly I can now do what years ago I was incapable of, — dally with my lust under the strong excitement of a fresh cunt. I can pull my prick out of it as my sperm begins to rise, await its subsiding, put my prick in again, again postpone the crisis, and get by this husbandry, this prolongation, as much voluptuous delight out of one fuck as I used out of two. I can at times look at a cunt which my prick has never yet opened, and by strong effort of will, contemplate it for a time even with a stiff and throbbing prick. I think at times, even, that I can prevent my prick from stiffening, when looking at a lovely naked woman, but this for a short time only. — Directly afterwards, when I allow desire full swing, my prick, in rapid throbs, jerks itself up erect. — It seems to me to rise to duty with the throbbing of my heart, when the restraint of my will is removed from it.

I have much, perhaps great, knowledge of sexual matters as it affects both male and female in their daily life, and feel sure that with that experience, coupled with the influence of my age, I can get mastery over women more easily than formerly. — Yet have I not been already sufficiently masterful with them? But my deeper knowledge tells, and adds to my power and pleasure. I can astonish the younger ones, whores tho they may be, by telling them as much as they know, and some of the young practitioners more than they know. — [Many a young pair of eyes I have, since this was written, seen to wonder at my disclosures.] Then finding I know so much of their sex, their mendacity, little dodges, artifices, salacious tricks, and lewed habits, they are frank and tell me much about themselves and of their class. That is to say, some do, — those who naturally are frank. — Those innately cunning liars — but little.

I like to notice carefully, quietly, the difference in cunts; to study the look of cunts. This taste for comparing them has been growing on me for years. But more — I can tell, I think, tolerably closely, the age of a woman by the growth of the hair around, and the general aspect of her vulva. — "How old do you guess I am?" — "Wait till you're naked my dear, and when I've looked at you from your arse hole to your navel, I'll guess." — "You are a funny man, — well look then — now tell me." — That often has occurred, and it pleases me to inspect and to guess.

I can look at a woman's bum hole without dislike, and like pressing it with my finger, when my prick is in her cunt, and, in the ecstacy of the spend, even to intrude it. — Have I not done now nearly everything? Is not everything which two people like to do together, fit and proper for them to do? Besides, some sweet Paphians whom I have had, and enjoyed my embraces, liked that anal plugging.

What often astonishes me is my desire to do again every thing sexual and erotic, which I have done already. Yet many things done, I fancied I should never repeat. I have frigged a man. — My curiosity satisfied, I said to myself, — "I shall never frig a man again." — Yet I want to do so. — After each nearly hairless cunt which I have fucked, I have said, "Bah! she is not so well worth a stiff one as a full grown woman. There's no squeeze in the cunt, tho it be so small and tight — less soft liquidity exudes to meet my sperm, I'll not have another." — But I want another, and seem even to forget the sensation and the distinct pleasure that the small cunt gave me. I still want to compare them with the pleasure from larger cunts. — Nay, I crave for a young, unfledged cunt to lodge my prick in once more, and for the very fact of its being young and unfledged, and without thought of the pleasure of the fuck in it.

I want to do every thing over again. All former gratifications which were a little out of the common, seem to have faded from my recollection somewhat. — I don't clearly enough recollect my sensations, or the quality of the pleasure they gave me. I wish to refresh my memory by repeating the amorous exercises. It is not my lust or powers which want stimulating by variety; it rather seems as if it were strong animal want which is stimulating my desires and exercising my brain to invent even voluptuous combinations. I should like now, I fancy, those amusements I have often objected to. I should I think like my prick sucked by a sweet red lipped mouth. — Many a time I have refused that. What made me do that trick with the three Italian Graces at F**r***e I wonder?

Certainly I should like to gamahuche a pretty, coral tinted, hairless cunt, between young thighs. And a large stiff white prick! — I should like to see the sperm start from it, whilst I handled it. — Big women and little, black and light haired cunts, cunts of fourteen, and cunts of forty, I should like to see and taste again.

And I am middle-aged, and as some would say, should know better. Bah! — why should I not enjoy myself erotically if I fancy it, even if I were a centenarian? — *"Vive le con, vive le vit."* — I will recommence as if I were young and ignorant. — Know better? He who knows how to get full enjoyment of life, be it done how it may, knows best.

I have perhaps arrived at the period of philosophical eroticism, but have I anticipated the period? Camille says that I have, and reminds me that she always said I should, whilst *"beau garçon."* — In fact I know everything about women: their sexual organization, the mysterious influence that the womb exercises upon them, and they upon us from the same source of vitality. — But whilst I flatter myself thus, I know also that I may be, and probably shall be, deceived by them, have their dust thrown in my eyes, — humbugged by them.

Any man may be humbugged by a woman whom he loves. Nay if he only likes her much, he is sure to believe her. It would pain him too much to disbelieve. This my opinion of masculine weakness, for many a year I have held. — It has saved me, I believe, from more than one false step, from several dilemmas. — It may save me from others, but who knows? If I should love, or only lust after, or only like, it will not, especially from gay women. — A gay lady is almost by necessity a liar and trickster — money, money does it. — But in love matters, all women, modest or immodest, are liars, they will lie like a dentist to serve their turn. *Trust them not,* shall be my motto henceforth, but fear it will avail *me* but little, if I love or lust for them.

[Thus ran my thoughts, during the time I was constant and true to one (and to whom I thought I should be constant and true for ever), and the period of hesitation which ensued afterwards. — Thus did sensual cravings surge and struggle with me till I yielded. — They worried me even afterwards, whilst I indulged my lust with cheap Paphians, whom I sighted, longed for, fucked, paid, and dismissed, oftentimes in half an hour; leaving me unsatisfied, almost doubting what had taken place, yet with a desire to see more of their seat of pleasure, which in my lustful impetuosity I had had but a glimpse of. That flash of the cunt before my eyes had a sorcery of its own, for I could rarely help thinking of it and wishing to contemplate it more at leisure, and to think about it when contemplating.]

[Such fugitive pleasures also left me with fear of ailment, not for my own bodily suffering, but for the disclosure of its origin and source, and of the anguish that the disclosure would cause to *her*. Often I vowed that never — never — would I incur the risk again. — Alas for such resolves. — A stiff prick has no conscience. — A lustful throb in mine at a pretty face, a neat ankle, a swinging backside in sight, and all was forgotten, till I saw my sperm rolling out of her cunt, and my regrets and fears returned.]

When I recommenced indiscretions (to use the accepted and modest term for going on the loose and fucking others than the legitimate one), I sought Camille. — Years had passed since I had had her, and the look at her was a pleasure to me. — *"Mon Dieu! c'est vous mon ami, je suis enchantée de vous revoir, j'ai cru vous avoir perdu.* — How well you look. — Ah, unchanged — as young and handsome as ever. — Ah, why have you so long neglected me?" — We kissed, in another minute my fingers were on her cunt, hers round my prick — our months were glued together in silence, and in a few minutes more, my prick was throbbing out its sperm into her heavenly receptacle, which gave out its tribute to meet mine whilst we sighed ourselves into voluptuous silence.

Camille was unchanged, excepting that she had got stouter, and the hair of her cunt was thicker and covered her motte more. — Her lovely, smooth, satiny skin, her quiet voice, her other perfections mental and carnal, were the same. — But I fancied she had more the manners of a Paphian, more those of a professional fuckstress than when last I had her. We resumed our conversations as of yore. — Fucking and frigging, gamahuching and minetting, sodomy, thumbuggery and tribadism — male with male — woman with woman — man with woman — all the changes were discussed. — All, we agreed, were permissible amusements, and that only fools would hesitate to get any enjoyments out of any parts of their body that they lusted for. It was the same philosophy — a theory of pleasure we had agreed upon years before, and we only reaffirmed it now, after increased experience.

But I wanted other women besides Camille. — Soon she perceived that want, for she asked me if she should get me this woman or that pleasure. She had had now the experience of some years of harlotry, and knew men's natures. — Well, for a short time I accepted her aid, but then went my own way and again ceased seeing her altogether. [Partly perhaps because she left England and partly owing to a change in my residence.]

Then I went promiscuously and took a clap. It was not so serious an affair as the previous one, and luckily, being then temporarily alone in my home, it enabled me to get cured without the ailment being discovered. — It made me more cautious, made me insist on rigorous washing, and cuntal injections, before embracing the ladies afterwards. Occasionally also I then used French letters, but I could not bear them, nor they me. The injections also even if only of soap and water, left the cunts so rough, that my sensitive prick was deprived of half its pleasure. I have lately noticed, more than ever, that some cunts have more natural lubricity than others, and that my pleasure in coition depends on that smoothness. That a sort of soapy, greasy, mucilaginous lubricity, gives me the most pleasure. That is found in perfection in girls about eighteen years old, and afterwards up to a certain age. I think it diminished in a woman after forty.

[Complete lubricity in the woman's cunt has now become a necessity. — Without it at times my prick suffers almost slight pain at the beginning of the fuck. — The second fuck in the spermatized channel is by far the most pleasurable, and on reflexion I am conscious that the liking I had always for an unwashed cunt, or rather for one not recently washed, was an instinct with me, the result of this very sensitiveness of my glans. — I used at the time to think it was purely fancy on my part, yet could not reconcile it with the desire which I had for intense cleanliness in the woman, whilst at the same time I sought lubricity.]

[Finding I could not break away from my sensuality, I gave up the victory to it, tho I never was able to get rid of my moral scruples, and thinking I was unfair to her whom I loved better than my life. But I forgot those scruples, or they troubled me less and less as time went on. — My fears about ailments also grew less, for I reverted to a former habit, and always began my acquaintance by paying the ladies directly I got into the bed room with them. The dialogue was usually this. "Here is the money, don't let me poke you if you have any thing the matter with you." — "I'm all right." — "Ah but if you've been poorly, or are going to be, the least stain will make me ill, my prick's so sensitive, I don't mind paying you a bit, I know you must get your living, so tell me truly, don't let me touch you if you've even the whites."

That has been received in various way. — "You do it, I'm all right. Come on and fuck me," and after the business. — "You're married, I suppose, but don't you fear, I'm all right." — Others on the contrary. — "I'm quite well, but my poorliness was only over this morning. — You mustn't push too deep." — Or: — "Well, I am expecting to be poorly every hour." — Or — "Well, do as you like." — Sometimes "Well, I'm a little poorly, but I'm quite in good health" — or — "I'm all right as far as I know." — Sometimes there was an evasive one. Others "Well, shall I toss you off then if you're afraid?" — or, — "A French letter then." A French woman. "Shall I do minette with you?" — and there were other little varieties of meeting my offer, and questions, and result.]

Here from my manuscript are two extracts illustrative of my notes as written almost day by day at that period — many and many a page there was of them. All were amusing, and writing them pleased me immensely at the time. Indeed I think that I had more pleasure in writing my narrative at this period than at any other, tho I had far less to write about. — Of these temporary infidelities I destroy the remaining notes now, excepting one or two curious ones told further on.

Had a woman named Susan ***** seemed twenty-five, a fat arsed, tho she didn't look so in her dress. — Discontented with what I'd agreed to give her, said I give no more, — where on she said. — "All right" and seemed quite satisfied. — Dark hair and eyes, plenty on her cunt, fucked well and, I think, spent; told her so. "Yes I nearly always spend with my first man if he's nice, perhaps I mayn't get another tonight." — She hated frigging herself. — No woman should touch her own cunt, she thought. — A funny one.

21 January. — A funny little bitch about four feet six high, thin. — A modest looking juvenile cunt. — One of the smallest I ever put into — quite tight as I pushed my penis up it — hurt me as I pulled prick out quite stiff — I'd spent, tho I feared — washed. — "You're in a hurry," said she — light haired, squinny face.

23 March — A hairy arsed, low, she. — Wonder I poked her, glad to get away — ten and six — dirty rooms.

A German — long nosed — big — spoke good English, said another woman was in house — would I see her — offered five shillings. — German laughed scornfully so I dropped the subject. —

Soon after said she'd go and see — and it ended in having a plump little whore, whose cunt I looked at, whilst I fucked the German, and for five shillings.

If I had any doubts, owing to the woman's manner, I got away as quickly as I could. Sometimes I said, "I won't poke, but show me your cunt." I almost always looked at *that,* and then left, and oftentimes was in a house with another woman ten minutes afterwards. — Once or twice the look of the cunt so excited me that, "Oh, I must fuck you." — "Perhaps you'd better not," — but they never alledged anything but their poorliness as a reason. — By adopting this mode of dealing with the women, I expect that I often escaped an ailment.

So for some time I had two or three different women weekly — feeling quite sure that I could do duty at home as well, but I had no woman whom I took to as a friend — or regularly visited. It was one continuous change in cunt, which I saw in all sizes, developments, and colors, and this variety largely increased my knowledge of the look, and capabilities of that feminine appurtenance, and the ways and manner in which women used it and permitted it to be used, and their movements, manner, and behaviour, whilst it was used.

I only select one or two funny and exceptional incidents which occurred me during this continuous change of women, and they stand in my manuscript in the following order, or something like it.

CHAPTER VII

*Caroline the ex-chambermaid. — Her lewed moment. — Handsome backside. — Acquaintance claimed. — Prologue, copulation, Epilogue. — I am known. — Caroline's history. — She disappears. — Madeline again. — The street, the cab, the brothel. — A solemn promise. — Sarah F**z*r. — Form, face, cunt, and tongue. — Micturating frolics. — Spending indications. — Her dress. — A poke in the open. — Legs in the street. — A male competitor. — He after me. — A titanic prick. — Sarah on gamahuching. — Her nose.*

One dark evening at about six o'clock, I went to a house with a woman who pleased me when I met her, she looked so fresh and plump, tho clad in a vulgar, staringly light coloured, but very good cloak. She had smiled cheekily at me as I stood under a gas lamp, to see the sort of looking woman she was, and said "Well you're coming home with me ain't you?" — on saying I was, she laughed heartily and put her arm thro mine to walk with me, in such a way that I thought she had been drinking — I sent her on in front, which was my customary mode in such affairs, and joined her in nice lodgings not far from L***h*m P***e.

She undressed quickly, and I found her a fine woman looking about twenty-five years of age, with dark hair and eyes, and with a fresh colour like that of a country woman. She had an unusually big rump and fine thighs, but with quite a youthful quantity of dark brown hair on her quim. — "Show us it, I've often wanted to see it," said she, alluding to my prick. — She handled it and gave it a kiss with an air of satisfaction. — "You've just come in the nick of time, *you* want a bit, and I want a bit," and she laughed again. Her mirth was contagious and I laughed too, but couldn't quite make up my mind whether she had been drinking or not.

"Not so quick my dear, let's have a good look at your cunt first."—She'd got on the bed and thrown her chemise up ready for me, just as women do when anxious to be fucked or to get rid of a man.—"All right, look as long as you like, but poke first and look afterwards"—I declined.—"There then," and she slipped to the bed side with thighs apart—"Now you'll want to see it the other way I suppose," and she turned arse upwards, kneeling, and showing a pretty brown haired quim, pouting between as white, solid, and handsome a pair of bum globes as ever I saw. "Now come on." "Are you in a hurry?" "Not a bit to get rid of you, poke me, and we'll talk afterwards."—I got on the bed, and she amatively kissed me.—I felt her cunt inside and out, and in few minutes my prick was lying up her, satisfied, shrinking, and sticky.—"You've spent my dear." "I should think I have, and will again," and she kissed me more than ever—I thought I'd got a doxy just at her thoroughly lewed moment, or who had taken a letch for me.—I've had such, and their manner then is generally unmistakable, tho the manners of women vary much.

I laid on her in full enjoyment of her spermatized cunt, smoothing her fat, cool, backside, till a sudden fear of ailment came over me. "I must wash," said I.—She put her legs round mine, held me tightly round my bum with both hands, and nestled her cunt up to my balls.—"Keep it in and wash when you've done it again, I'm all right." "But I must get home to dinner." "Shan't let you go till you've poked me again."—She was chirpy in manner—there was a vivacity in her, strongly resembling that of big-eyed Betsy Johnson of whom I have told.—"I must go, I shall be late, and shan't be able to do it again for half an hour," and I wriggled a little with the intention of quitting her body, yet was half hearted about it, so nice was she to handle. "Yes you will—what will you bet?"

I laid a little longer wondering at her manner, feeling somehow now sure that she was sound in body, thinking she had taken a letch for me, began feeling her bubbies, and investigating her armpits.—"I haven't seen you for a long time," she said laughing. "I never saw you before," I replied astonished.—"Oh haven't you tho, are you sure?"—I raised myself up to look at her face, and began to fancy I had.—"Oh, it's all running out of my cunt, haven't you put a lot in,"—saying which and moving me with her, she turned partly on her side, putting her leg over my haunch as she did so, still held me close to her, and caught hold of my prick, which uncunted with the movement. — "You've had a drop." "Yes — but nothing but tea. I never drink liquor till night," said she, squeezing gently the glans of my prick. — It was a most delicate, refined performance, and already a voluptuous feeling at the tip and running thence everywhere, filled me with desire for her.

The pleasurable sensation of a soft female hand coaxing my prick, now gently clasping my balls, now twiddling round the foreskin, now pinching gently below the tip, brought me to voluptuous silence. My hand sought her clitoris, the spermatic moisture on her quim increased my lewedness, and again our mouths met. — "Ohoo — I want it again — put it in. — Aha — how stiff it is." "Aha, how spunky your cunt is," I murmured amidst wet kisses. — It was all that was said, till I'd had a gloriously voluptuous second fuck. — Then we lay joined together till my prick would keep in her no longer. — Quickly I washed, and left her promising to see her again, and meaning it. "Don't be long first or you won't see me again at all, shall I write to you?" were the last words she uttered after chaffing me, and saying she knew me well enough, which I denied — I fancied I had somewhere seen her before, yet dismissed that from my mind, for I rarely quite forget the face of any woman whom I have had.

In a few days I saw her again. — Directly she noticed me, she turned and walked towards her lodgings, as if making sure I had come to have her.

"I knew I should see you again," were her first words when in her bedroom. "Why?" "Sure you'd come to see an old friend." "I never saw you till the other night." "Quite sure?" "Quite." "I know well all your names, and where you live, and all about you, what will you bet I don't?"

As before, she stripped rapidly to her chemise, as if anxious to be poked — sitting down whilst I undressed, she seized my prick directly I approached her, kissed it, and then with a gentle, almost imperceptible delicacy of handling, passed the stiff stem through her soft hand, alternately looking at it, then up at me, and holding with her other hand my shirt well up, so that she could see my procreator without hindrance. Then she began chaffing about her knowledge of me. — I returned the chaff, saying that now I recollected having her one or two years before. — "That you didn't, for I have only been poked eight months, and a gay woman three." For a second she was then silent, as if my remark had annoyed her.

"Tell me what you know," I resumed. "If I do you won't see me again." "Yes I will, let us poke first." "No." "You shall, I have only been chaffing you," said she, getting on to the bed. I believed that, said no more, laid by her side, and delicious reciprocal preliminaries began. I looked at her lovely cunt, pulled apart the red lips, kissed her motte and belly up to her bubbies, and then more tranquil by her side, felt over all the surface of her cunt, now thrusting a finger up the red prick tube, now rubbing gently the clitoris, whilst she continued the delicate, slow, masturbating movement on my prick from tip to balls. Our mouths joined in moist contact, then in silence I mounted her, clasped her smooth solid arse, and thrust my prick to its roots up her. She sighed with delight as it struck the end of her cunt.

After a short voluptuous rest for my prick, tho my brain during such times is in its baudiest state of thought, I fucked. — Up and down went my prick in her sheath, with our sighs and murmurs of pleasure mingling, till all movements finished with a throbbing prick, a gripping, clipping cunt, tightening arseholes, wriggling bellies, spasms of pleasure, thick white spunk spurting from me into *her*, salt slimy juices exuding from her vagina — amidst our sighs and cries of ecstacy. Then with relaxed hold, with limbs stretched out, tranquil we lay, prick still in cunt, cunt clipping, prick loosely but deliciously shrinking in the fecundating mucilaginous bath of our mixed spendings, our tongues still joined, and salivas mingling. Thus for minutes in a blissful Elysium, as if our souls and bodies were dissolving. What a happy death to die.

The pleasure over, I slipped off on one side. She turned to me, laying hold of my tool. I put my hand over her upper buttock, and laying together thus in salacious companionship she said laughing, "I *do* know you tho." "Tell me then." "Your names begin with *** and **** and ****. — The number of your house is 34 — and the street name begins with A." — It was so exact that I started, but said, "No." She laughed, told me all, and finished up by, "Now fuck me, it's quite stiff," and I did.

These were the circumstances. Three years or so before, an

Australian family, the lady of whom was distantly related to me, came to England and stopped six months nearly at the ***** hotel. I visited them often, dined there, went to the theatre and everywhere with them. She was chambermaid there, had waited on the ladies, taken messages to them from me, taken letters to the hotel box addressed to me, had heard me often spoken about, and thus knew much about me. I had kissed her once, and putting my hand down to her belly gave it a gentle tap and said, "There's a baby there I think." — I'd forgotten her, tho her face had seemed familiar to me.

Surprized and a little annoyed (such tricks have been played, by women), that I could not help for the minute pondering on the incident, tho there really is nothing very singular in it. I have often wondered that out of the hundreds of women of all classes I have fucked, or toyed with baudily, that I have met so few of them afterwards, when I have once parted with them. Said she with her pert manner, "Ah — you're wishing you hadn't seen me, and thinking I'm going to leave my card on you — but I'm not, for I'm going away altogether, I shan't be what the French women about here call a *Dame Galante* long," and she laughed. Then I wanted to know her history fully. She wouldn't tell me. — "If you want to hear that, come and spend the evening with me, I shan't be here long." — Perhaps I would I said, "No, you're not going till I've had another poke — I'd have let you had me first two years ago, but you didn't see it and shied off."

I poked her again, and said I would see her that day week, knowing I should then be by myself in town. — She counted on her fingers. — "I think I shall be poorly, come the day before." "I will." — That evening I had my dinner first, and at her request took a bottle of champagne with me. I'd been four days without a fuck, and wanted one. — She'd had her dinner. — "I waited for your phiz and haven't had any thing to drink, but wasn't sure if you'd bring it," and she began drinking.

She was ready when I got there, nicely got up with a silk open gown or dress, over a fine chemise. — "Look! that's what my young man's given me," said she drawing my attention to it. "You've silk stockings on" (she'd not worn them before). "Yes, bought them for you, you may give them me if you like." "Well I will." She got up and kissed me. "You ought to have had me first."

"I wish I had, tell us all about it." "Take your trowsers off, and make yourself comfortable." — Whilst I undressed she stirred up the fire, and we sat down. "Show me your cock." "Show me your cunt then." She lifted her chemise to her navel, the sight of her motte and legs which were handsome, made me stiffen at once. I lifted my shirt. — "Hoh, hoh, ho," saying which she got up and laid hold of my pego. I clasped her bum, and fingered her notch. — She stooped and our mouths joined. — "Not yet," said she disengaging herself and sitting down; but in a few minutes, our backsides were heaving reciprocally on the bed.

Then we sat before a good fire drinking, I smoking — our passions temporarily assuaged. — She with chemise above her knees, to let the warmth of the fire reach her quim. I, with its warmth playing on my buttocks and ballocks. — This was her history — which I now abbreviate as much as possible, tho as first written, it filled seven pages of foolscap.

Caroline **** was her name. — She was only twenty-one years old now, tho she looked much older, had been in private service. Her eldest sister, who was chambermaid at the hotel, persuaded her to go there. Both were there, when my Australian friends were. — Caroline found it pleasanter than a private house, but much harder work. They saw lots of life, single men larked with the chambermaids, and married men as well, but furtively. — "Yes," she said in answer to my question, "many men have shown me their cocks when I took water or things into their bedrooms, some made a sham of being caught with it out," — but she knew it was "all my eye" — they meant her to see it. Her sister who was thirty and a widow, told her it was the same with her. The waiters tried to get over her, lot of gentlemen at the hotel had asked her to go out with them, but she never had. All the female servants talked baudily, most of them she thought fucked on the sly, her sister included, but *she* always gave Caroline good advice.

She'd been there but a few months when I visited my Australian friends. — "Nine months ago I went wrong. I went out one night with a young man, a gentleman who had been at the hotel some time." — He'd kissed her several times, she thought him nice, and it ended in his getting her to have dinner, then to a house, and taking her virginity. — He'd said he'd keep her. Whether that induced her to let him have her or not, she didn't know. — "I expect I wanted it badly. I often did just then, I was always hearing about fucking, and was tired of frigging myself. — Directly he got his hands between my thighs in the cab, I thought I'd let him do me." She left the hotel, he kept her a few months, went abroad, and she'd never seen him since. He gave her fifty pounds when he left, and she turned gay at once.

"I believe I'd have let *you* do it, I liked you, and put myself in your way, don't you recollect asking me if there was a baby there," pointing to her belly. — "A young waiter that very day had offered to marry me. — The maid who slept in my room just then, talked about nothing else but fucking every night, and I was clean upset by it all. — *You* never saw your chance." — Her sister used to say, "What are you hanging about there for, when that gentleman's here." Then Caroline said — "I wanted you directly I set eyes upon you a fortnight ago."

I pulled my chair closer to hers, our naked thighs touched, she laid hold of my tool, my fingers sought her notch, our mouths met, and we sat in voluptuous silent play, till with a wriggle. — "Ahar, come and do me." — Then on the bed at once our backside joggings recommenced.

Then she told me she thought she was going away with a gentleman "I wish it were *you*." He'd given her that cloak and other things. She didn't like the life, tho she'd done very well at it. — Her sister advised her to go to service again. "But I can't do without fucking now, and wonder I did without it so long, and like my liberty, tho I wish I'd married the waiter." — We embraced again, I had been with her some hours, and was getting hungry, so was she. The champagne was gone, but I was quite comfortable, and didn't like to quit her she was so unusual in manner, and there was such an evident letch for me that I felt flattered; for I like a woman to enjoy me, it heightens my pleasure.

"I'm so hungry." "So am I, and shan't go out tonight — you can get ham and beef round the corner, and they have good hot saveloys up to midnight. — They sell good whisky and wine at ****." "Send your servant." "No *you* go, they'll serve you better, I can't dress in time for it's just twelve, or I would." — Off I went, and came back with hot sausages and a bottle of whisky, and we sat eating and drinking till it was two o'clock. — When I rose to go, "Do me before you go, you may never have the chance again." "I can't." "I'll make you. — Ah, I must piddle first."

"Stop, let me see you," — my old letch came on suddenly. — I put her on the bed, a basin under her, and from her red slit saw a quart of the yellow fluid splash out. Her big round buttocks and white thighs made a charming setting to the red cleft. By the time she'd finished my prick was rampant at the sight, and with the glistening drops of moisture still on the vulva and its hedge, I fucked her at the bed side. — "You're a real man, and no mistake, I wish you had me first," she said as my prick left her.

A week after I had her again. — I kissed her white bum. — "Say good-bye to it," said she laughing. "Why?" "I don't think you'll see it again. — I'm going off. I hope so at least. — If you don't see me out, call and ask, but I'm expecting every day to leave this life. My friend says he'll keep me." — I never saw her after that night, and called at the lodgings. She had left, gone they knew not where, and with a gentleman, "Oh quite a gentleman."

I have often noticed that one surprize follows another. Within a few weeks after the ex-chambermaid vanished, I met, point blank, Madeline, the sweet young milliner over whose thigh I first spent, — and whom I subsequently relieved of her virginity. It is between two and three years since I had that pleasure.

It was in the afternoon just before dusk, both of us were turning a corner out of R*g**t Street. Both started, and stopped as if petrified. — "You?" "My dear Madeline, you?" — We shook hands. — "It won't do if we are seen," said she anxiously, "for I'm married." "Who'll see you? and if you are seen, surely you may talk to an old friend — but who'll know, let us walk on," — and I did by her side. — "Tell me all about yourself, and husband," questions rapidly put. — Yes, she'd married Richard. — "No children?" "None." "You lucky one, you can have any fun you like, without fear." "Oh! fun? I'm married." — She wanted to get rid of me, apparently fearful. — "I won't go, I must talk with you, may never see you again, get in this cab and you can tell me all, nobody can see us in it." — I hailed a passing cab, in a second we were in it and off we drove. — I had almost to hustle her into it, but the fascination of our former delight was on *her*, as on *me*. We were both yielding to the inevitable curiosity.

She was agitated. Old endearments I know came to her mind, how can any woman meet a man who has fucked her without thinking of it? — We kissed. "Do you recollect that night Madeline when, etc. etc." "Oh you mustn't talk of that, we must forget it." Then she told me that her husband had a good situation, was very kind, she'd never had a child. — "He fucks you doesn't he?" "Oh — well — oh — you always were such a — Oh! — Where are we going now? — I mustn't be late — let me go."

"No you shan't, I may never see you again. — My God, how I long to see you naked, how much stouter you've got, how lovely your arm feels — fucking agrees with you, your legs have grown larger like your arms I'll bet, haven't they now?" "Oh don't go on so, don't." "Oh let me feel for a moment only."

Stooping, I pulled up her clothes to her knees, and got my hand just above her garters. — She struggled violently. — "Oh now — don't — you shan't. — Oh leave off." "I will by God, Madeline, I will feel that lovely cunt once more." — It was a real hard struggle. She meant to prevent me, I resolved to feel it — A whirl of lust passed thro me, I thought of fucking her in the cab, or any where, but somehow. As we struggled, my head was over her shoulder, my mouth against her neck. After I'd once got my hand above her garters, that position kept her from stooping much and helped me, for in a minute or two (but how time flies in these lovely erotic combats) my hand was well between her thighs, my finger tip on the vaginal mouth, my open hand covering her whole cunt, I had grasped the whole of her cunt so to speak, my fingers squeezing apart the lips. The next minute I had placed her hand round my erection, placidly her hand closed softly on it, and our mouths met.

She murmured, "What a shame," — then gave herself up — vanquished — silent — and now enjoying it; for lewedness once possessed of man and woman, absorbs all thought, — pervades the whole physical frame with a subtle languid pleasure, from the crown of the head to the soles of the feet, it enervates. Thus in silence we sat for a time as the cab rolled on. — How useful four wheeled cabs have been to me.

It grew dark, whilst we handled each other's genitals — the

sensations our fingers gave us made us forgetful of all but our love. — "Let us just look at each other once again, you've more hair on your cunt I can feel. — My God how my prick's throbbing for you. — Frig me." — "I won't." — "Come with me, and I swear if ever we meet again I'll take no notice of you. That shall be agreed between us. — We shan't be half an hour. — My beloved Madeline, let me have you once more. — Come darling," and my fingers moved unremittingly over her cunt, rousing her lust to insensible compliance.

In ten minutes afterwards we were in a house, the scene of many a former pleasure, she knew it well. — Within an hour we had fucked thrice and separated, but what maddening Elysium that one hour was, what disclosures we both made. I told her as much as she told me, it was pleasant to tell her of my social happiness. — She had got stouter, her thighs were large and round, she had still her marbly backside, and it was a larger one. She'd now a well-haired cunt — quite thick hair now, and it fucked as deliciously as ever. — We talked over all about our liaison from first to last, sponges, French letters, and all. — She soon lapsed into lasciviousness after I had once fucked her. — When we parted she said she should be ashamed of saying her prayers or to go to church next Sunday. — "My love, your husband never found out that you had been poked before he poked you, and he'll never find this fucking out." — I've never seen her since to speak to, tho I have once or twice in the distance, but our paths lay apart.

It was a most delicious incident — a break in the monotony of harlot loves and pleasures to which I shall be for the future limited. — But I don't regret that. — I regret my infidelity more. — Mais que voulez-vous? — I am made so — made I suppose to be unfaithful. But I always reserve enough sperm for connubial duty, and *she* is satisfied.

In the year 18** I walked up P***l**d P***e at about ten o'clock at night, and saw a tall woman standing at the corner of L**t*e P***l**d Street. Her size attracted me, I spoke, and offering half a sovereign with the understanding that she would take everything off — went with her to a house in L**t*e P***l**d Street.

She kept her word and stripped whilst I sat looking on. — When in her chemise, — "Do you want me quite naked?" — "Yes."

Then she slipped it off and stood start naked, boots, stockings, and garters, excepted. — I may as well describe her at once, as for quite four years, she satisfied almost every sexual want, and helped me to satisfy every sensual fantasy.

She was with the exception of the second Camille (the French woman) almost the most quiet, regular, complacent woman I had had since that time, and moreover was most serviceable to me in all my pleasures, ministering to them as I wanted them — but rarely herself suggesting them. — Ready to undertake anything for me, and after some length of intimacy participating in, and well pleased with, our erotic amusements; never attempting to exact money, but always content, and at length getting so accustomed to me that she let me into much knowledge of her private daily life.

She was I should say five feet nine or nearly ten high, which is tall for a woman. Her hips were when viewed from the front, of the proper width for such a height — but her shoulders somewhat narrow. Altho so tall, she was small boned and plump all over, yet she had not an atom of what may be call fatness; had a small foot, a fine shaped calve, and thighs not quite so large proportionately. Her bum with fine firm round cheeks was not heavy at the back, was rather broad across the hips than thick and prominent behind, yet her backside looked handsome. — In fact she was straight and well shaped from top to toe, but if anything might have had broader shoulders with advantage, to make her proportionate to her height; yet only a sharp critic would have noticed that deficiency.

Her cunt, that important part of a woman, was large, but tight, fleshy inside, and muscular. It clipped my prick as deliciously as if it had been a much smaller one, and it was so healthy and deep, that often as I tried, I never could touch the orifice to her womb, either with my prick or my fingers. Nearly black hair, crisp and in full quantity was on her mons, and down the lips, and almost to her arsehole, but not round that brown orifice. The lips were thick and full, yet if she put her legs apart, they widened at once, showing deep crimson facings, and when shut a thin crimson streak. — Her nymphæ were small.

She had dark brown, bright eyes, dark hair and good teeth — but her nose had been broken. That spoiled her face which otherwise would have been very handsome. As it was it did not make her ugly, but decidedly spoiled her.

She had the longest tongue I ever saw. She could put it further out of her mouth altogether than any one whom I have seen do that trick. — She was somewhat an unusual woman in every respect, and was I think twenty-four years old when I first saw her. — She had been a ballet dancer at some time, altho I only found that out after I had known her some months. — Her name was Sarah F**z**r.

She laid on the side of the bed, pulled her cunt open, knelt on the bed backside towards me, shewing cunt and arsehole together in quick succession as I asked her, and without uttering a word, but simply smiling as she obeyed. It had the usual effect, — a stiff-stander of the first order. It always is so with me. Objections, and sham modesty, a refusal to let me touch, and feel, or see, instead of whetting my appetite for a gay woman, always angers me and makes me lose desire. — With a woman not gay the case is different. The next minute I was enjoying her with impatience, then I lay on her stiff still, and full up her when I had spent. — "I shall do you again." "All right," she replied. My prick never uncunted, but whilst reviving, my hands roved in all directions. She moved first this leg, then that, lifted her backside up, and seemed by instinct to know where my hands wished to go, and they were restless enough. — She was like Camille. — To something I said, she remarked. — "You're fond of it." — As I recommenced my thrusts she said. — "Don't hurry, I want it," — and we both spent together. — I forgot to mention that her flesh was of surprizing firmness, and her backside solid and smooth. — I gave her the half sovereign as agreed — she did not ask for more, and we parted — but not for long.

The readiness with which she complied with all my wishes, together with the recollection of her personal charms, and the pleasure of her cunt, dwelt in my mind. I had her next night, and the night after, and then began to see her once or twice a week, and to indulge in voluptuous freaks which I had not done for three years or more, and which my imagination increased in its powers by what I had seen, read, and done, supplied me. — I am not going to tell of tricks I have done with other women, but only such varieties and vagaries as were newish, and one or two which I had, I think, not done before with any women. If I had, I have forgotten to tell them, tho I am not sure even of that.

My piddling letch, which seems for a time to have been dormant, returned. I began to make her piddle in all sorts of attitudes, first in a pot, then in a basin — at times with her cunt opened naturally, then holding the lips open, so that the little red piddle-vent could be seen almost. — At no time of my life had I such variety of frolics with urine as I then had. — It may be termed my pissing period. I began to piss with her, would keep myself from watering for hours before I met her, so that I might deliver the fullest, longest, and strongest stream of urine possible. — She was famous at it. I have seen the piddle stream of scores of women, but hers was the hardest, and strongest that ever wetted a pot. — I hit on the idea of bringing her to the bedside, laying her back, putting a basin under her bum as close as the bed would permit. Then she would hold the lips of her cunt wide open, and I pointing my tool, would empty my bladder. The yellow stream hitting either prick hole, or broad surface of the cunt, splashed in a thousand little bright drops on her thighs, or lodged in the crisp black hair, then ran down to where the quim nears the bum hole, and dropped into the basin beneath. Directly I had pissed, my prick would stand, I joined my body to hers, and capable no longer of delay, bedewed quickly with sperm the inside of the orifice which I had just bedewed outside with a thinner fluid.

Pissing against her cunt, she declared, no man had ever done to her but me. She enjoyed it, it seemed to make her lewed, and she always spent with me afterwards. — When spending she shewed it plainly, and did not attempt to hide it as some do. — Indeed she could not, for her cunt *would* close so strongly round my prick, that there was no mistaking what it was up to. — Besides that, her face first went scarlet — perfectly scarlet, — a minute afterwards, perfectly white — and then gradually recovered its natural color — I never saw that change in any other woman's face. She always kept my prick up her as long as she could, — twining her long legs round me to hold me up her, whilst her long arms held me firmly round my arse cheeks, as she lay perfectly quiet with her eyes closed. — At other times when she did not spend herself, she took no trouble of that sort, but got up and washed the moment I released her.

The house I went to with her was usually in L**t*e P***l**d Street. — It had some advantages, but there was no looking glass of any size. As I wanted now to see our limbs and muscles move under our embraces, I went to a well known house, — the A*ma in ***** St. (There were several houses in the same street then, in this one there were glasses in profusion.) — It was now my additional delight when looking at her cunt, with her thighs wide open, with the basin beneath preparing for my salt splashing, to glance about and see her long plump flanks and thighs, half hiding the basin, my own nudity, and our erotic tricks.

In the various ways which I amused myself with her, one very large cheval glass increased my pleasure. I mostly managed to get the room in which that particular glass was, for I soon became known. They gave me what I wanted and never disturbed me however long I stayed.

Two other modes, in which we used to amuse ourselves with our bladders were these. — We used to strip ourselves start naked, shoes and stockings off even, and arrange the cheval glass, so that with other glasses I could see her both back and front at a glance. Then lay on my back with hands under my head on a pillow, so raised as to enable me to see the picture we made. Then she would stand for a minute straddling over me, and the sight of the red stripe peeping out of the black hair would stiffen my penis. Then sitting down on me as she would on a chamber pot, she would take my stiff prick and engulf it in her cunt, the dark hair of her quim meeting mine, her bum cheeks just touching without weighing heavily on my thighs. Then out would come her warm stream, hitting my belly below my navel, and running down in two little streams by the side of my balls, uniting beneath them, washing over my arsehole, and depositing itself on the carpet on which I was lying.

At other times I reversed her, and she engulfed my prick in her cunt with her backside towards me. — Then I could play with her cool, firm, smooth backside, and feel round the stem of my prick just where it was lost, and hidden in her warm juicy tube. I could feel to her bumhole — or back bone. In the glasses I could see my prick rising out from the balls, and losing itself in the dark black thicket on her cunt lips. — "Open the lips, Sarah." — Immediately her two fingers would separate the lips, leaving the broad red surface, at which sight my prick would throb with desire to spend. — "Piss, piss dear, I can bear it no longer." — Then it would fall like a cataract in front of my balls, and partly on my thighs.

At times wrought to an irrepressible pitch, no sooner had the last dribble fallen on my ballocks, than with a few upward shoves I finished my pleasure, feeling her arse, and gloating over the luscious picture we made; holding her on me until my prick slipped out, and drew with it some of my sperm, as it flapped down on to my balls, still wet with her piddle.

By that time the piddle had cooled — my arse used to feel as if it had fallen into a ditch — we both rose, wiped and dried ourselves, and sat down to talk until desire again asserted its empire over me, or over us, for she enjoyed this fun.

Another way I have tried unsuccessfully with another woman. — With Sarah it was practicable on account of her height — for in tall women, the extra length is nearly always in the legs, and not in the body. Stripping ourselves start naked, I stiffened my prick by her incitements, or perhaps by a few preliminary shoves up her cunt, then both standing up before the glass, I used to put my prick up her and she would piss, and the warm stream run dripping round my balls, falling on both our thighs, and descending till we stood in a pond. — Then standing, I would fuck her, watching our movements in the glass.

And all this is practicable, if a man who is lewed as I was takes the trouble, and has a suitable woman. With Sarah I could do this scarcely bending my back, for upright by me my prick was nearly at the level of her cunt. — When the twisting and wriggling of our backsides and genitals had ceased, I have without uncunting, waddled with her back towards the bed, and leaning her on the edge, leaned on her, and took what rest I could in that position, until my prick slipped out. — Such was my force, and the rigidity of my penis, that several times I have done this. But it is a laborious, erotic amusement tho worth trying [I could not do it now].

I used at times, because of the convenience which her height gave for such amatory eccentricities, put my prick up her, and then clasping each other we used to wadddle round the room, laughing as we viewed our movements in the glasses. That exciting amusement could not endure long, for there is an involuntary action in a cunt when the prober is in it, which compels the penis to move towards a consummation. After a minute or two, a constriction of her cunt muscles on my prick tip compelled it either to push or withdraw. Then came an involuntary shove or two, and then the sequel came, which was either the perpendicular shag in front of the glass — or an uprighter against the wall — a sloper against the bed side — a horizontal, old fashioned fuck on the bed, or on the floor — or a bum to belly fuck in dog fashion on the bed or on the carpet, bringing their usual crises of pleasure and relaxation of limb, luscious dreaminess, a sensation of cool dampness round the prick stem, and a desire for a doze.

I have fucked and awakened, still finding my prick in her — for she had only to raise her thighs, and bend her knees up somewhat, to bring her cunt in such a position, as to press my balls against her buttocks, and keep my prick in if only the size of a large gooseberry. The same facility enabled me to get my prick up her when limp — I took much pleasure in doing that, and letting it stiffen up her, under the compressive movement or grip of her cunt — I have never known a woman who could give my prick a longer lodging than she could; tho I have known many who could do it well. She knew it was my pleasure, and gave it to me to the full when she got accustomed to me.

I used to be thinking constantly of what voluptuous tricks I could do when we met, but for a time, a preliminary usage of our organs, in pissing some way or another was my delight. — Then it took such possession of me that I thought of nothing else. My letters to her to meet me used to run. "Tonight — seven — keep in P." — By which I meant her to have her bladder full. — So she used — so full at times that she said, "If you don't do something directly, I must piddle, I can't keep it in any longer." Then the evening's amusements began. — The quantity she spouted oftentimes, I am sure, was a quart or more.

There is one thing in these amatory micturating bouts, which I only recollect having done with her and one other woman. — It was pissing when up her cunt. — She told me she had allowed a man or two to try, but that they could not succeed. — Indeed it is difficult. For when a prick is stiff and in the state of nervous strain which fits it for penetrating a cunt, its ejaculatory muscles struggle to shoot out sperm, and so I suppose contract the opening to the bladder, and prevent piddle issuing. — But one night she was undressed, and lying at the side of the bed with thighs wide open, up I thrust my prick bursting, and as I thought with piss so proud, that nothing could prevent the jet. When up her cunt I tried to piss, but my prick began to throb, and her cunt, as I thought, to squeeze it, altho she declared it was quiet. I strained till I farted like a cow after beans, but not a drop would come. — The more I strained, the more difficult I found it to restrain myself from oscillating my buttocks, for an outshoot of spunk.

My prick would not be cheated. Her cunt resented its being treated as a pisspot, and asserting its right to a stronger and thicker injection, closed round my prick, and worked it so, that getting its way, it drew from me its natural embrocation. — As my sperm throbbed out, it caused me such pain that I groaned.

Directly my seminal reservoirs had emptied themselves, with a little effort my bladder opened, and I pissed for two minutes I am sure. — My prick kept gradually shrinking but until it had done its full duty as a sperm spouter and water pipe, kept in her cunt. Pressing out from her cunt came my stream, running over my balls, and down by her arse split on to bed and floor. — At length cut flopped my doodle, bringing with it the remainder of my injection both thick and thin. — Up I pulled her, laid down in her place, but sloping off from the edge of the bed and she standing up, I thrust my body between her thighs so that my prick was just under her cunt. — Out came her piddle copiously over my belly and ballocks, and that completed the fun. — She cried out, "Oh, no, I shall wet my boots and stockings," for in our lustful hurry she had kept them on. "Damn your boots — piss — piss." — Out came the stream and I was happy. But we made the bed in such a mess that I was obliged to pay extra for its use.

Then I seem to have ceased eccentric micturating amusements, and erotic pleasures of a different kind took their place; tho as long as I knew her, I made her squat and piddle before me. I shall always I am sure, love to see a well made pair of white thighs, and their oval terminations in rear, whilst from between them the red line opens its hairy lips, and the sherry tinted stream spurts.

She was a scrupulously clean woman, always had the whitest linen on, but it was not of the finest quality, and was without ornament excepting a frill just round the top of the chemise — I never saw her in any dress but black silk. She said it was economical, that one dress helped to repair the other, that in coloured things she looked too big and vulgar — that her friends were mostly quiet men, who did not like women whom every one turned round after. — She usually wore a black veil, which were much worn by women then, lifted it up when she spoke to a man, then dropped it again. — I have watched her several times. — At that time gay ladies were fond of lifting up their petticoats if the streets were muddy, so as to show their legs a little. Sarah rarely did unless as she said she was "hard up." — If she showed her legs she always got a man, yet could not bear doing it. — Odd! — How odd! — She would do anything with me in a room, and perhaps with any other man, yet did not like shewing her legs in the street. — Humbug?

When I came to appreciate her very handsome feet, and legs up to her knees (her thighs and haunches were scarcely as fat and fine) I found her stockings were sometimes a little coarse, so gave her boots, and silk stockings of the colour I admired. They were then light kid and pink silk — and also beetle-brown kid and white silk. — I gave her also splendid garters and expected her only to wear them all for *me*. I think she did so, for I tried to catch her with them on at odd times, and only found her with them on once. — When we had pissing bouts, she took off both boots and stockings. — Altho fond of a naked woman, I always made her keep boots and stockings on at other times.

Among my delights, was to make her squat at the edge of the bed with her knees up, and heels drawn as closely as possible to her bum. This she did with an ease, flexibility, and completeness which surprized me (the reason will be seen). — Then the dark mass of hair on her cunt, with the red lined lips, shewed up in perfection between her thighs, kid boots, and pink silk stockings. — I used to keep her so for a quarter of an hour at a time, I sitting on a pillow on the floor, so as to be able to look up at her cunt, holding a candle under it almost touching it, and opening, twitching, and fingering the cunt, as the impulse seized me. Then I viewed it from all parts of the room, until my pego would bear it no longer, and I rushed it up her. On several occasions I met her when she had no expectation of seeing me, and she went with me into the first dark place, I felt her limbs, and saw what boots, etc., etc., she had on, then I felt her cunt and went my way. I began again about this time occasionally to feel women's cunts in the street. I had not done so for a couple of years. I taught her when I met her, on a signal, to go ahead of me, lifting up her petticoats as high as she dare. — It amused me to see men turn round, follow, and speak to her. — Then she, if I wanted her, turned into the baudy house, I after her. But it was risky, for the sight of her legs used to give me such a cock-stand, that I was always in danger of wanting a fuck in the open. — One night I had her up against the door of a house in a back street. — She refused at first, but at length we did it, after my swearing that if *she* did not, I would do it in the street with *some other* woman. — But I never had her in the street but that once.

One muddy night she lifted up her clothes and walked up P***l**d P***e. — I followed her at some distance, then she turned and went to the house in L**t*e P***l**d St. As she was going there, a man spoke to her just before she got to the door. — In looking at her legs, I had not noticed him till then. In a second I was at the door. The man stood and insisted on going in with her. — She would not let him, and there was quite an altercation. — I slunk off to the other side of the way till it was finished. — The man saw me join her and looked very savage. I went in, had my evening's pleasure, and was there perhaps two hours. When I came out, I saw the same man, and he entered the house directly. — I knew he was after her. She did not come out, and there I waited an hour. — I had begun by laughing to myself at the man for waiting two hours for a woman. Now I waited tho I did not know why. But I thought of what they were doing together. — Now he is perhaps feeling her, now fucking — now she is feeling his prick. Has he fucked her — twice — or thrice? — These and a hundred similar thoughts floated through my brain, until I got as randy as if I hadn't fucked for a week.

The longer I waited, the more impatient I got, yet determined to wait all night if needs be, thinking of nothing but what he was doing with her. — I resolved to see if she would tell the truth or a lie. — At length out I saw him come. I went down towards Ox***d St., — for I knew then the way she went home, — and peeped round the corner of a street until I saw her come along. Then walking I met her as if by accident. — "What you?" said I. — "Yes." — "Where have you come from?" — "From **** — I have never left." — Then she began to tell the truth, and I went back to the baudy house with her.

I am telling this part of my history a little out of order, for it occurred somewhat later on, when I had then got her confidence, and she used to talk to me like an old acquaintance. — In the bedroom she began to laugh. — "You saw the man who followed me. — Well! he waited for *you* going out, came into the house after you left, and asked if a tall dark woman was up stairs. — Of course Mrs. A said — 'No' — He said he was sure she was, for he had seen her come in with a man two hours before, and she had not left. — Mrs. A then came up, and asked me — and I said — let him come up. — He came, I had my bonnet on." "I have waited for you two hours, to have you — how often have you been fucked?" "I told him not at all — that my friend had only looked at me." — "Ah! you frig him, and that is what I want — but I like to be frigged by a woman who has been fucked the same night." "Then I told him you did it to me once, which *excited* him. He put his hand up my clothes immediately. I asked him what he was going to give me, and he gave me three pounds at once, and said he would give more if I pleased him.

"He made me undress, except my stockings, and stripped himself. — Well — I have seen a good many pricks in my time, but on my soul I think his was the biggest — It was as stiff as a poker when he undressed. — He had not seen me naked then. — Then he asked all about your prick, and what you did — how you spent — I told lie after lie, just as I thought would suit him. Then he laid me on the side of the bed and began to lick my cunt." Sarah often dropped her voice and hesitated when she said a baudy word (women differ in their ways). "Then he turned my bum towards him, and he hit me all over with his prick, as hard as if it was with a stick, and asked if I had ever seen a stiffer, or larger one — then he turned me and said he would put it in — I got ready saying I feared he would hurt me. — He put the tip in which stretched me, gave an awful shove which hurt me, and I cried out. He pulled it out, put me between two chairs, just as you do when you make me piddle (I do that) and sitting down, licked my thing till I could bear it no longer, and laying hold of his head I spent. Then he frigged himself so that his spunk spurted up on to my bum.

"He licked me again, and wanted me to suck him. Then he frigged himself again. — Then he went away and gave me two sovereigns more." — Sarah showed me five sovereigns, together with mine — said she — "I will treat *you* with a bottle of champagne if you like."

His licking her cunt — his big prick — his desire to know all about me — sank into my mind, but as before said, this story is told one or two months too soon. — I fucked Sarah, and departed without the champagne — thinking of his big prick which Sarah never seemed tired of describing to me afterwards, and I quite felt jealous of it.

I had then known Sarah many months, but had never licked her cunt. — Two or three years had elapsed since I had done such a thing. — Sarah altho fresh colored, firm fleshed, and about her cunt a fine woman, had never made me desire that. — Nearly hairless cunts, are those only which I have generally desired (with few exceptions) but *his* licking and *her* description of the effect on *her*, made me curious. — "Why could you not bear it?" "No woman can long — you can't help yourself, — you must make a man leave off, or you can't prevent yourself spending." "I never did it to you." "No *you* never did, but some men are fond of doing it to me." "Do you like it?" "I like a poke best, yet you can't help liking it if a man begins — and you happen just then to want anything." — Now I will go back, to where I left off about her boots and silk stockings.

Soon after I had known her, I increased and unasked, from ten shillings to a sovereign for her favors — and often stopped later with her. — As she liked champagne, I began to take a bottle which we drank between our fuckings. — When it was warm I used to put her naked on the bed, and sit in a chair so as to look at her cunt and other charms. — When cold we used to sit by the fire both half naked, and talk baudy things — or the news of the day — I used to read the paper — and if there was anything about a woman being ravished — or a fellow showing his cock, — or feeling another man's cock in a pissing place — or an adultery — or anything of that kind, we used to discuss it. — She would tell me her views, and I gained further experience of women in such matters. — She became frank, and told me why and wherefore, in a way that few gay woman had since Brighton Bessie, Camille, and one or two others.

More than once I alluded delicately to her nose. She did not like the allusion, and altho not given to swearing — damned and cursed at *him* about it. — When I asked who *him* was she said. — "No one" — or — "Nothing." — She told me, she was thought a very handsome woman before her nose was damaged, and brought me a photograph [early days of photography] to show me. — In that she looked extremely handsome. — I said so — which set her off swearing at *him* again. — Another night, furiously she said, "If he were here, I would knife him. I'd fuck before his damned eyes. — I'd murder him." Then after a short pause, "But I have served him out." "Who?" "Nobody you know," — said sullenly — and no more could I get out of her — I never knew who *him* was — I have tried to get it from her when half groggy — when ready to spend — and when revelling in baudiness with me, but never did. From chance words dropped from time to time, and the odds and ends of talk, I came to the conclusion that *him* was her *husband,* but its only a guess.

[Much that I did with Sarah I have done with others, but every woman has a way and manner of her own even in the most simple baudy gambols. That is the charm in having a change in women. The variety gives me exquisite delight. But with Sarah some of my lascivious frolics were the most complete in their performance — and some I never yet have done with other women, as I find in my narrative further on.]

CHAPTER VIII

A fair haired giantess. — Face, form, and cunt. — Two big ones together. — Sarah upon Eliza. — Who was Eliza? — Sarah's agile tongue. — Listening at a brothel. — A hole bored uselessly. — The donkey-hung one. — His letches. — A brothel with a spy-hole. — A hundred couples fucking. — A young couple. — Involuntary onanism. — Five shillings extra. — Sarah's curiosity. — A lady and gentleman. — The lady's fears. — The rickety sofa. — The scare. — The baud's cautions. — Common coitions.

Things had gone on so nearly a year, when I saw in P***l**d Place a woman as tall as Sarah, who had fairish hair. I thought I should like to see them both together naked, and proposed this. Sarah supposed I was tired of *her*, said she would find the woman and bring her to me, but she delayed until I got annoyed. Then she said, "It is not that I mind your having another woman — but if I bring her she is sure to do me harm, for all women try to get each other's men. — Why do you want *that* woman?" — I did not care, I said, so that it was a very big woman, the bigger the better, and with light hair.

If I would not mind five pounds she'd get me a taller woman than herself — such as some men would give any money to get — and she so described her, that I agreed to give it. — "But," said Sarah, "I must be in the room with her, and you must promise not ask her name, or anything about her." I agreed to all that tho it seemed singular — thinking to myself that if I liked her, I would find means to get her again.

Sarah said the lady must name the night, and on that night Sarah told me — and not before. "She is not young, she is thirty-five." — I shied at that, not liking a woman of such age and thought

I was going to be humbugged. — However I let the affair go on, went to the Ama full of lascivious anticipation, but vowing to myself if the woman did not please me, that I would pay and go off — and if she did — how I would place her and Sarah together, making them stand up belly to belly — bum to bum — lay on the top of each other, and so on.

I went to the house first. Sarah entered followed by a very tall woman with her veil down, who stood and looked through it at me. Sarah having locked the door said, "Take off your bonnet, Eliza." — The woman only looked curiously round the room. — "Take off your bonnet." — Then she took the bonnet off, and stood looking at me. — "Sit down," said Sarah — and down she sat.

She was full thirty-five years old, but what a lovely creature. — I think I see her now, altho I never saw her but that once. — She had beautiful blue eyes, the lightest auburn hair crimped over her forehead, a beautiful pink bloom on her cheeks, and flesh quite white. — She was dressed in black silk, which contrasted well with her pink and white face. — She was big all over. — Big breasts jutted out in front — the tight sleeve shewed a big round arm — her ample bum filled the chair. — She was exactly what I wanted. — I never could wait long to talk with a woman whom I liked the look of, without proceeding to see, if not to feel, some of her hidden charms. — A burning desire to see what she had hidden seized me. I don't know if I spoke or not, but filled with desire, dropped on my knees and put my hands up her clothes, one round her thighs towards her bum, one towards her cunt.

As I touched her thighs, she put both hands down to stop me with a suppressed "oh" — neither action or word, those of a woman who was shamming. — It wasn't the fierceness of a girl who first feels a man's hand about her privates, nor the sham modesty of a half-gay woman. It was the exclamation and manner of a woman not accustomed to strange hands about her privates. The next instant, I had reached both haunch and cunt. — She gave another start, my arms had lifted her petticoats, and I saw a big pair of legs in white stockings, and the slightest flesh above the knee nearly as white. — I placed my lips on it and kissed it — my hand slipped from her cunt round to her bum, and both hands now clasped one of the largest, and smoothest, and whitest backsides I ever felt. Then burrowing with my head under her petticoats, I kissed my way up her thighs till my nose touched her motte, and there I kept on kissing.

The warm close smell of her sweet flesh, mingled just with the faintest odour of cunt, rendered it impossible to keep my lips there long. The desire to enjoy her fully was unbearable — I withdrew my head and hands, and got up saying. "Oh! — undress dear, I long to fuck you." — They were the first words I had spoken to her, and she had not spoken at all. — She then rose up, and slowly began unbuttoning looking at Sarah. — "Lord, what a hurry you are in," said Sarah to me.

Off went the black silk dress, out flashed two great but beautiful breasts over the top of the stays — and a pair of large, beautifully white arms shewed. — Then I saw the size of the big bum plainly under the petticoats. Off went stays and petticoats all but one. — Then she, "*There*, will that do?"

I wanted all off. — "Oh — I cannot take off any more." I appealed to Sarah, who said. "Now don't be a fool, Eliza" — Eliza then undressed to her chemise, and positively declared she would keep that on — I had taken off my trowsers and was standing cock in hand. — My impatience to discharge my seed into the splendid creature before me, made me careless whether she stripped or not. — I had drawn near to her — was feeling all round her bum with one hand, and wetting the fingers of the other in her cunt. I placed my prick so that it rubbed against her thigh, and feeling her, was at the same time pushing her towards the bed.

When we touched the bed — "I can't with Sarah there," said the woman. — "Go out," said I to Sarah. She looked savagely and replied, "Nonsense." Then I had a moment's dalliance and no more, forget what more was said or what took place, but saw Eliza on the bed, threw up her chemise, saw a mass of white flesh and a thicket of light hair between a pair of thighs, the next instant was between them, and my prick was up her cunt.

It was an affair of half a dozen shoves, a wriggle, a gush, and I had enjoyed her. Then I became tranquil enough to think of the woman, in whose vagina I had taken my pleasure. Resting on one arm and feeling her all over with one hand, I looked at her, and she at me. I said a few endearing words, as she lay tranquilly with my cock still stiff and up her.

I could have done it again right off, but had not yet looked at her hidden charms, and desire to inspect her quim made me draw out my cock and rise on my knees between her legs. Few strange women like their cunt looked at, when sperm is running out of it. She pushed down her chemise, I got off her, and then without saying a word she washed. When I had washed my cock it was as stiff as ever. I went to the side of the bed where she had just begun piddling, and held my stiff one in front of her eyes. For the first time she smiled.

She began to dress, but I told her I had only begun my amusement. I had brought bottles of champagne, for I knew how that liquor opens the hearts and the legs of women. — We got glasses and began drinking. — She drank it well and soon began to talk and laugh. When I again brought her to the bed she was an altered woman, but still did not seem to like fucking before Sarah. "Why I have seen all you have got to show often enough," said Sarah angrily. — On the bed now for a good look at the cunt. — It was a big one. — An inch of fat at least covered the split, stoutish middle-aged women get I think fat cunt lips, and hers were very large. — She had a very strongly developed clitoris, and such a lot of light hair. Large and fat as the cunt was, I do not recollect if the prick hole was large or little but know that I enjoyed her as much as a man possibly could. I delighted in laying my hand between two, long, fat cunt lips — I rolled over her, played with and kissed her from her thighs to her eyes, frigged her clitoris till she wriggled, and as at length my prick slipped up her cunt again, she whispered, "What a devil you are." She pushed her tongue out, mine met it, and then all was over. — She wagged her big arse vigorously when spending.

Ballocks and cunt again cleared of sperm, to the champagne we again went. — Sarah had not yet undressed, I had almost forgotten her. Now I made her strip, and my two big women were nearly naked together. — A little more pfiz and we were all on the spree. — Eliza still had the manner of a woman not accustomed to expose her charms, but insisted on by me and Sarah who seemed to have control over her, off went her chemise at last. — Off went my shirt — and there we all stood naked.

I never before had two such big women together and did with them all that my baudy fancy prompted. — I put them belly to belly, then bum to bum. — Then standing up before the glass. I put my prick between their two bums, making them squeeze it between their buttocks whilst I groped both cunts, and frigged at once both of them. Then putting Emma at the side of the bed with open thighs, I put Sarah between them as if she were a man — and pushing my prick between her thighs just touched her split. — She laid hold of my prick and slipped it up her own cunt. — But I did not mean that, and pulled it out. — Then I had them both side by side on the bed, and scarcely knew which of the gaping cunts to put into, but the fair haired one again had my attention. Then I put Sarah upside down on the bed so that her arse and cunt were near the pillow, one leg partly doubled up, and one cocked up against the back of the bed, and looking at her thus I fucked Eliza by her side. Sarah said she must frig herself and set to work doing it, whilst with the one hand stretched back she played round my prick stem in Eliza's cunt which was tightening under the pleasure of my shoving and probing. Eliza's amativeness had been awakened, she clasped me tightly with her large white arms, kissed and thrust her tongue into my mouth, in a state of the fullest voluptuous enjoyment.

We finished the champagne and sent out for sandwiches, stout, and brandy. — I had taken the room for the night. — Sarah never was, and her companion was not in a hurry now. We eat, drank, and got more erotic. — Eliza's fat bum was on my naked thighs, she put her hand on my prick, and grasping it for a minute whispered, "Come and do it again." — Sarah said, "What are you whispering about?" — She had been looking at times annoyed at my taking no notice of her. — Again I put Eliza on the bed. — Sarah who had alternately been quiet and then baudy, said, "It's my turn, why don't you poke me?" — "You will have it another night." — She then got on to the bed, and on to the top of Eliza, kissed her rapturously, got between her thighs, and my two big beauties were like man and woman in each others arms. — Eliza threw up her legs until her heels were on Sarah's back. Sarah nestling her belly close up to her, the hair of their two cunts intermingled. — Sarah's arse wriggled in a quiet way. "Don't now — don't" — said the other — Sarah took no heed, wriggled on, then lay quiet, and after a time rolled gently off Eliza, left the bed, and sat down in the arm chair. — I looked at her very white face. "You've spent," I said — she laughed.

I fucked Eliza then, and laying with prick in her asked her in a whisper to meet me again. "I cannot, I dare not," said she. — I could not get out of her her name, or where to find her again.

Eliza was now half screwed. No sooner had I fucked her than she began squeezing my prick. — She opened her large thighs, placed my finger on her clitoris, kissed my prick, thrust her tongue in my mouth, and did every thing which a randy-arsed woman does to get more fucking. — I fucked her four or five times, perhaps more, and till neither she nor Sarah could make my cock stand. The house was closed, off I went, but not until Eliza had gone long. — Sarah insisted on that. — Then said Sarah, "I'm not going without a poke." With infinite trouble she got a fuck out of me, and both of us groggy, we separated.

Some nights after talking of Eliza, whose legs in boots and silk stockings had charmed me, Sarah laughed. — "Why, they were mine, I lent them to her." Then I recollected that Sarah had not had her usual boots on.

I wished her to get me Eliza again. She refused. I said I would find her out. — She was sure I should not! — I went to one or two places on the chance of finding her, and Sarah laughed when I told her. — I used to get awfully randy when I thought of the two big women naked together. "She is not gay, altho you may think so, it was only because she was so dreadfully hard up that she came," Sarah averred.

"If she wasn't gay, she did all I asked her." "As she was getting screwed, and I had told her what you expected her to do." "And she spent like fun after the first time." "Oh yes I saw, and I told her about it afterwards." "Where did she go that night?" "To my lodgings and slept with me." "If you don't bring her, I won't see you any more," — and for a fortnight I did not — I used to go up to her in the street and ask her. She said she couldn't even if she would. — "You are lucky to have had her at all." "I paid handsomely." "If you hadn't you would never have had her." — I expect that now and then married women make a bit of money by their cunts.

Then things went on as before, but as I pulled Sarah's cunt about, I used to compare it with Eliza's. — Sarah seemed to me to know Eliza's cunt as well as if it had been her own.

One night Sarah was in a strong fucking mood and put her tongue into my mouth, and I said something which made her remark, "You did it with my friend Eliza, and I have as good teeth as she has." — Altho I had known Sarah so long, I had never put my tongue to hers. Then it was that I found out that she could put out her tongue further than any one I ever knew. She could reach half through my mouth with it. — When she was being fucked, she used after that to glue my mouth to hers, and I gave way to her. But altho she had a nice mouthful of teeth, I never cared about mixing our spittles — which is curious.

It was just before I had the big Eliza that the man with the big prick watched me into the house, and now I go back to him.

I still went at times to the baudy house in L**t*'e P***l**d St. It was dilapidated, the paper partly torn from the walls, and in the upper rooms (it was a two-storey house) the division between them seemed to have been temporarily put up, making one room into two, and was papered and canvassed over; but it was so thin, that you could hear distinctly what was said in the adjacent room. They had been afraid for a long time of the house being indited, so did nothing to repair it. But it was convenient, and why I went there was that I could hear the bed creak when the couples were at their pleasures, and also what they said. On the first floors you could hear, but not so well. The baud somehow found out my taste and told Sarah of the top room. — But altho I could hear, I could not see. The partition was canvassed on both sides, if one side was torn and there partly opened, there was the canvas on the other side.

I bored through it, and tried to make holes as others evidently had tried — and saw, but could not get a good glimpse. The keeper to whom Sarah spoke, refused to allow holes to be made, so I had to content myself with laying on the bed with Sarah, and feeling her cunt, until a couple came in. — Then we listened and it seemed to amuse her as much as me. — When we heard the bed creak, on to Sarah I got, and the delight of my fucking was increased by thinking that close to me was another couple fucking.

The man and woman wrangled about money at times, and I heard many funny things. But one night I slipped outside our door and bored, with a gimlet, a small hole in the door of the back room, and there would stand until Sarah beckoned me to come in.

I was not likely to be surprized by the baud, for I could perfectly hear if any one came into the house, and there were no rooms over head.

I could however see but little, could not see the bed, but saw the women washing their cunts, and the men washing with their backs turned to me. Occasionally a woman undressed on that side of the room, then disappeared on to the bed side. I began to crave to watch a couple go thro the amatory preliminaries, and to see the man's prick — But, I was always in fear that some one might come to the door, open it, and catch me.

Just then Sarah met the man with the donkey prick, whom she told me did then exactly what he had done before with her. This recital made me wild with desire. — I told her I would give her something handsome, if she could find a house, where I could see couples fucking. She had heard there was one, but those who knew would not tell, and some time slipped away. — With a smiling face one night she said, "If you don't mind a sovereign for the room, and five shillings afterwards for each couple you see, I know now where you can get what you want. — Off we went the following night to the house, and through a carefully prepared hole beneath a picture frame, I had a complete view of a nice room. — The washing place, bed (no sofa), looking-glass, fire place, were all in sight. In fact only that side of the room in which the eye hole was made in the partition, was not perfectly visible.

I recollect that first night well. — The woman of the house said to me, "You won't tell people will you?" — then — "Put out your light when you are looking." — There was gas in the room. — "Don't make a noise — and don't look till you hear, or think they are on the bed." — Then she lifted a picture up on to a higher nail in the partition, which disclosed a small hole. — Then she went into the other room, and did the same to a picture there. It was in a huge, old fashioned, projecting gilt frame, which when hung higher up, just cleared the hole but well shadowed it. — There was one good, strong, gas burner in the room, but no candle to enable people to pry about with.

The hole was so high up, that it was necessary to stand on a sofa placed just against the partition. There was no fire in our room when first I went there, and it was dark at about seven o'clock, Sarah had gone in first. — The woman when she had got my sovereign said, "I don't suppose any one will be there till about eight o'clock."

I undressed Sarah, and sat in excitement feeling her about, and looking at her legs, and talking. — I heard couples going into lower rooms, and the woman saying, "This way, sir" — a gruff voice reply, — "I won't go so high." — At length a couple entered. Sarah turned down the gas in our room, and up I got on the sofa. Oh my delight, — how I wish it were to come over again. There was a fine young man and a niceish young woman — I watched them with an intensity of lust quite indescribable. — I saw him first pay her, she take off her things, piss, and then stand naked expectantly. He took off his trowsers, she took hold of his prick, and he felt her cunt. — Then it was kiss, feel, and frig on both sides. I could hear him ask questions, and she reply. Then he put her down on a chair, and pushed his noble prick up against her but not up her. Then he brought her to the side of the bed. I saw her thighs distended, a dark haired cunt opened and looked at. He pushed his prick up it and had a plunge or two. (His back was towards me then.) Apparently not satisfied, he then pushed her straight on the bed — got on himself, laid by the side of her, and then I saw his prick in all its glory. — She wanted to handle it, he would not let her, but fingered her cunt with his hand nearest to her.

At length kneeling between her thighs I saw it again in all its prominence, stiff and nodding — until dropping on to her belly, it was hidden from my sight. — I watched the heavings and thrustings — the saucers which came in his arse cheeks, and disappeared as he thrust up and withdrew his penis, her thighs move up, and then her legs cross over his, as she heaved to meet his strokes. — Then the shoves became mere wriggles, then were loud exclamations of pleasure, then all was still. His limbs stretched out, her legs came tranquilly down to the side of his, a long kiss or two was heard, then absolute silence. — It was a delicious sight.

Almost before he had finished, I had put the cork in the hole in the partition, pulled Sarah to the side of the bed, felt her cunt, and was about to put up it, when alas I spent all over her outside, on thighs and cunt, then with my cock still dripping I got on the sofa again. — Sarah with me, for she seemed to enjoy looking as much as I did.

He had risen on to his knees between her thighs, and held his prick in his right hand, I could just see its red tip. — "Don't move, I'll fuck you again." "Well, you must give me some more." "I will give you five shillings." "Very well, shall I wash?" "No stay as you are." — Slowly his bum sunk on to his heels — his head peered forward — his left hand went to her cunt. — "My spunk's running out," he said. "Oh you beast." He flopped down on her without another word — and I saw by the action of his buttocks that he was driving his pego up her. — His hands clasped her again, I saw the saucers in his arse — his short shoves — her wriggles and jerks — and heard his sighs and "oha's." Then soon his silence shewed that his pleasure was complete.

During all this I kept telling Sarah in a whisper what I saw — she got as impatient as me and wanted to see as much. — It often was, "Let me have a look." "I shan't." "What is she doing?" "She is doing so and so," — then I let her peep and *she* would tell *me.* — I sat on the sofa whilst she was standing and looking, grasped her arse, put my lips on her cunt, and pulled her towards me, giving utterance to all sorts of baudy extravagances in whispers. — It is odd it occurs to me, that all *she* wanted to see was what the *woman* was doing — what *I* principally wanted to see was what the *man* was doing. — At all times that I was at that peep hole, the same feelings were predominant in both of us.

The man was pleased, gave the extra money, told her he would meet her again, washed his prick and went off — she leisurely washed her cunt, and off she went — then lighting the gas, I ballocked Sarah — not letting my sperm be wasted outside this time. — "It's exciting," said she, "I have not seen such a thing since the night you had the fine, tall, fair woman — and it makes me as randy as be damned" (her favorite expression). We finished fucking just in time for another couple. We saw three couples the first night.

I am not going to tell all I saw — much of it was commonplace fucking enough — yet some had the charm of novelty, and although I was there perhaps in the course of a year or two, in all fifty or sixty times, and saw nearly a hundred and fifty couples fucking, never grew tired of seeing.

The most amusing thing to me was that Sarah wanted to see so much. — After a time I put her occasionally with her back against the partition, and my prick up her — and then applying my eye to the hole over her shoulder, fucked her, and looked at the fucking couple in the room, until I lost sight of them, in the excitement of my own physical pleasure.

That was a risky thing to do for they could have heard us, as well as we did them. But usually the couples were so absorbed by lewedness, so preoccupied by fucking or anticipation of it, that they rarely seemed to notice anything.

One night a couple came in, she about thirty, he about thirty-five years old. She was not gay, was deeply veiled, and shabbily dressed. — At his request she undressed to her petticoat and I saw she was beautifully white in her linen. She was a fine tall woman. — "We have never been here before," said she, "why did you not go to the old place." "It's not safe to go always to the same place." — They spoke in a very low tone. — Sarah looked, and said she was a modest woman, indeed it was quite evident that she was not gay. She unlaced her stays, and whilst doing so, he knealt and putting his head under her petticoats, kept his head up against her cunt or her thighs. Withdrawing it he said, "Oh! I love you so, I love the smell of your cunt." "Oh darling for shame, how can you?" He took off his coat and trowsers, they kissed and toyed, he got her on to the bed, threw up her clothes, and disclosed as fine a pair of thighs as I have ever seen. — He kissed her all over and buried his head between her thighs, then rising I saw his prick. He took her hand and placed it round it. — "Feel how stiff it is before I put it up you." — Then he threw himself on her and began his poke.

Their loving voluptuous manner so stimulated me, that making some remark to Sarah, I clutched her round her rump, and pressed my stiff cock up against her thighs. — At that instant a leg of the sofa on which we were standing gave way. — It had, as we afterwards found, only broken off just above one of the castors. — It threw us both violently up against the partition with a bang, or indeed two, for my head went with a second bang against it. — We kept silent instinctively, after we had recovered ourselves.

"Oh my God," said the female voice quite loudly. "What is that." "It's some one under the bed — get up — get off, — I will get up," said she almost with a screech. — After a pause we heard them both walking about for some minutes. — We feared to look. — "Nonsense — under the bed." "Oh look there," I peeped, Sarah holding me for fear the sofa should go worse. — He lifted the bed valance. — "It's in the next room then, I am sure some one sees us." "What nonsense, is it likely, it was over head I am sure." "Well I am frightened," and she got off the bed, and sat on a chair.

They dropped their voices again, but I heard that they settled that it was something over head, and with a little loving enticement, on to the bed they again got, and soon were in each other's embraces. — How they enjoyed it, their kisses and murmurs were quite loud. — They lay when finished such a time with limbs interlaced before he got off. — "Don't she like it?" said Sarah who was much interested in this couple. — I was I suppose unusually randy that night — for I brought Sarah to the edge of our bed — fucked her — and directly afterwards going up to the sofa, which was not now easy to stand on, and which wobbled so that it was not safe for both of us, found him just getting off.

Without washing, they both went and stood in front of the fire, talking about the noise. — "It frightened me," said the woman. "I'm always frightened at these places. — I felt frightened as I came in — as if I should be found out, as if some one would see me. — I know it's stupid — but I never felt like it before — or not so much so as I do to-night." It was said in a low clear voice and I heard it distinctly. — "Who can see you, it's nonsense." "Yes, but I feel as if we were found out, as if some one knows what we are doing in this room." — It was really wonderful (and I've often thought so since) to hear this. What would she have said, had she found out that two eyes had seen a man between her thighs?

"I must get back," she said. "Wait a little." — He took a chair to the fire, and sat down — sat her on his knee, and his hand went up under her chemise. They faced our partition then. — "Oh don't dear — don't now — I am not washed, it is so dirty of you." "Never mind," he replied and kept her there feeling her, until up came his cock quite stiff. He pulled it from under his shirt and shewed it to her laughingly. Then she felt it, and they sat kissing and toying, and saying how they loved each other, putting their tongues together almost without speaking for twenty minutes, until her thighs moved restlessly under his titillation, and gently he again led her to the bed.

She got on to it cheerfully enough, forgetting her scare. They laid two or three minutes kissing and toying, they scarcely ceased tonguing, they moved in various attitudes, she threw her leg high up over him, he put his prick into her, and then they rolled on to one side clinging to each other, her bum then was towards our partition. "Put your leg up again dear," he said. She obeyed. He thrust for a minute, then pulled his prick out, and pushed his fingers up her cunt. Then in again pushing his pego, they at last consummated their enjoyment, with the utmost love and voluptuous energy. — They spoke so low on the bed that I could not hear much, I only heard murmurs until he got fierce in his lust and spoke louder, but their kisses were loud enough to be heard on the staircase. — They were both as fond and as randy as a man and woman could be. — It was one of the most voluptuous sights I have ever witnessed.

They now dozed, he nestling his balls between her thighs, and keeping one of her thighs up under his arm. Her chemise was just sufficiently up to show where the arse cheeks began to divide at the backbone. — I let Sarah get up and look, then I put her on the bed, fucked her, and went back.

He was putting on his trowsers, she washing her cunt. I could see her head just over the bed and hear the slopping. — Again they stood near the fire whilst she put on her petticoats. They now talked in so low a tone that I could hear nothing. — He put his arm round her waist, and leant his other arm on the mantel piece. — I could see their two faces in the glass, and they were both very plain — but she was a beautiful shape, that is, what I had seen of her. — "Oh, I must go, what will they think?" said she as she broke away from him. "What can I tell them?" — Then they went on dressing and when all but finished, "Let me give it another kiss," said he as she put her bonnet on. — Down he knealt and put his head up her clothes, kept it there a minute or two, she standing quite still just facing me. I could see the bunch his head made under her petticoats, and kept telling Sarah in a whisper what I saw, and was watching the woman, when suddenly she closed her eyes. "Oh don't dear," and she drew her bum back. He got up with his hair in disorder. — "I think he's been licking her cunt," said I to Sarah. "Ah," said Sarah, "she is just as bad as a gay woman."

"I will go out first, you turn to the left when you get into O*f**d St and get into the cab standing by the kerb. — I will put my stick outside the window, so you will know its me. — Wait about five minutes after I have gone in case I can't get one directly." He went to the window and looked out (the room is at the back of the house), and said it didn't rain. They kissed and murmured to each other — their faces close together, his arm round her. — Then, "Oh! let's do it again before we go," he said quite vivaciously. "Oh, I can't — I can't — look at the time," said she taking out a watch. "Oh William, I must go, what can I tell them. — Oh, don't now, pray don't," said she, for he had pushed his hand up her clothes again. — "Oh pray don't."

He threw off his hat and pulled off his coat like lightning. "I will — I must. — We won't be five minutes." By the time he had said that, his prick was jutting out in front of his trowsers. — His impetuosity, the sight of his prick (that wonderful persuader) conquered. She pulled off her bonnet, he tilted her backside on to the edge of the bed, threw up her clothes, her belly and thighs came for an instant, and for an instant only into view, and received him; the next instant he was ramming into her, holding her thighs under his arms, and in five minutes was quiet, leaning over her belly. They had taken the foot of the bed and I saw them sideways.

He wasted no time, "mind my chemise" said she as he pulled out his prick, and he did it with care — buttoned up, and without washing went out. — She washed, threw off her cloak, pulled up her chemise, and looked at it in all directions, as if to see whether there was any spunk on it; then dressed, put on a thick veil, and out she went. — "Modest women are worse than gay women, for there is no excuse for *them*," said Sarah.

The baud begged we would not make a noise again for she had heard it, but how could we help the sofa breaking down? We promised and begged her to get in couples, when she thought the woman was not gay. — "I know them," said she, "cause of their veils are down, and they never looks at me; but then your will have to wait, and of course I wants my rooms let." But afterwards we certainly saw many couples, of whom the women were what is called modest, tho necessarily the bulk of the fucking was with strumpets.

I may tell of one or two odd occurrences, but for the most part the couples went through the fucking business much in the same way. If the man was quite young he felt the woman's cunt directly he was in the room, then made her partly or quite undress, and if he did not pull off his trowsers, he pulled out his cock, which was usually stiff by that time (if she undressed). Then she gave his cock a squeeze, or a shake or a frig or two, he groped her cunt, and had a hurried look at it, they got on to the bed, fucked quickly, and then off they went. The middle-aged went to work more leisurely; and carefully looked at the ladies' cunts.

[It is well to mention here that but few vehicles passed through the street, but when they did, their noise prevented me hearing what the couples in the back room said.]

CHAPTER IX

Penis in excelsis. — Pride in his Priapus. — A whack on a bum. — A whack on a table. — Between two chairs. — Over silk stockings. — A male sixteen and female fifty. — "My little cunny." — An old man and his servant. — A virginity taken. — Tooth brush, anus, and suction. — The omnibus next day. — My letch for minette. — A sodomitic parson and catamitic harlot. — A bum hole licked. — A bum hole plugged. — The pains and pleasures of sodomy. — A digital anal experiment. — One stumpy, frousy, and middle-aged. — Fruitless exercise on a stomach. — "You'll fuck my bottom out."

Two or three weeks after I had used this peep hole, Sarah said she had again met the man with the titanic prick. — We had by that time got so intimate, that she told me any funny adventures she had with men. — He had behaved in just the same manner to her, and was to meet her that day week. — "Oh! I long to see him with you — bring him to the next room," — and it was so arranged. — The spying room was to be kept for me — the back room I was to pay a pound for, and it was to be kept for Sarah. The old baud knew what we were up to. — I told Sarah to keep the man as long as she could, whether he paid much or little (he gave her treble what I did), and above all to manage so that I could see his prick well.

The evening came, I was there before the time, and thought that they were never coming. — At length I saw them enter — I had been in a fever lest it should not come off. — The whole evening's spectacle is photographed on my brain. — I recollect almost every word that was said. — What I did not hear, Sarah told me afterwards, tho that was but little.

"Take off your things," said he. — Sarah undressed to her

chemise. — His back was towards me, his hand was evidently on his prick. — "Ain't you going to take *your* clothes off, you had better — you can do it nicer." — He evidently had not intended that, but yielded to her suggestion. — When in his shirt he went up to her, she gradually turned round so that *her* back and *his* face were towards me, and her movement was so natural that no one could have guessed her object, altho I did. — Moving then slightly on one side, she put her hands to his shirt, lifted the tail, and out stood the largest prick I ever saw. "Oh what a giant you've got," said she. — He laughed loudly. — "Is it not, did you ever see a bigger?" "No, but your balls are not so big." "No, but they are *big*." "No," she said. "You can't see them," — and he put one leg on a chair, — Sarah stooped and looked under them. — Whilst doing so, he tried to give her a whack on her head with his prick — and laughed loudly at his own fun. — "Why," said Sarah, "if your balls were equal in size to your prick, you wouldn't be able to get them into your trowsers." — He laughed loudly, saying, "They're big enough — there is plenty of spunk in them."

Sarah went on admiring it, smoothing it with her hand, pulling up and down the foreskin and keeping it just so that I had a full view. "You are hairy," said she, rubbing his thigh. — Then I noticed he was hairy on his legs, which was very ugly. — "Yes, do you like hairy-skinned men?" "I hate a man smooth like a woman — take off your shirt and let me see." "It's cold." "Come close to the fire then." — She talked quite loudly purposely, tho it was scarcely needed. His voicc was a clear and powerful one. — Without seeming anxious about it, but flattering him, she managed to get his shirt off and he stood naked. — He was a tall man, very well-built, and hairy generally. Masses hung from his breasts, it darkened his arms. It peeped out like beards from his armpits, it spread from his balls half way up his belly, he had a dark beard, and thick black hair. — In brief he was a big, powerful, hairy, ugly fellow, but evidently very proud of his prick, and all belonging to him. Her flattering remarks evidently pleased him highly, and he turned round as she wished him, to let her see him well all over. — His prick which had been stiff had fallen down, for instead of thinking of the woman, he was now thinking of himself; but it was when hanging, I should say, six inches long, and thick in proportion. "Dam it, it's cold, we are not so accustomed to strip like you women." — Then he put his shirt on and began business.

He made her strip and told her to go to the bedside. She went to the end and leaned over it with backside towards him. — He tucked his shirt well up, came behind her, and with his prick which had now stiffened and seemed nine inches long (I really think longer), hit her over her buttocks as if with a stick. It made a spanking noise as it came against her flesh. Then he shoved it between her thighs, brought it out again, and went on thwacking her buttocks with it. — "Don't it hurt you?" she asked him turning her head round towards the peep hole. — "Look here," said he. Going to a round small mahogany table and taking the cloth off it — he thwacked, and banged his prick on it, and a sound came as if the table had been hit with a stick. — "It does not hurt me," he said. — I never was so astonished in my life.

"I mean to fuck you," said he. "That you shan't, you will hurt any woman." — Again he roared with laughter. — "Suck it." "I shan't." — Again he laughed. — Then he made her lean on a chair, and again banged his prick against her arse. — Then he sat down, and pulled her on to him, so that his prick came up between her thighs just in front of her quim. — "I wish there was a big looking-glass," said he. "Why did you come here, there was one at the other house." — Sarah said this was nicer and cleaner, and he had said he wanted a quiet house. — "Ah, but I shan't come here again, I don't like the house."

"Get on to the chairs — the same as before." But the chairs in the room were very slight, and Sarah was frightened of them slipping away from under her. — So she placed one chair against the end of the bed, and steadied it; and against another which she put a slight distance off, she pushed the large table. Then mounting on the chairs, she squatted with one foot on each as if pissing. I could not very well see her cunt for her backside was towards me, and shadowed it.

He laid down with his head between the chairs, and just under her cunt. He had taken the bolster and pillows from the bed for his head, and there he laid looking up at her gaping slit, gently frigging his prick all the time. At length he raised himself on one hand, and licked away at her cunt for several minutes, his big prick throbbing, and knocking up against his belly whilst he did it.

Said he again, "I wish there was a glass." Sarah got down, and put on the floor the small glass of the dressing table, and arranged it so that he could see a little of himself as he lay. — But he was not satisfied. — He recommenced cunt-licking, and self-frigging, and all was quiet for a minute. — Then he actually roared out, — "Oh — my spunk coming, my spunk, — my spunk, — spunk — oho. — Come down — come over me." — Off got Sarah, pushed away the chairs, stood over him with legs distended, her arse towards me so that I lost sight of his face, but could see his legs, belly, and cock as he lay on the floor. — "Stoop, — lower, — lower." — She half squatted, he frigged away, her cunt was now within about six inches of his prick, when frigging hard and shouting out quite loudly — "Hou — Hou — Hou," his sperm shot out right on to her cunt or thereabouts, and he went on frigging till his prick lessening, he let it go, and flop over his balls.

Sarah washed her cunt and thighs, and turning round before doing so, stood facing me and pointed to her cunt. His spunk lay thick on the black hair tho I could barely see it. — She smiled and turned away. He lay still on the floor with eyes closed for full five minutes, as if asleep. Sarah washed, put on her chemise and sat down by the fire, her back towards me partly.

He came to himself, got up and went to the fire — then he washed (his back towards me), then stood by the fire, then fetched the pot and pissed. I saw his great flabby tool in his hand, and the stream sparkling out of it, for it was done just under the gas light. — Again he stood by the fire, his tool hidden by his shirt which he had on, and they talked. — Then he strode round the room and looked at the prints on the wall, looked even at the very picture beneath which I was peeping. — "What a daub," he remarked and passed on (it was a miserable portrait of a man), then from the pocket of his trowsers he gave Sarah several sovereigns.

That lady knew her game, and had thrown up her chemise so as to warm her thighs — and after he had paid her, he put his hand on to them. — She at the same time put her hand on to his tool. "Oh what a big one." — nothing evidently pleased him so much as talking about the size. — "Did you ever see so big an one," said he for the sixth time I think. "Never — let's look at it well. — Hold up your shirt." — He did as told. — Sarah pulled his prick up, then let it fall, handled his balls, pulled the foreskin up and down, and shewed him off again for my advantage. — "Why don't you sit down, are you in a hurry?" Down he sat, his tool was becoming thicker and longer under her clever handling, and hung down over the edge of the chair. He was sitting directly under the gas light, and I could see plainly, for Sarah cunningly had even stirred the fire into a blaze. He was curious about other men's cocks — what their length and thickness was. — She shewed him by measuring on his own, and kept pulling it about, her object being to get it stiff again for me to see his performances. — My delight was extreme — I could scarcely believe that I was actually seeing what I did, and began to wish to feel his prick myself. How large it must feel in the hand I thought, how small mine is compared with it, and I felt my own. — As Sarah pulled down his prepuce, I involuntarily did so to mine, and began to wish she were feeling mine instead of the man's.

Then only I noticed how white his prick was. His flesh was brownish — and being so sprinkled with hair it made it look dark generally. — His prick looked quite white by contrast. Sarah must have been inspired that night, for no woman could have better used her opportunity for giving me pleasure and instruction. Repeating her wonder at the size, she said, "Let's see how it looks when you kneel." — He actually knelt as she desired. I saw his prick hanging down between his legs. Soon after in another attitude, I noticed that hair crept up between his bum cheeks, and came almost into tufts on to the cheeks themselves. — I saw that his prick was now swelling. — Sarah taking hold of it, "Why it's stiff again." He grasped it in the way I had first seen him, and said eagerly. — "Let's see your cunt again."

Sarah half slewed her chair round towards him, opened both legs wide, and put up one of her feet against the mantelpiece, as I have often seen her do when with me. He knelt down and I lost sight of his head between her legs — but saw his hand gently frigging himself as before, and heard soon a splashy, sloppy, slobbery sort of suck, as his tongue rubbed on her cunt now wetted by his saliva. Then he got up and pushed his prick against her face. — "Suck, and I will give you another sovereign." "It will choke me — I won't," said Sarah.

Then he began to rub her legs and said he liked silk stockings, that few wore silk excepting French women whom he did not like, — but "they all suck my prick." — Again Sarah put up her leg — again he licked her cunt, and then said she must frig him, which she agreed to on his paying another sovereign.

He told her to go to the edge of the bed and he then went to the side nearest the door, which put his back towards me. — He called her there. — "Come here," said Sarah, laying herself down at the foot. "No, here." "I won't, it's cold close to the door" (she knew that there I could not see his cock). He obeyed, put up her legs (just as I used to do) opened them wide, and I could sideways see her black haired quim gaping. "Close them," he cried. She did and lay on her back, her knees and heels close together up to her bum, "I'll spend over your silk stockings," said he, now frigging violently. Sarah to save her stockings, just as his spunk spurted, opened her legs wide and it went over her cunt and belly. — He never seemed to notice it.

I had passed an intensely exciting couple of hours by myself, watching this man with his huge fucking machine. Sarah in her attitudes, altho I had seen them fifty times, looked more inviting than ever. My prick had been standing on and off for an hour. — I would have fucked anything in the shape of cunt if it had been in hand, and nearly groaned for want of one. As I saw her legs open to receive his squirt, heard his shout of pleasure, and saw his violent, frig, frig, frig, I could restrain myself no longer, but giving my cock a few rubs, spent against the partition, keeping my eye at the peephole all the while.

He wiped his cock on her cunt hair, washed, and went away seemingly in a hurry. — Sarah came in to me. — "Don't you want me," said she. — I pointed to my spunk on the partition. "You naughty boy, I want it awfully." — Soon after I was fucking her. — With all her care to save her silk stockings, sperm had hit her calf, and while I fucked her at the bed side, I made her hold up her leg that I might look at it. — It excited me awfully. What a strange thing lust is.

I never saw the man afterwards. — She did, but he would never go to that house again. — She thought that he lived in the country. He seemed a gentleman.

One night a couple went in. It was a thin woman about fifty years old I should say, and a youth of about sixteen. — He looked like a Jew. She asked him, directly he was in, for the money; he gave her five shillings, put down his hat, and went up to her. —

She had never moved from the door side of the room, and stood with her back to the bed, her face towards us. He seemed shy. She said, "Let me feel your cock." His back was to me, but I could soon see she had hold of his doodle. He was quite quiet, and when he spoke, he did so in a low tone of voice so that I could scarcely hear him. — Her voice on the contrary was that of a magpie, the clack of an old woman. — "Feel my cunny my dear," said she, "it's such a nice hairy cunny." — He put his hand up her clothes and wanted to look. — "Oh, no, you want to know too much, I can't shew it — it's made to feel, not to show, but feel it, it's nice and hairy." — "Oh what a nice cock it is — how it longs to go up my little cunny — how stiff it is — oh what a nice cock," and she stooped and looked at it — I could not see it. — "Oh no I can't let you see it — another time," she said, in reply to something he said. — "Oh put it in, put it in, it's longing to go up my cunny." — Leaning back against the bed, she hitched up her clothes, and I saw a pair of dirty spindle shanks nearly to her thighs. — She never left go of his cock, but pulled him towards her by it. — "Oh it's up my cunny, how often do you fuck, — Oh it is up my little hairy cunny my dear, is it not nice? — Oh fuck it, fuck, fuck, fuck, — Oh isn't nice?" — He had clasped her somehow and was shoving rapidly, and spent almost before he began, for I heard a deep sigh from him and he was quiet; whilst she kept on cackling, "Oh is it not a nice little cunny."

He was in a hurry, or did not like his bargain, for he buttoned up the instant he had done, and put his hat on. — She went across the room, took a towel and gave her cunt a dry rub but did not wash. — "Give me a shilling for luck," said she. — He gave it her. — "I'll give you more pleasure next time, and you shall see my cunny." — Off they went. They had not been in the room ten minutes. — She never took her bonnet off.

Sarah always anxious to see the women, used to say if she knew them or not. — It was, "She is lucky with men," — or, "She used to be about but I have lost sight of her," — and so on — once, — "Oh that woman's been laid up with the pox — I thought she had gone home." — There was always amusement for both of us.

One night a fine looking, white-haired old man, I suppose sixty years old — brought in a young woman resembling a servant. — She sat herself down solemnly, and let him take off her bonnet and shawl without a word. "This is one of those houses," said she when she first spoke. — He tried to feel her and she resisted. — There was a mild scene. — "Oh my goodness! what would Mrs **** say if she knew I was here?" "She never will," said the old buck, "and I will be a friend to you for life — now don't be foolish — have I not got your father out of debt, have I not helped you all?" — He was a big old fellow, walked round her, undid her dress which at length she pulled off, and then he attempted a grope. — She resisted, and in the scuffle sank on the floor at the foot of the bed. — He dropped on his knees and put his hand up her clothes. "Oh for God sake, sir. — No. I won't let you. — I am sorry I came, I didn't mean to come." — The old boy then apparently got a finger or two in her cunt, for she gave a small shriek. — Then he spoke angrily. — "If you don't, I'm damned if you stop with us another week." — He left off, puffing and blowing with the struggle, and got up. There she sat on the floor crying, her bosom was bare as he had pulled it open, her clothes up so that I saw to her knees — and that she had striped, dark stockings on, thin legs.

After a little time he lifted her up, and they sat on two chairs, he with his arms round her coaxing, kissing, and talking, but I could hear but little. — Sometimes he got in a temper and then he talked loud and threatened. — "There is a virginity," I said to Sarah. — She thought at first it was all a sham, and that the woman knew what she was about, that she would — "humbug the white haired old cove" — but as time went on, came to the conclusion that the old cove had got one of his servants into a trap. — Soon afterwards, he got his hand up her clothes again, and after a time by coaxing, hugging, and handling, got her on to the bed and himself there too. — She had only taken off her dress, he only his coat.

When on the bed, for a minute she buried her head in his breast. The old boy had then got his hand seemingly round her bum, but her clothes covered it, and I could not see exactly where his hand was. — But he soon took it away, and I saw him fumbling between himself and her, and knew he was getting his cock out of his trowsers. She was now silent, passive. Then holding her close to him with his left arm, which was under her, he managed with his right hand to pull his trowsers quite down. — I saw his large fat haunches, but not his tool. Then he pulled up her clothes — nestled his belly against hers, and rolled over on to her. She turned quite on to her back. — He kissed her. — "Now be a good girl, I shall not hurt you — or do you any harm — be a good girl." — She laid quietly with eyes closed. "Now be a dear good girl, there's a dear," and he pressed on her and gave a shove. — She gave immediately a cry, quite a loud one—and only one. — He put his hand right over her mouth, rammed quickly, and soon his wriggles told of his consummation. Then his head sank by her side. The girl was crying violently. I both saw and heard.

He lay on her such a time endearing her, to all of which she made no reply that I could hear. Then he got off in a temper. For half a minute she lay still scarcely moving, and then got off the bed still crying, which seemed to disconcert him. He sent for brandy, and made her take some with water. Then he sat her on his knee and they talked. Then he looked at the tail of his shirt and said triumphantly and loudly. "You have bled a little, never mind — it's all over, you'll be all right to morrow — do wash dear — do — you needn't mind me now — wash your thing my dear." She went to the side of the bed and put the basin down on the floor. The old boy began at once frigging away at his prick with the view of it making it stiff again — but it seemed no go. — The girl washed and sat down looking at the fire, and began crying again. — He then washed and soaped his prick and recommenced frigging it, turned round with it quite stiff, and for the first time I saw it. — He walked up to her with it stiff. "Look dear, that's what has done the mischief," and sat down with his back towards me, but he kept at times frigging his cock I could see.

The landlady knocked at the door, she was always interrupting couples. — "Shall you soon have done?" said she. — He started up putting his shirt over his stiff cock. — She started up seemingly in terror. — "I shan't be long," said he, and then turning round. "Dam the woman for frightening me so." — They both went away soon after. — She still crying, and he saying he would be a friend to her as long as he lived. — Sarah remarked. "Well, — I really think the old boy has had the first of her, and he's old enough to be her grandfather.—I'll warrant that the old beggar has a large family, he looks like it—there is no trusting any man."

One night a fine looking man with a dark moustache, looking not forty years old, came in with a poorish looking woman.—They talked for some time, then he said, "I will give you five shillings extra if you'll suck me."—After refusal, and a declaration that she had never done it before, she agreed to it.—I told Sarah and let her look.—"I know that woman, let me see her do it, I never saw a man's prick in a woman's mouth in my life."—He gave her ten shillings and said he would give the five when she had sucked him, took off his coat, and feeling in the pocket took out a paper, from which he produced a round handled tooth brush, and put it in his waistcoat pocket.—Then in the centre of the room he dropped his trowsers down.—She laid hold of his tool which was quite flabby, and pulled the skin back, and squeezed it. "Wash it first."—He scuffled with his trowsers down his ankles towards the wash stand, washed and came back. She dropped on her knees. He had refused to lay on the bed as she asked him.—If they had placed themselves so as to let me look at them, they could not have placed themselves better.

She took it into her mouth, and moving her head backwards and forwards fucked his prick so to speak with her lips. Then she spat on the floor, then into her mouth his prick which had begun to swell again went. As it came out it was now quite big.

She stopped, looked up and said.—"You must not spend in my mouth, tell me when you are coming." "Yes I must—there is no pleasure unless I finish." "Oh I can't." She left off and stood up.—After an altercation, he agreed to give her ten shillings instead of five, if she would let him, and she to make sure, had the money first.

She stood besides him for a time, holding his cock and frigging it—for unless a woman loves a man, or is really fond of having a prick in her mouth, as some are, she likes to make the prick suction short, and bring it as much forward by fist-fucking as she can. "Do you never fuck?" said she. "I was wounded some years ago, and have never been able to fuck since."—It was not clear to me why a man whose prick already stood, could not put it into a woman's cunt, as well as into her mouth. — He had then taken the tooth brush out of his pocket. — "What are you going to do with that," said the girl. "I tickle my bum hole with that, it increases my pleasure, you will see."

She dropped on her knees — and his prick which had drooped again, got stiff under her sucking — but she had to go on for such a time, that she rested and said, "Oh you can't spend."

He said he could. — Then I saw him wet the handle of the tooth brush with spittle, and laying hold of it by the bristly end he pulled up his shirt and passing his hand to the rear, began to move it rapidly. — "Have you put it up your arse hole?" said the girl, leaving off.

"Yes — yes — go on — suck — I shan't be long." — On they went, her head bending up and down as his prick came in and out, his hand bobbing from his backside. — He was just beginning to shiver with pleasure, when the landlady knocked at the door. — "Make haste please, we want the room." — I have heard her do this several times when the couples seemed too long — but this couple had been but a short time in the chamber.

Out came the handle from his arse hole, out came his prick from her mouth, up she stood. He called out "I will pay for the room twice." "All right, sir," said the landlady, going away.

"Damn her," said he, "I was just going to spend — go on." — "Oh what a time you are — you ought to give me another five shillings." "I will, I will," — he said hurriedly.

Sarah who had been looking at intervals thro the peep hole, remarked, "That poor girl will have all her trouble again."

She again dropped on her knees, again engulfed his doodle which had gone to the size of a gooseberry — again the tooth brush jigged up his arsehole, and after much hard work for the woman, he cried out, — "I'm coming, I'm coming," drew out his tooth brush, and holding her head with both his hands, whilst the tooth brush stuck out from one of them, fucked hard in her mouth, till his head fell forward, with eyes closed and his mouth wide open. She slowly mumbled at this doodle for a minute, then emptied her mouth into a towel she had.

Sarah had glimpses, and I told her what was going on. — "Is she still sucking — what is he doing?" were whispers frequently made. — I had never seen her in such a state of curiosity. — "Well!

I never saw that before altho I have seen much — I wouldn't make a baudy house of my mouth — or turn it into a cunt for five shillings, or fifty shillings."

I was amused, tho the tooth brush business so disgusted me that I retched, and sent out for brandy. But the cock-sucking made a great impression on me, I'd had it done a few times in my life under excitement which left me almost without knowing what I did. Soon after I thought I should like to try it, and I looked out for that very woman, but never saw her — I reserved my want, not liking to ask Sarah. — The sight she said had made her as sick as it had me. — Wasn't she lying? — A desire for Sarah to gamahuche me sprang up that very night, tho I didn't then ask her.

I thought about it repeatedly afterwards for the enjoyment of the man seemed so intense. — His whole frame writhed as he stood, and what struck me was the extraordinary quivering of his thighs; they shook as he spent like an aspen leaf. I noticed *that* more than anything else. He had tucked up his shirt round his waist in a roll, as if quite accustomed to the operation standing.

The girl rinsed her mouth. — He washed his tooth brush and put it carefully up in paper, pissed and began to button up. The woman again asked him if he never fucked, and he made a similar reply; he had not fucked for years. — It is noticeable that he'd never touched or looked at the girl's quim, nor made her undress, nor felt her in any way. — She, curious, asked him many questions. Replying, he said he found no difficulty in getting women to suck him, that some did it much better than others, that he did not often do it, and never twice the same day for it made him ill. Then he drew the girl's attention to something under his balls, but I could not hear what he said for he turned his back, and his belly was to the gas. The girl felt and looked, kneeling to do so. He was an exceedingly fine man and in the prime of life — his prick by no means large.

Next day I got into an omnibus. — A minute afterwards a man got in and sat opposite to me, and I saw it was the same who had the night before tooth-brushed his arsehole. — I was under no error, his eyes, manner, clothes, the ring on his finger, I recognized all. I sat staring until he raised his eyes to mine. I still stared resolving in my mind what I had seen him do, and felt such an aversion to him, that I stopped the omnibus and got out.

Sarah laughed. "Well I have done most things and am not particular, but blessed if ever I had a man's spendings in my mouth and never will." — Yet before a month had passed, she had mine — I expect she lied, but it is never safe to say you won't do anything in love matters. All women I believe have had a man's prick in their mouths, it's human nature.

One night a man of about thirty years old came in with a woman. They had evidently met before, and she knew his ways and wishes. — He was coated and muffled up almost to his eyes. When he'd unwrapped, I guessed by his well-shaven face and long frock coat, that he was a clergyman. He spoke so low until towards the end of his amour, that I could scarcely hear a word. — Before she undressed, he made her kneel on a chair, and throwing up her petticoats exposed her buttocks, and a remarkable plump, well-made woman of about twenty-five she was. Then he walked to the other end of the room and contemplated her. Then he turned her round and made her sit with her clothes up, stand with them up, lay on the floor, backside up, and then belly up, and in fact put her almost into every possible attitude to expose her private parts. — But he never put her on the bed, and as there was no sofa, he placed her always at the corner of the fire place under the gaslamp, so that Sarah and I had the finest view of her. — After having seen her in one or two postures, he, dressed altogether in black, pulled out a stiff cock and his balls, he walked about, still looking at her but without putting his hands on his machine, of which we had a good view. It was rather large, and stood out stiff enough for a time, then it flopped down over his stone bag. — Then he made her strip to her chemise, he stripped to his shirt, and put her through the same postures, but principally with her arse towards him, to which he knelt down and began to fumble about and kiss, and at length to lick.

Almost at the outside Sarah said, "I know that woman, but I haven't seen her for some time," and told me her history which I quite forget. — Then she got anxious to watch her, continually saying, "Let me have a look — do." But it was a sight I much desired to see myself, for the woman looked so nice, that I began to long to have her, and resolved in my mind how I should get her. —

Then I got such a stiff-stander, that excepting for losing the sight, I should have put it into Sarah. But there I stood, feeling Sarah's arse and tucking my fingers between its cheeks, and twiddling her cunt and looking.

The man whose prick again got very stiff, began poking it at her. — He pushed it in her face, up against her breasts, her sides, and her bum, but principally her bum. — Sarah looking one minute, said, "He likes her arse better than her belly." Then he put two chairs close together so as to let her kneel with knees wide open, and came close to the partition thro which we were looking, and stood gazing. Now just beneath her distended thighs I could, tho sideways, see her cunt gaping but it was in shadow in the dark fringing hair, which in quantity in front, was thickish behind.

He went close and pulled open her arse cheeks with both hands, and began licking her brown hole furiously — at intervals leaning back, looking at the hole, and what seemed to us to be thrusting his finger in it, but his head was in the way and we could not be sure.

"He will keep her all night," said I, "let's fuck, my spunk's nearly coming." "Wait, wait, he won't be long now, he is feeling his prick," but Sarah was wrong. — He came back and again stood looking so long, that impatiently I pulled Sarah off the sofa, put her at the edge of the bed, and in a few shoves discharged up her cunt, my seminal libation.

Scarcely waiting for my prick to shrink out I pulled it out of her. — She with cunt full, got on to the sofa before me, and looking attentively for a minute whispered, "Oh! oh! he is going to bugger her — he is greasing her bum."

I could scarcely get her head from the peep hole; when I did, saw he had got a pot of grease and was greasing his prick. — "He's greased her arsehole," said Sarah to whom I kept whispering what was going on. Then he placed her at the bottom of the bed, and their flanks were towards us. — The woman said, "You will give what you did before." "Yes, yes," he replied, but he was scarcely audible. Then she again turned her arse towards him, her legs distended, her face and arms over the bed, he had pulled off her chemise, he his shirt and they were both naked. — His prick stood upright against his belly, with his left hand keeping the bum cheeks open or fumbling, his right hand holding his tool, he put it in her. I saw his arse oscillating and heard her with muffled voice say something which sounded like, — "Oh you hurt so," just as his belly closed on her arse. Then he placed both hands round her haunches holding her tightly. — "He's up her, I wonder if he is up her cunt or her arsehole." "Up her arse or why did he grease it and his own prick as well, — let me look. — I want to know what that woman does, she's cheeked me, and I want to know."

I let her look for a second. — "He is buggering her I am sure from the way he stands." I pushed her head away for she would not move, applied my eye to the hole, and saw him ramming away hard, his bum wag, his thighs shake, his whole form move quiveringly. Beyond "Yes, yes" — when she'd asked him first about the money — I'd scarcely heard him, so low was the tone in which he uttered what little he said. — All at once he drew his belly back from her bum, and looked down, gratifying his eyes, but for a second only; for with a quick shove followed quickly by others — he shouted out in a loud voice, — "I'm up her arse, I'm up her arse, Oh! — oh!," and then still louder, — "My spunk in your arse, my spunk in your arsehole." "Oh! some one will hear, don't," said the woman, lifting her head and turning it partly round. "Don't! hish! don't!" — but he shouted still "arse-hole, spunk," and then was quiet — bending over her, holding her tightly, and gently wriggling his arse about with enervated muscular action.

"He has buggered her, look." "Yes he has buggered her," said Sarah, looking, "a dirty, nasty bitch, she ought to be shown up — dirty bitch, I have a good mind to tell one or two of her friends what I have seen her up to. — I wonder if it hurts her much," said she enquiringly after a pause — I wondered too.

He kept close to her backside, leaning over her and grasping her round her waist. — His head laying on her naked back, his face slightly turned towards me, and I thought he never would get off. At last she moved and I suppose threw his prick out, for he relieved her and threw himself naked as he was on the bed, his arse towards us, and there he lay as if in sleep for I suppose ten minutes.

She took no notice — but opened the door, and asked for warm water, washed, put on her chemise, then put her finger evidently on to her arsehole, and looked at her finger. She did that more than once at intervals of a minute or so. — Then she said I *think* (for she dropped her voice), "arn't you going to get up," — He rose, washed and dressed, and they went away. She was a sweetly pretty woman, had a charming plump figure, and was I should have said a very appetizing fuck, — but she was not well dressed.

Before they went away — he turned her up after she was dressed, looked at her arse hole and kissed it, and they both laughed — but they spoke during the whole entertainment in such a low tone, that I could hear nothing but what I have told.

Sarah and I talked about buggery in general. — "It does not hurt," said she, "to put your finger up, but a big prick must." — I thought it must hurt to put up a finger. — "You can try on yourself." "I would," said I, "if he had left his ointment." She laughed, "We will try it together some day, you shall put your finger up my bum hole and I up yours." "All right you bring the ointment." "I will get some cold cream." We joked about the parson's fun for I was sure he was a parson. — Soon we had another couple to look at, and another, but when we talked we got back to the sodomitical subject — and when I fucked Sarah that night, we both talked as we lay in copulation, of the difference of sensation there might be between arse hole plugging — and cunt plugging. Said I, "The pleasure really must be all on one side." "I have heard that some men and some women too, are fond of the sensation of a prick in their bum holes," said she. This was said whilst I was up her. When in that sensuous, stimulating, lascivious, position, it takes away one's sense largely; all is pleasure, but I know what I have written was said then.

Afterwards I thought of my adventure in my youth, with the fat, squabby, Devonshire woman's bumhole — and wondered if going up that round hole gave greater pleasure than fucking. I longed to try but dismissed it from my mind. Then I wondered if it hurt to put anything up the bum, so greased my finger one day, and to my surprize it slipped up without pain, but with an unpleasant sensation. I asked Sarah about what she had said, and one night she got cold cream, and as we lay on the bed together, I induced her to try on me; and we both poked up each other's arseholes. It rather upset me, and I was ashamed of it. — It gave me no pleasure and gave her none she said, so we never did it again. But from time to time I could not help thinking about it and had a desire to have the woman we had seen buggered.

An odd couple came in one night — A common place young woman poorly dressed, with a very short, middle-aged man in black, whom I recognized as a clerk in a public department, and had seen for years. — He was about fifty years old, perhaps more, and awfully ugly. — There was that night a fire in the room and they both at first sat in front of it. — Whilst there, he pulled out his prick and tried to get it to stand, but could not. I heard the girl say "Let me try." She frigged it a long time, but it was of no use, for she remarked, "I don't think that will stand to night." — I could not see his cock for she just hid his middle, but saw well the movement of her arm whilst she frigged.

After a time he said in a low gruff voice. "It will be all right when I get on you — get on the bed." — She complied. — Pulling her gown off, he his coat, they laid down side by side — she put her hand to his cock, and fumbling it said, "Why don't you let your trowsers down, I can get at it better." — He let them down, she then pulled up his shirt which looked black and dirty, and took hold of his cock which must have been very small for I couldn't see it. — I suppose it was flabby. "Why don't you feel me," pulling up her clothes as she said so, and showing a chemise also not of a very inviting color, and limbs not too beautiful. — He put his hand there, and turning on his side as she turned on her side as they lay together, began feeling, and she frigging for some time. Then — "Oh, you can't do it," but he went on frigging.

He said in about ten minutes, "I want to piddle and shall do it afterwards." The stumpy little man got off the bed (he was on the side nearest to me) and toddled round to the side where the piss pots were, and stood long making water I suppose, for I saw that he had the pot in his hand. She laid looking at him and scratching her cunt or thighs high up, but her clothes just covered the bottom of her belly — and I could not see exactly where her fingers were.

Turning round, he pulled up her clothes to her navel, and I saw she had a sandy haired grummet. — He made her open her legs wide, pulled open the cunt lips, and looked. "You're a long time, you must give me more or I can't stop longer." — He made some reply I could not hear.

Emptying his bladder and fumbling at her sandy haired opening, apparently had the desired effect. — He told her to move further off, and got on to the bed from the pisspot side and facing me. — As he did so I saw a smallish sort of sprout from under his shirt. His trowsers so embarrassed him that he could scarcely shuffle into position, so she helped him by cocking up one leg, and just shifting herself so as to bring him between her thighs. — Down he went on to her like a lump of lead, and began shoving.

If he was on the woman one minute he was half an hour there, shoving and wriggling more or less the whole time; he got fatigued, blowing and snorting like a pig — I could hear the wind whistling through his nostrils quite plainly, I shall never forget it.

The affair was amusing at first, but I had then seen such lots of couples in coition, some nice, handsome, clean and voluptuous, others quaint and novel in amusements, many inciting in some way — so got tired of this poor couple and left off looking. — Sarah looked — then I looked again. — There was he still ramming and blowing away — I heard the woman say "You can't do it." — The woman of the house just then knocked at the door as usual.— He stopped short, and the girl called out, "We shall be out directly," — then to the man, "Get off you've had enough." — He muttered something and continued shoving.

Again I and Sarah looked, and left the spy-hole. "He means to keep on that poor woman all night." Looking five minutes afterwards I heard her say, "I'm damned if you won't fuck my bottom out." — Then was an agitation of his body, he laid quiet for an instant, then puffing and the sweat streaming down his face he got off — whether he had had a spend or not I don't know.

The woman went off leaving him sitting by the fire, seemingly quite done up, until the landlady went in and asked if he wanted the room again. He grunted out "No" — and left.

CHAPTER X

The baud's avarice. — The couples hurried. — Cyprians remuneration. — A tight cunted one. — One who knew the spy hole. — A loving, handsome couple. — The mother's maid. — Amorous impatience. — His lustful power. — Varied postures. — Copulations reckoned. — Brother John's cock exhibited. — Gossip with Sarah on gamahuching. — The fourth poke. — The pocket handkerchief. — Laxities with Sarah. — Heads to tails. — Sarah's letch for gamahuching. — On female cunilingers.

I have said that the landlady did not give the couples too long a time, especially if business was brisk. — She had an eye mainly to the double fees, for in addition to the pound, I paid five shillings for each couple. They charged the couples three and six pence and sometimes five shillings, never more. It was only a second class house, tho I saw swell women there.

One night she turned seven couples in between eight and twelve o'clock — all of whom we saw copulating — I did not mind the ordinary run being got in and out soon, for they usually went to work with small prelude, and the more petticoats I saw hoisted, the more cunts I saw, and the more pricks wagged and stiffened in my view, the better. But when a spoony couple were in — or the man had funny letches, — I was annoyed at their being hurried so asked again the landlady to try to put couples of whom the woman was what is called modest (altho every woman is immodest enough to show her own tail, and feel a man's tail at times), and not to hurry them. — The ordinary couples needed no hurrying, for the gay ladies urged on the shagging.

I soon discovered the very unequal fees paid, and what small sums at times were paid even to exceedingly well dressed women.

— Many had only ten shillings and often five, although at times they got two or three sovereigns, and from men who did not look very rich. — I once saw a girl come in twice the same night and be fucked for five shillings, and heard her say it was very little. He gave her a shilling more for a glass of wine. — The second time she got a couple of sovereigns. — I chaffed Sarah about the nice cunts to be had for ten shillings, but in my young days I knew that. Yet having for so many years given higher compliments, it came quite new to me, that a clean nice looking woman, would give up her privates for five shillings, yet well dressed women did.

There was a woman looking twenty-two years old, whom I saw many times. — She was well made and had a pretty face. I took a fancy to have her, but did not like to ask Sarah to get her. — One or two men said, "What a little cunt you have," — at which she used to laugh. — I went about this time in the middle of the day and saw the landlady, who made objection, but principally about Sarah knowing of it, but as I vowed I would not tell, I got the spy room by myself, and passed the evening looking — I told the landlady of the girl I wanted but she would not get her for me, few women, knew of the peep hole room, and I should tell the woman, and that would blow the house — I did not see the girl that night and felt not so comfortable alone. — But the small-cunted woman ran in my head. Again I had the room by myself, and that night she came in. I got awfully randy at seeing her fucked, and directly it was over left the baudy house. — The woman shortly afterwards came out, and turned towards **** St. — When she was just in **** St. I spoke to her, and we went to another house. I bargained for half of a sovereign which I knew she had just been paid. — She accepted after swearing she never had less than a sovereign.

She was perfect in shape, and her cunt one of the smallest for a full grown woman my prick ever entered. — Two fingers went in with greatest difficulty, yet the vulva looked as large as an ordinary one. — There was black hair on it. I enjoyed her immensely and fucked her three times, paying her for each fuck. — What amused me was my asking her if she had it done to her before that night, and she swearing that she had not.

I fucked her at the side of the bed at first, to see my prick draw in and out of the small orifice. When I had recovered from my pleasure, I put her legs over my shoulders, and drawing her bum to me, kept my prick in whilst I asked her questions. She did not hurry me. I had noticed she never was impatient with men. — Pulling my prick out, and telling her what I was going to do, I watched my sperm laying at the mouth of the tight hole, and soon began to work again in my own sperm. — "Oh come on the bed, I want it, let's do it nicely," — and on the bed a more voluptuous little devil never wetted my ballocks.

She would make no appointment with me saying I should see her about, but I never did. I asked the landlady at ***** St. She recollected her, said she sometimes came with men often for a week or so, and then did not for a month. She did not know her name nor anything about her. — I never told Sarah.

One night an ordinary woman was on the bed with a man when Sarah, looking, remarked — "That woman knows there is a peep hole, see how she keeps her eye on it." — Certainly she did keep looking, and she pulled her clothes over her thighs as much as the man's lying between them would permit. — She pushed the man away directly he had finished, and got off the bed looking in our direction. — Sarah let down the picture and waited till the couple had gone. — The landlady had told her to do so in case we thought any one looked at the spyhole. — I saw only two or three women out of the whole number, who eyed the spot suspiciously, and never a man, altho I saw a dozen walk up to the picture and look at it — it was most cunningly contrived. [I wonder if it was ever found out afterwards and there was a row, for the house was closed all of a sudden.]

Another night a couple came in together both muffled up, she deeply veiled. — Directly he had locked the door he took off his hat — she her veil, — both laughed, rushed into each other's arms, and stood kissing long as if they'd never have enough of it. — "Oh I am so glad," said she, and again they kissed. "What a time since we met." "Is it not." "Oh I am so glad," — and similar exclamations of joy whenever they got their lips apart. — They talked loud, they kissed loud, in a state of mutual delight at meeting. — They had no fear — no thought but of each other. — "It's a spoony couple," said I to Sarah. "Yes," said she when she had a look, "and what a fine woman, I wonder how she will do it, as she calls herself, I suppose, modest." — Sarah hated the modest fuckstress — I pulled Sarah's head away, begrudging her looking.

They finished kissing for the moment. He threw off an over coat, she her bonnet — and as handsome faced a couple as ever I saw stood there. — He a gentleman, seemingly about twenty-six years old, tall, strong, with dark brown hair. — She a fine grown woman of perhaps twenty-one, with dark hair and beautiful blue or grey eyes, I can't say which, and such long eye lashes that they were a marked feature in her face. — That done, they again rushed into each other's arms, and kissing recommenced. — Her back was to me as he clasped her, and I saw his right arm move gradually lower, from her waist to her bum. He was thinking of her cunt.

"There is no sofa, I hate a room without a sofa," said he sitting down on a chair and pulling her on to his knee. For a minute they again kissed. — "Now tell us all that has taken place since I saw you." She began to tell, and from what I heard, it seemed that she was in service in his mother's house.

She had scarcely begun before he pushed his hand under her clothes. "Oh Charley, don't dear," said she with a little faint resistance. I could see that his hand in a second or two was between her thighs, and a lovely leg came into view, as his arm hooked her petticoats over it. — Then all was kissing and murmurs, or restless moving of his right arm, a restless movement of her bum on his knee, and a shuffling of her feet. The titillation of her cunt had told on her, and was filling her with voluptuousness.

His hand was withdrawn, he pulled open his trowsers, and out came a magnificent prick. Without a word he placed her right hand on it. — She felt it, and hung her head over his shoulder. — Up went his hand beneath her clothes, their mouths met, nothing but kisses were audible, but her body moved uneasily from her waist to her bum, and both their feel shifted places continually — pleasure made them restless.

"Come to the bed dear, come — I want you so." — He pushed her from his knee and stood up, his prick stiff out of his trowsers.

— He led her hurriedly to the foot of the bed, and seemed wild for her.

"Oh Charley dear, what a hurry you are in — oh don't, don't, I shall spoil my dress — don't, wait a minute." — He had her bum against the bed, had lifted her petticoats, and with both arms under her thighs was trying to lift her on the bed, but desisted at her wish. "Make haste dear — I am dying for you — look here," — shaking his pego which with the skin down, shewed a flaming tip, and a noble prick it was.

She began to undo her dress. — He threw off coat, waistcoat and trowsers, and had finished before her gown was off. Then he helped her. A beautiful pair of calves and ankles came into view, her breasts attracted him, he put his hand on them. — "Take your stays off." — Smiling she began — there was a hitch — "Oh damn it" — laying hold of the lace, with a violent tug he broke it. "Oh don't, I shan't be able to lace it again." He pulled the stays off, threw them on the floor, pushed her on to the bed and threw up her clothes. — I saw a dark haired motte, and the next instant he had covered it, then laid in tranquillity for a few seconds.

What a splendid-limbed woman. — Altho she had all her petticoats on, I saw one side of her fine haunches and faultless legs. In a few seconds, one hand was put between their bellies, feeling his prick, or the warm lips which embraced it. — His drawers which he had not pulled off annoyed him, for withdrawing his hand, he pushed his drawers down, and with a loud kiss his arse began that oscillating motion, which brings the pleasure to the couple whose cunt and prick are joined.

He went on slowly, their kisses and murmurs were enough to have made a saint who saw them, randy mad. — Soon her thighs began to move responsively to his thrusts. Her hands came on to his back, his drawers worked down under his movements, his shirt got a little hitched up, and the lower half of his buttocks came in full view. With kisses and murmurs of love, he now oscillated his rump rapidly, till their limbs at length stretched out languidly, almost lifelessly, and both were silent. Never to me is a woman so loveable as when the ecstatic gush is over, and I lay half dead with voluptuousness in her arms.

I could scarcely hold my sperm in me, but was so anxious not to lose an atom of the sight, that I would not leave the peep hole to fuck — I had been feeling Sarah's cunt as she stood besides me. — "They have fucked," I whispered, — "I'd give twenty pounds to be up her, lay down." — Sarah went to the bed and I fucked her.

Even in my pleasure I did not forget the couple, and as fast as possible, with prick dripping from Sarah's cunt, got to the peep hole. He was lying on her, his face on the side of the pillow and turned towards her, she was on her back. He had partly left her belly, and I saw her right thigh fully, part of her belly, and a glimpse of her mount.

Sarah looked. "She has a fine leg really, and is a fine woman — hasn't she got your steam up — what a breast she has — she isn't gay. — She's been enjoying it — they will do it again before they get off the bed I'll bet," said Sarah, who understood human nature well in its copulative instincts and habits.

Sarah was right. He moved, she opened her eyes, they kissed, he got full on to her again, but apparently changing his mind rolled off on to his side, and rose to look at her belly, over which she pulled down her chemise. I had only a glimpse of the motte. Then he turned towards her, his hand moving under her chemise, and she partly turned towards him. His hand in getting to her buttocks had lifted her chemise, giving a glimpse of a large white backside, and showing one side from feet to waist. She was as fine a made woman as ever man clasped in copulation. A splendid creature.

Again he got on to her and they began joking and kissing, and they both talked loudly. — "Your clothes are in the way." "You wouldn't wait to let me take them off." — Then he got off the bed and dragged off his boots and drawers. She sat up, undid her petticoats, he pulled them from under her as she lay, laughing. Chemise, shirt, and stockings were now all they had on. He stood, gently pushed her back on the bed kissing her, threw up her chemise to her breast, and began to kiss her belly. He thrust his fingers up her spermatized cunt. — She squirmed, "Oh Charley — don't — how dirty — dear — don't." "Isn't your cunt wet!" — Withdrawing his fingers he jumped rapidly on to her, but enclosing her legs with his, and so they lay kissing and talking but inaudibly. His thighs were quite distended, his balls shewed between them as they hung over her split, I thought I had never seen anything more voluptuous.

Then his hand roved about her haunches. He rolled on to his

back and lay for a minute with prick again quite stiff. She turned on her side and handled it. Then putting his right hand under her bum, and his left across her, he heaved her over on to his belly, and they lay belly to belly, she arse upwards, his hand roving about from her blade bones to her arse cheeks, and exposing all to my delighted view. I saw the hairy notch well, as she lay over him with thighs distended. Their baudy frolics had now brought their passions to the highest. He got her off of him to his side, he turned, and so they lay kissing, and close together. I could hear nothing but kisses. Then up he pushed one of her legs and drew it over his flank, his hand went between her thighs, and he handled her moisted cunt again. I caught a glimpse of his stiff prick as he inserted it. Then they sank into an attitude which brought her three quarters on to her back, her right leg still high up and over his left haunch, fucking began, and then more he raised up her leg — bringing into view at intervals his ballocks. Their mouths were glued together — their whole frames vibrated and with loud kisses and sighs they spent again. — Their second fuck had been finished I think within twenty minutes from the time they entered the room. — All that time as far as I could hear they scarcely spoke — fucking in all its preliminaries and consequences had absorbed them — they thought of nothing else.

Reposing in each other's arms, they nestled to each other with limbs interlaced. Altho it was warm, she I suppose felt cold, for he more than once pulled her chemise down. They half turned and her backside was then towards me, but through his feeling and fumbling, her chemise was never long before it worked up again. — "I told you they would do it twice before they got off the bed. — He'll get her in the family way and then she'll turn gay. He's a gent and won't marry her, fucking like those two will do the job, unless she is very lucky. Oh! he wants to put his finger up again and she won't let him," said Sarah who was looking through the peep hole. I was sitting on the sofa feeling her cunt.

Had it not been for our conversation, Sarah would often have had a dull time of it. Our room we kept so dark that we could not see each other's faces, and I only let her look at intervals. — But I kept up a running description of all I saw in whispers, which amused her I suppose, and she did the same to me when looking, but then I always was feeling her cunt or nudity somewhere.

He was poking his hand between her thighs, she preventing it, when I next looked. "Now Charley, that is really dirty, do let me get up — I am so wet and I want to pee so badly, I really do." Up both got, he stood affectionately over her whilst she pissed, and washed her cunt. He washed and pissed and then he sat her on his knee again, and they began talking. I could now hear all they said.

There was a large easy chair without arms and I think two such chairs but am not sure. — There was no sofa, an omission the baud told me intended, so that the couples might take their pleasures on the bed and in sight of the spyhole. — There was but one place indeed where a sofa could be placed, which was just against the peep hole partition, but with couples so close to each other on either side of the partition, we might, had there been a sofa there, have been more easily heard and found out. — With bed in full sight, the washing place on the other side of it and near the window, the fire and bright gas light, beneath which nearly all the men placed the women when they wanted to look at them naked, and all being away from the peep hole side, there was very little in the room which could not be seen by us. Evidently the whole arrangement was purposely made, tho the plan of the two rooms aided it.

The gas burner also was large for a baudy house, and made so to show up the occupants. I saw some gay women turn it down, and the men turn it up. One girl grumbled to the landlady about there being too much light. — After a time, to my disgust, a smaller burner was put in, then a larger again replaced it. — But I've no doubt the peep-hole room paid well. Several times when I went there by myself, I found the room engaged, and at other times with Sarah, couldn't have it.

The handsome couple sat down just under the light facing us, after he had said again "This is not a very comfortable room, there is no sofa. — Do you recollect what we did on the sofa the last time but one." "Yes," said she, and laughed.

His hand went under her chemise. — How is it that a man cannot keep his hand off a pretty girl's cunt? — "How many times have I fucked you?" said he. "Ho! Charley — oh! you do speak plain — I don't know." "Fifty or sixty — let us count them," — and he began to reckon their meetings. — They were so joyous numbering them. Then I heard places named, they made mistakes, and recommenced laughing. She'd seen several houses I found.

"Oh Charley, your brother John put his hands up my clothes the other day." "John — my brother?" said he surprized. "Yes, he has been always getting in my way ever since you left, and trying to look up my clothes if he gets a chance — he is getting on fast — I gave him a good cuff one night — and then he pulled it out and said, 'Look here — this is what you want.'" "Pulled out what?" "Pulled *that* out." "What, his prick?" Laughingly she said, "Yes." — The man swore. — "Damn him, I'll give him a lump on his head." "Oh you can't, he mustn't know I told you." "Damn him, — did you see his prick?" "Yes." — Then they both roared with laughter. — "Oh, if I could catch him, what a hiding he'd get, why he's only fifteen, he beats me." They talked on and every now and then he groped her — then they took to kissing and feeling each other. — "When do your monthlies come on?" "Oh, I feared they'd come on to day." "Oh, how lucky."

I could hear nearly all they said for they were inexperienced, and seemed quite fearless directly they were within the room, and never thought if any one could see or hear them. — The street was also that night free from vehicles, on other occasions when passing they prevented me at times hearing what couples said. — I heard now nearly everything until they got lewed, and then only snatches, and his exclamations of amatory delight. But I had a bad cough — altho it was warm weather — and I feared they would hear my suppressed barking. — They never seemed to do so. — She had changed from one knee to the other, I suppose because she had fatigued him. — Now on his right she was nearly facing me — I could see his left hand up between her thighs — and his prick standing up. He pulled her right hand down to it, and they sat feeling each other and kissing.

Just then my cough became so bad, that I got down and buried my head in the bed clothes. When I got back he had laid her on the foot of the bed and was standing kissing her. I heard what seemed like modest objection, but he heeded not, and opening her legs wide, I saw sideways the red gap between her thighs. He opened the lips with his fingers and contemplated, he opened and closed them again and again, then put his head against it and it seemed stationary, her limbs moved, and quickly she raised herself up on her elbow.—"Oh, Charley what are you doing?—Aha—you dirty man."

A little resistance on her part—and coaxing on his—then down she fell on her back and again his head went between her thighs. Turning to Sarah I said, "He is licking her cunt."—She looked.—"So he is, I wonder if she likes it."—He licked on, her limbs quivered, her thighs seemed to open, then close tight round his curly haired head, her belly heaved—and suddenly she half-rose crying quite loud, "Oh—don't—I won't—oho—oho,"—and fell back again.

He rose, pointed his stiff stander to her crack, and canting both thighs over his hips, fucked her again.—Then bending over her with his hands still under her thighs, they again were quiet.

Then they sat down and talked about cunt licking.—"I am ashamed of you and myself, what made you do so?" "I don't know, I never did such a thing before," said he. Then he was curious and questioned her about her sensations whilst being gamahuched.

"I did—it is something like the pleasure when we do it together—but I don't like it." "You don't mean to say you spent." "I did—it got more and more nice, and was all over just as you got up—I wanted to stop you and could not, it got the better of me." "I'll never believe that you spent, or that any woman can by being licked," said he. "How salt your cunt tastes." "Oh Charley, how can you go on so."

He called out and ordered sherry, took it in standing in his shirt, and the landlady said, "You won't be long sir, shall you?"—Angrily, "I took the room for the night didn't I?" "Oh yes, yes, but you said you might not stop and we are so busy, sir, that's all."—He slammed the door.—"The old bitch says she wants the room—and so she may."—"Oh," said the girl, "it frightened me to hear her say that, and I only with my chemise on, suppose she'd come in."

They took sherry and he said, "What beastly stuff, don't drink it, it will make you ill."—Again he called and rowed about the quality, got hot water and brandy, and gave her some, lighted a cigar, sat her on his knee and with cigar in his mouth, put his fingers on to her cunt—the cunt he had licked and fucked, and which then had his spunk in it. I whispered to Sarah.—"Girls like that are never so clean as a gay woman," said she.—Their voices dropped low and what little I could hear was partly baudy. I had been standing an hour and a half with my eye to the peep hole, grew tired, put in the cork, dropped the picture over the spyhole, turned up the gas, and talked.

It was shortly before this that I had seen the girl suck the man's prick, whilst he buggered his own arse with a tooth-brush handle. — Somewhere also about that time a French doxy — unasked took my prick in her mouth and whom I made desist — I had rarely had it in a woman's mouth excepting in half drunken orgies. Now at once came on a desire for that luxury, it was though seeing this woman's cunt licked. — "Suck my prick," said I. "I'll see you damned first," said Sarah.

I never relinquished a letch till I satisfied it, I talked about what I had seen, what heard, what done that way with women, and got her to admit that she had been asked to suck. I wondered whether it was more pleasure than spending in a cunt. She wondered (I know now it was bosh). We talked about the gamahuching just seen, and prick sucking. Then she said, "Why don't you lick my quim then?" "Do you like it — do you spend with it?" "Of course I like it, every woman does, you can't help spending if a man keeps on at it."

"Suck my prick — do." "Lick my cunt then." I have gone thro this talk with other women, but with Sarah it seemed quite novel.

The couple were laughing and getting noisy. Suddenly I heard thro the partition, the woman laughing loud and say, "No I won't, I won't now," and feet moving hard on the floor. Sarah turned down the gas, and in a minute I had my eye at the peep hole.

He had her in the middle of the room, and was trying to pull her chemise off — she resisting. — "I *will* see you quite naked." "You *shan't* — oh don't make such a noise, we shall be heard," said she.

He desisted a minute, then recommenced. She would not let him — but in a modest way dropped her chemise down to her cunt, then put it up on her shoulders, and let him pull it up to her navel. Half naked each pose, he turned her round, admired, and kissed her flesh, exclaiming. — "Oh ain't you beautiful — oh what a bum you have — oh I am so randy again, look here," and he pulled up his shirt to show his stiff one. — "I want another fuck." — Then he sat down with prick standing upright before her admiring eyes, and said. — "Do you mean to swear you spent — that you had pleasure just as if my cock was up you?" — "I don't know that — but it seemed so, I seemed to wet with pleasure, and yet I didn't like it — but it was pleasure, and great pleasure — nearly like the other."

"I'll never believe a woman can have pleasure and spend by being licked, just as if she is being fucked. Let me try again." — "He's never done it before really I think," whispered Sarah, "he don't know much."

She refused, it was dirty, how could he want, wish such a thing. — But how can a woman withstand a man? — Refusing whilst she yielded, he threw her on the bed, and putting a pillow under his knees, again I saw the white thighs distend, the dark haired lips pulled open, the red gash appear, his head close up to it, and the licking begin.

All was silent. I placed my ear at intervals to the hole, heard the sossling of his tongue on her clitoris, when his saliva had run over, and then in low tones he said, "Does that give you pleasure?" — But I heard no reply, I looked, and he had drawn back his head — whilst she lay with her limbs hanging down.

Then a little conversation, and again the licking began — her thighs crossed on to his shoulders, she cried out, — "Oh don't, now — do it properly." "Be quiet, only this time." Breathless with agitation, I kept putting first my eyes, then my ear to the hole — heard her murmur with pleasure, saw her belly heaving, her thighs twitching round his head, and no more. Then he rose, pushed her further up on bed, and for the fourth time fucked her as she lay there.

I got down. — "Suck my prick, do — you shall, and I'll give you another sovereign — two — if you will. — If you don't another woman shall." "Lick me then." — I thought she was joking, but soon it was a reality — I did not like it, but said I would. — She sluiced her cunt, she placed herself at the bed side, my tongue touched her cunt, I gamahuched thinking of my pleasure to follow, till she writhed under her sensations. — Now I ceased, for it struck me that when I had done her, she would not fulfil her part of the bargain. — "Oh! go on, I am coming."

"Will you suck me afterwards?" "I will, I will, and you will give two pounds." "Yes," and again my tongue and her clitoris met.

"Let's do it at the same time." "All right." I took off my trowsers and drawers — we placed ourselves side by side, one of her thighs over my head my head laying on the other, my prick touching her face — I recollect no more than that I tasted her cunt, that I felt as if a cunt had got hold of my prick, that I put my left hand to it, that her belly shivered, that my nose went against her cunt, that I spent in her mouth, that I tasted her ejaculation, that in a baudy frenzy she had sucked my prick for the first time, but not the last, and that I had gamahuched her.

"You need not hurry," said Sarah, "they won't stir now in such a hurry." — It was true. When I looked they were laying quietly. — At length he rose, looked at his watch and said she'd better get up — "for darling you must not be too late." She got off the bed and they kissed. — Never was a more loving couple — they had kissed every two minutes for four hours. — Again she sat on his knee, but I could not hear what they said.

To the door he went and asked if they had a daily paper, and told them to go somewhere and get one, which was soon done. — He stood under the gas light and called over a list of plays. — "Say you have been to the Lyceum, they play Hamlet." "Oh but I have seen that." "So much the better, you'll know all about it." "They will wonder why I went again." "You say they took you." — Then they laughed, and I gathered that the woman was supposed to be at the theatre.

He looked at his watch. — "We can stop three quarters of an hour more. — Wash your cunt — you had better always do so soon afterwards, they say it stops getting in the family way." — Then he sat down and lighted another cigar.

The girl put a basin on the floor. As she washed I just saw the top of her head above the bed. Then she pissed. — Whilst doing so she made some remark I did not hear — but he put down the paper and said, "Oh the devil."

As she rose from the pot, — "Yes, I am afraid so, I am a month behind my time, they ought to be on to day." — Her voice was sad, she sat on his knees again, her back towards us now, and I could not hear what they said but they talked earnestly.

He changed the position — pulled up her chemise, and sat

her naked bum on his thigh saying, "I like your flesh against mine." — He drank more brandy and water — his cigar had gone out, he lighted it at the gas. "Is John's cock big?" She laughed, "I scarcely know, he showed it only an instant — but it was stiff." "Was the skin off?" "It was quite red." "I should like to catch him, I'd knock his damned young head off." "*You* told me *you* did something like it to one of the girls, when you were about his age." "So I did, but I don't like John doing it to you."

He began walking about the room with his hand on his prick, and said she had better dress. "I should like to do it again." "Oh, I can't let you, you have tired me so." — He dressed and again walked up and down the room, frigging his cock as if determined to make it stand. — "Look at you," said the woman laughing.

"You don't know what a number of ways there are of doing it," he said. "Don't I?" "No, come here, people often do it this way." — His cock was not stiff. — She was nearly dressed. — He sat down and pulled her on to him, placing his legs between her thighs, her cunt close to his cock. — "They do it like that." — Then he turned round and sat her with her bum towards him. — She laughed. Then he said something and both laughed loudly. — "They do it so — come here," and he got up. "I shan't." — But making her lean over the bed, he threw up her petticoats, exposing her fair round backside, and pressed his cock against it, she wanted to move, but he kept her there fumbling her bum, and, frigging at his cock at the same time.

"I must go — if am not in by twelve — there will be a row — your mother always sits up you know." — He looked at his watch — both finished dressing, but he kept his cock out of his breeches, and it had stiffened whilst putting on her bonnet. — "I mean to do it again." "Oh! I can't, — I can't stay, it must be time to go." "I will do it, — I will — lie down and I won't be a minute." — In vain her resistance, he got her on to the bed, and again fucked her. They seemed to enjoy it more than ever, for it was a long job, and they groaned and sighed loudly with pleasure. In another minute without either of them washing, off they went.

The baud went in the room, looked at the rumpled bed clothes, muttered, called to the servant, and told her to bring a clean counterpane. They had left spunk on the bed. Then she took up a white handkerchief which the young man or woman had left, put it in her pocket, and looked at the peep hole, and seeing that she was being watched, dropped the picture on her side.

I was in a fever of lust — never have I seen a sight which for its prolonged voluptuousness was equal to it. — I have seen more erotic sights, but for pure voluptuousness — never — I doubt whether many have seen a fine young man and woman in the height of sexual strength, abandon themselves without fear or thought, to all their voluptuous desires for the space of four hours, as this couple did.

I stripped Sarah, examined her cunt, compared it mentally with the young woman's, rolled over her, rubbed my prick against her arse, impaled her on my doodle as I sat on a chair, first with her belly, then her bum towards me. I followed every thing I had seen the young man do — and then fucked, talking of the couple, till Sarah said she was sick of hearing about them.

Then we got brandy and water. My desires ran on having my prick sucked — I doubted if Sarah had done it to me properly, I wanted to be sure, and the sperm to go into her mouth — I was reckless, and said that unless she did it, I would go out and get another woman. — At last Sarah kneeling over me, again sucked my prick and took my sperm into her, whilst I with her arse close to my nose licked her cunt.

Exhausted, on the bed I laid, whilst Sarah was washing her mouth. — "There is another couple." — To extinguish the light and get to the peep hole, was the work of a minute. There was a man just getting off a woman whom he had fucked, whilst we, engrossed in our physical pleasure, had never heard them there; which explained how little people notice who are randy, and thinking about their own performances, and why they never noticed the spy hole.

This spy hole amusement was spread over the best part of two years. Many lustful amusements I had between the various sights, which would better have been told in their place, but I shall from time to time refer to them.

After this night I had a letch for being sucked. — When I next met Sarah, we spent the whole evening in talking about that and gamahuching. Sarah confessed to liking it being done to her *occasionally*, and on her undertaking to tell me when she was spending, I did the job for her, and also had the pleasure of spending in her mouth for the extra fee. But I soon grew tired of that pleasure, unless so fucked out that I could not get a cock-stand. Many times after, when looking thro the peep-hole, she knelt on the sofa and gently sucked my prick.

Gamahuching *she* always wanted, when she'd had a drop more than usual, and I believe really had a great liking for it — I did it at times to please her, but couldn't bear the taste of her cunt, and whilst operating used to keep slobbering, so that her cunt was soon much like a spittoon. — "Aren't you coming?" "Yes, stop, lick just there," and with her finger she indicated the exact spot. — I suppose finding that I did not much like it, she ceased after a time to ask me to do it to her.

But we often described our sensations to each other, and she told me very funny stories about women who were fond of having their cunts licked by other women — I was increasing my experiences largely with her, yet did not know what I since believe to be the case, that *she* was a little fond of having another female tongue on her clitoris, and perhaps another clitoris against hers as well.

CHAPTER XI

A juvenile strumpet. — Two saucy little bitches. — One selected. — Sexual manipulations on the highway. — Omnibus riding and jam tarts. — My moral compunctions. — Sarah dissipates them. — An unsuccessful assault. — On the fornicating facilities of four wheel cabs.

I go back a while. — When I had known Sarah some time I wished to go to her house, having to pay heavily at the baudy houses for stopping long there. — Besides I always feel so much more comfortable at a woman's lodgings. J***s St. bagnio was an exception, but that house has been long closed — Sarah objected at first, but as we knew each other better, said that her rooms were comfortable but very homely, that I should not be pleased with them; and moreover her friend was often there, that then I could not, and so on. — On being pressed, she admitted that she lived with a man, had done so for three years, and she showed me his miniature. — I said that nevertheless I should like to go there. — Then she told me the address, but I was never to call. — She would meet me in the street, and if she could take me home she would. He was a traveller for a firm of **** makers, and often away. For a long time I did not go there.

I had letches for big women. — Sarah was one, big Eliza another, and I had other big ones (tho but rarely) who were about town. — Big women, with big arses, and lots of cunt hair had been pleasing to me to see and feel, even if I did not poke them. Now suddenly I desired a little one. At L**c**t*r S****e one night, a group of girls so little that I thought them at first only rude children, spoke to me; and it ended in my going to a house with one about half my height, but who stripped and talked as baudily as if she had been fucked twenty years. — I fucked her, wondering at the little hairless quim my prick was closed up in, and such seemed the difference between the deep, thick lipped, dark, fully haired, large cunts, I had had for a long time, and the thin hairless split, and slim little form I was enjoying, that it roused desires for another.

It was late autumn, I was going along a suburb of London one night at about six o'clock p.m. It was in a dull tho widish road, where the houses lay back from the road in gardens. — A slight fog came on. — On the opposite side of the way, I saw thro the mist two young girls, singing, laughing, and talking loudly whilst walking on. — A man carrying a basket on his back passed them, and I heard him say. — "I should like to tickle up both of your legs a bit." "Tickle us up then," said one in a loud cheeky tone, and then both ran across the road, and down a turning close by me. I heard them laughing loudly when just out of sight in the mist, as if they enjoyed the baudy suggestion.

This stirred my blood. They must be fast young bitches I thought. Soon I heard a shrill voice say. "Come on, he's gone a head a long way." It was one of the two girls. The turning they were up I found was no thoroughfare, altho then I did not know that — I turned at once up it, met them, stopped them, and asked them the way to some place. — I saw the face of the tallest, and as far as the fog would let me see by a lamp, it pleased me. I began to talk, and said they were both pretty girls. — "Give me a kiss and I will give each of you sixpence." — They laughed, said no, but in a minute I gave each a kiss and sixpence. — As I kissed the biggest, I whispered her, "I'll give you a shilling if you will do something for me and get your companion away." "What?" said she boldly. "Send her away." "No, she'll tell, but at **** Street she goes another way — you come back, then."

She said she should not. — "Come on Betsy," and off they went together — I followed just at such a distance as the fog enabled me not to lose sight of them, saw them part, then quickly made up to the tallest, and by degrees persuaded her to stop and listen to me. I know how to deal with young lasses well, having had experience now. — "Now don't be angry — don't be alarmed, it can't hurt you, and if you won't do it there's no harm done. — If you do what I want, no one will know it, and I'll give you a lot of money when I meet you." "What is it?" — Oddly enough, I could not make up my mind what to ask her to do — I wanted to feel her cunt, but guessed if I said so, she would run off as fast as she could go, so went on talking awhile, and at length said, "Here's a shilling for you if you will tell me one or two things. — Have you a brother?" "Yes." "Have you seen his cock?" She began to laugh. "Shan't tell you," and she began to walk away. "Never mind, here is your shilling." She turned round and took it. — "How foolish to go away, you might get more money, and no one but you and I know any thing about it — and directly I ask you a question off you go." "You talk improper," said she. "Never mind, you know you have felt your brother's cock if he is a baby." "He's three years old, and I nurse him when at home." "Then you have felt his cock." — She laughed.

"What are you doing about here?" said I turning the conversation. "Going home from work." "What do you work at?" "Folding up seeds at **** nursery," and she told me where. "What do you get a day?" "Nine pence — we both work there" — (meaning the other girl). "You can get half a crown if you'll do what I wish." "I can't do anything." "Yes, you can feel me." "Feel you, what's that?" — I rattled the money, — "Here are two and six pence, none will see us." We were by a long wall, and the fog was now thickish. "Here is the money — give me your hand."

I unbuttoned my trowsers, my prick was stiff, I put it outside, but under my greatcoat. She gave me her hand in a reluctant way, and I guided it to my penis. — "Lay hold of it." "I shan't, let me go — I'll hollow." "No — feel it, put your hand round it and here is your money." — Her fright got over, she put her hand round it. — Curiosity got the better of her fears, I saw her tho she couldn't in the dark see it, looking down at it. — "You old beast, let me go," — but I kept her hand on the stem, then put it in my trowsers and under the balls. — "Now let me go." — I relinquished her hand, she turned away, went two or three yards off and stopped. "Here is your money, now you have felt my cock, tell me, is it bigger than your brother's." She broke out into a laugh, turned and ran off — I followed and overtook her standing still some distance off. — "You did not give me the money," said she. "That was your fault, here it is, but come back, people here will see us." — She came back saying, "I must go or I'll catch it." — At the corner I gave her half a crown, and said "Every night you feel my cock I will give you a shilling, and I'll give half a crown if you let me feel your bum." "You old beast," said she again, as the money dropped into her hand. Then she bolted off like lightning.

I went to the spot at the same time next night, but she did not appear. On the third night I saw her and she was alone, there was no fog, but it was between dark and daylight, and the lamps were not lighted. — She recognized me. "Go away or I'll run," said she. "I'm not going to hurt you, give me a kiss and I'll give you a shilling." — I induced her to turn up the same place, and there gave her both. Then she felt my cock again and had another shilling. — She was not in a hurry to take away her hand from my cock as on the first night. I fancied she liked feeling it. "Meet me every night," (it just suited me then). "I can't, cause *she* comes home with me," — meaning the other girl. How cunning young sluts are!

Her feeling of my prick, and the whispering baudy talk in her young ears, took my fancy, but I wanted more. I saw her the next night. She was with the other girl, and like a fool I was going up to her, when they ran off. Another night I caught her alone. I was that night in a frenzy of randiness, put her hand round my prick and my own hand outside hers, and so frigging, I spent copiously. — "What is the matter sir," said she looking up in my face, for I dare say I was sighing and giving evidence of sexual emotion.

Then I missed her, and gave up all idea of getting into her, for that had been in my mind. About two weeks afterwards, by mere chance passing by there, I saw the little devil loitering near the turning where she had first felt me. — Crossing the road, I said in passing, "Come on," — and in two minutes she stood by my side.

She had been ill, her mother said it was fever. But with a chuckle — "I know what it was — I eat too much of them sweets and fruit. — Mother said it was the smell from the privy, and told the doctor so. — He asked me what I had been eating, and I said nothing." — Then I found that she spent her money on fruit, sugar candy and bull's eyes, and in riding in omnibuses. When she felt sick she got some brandy, and she only gave her companion a little bit of sweet. — "Because she'd wonder where I got the money and would tell." — This much amused me, and reminded me of a girl, or rather two girls I had known many years previously. A girl of fifteen riding in an omnibus by herself for pleasure, and gorging herself with sweets out of money got by feeling a man's prick in a street, seems an amusing fact.

She missed the money evidently, and *her* want was *my* opportunity. Said I, — "I can only give you money if you let me feel your bum." "Oh no, not that." "Well, it's no worse than feeling my cock. — If you feel my cock, let me feel your cunt." "Oh! that I shan't," — but she lingered. — "It could not hurt," I said, "and who knows you have felt my cock?" — "Who will know it if I feel your little cunt? — Here is the money." — She looked round (it was dark). — "No. No," — but she stood quite still — I stooped and put my hand up on to her bottom. — "Oh! have done now, let me go, give me the money." "Let me feel properly." "I won't." — With the hand which was on her naked bum, I drew her close to me, and with the other, pushed up her clothes till I felt the top of her cunt. — She struggled tho quietly, and escaped me, but as before stopped till I went to her to give the money; then she went off. — I felt sure that she had come out to meet me that night.

One night soon after it was lighter than usual and some man passing the main road shouted out. — "Leave that girl alone." — I went further up the turning, she with me, and was just stooping to feel her little bum, when some female came out a house and passed us. I stood upright, but soon saw the woman standing at the end of the turning, and seemingly looking back. — No one had ever passed out of the houses during my previous fun. This woman who had eyed us narrowly as she passed, or had certainly turned her head to look, I thought would turn back. The girl was more frightened than me. — "Oh don't again, don't, I won't any more, and I mustn't stop, I'm frightened of mother," — and she walked towards the high road, I following.

A cab passed, few do pass at that spot or indeed much other traffic. — I hailed it. It was empty and stopped. — "Come into the cab, we'll drive, you can feel me there and I can sit." She hesitated, but I hustled her in. — "Drive to **** Park," and off he drove. — How many times have I got women into a cab for my pleasure, how many times more shall I do so? They like it.

She got frightened and wanted to get out. I pacified her, promised her five shillings instead of the smaller sum I usually gave. — "Where to?" said cabby turning round as he entered the park. —

"Go on till I stop you."—On he drove, it was getting darker, I had not yet kissed her that day as I usually did—but in the cab, she stood by the side of me, and I kissed and she kissed again.—Kissing always soothes a female young or old.—Gradually I got one hand round her bum, and the other outside her quim, but directly I tried to insert my finger in the split, she strongly resisted, threw herself on to seat opposite, and cried to get out.—"No, no, I won't—you'll hurt me—yes you will."—So I desisted.

"Well dear, lay hold of my hand—lay hold of this finger—put it yourself there,—just let it go where you piddle from, and no further."—"There," said she, holding my finger so that I just felt the clitoris. Then thrusting away my hand she again sat on the opposite seat, holding her clothes down; but I soon got her by my side again. The baudiness, I know, pleased her.

I was furious with salacity and talked baudy to my heart's content. I had said a little of that sort before, and the little slut had listened to it without uttering a word, but stood drinking it all in with her ears, and as if she knew quite well what I meant, and as if she liked it.—I never liked frigging myself, but now my cock became unmanagable, as I felt her little buttocks, and coaxed her lewedly, and lovingly.

"Frig me my dear,"—I had taught her the meaning of that word.—"I can't." Taking her hand I put it round my prick.—"Now I'll lift your clothes—there—it's against your thigh—that doesn't hurt you does it?"—I slobbered my prick with saliva, and taking her hand and putting it round my prick (which she now liked doing), frigged myself with it.

I always frig myself when I commit that wasteful action, with my foreskin nearly up, unless using soap or oil as an emollient; my tip being so delicate.—As the sperm left me, I pulled her hand up so as to quite pull up the foreskin, and cover the orifice, and much was ejaculated into her hand, whilst oscillating my arse, holding her by her bum, and kissing her in my ecstasy.—Trying to relieve her hand, "Let go," said she, "you've done something sticky with your thing.—Oh! let it go, it's nasty,"—but she seemed pleased with the fun for all that.—Then she got anxious to go home, so telling the cabman to drive to a convenient spot, I let her out.

The affair fascinated me. I went again to that quarter of the town at the time the girl left work, but never saw her for a fortnight. — She I believed had avoided me, till she had spent all her money. — Then she only felt my cock, got her shilling and went off. She resisted everything else.

I didn't see now much chance of getting into her, circumstances did not favor me, and I had a long distance to go even to get the chance, so desisted; I had, besides, compunctions, thought it a pity to make the girl a harlot, and so told Sarah all about what I'd done and what I'd thought of doing. — Sarah said I had better leave it alone, but that some one would do it to that girl before long, for she evidently knew more than she should. One of the lads at the nursery would have her. She was more likely to let a lad have her than to let me. Perhaps she'd been fucked already, spite of her resistance. "Those little bitches are so damned cunning that it would surprize you, she'll be gay, whether *you* do it to her or not." — That gave me comfort, and again I thought I'd try to get the girl. — Time had run on, it was now dark at four o'clock.

So a fortnight after, I met her. It was so clear an evening, that I did not like talking to her in the road, and again waiting, got into a cab with her. Familiarity had, I found, removed her fears. I had talked baudy in the street, and in the cab, so far from having to hold her hand on my prick; on saying "feel it," she put her little hand on to it, and grasped and felt about it. — I told her I wanted to feel her cunt, and promised never to move my fingers from her belly to between her legs — I had kept my word before, when she had helped me to frig. — After I had had her some minutes so, she holding my cock, I said, "It twists me so, sit on my knee." She did, but still kept her legs close together. — "Let me put my cock against your leg again." At length I put it against her flank, whilst she still held it. — "Do you know what fucking is?" I said, to which she made reply, "I only knows what you tells me."

I asked her then to come to a house, but got a positive refusal — I got awfully lewed, and by coaxing, at last she stood in front of me and frigged me herself, but she hurt me. — "Hold my cock against your belly, just as it was at the side of your bum." She did. — Then with one hand I pulled her to me, the other was on her naked arse. I'd lifted her clothes, and my prick touched her belly just by her cunt. She was still holding it — I shoved my prick against it up and down through her hand for some time, it was inconvenient, but the lewedness pleased me. — The cab kept slowly jogging on.

My pleasure increased, and with it the desire to fuck. — "Oh! I will give you half a sovereign if you'll do what I want," and I left off frigging. "Ten shillings?" "Yes, ten shillings." — She seemed reflecting. My desire grew stronger, — "I'll give you a sovereign if you'll let me put my prick between your legs — not in your cunt, but only between your thighs, and you shall hold it there."

"Oh no, — none of that," — said she, hastily, "I ain't a going to let you do that — I want to get out of the cab, let me go, oh do." — She was taking fright and beginning to struggle.

I let her talk on. Opening my purse I took out a sovereign. — "Here's a golden sovereign," showing it to her as we passed one of the few gas lamps. — "You shall have it if you let me, you can wrap it up in a piece of paper, then make the paper muddy, and tell your mother you found it." I once taught another girl this.

The girl was silent long, looking me in the face (as it seemed) in the dark. — Then, "No — oh no." — Disappointment in her manner and tone, I saw she would yield. She'd laid hold of my prick again unasked, and I replaced it and my hands as before.

"If you won't I shan't see you again, I can get fifty girls to feel my prick for a shilling." "Has any other girl done it? you didn't tell me so." "A dozen have." "Lor," — and she seemed to be reflecting on the information. "They will all do it my dear if they get the chance." — So we talked. — The cab had gone once round the park, and still drove on. — I expect the driver knew the games we were up to, but never looked round that I noticed. But it was quite dark now.

Little by little I induced her to straddle across me with her clothes up, my legs between hers — I declared I wouldn't touch her cunt, but pushed my body so forward that my knees nearly touched the opposite seat, and holding her close up to me, her legs got more distended, and I more and more reclining. — At length her feet scarcely touched the cab-floor. — She fell half forward on me, her face touching mine. — Promising her more money, she let me with my left hand clutch her little naked backside, my right was at the same spot but outside her clothes. — "Put your hand down, and hold my prick just against the bottom of your belly." "I can't," said she, but she did it, and my prick tip was now near her cunt, and touching her thigh. I began oscillating my backside as well as I could, and got some rough friction against her dry flesh. — "That doesn't hurt you does it?" "No." She seemed amused with the trick.

I slipped further forward, hoping to get my prick against her cunt, then my position was so difficult that I could scarcely jog up and down. — "Let my cock go higher up dear." — I put the hand which had been outside her bum down to hers, and pushed it so that it, with my prick, went nearer to the goal, but bending, its rigidity hurt me. — The idea of its being close to her little cunt then drove me wild — I pushed both hands round her backside, clipped with both; violently oscillated my buttocks, which opened her legs wider, her feet left the floor, she let go my prick, and put her hand on my shoulders to prevent her falling on one side. She was then half lying on me; my prick lodged somewhere in the furrow of her backside, and she cried out, "Oh don't, you're a hurting," and struggled to get away.

Maddened with lustful delight at her cry, now I put one hand round her waist, kept the other on her bum, and grasped her so that she couldn't move her bum, and jerked my arse furiously; my prick left its lodging, and jerked about blindly on thighs, buttocks, and cunt valley, moving recklessly but always rubbing. — I was nearly at the crisis. — "Be quiet dear, I shan't hurt you." "Oho — don't — oh you beast — I'll scream. — Cabman, cabman — let me out," she yelled — and struggled.

Tighter and tighter I held her, and thrust and wriggled in the hopes of finding a soft lodging for my prick tip. — My spunk was rising from my balls when again my tool stuck tight. —Where I don't know, but think it was between her cunt lips. Holding her backside firmly on to it, spite of her struggles, and then wriggling my arse and rigid tool, I spent a flood of sperm, somewhere between her bum bone and her clitoris; felt some of it fall on my hand which was nearest her thighs, and then I relinquished her. She was still yelling. "Oh! you beast — don't — you hurt me — let me go out — cab — stop," and getting away from me. Yet in the faintness of my pleasure, I was lewed enough to bring my hand round from her bum, and thrust it between her thighs — and in a glutinous state I withdrew it. The driver if he heard took no notice, but she got so vociferous, that I stopped the cab. She got out, ran off, not waiting for her gift, and in a second was lost in the darkness. — A little further on I stopped near a foot bridge, paid the cabman liberally, and went off. — I never saw the girl afterwards, for the scene of my amatory doings was not near my home. I was going to visit a friend when I got this piece of luck, and first met the little stupid, who might have had the pleasure of a fuck, and profit as well. — As it is, I dare say some dirty young boy will open her cunt, and give her a black eye if she upbraids him if her belly swells. That is the course of events in her class. — It is not the gentlemen who get the virginities of these poor little bitches, but the street boys of their own class.

There was sperm on my shirt and trowsers, but no evidences of a shattered virginity. — Was she a virgin, did I hurt her much, how far in her did my prick go, or at all. — What did she think when she had gone, and felt my spunk on her cunt, for certainly I spent against it, if not up it. — A risk I ran, yet missed the mark after all. — That baudy tuition, that titillation of our privates, that spend outside a little cunt in a cab, and all at a cost of a pound or two, amused me, as all chance adventures do. They break the monotony of matter-of-fact hard fucking — yet that I should have taken all that trouble for a dirty little work girl, whose face I never saw excepting by the light of a street lamp, astonishes me often when I think of it.

What convenient accessories to love-making are four wheel cabs. — Some dozens of cunts I have felt in them, some that I should never have felt at all, had it not been for the opportunities the four wheelers gave me. Several women I have fucked in them, as they rumbled along with a discreet cabman. — No doubt other men have found them as useful. — Thousands of women I am sure have fornicated in them, and scores do it in them daily. — Every cabman knows of their amatory utility, and the profit that it gets him, the profit of ambulating brothels. — Dozens are used every night I'm sure. I never spoke with a man yet, who had not fucked a woman in a four wheeler.

CHAPTER XII

*My letch for a little one. — Sarah's lodgings. — A new dress wanted. — A virgin proffered. — The deaf little Emma. — The tailor's family arrangements. — The price of the hymen agreed. — Doctor H**-m**d. — Sham medical investigations. — Aperiant pills — Sarah's advice. — An aperient Priapus. — Emma leaves Sarah. — The grocer's in B**w**k Street. — On the fucking facilities a little bum gives.*

When I told Sarah F**z*r this finale, she laughed heartily. — The desire for a youthful virginity seems to have been strong on me. — Sarah said she'd try and find one. Then I became exacting, and wanted one without any hair on her cunt, and I would see her virginity also before I broke it. I told her of the lovely little lass Betsy Johnson had got me, what I paid her, of the little virgin I got at the L**c**t*r S****e brothel, that I'd had both at brothels, and I must now have the girl whom Sarah got, at *her* lodgings, or at some quiet place, not a brothel.

The night we spoke most about this, we were jolly. — Sarah remarked, "I wish I could get you one, for it's cold, I want a new silk dress and warm clothing for the winter, and don't know how to pay for it — but I don't see my way." And it couldn't be at her lodgings. — Then I dropped the affair.

Once or twice after, it was mentioned casually — when my prick was stiff, and a good dinner was in me — for the letch was still on me occasionally, tho I had ceased to expect to gratify it. Sarah began to say as she'd said before, that her lodgings were common, that I shouldn't like them — that she could only let me go to them at particular times, when her husband was not at home — it was impossible — and much more of the same sort. At last, would I promise to tell no one if she let me go to her rooms. — I wondered who she imagined I should tell. — It was ridiculous to suppose I should. For a week or so then, I was mostly at home of a night, and only saw Sarah once. The next night I had her, she said she had got what I wanted, and named the day after for me to go to her lodgings, of which she'd given the address.

I went to her lodgings. — Two rooms on the second floor in G***k Street, Soho. The front looked into the street. — The back into a yard which might once have been a garden, and in which was the watercloset. — The rooms were far better than I expected, they were thoroughly comfortable, and not like those in which courtezans receive friends. The bedroom led out of the sitting room, thro a passage which also had a door on to the landing of the stairs. The staircase went up in the middle of the house. Her sitting room was carpeted, there was a good stove in it with boiler and oven. — She said that was her own putting in. — A large sofa of old fashioned look stood against the partition, there was room to fuck on it and roll off by the side of the woman. — It was really a sofa bedstead, and there were two easy chairs.

The bedroom was equally comfortable. — There was a very large bed with red hangings, and hangings to the windows also. A thick padded curtain across the door opening on to the stairs, which she'd made herself to keep out noise and cold (perhaps to prevent listening). — The rooms looked as if the furniture had been bought at good sales, as I afterwards found it had been. Altogether they were very snug, and when she lighted a lamp and we sat down before the fire, I felt quite at home. I was surprized to find so much comfort. — She had occupied them three years.

She let me in herself. — "I have a new little maid, and don't want her to see that you are strange here — I have told her I expect a friend, a doctor. — If you like her, I will see what can be done. — She'll be in, in a quarter of an hour. Her name is Emma."

The girl who had been sent on an errand was about fifteen, or barely so, short and thickset and had large dark earnest eyes — but not a handsome face. She was rather deaf. — The idea of having her pleased me, I began thinking how I should like to please *her,* hurt her virginity, frig, lick, fuck, and generally teach her the art of love, in a snug private room like Sarah's.

Sarah told me she had no mother and was of German extraction, her father was a drunken tailor. The girl had kept his rooms. There was another girl nearly her age, who he thought now could do this, and he had told this one to get her living in service.—Sarah had taken her, and dismissed her other maid.

I sent the girl out for gin, brandy, etc., etc., giving her always the change, my custom of ingratiating myself. Her face brightened at the gifts.—She sat at needle work whilst we talked.—"This is my friend Dr. H**m**d, he has often attended to me.—Now he shall see to you, if you don't get better," said Sarah, telling me that she had indications of her first poorliness, and that she had advised her to let a doctor look at her when alone.—Then to me when alone,—"And as you are the doctor, you can satisfy yourself." Was she a virgin?—Sarah believed so.—When her husband (her man), was away, she let her servants sleep with her.—When he was at home they slept on that sofa in the sitting room.—He had been away a week, and the girl had slept with her. She had seen her undress, strip and wash. She always made her servant do that every week, or they would not be in the same bed with *her*.—The girl had the slightest sign of dark hair on the motte, but not a bit on the lips. When asleep Sarah had felt her, and so far looked.

Said Sarah, "When we are drinking, *you* give her a little brandy and water,—I can't make her take anything. Make her jolly screwed, and then see her cunt, or we'll do that together."—I let Sarah do it after I was gone, which was a weak caprice of mine.

There was a fire. Sarah sat lifting her petticoats so that the warmth could get up her legs. The girl was told to remain where she was till she was called.—We went to the bedroom, and on Sarah's virtuous bed, I fucked her for the first time in her lodgings.

"I mean to let her know I am gay," said she,—"get her lewed and it will all go right.—Your being a doctor will do it. My poorliness is coming on, and I have told her I have shown you my cunt.—That doctors often see the cunts of women who want advice about poorliness"—only Sarah usually said "my thing," when she spoke of her cunt.

I met Sarah out two nights afterwards by arrangement.—"She is all right, no one has been up her, you can come to night and see for yourself. I have seen her thing, and if you say you must look at it, she'll let you—I have told her that she must have no nonsense with a doctor."

"But she'll expect medicine." "Well, you must give her something which will open her bowels. She'll never think you are going to do her good unless you make her belly ache."

During that evening I made remarks to Sarah of a medical nature. — Sarah said, "I think I must get you to give something to my little maid. — She is not very well, her poorliness won't come on. — It is her first."

"Come here." She put her work down and came. I asked her questions about her bowels, her urine, and felt her breasts, put my hand up her clothes, and pressed her belly, all as nearly as I could in a cool, medical sort of way. — She flinched a little when I said, "Let me feel your stomach," and looked at Sarah. "I must examine her well," said I. — "When next you come — you shall," said Sarah.

How my prick throbbed when my hand pressed the little belly. I could feel no hair, or scarcely any. It is strange, that altho Sarah thought I had better proceed to look at her at once, that I put it off — I can't understand why I did it. We had shrub, the girl disliked spirits, shrub she liked. I have always found young girls will take shrub, it warms the stomach, rises to the brain, makes the cunt heat and tingle, and the girl think of fucking. There is no better term to express a woman's sensation of randiness, and I borrowed it from Sarah.

I again felt her little rising breasts and her belly, and said that in two days I would see her again.

I saw Sarah next night and did not fuck her, said I would not till I had spent up the little deaf maid. Sarah, with the girl in bed, had talked on sexual subjects, had heard that twice men had tried to take liberties with her. — Once a tailor put his hands up her clothes, it was on the stairs. She didn't like to tell, for a tailor had once done something of the same sort to her sister, and she had told her father, who boxed her ears, and said it must have been her own fault. — She had had a sweetheart, who had coaxed her down a yard, kissed her, then pulled up her clothes, and felt her, and she felt for a second, what must have been his cock. — He put her hand to it. She ran away, and had not seen him once. "All poor girls get these chances early," said Sarah. "She says she has frigged herself. — I made her feel what a lot of hair I had, then I felt hers, and I told her it would grow quite hairy when a man had put his thing up her. All girls are anxious to get hair on their things." — Then they got talking about how fucking was done, until, "I believe the little devil got quite randy, I told her that I had had it done to me before I was her age, that a girl need not have a child unless she liked — that half the girls did it with men but never told." — Sarah strove to fill her mind with desire to be fucked, told of the ease and secrecy with which it could be accomplished, and the benefits accruing. — Any woman I am certain can persuade a girl to let herself be fucked, if she stimulates rising passions, and incites her to compliance both for sexual gratification and interest, and women like teaching them.

Sarah told me she didn't like doing this. "But she will be sure to have some man do it to her, so you may as well have her as any one else, and I shall get my new dress. It will do *me* good and do *her* no harm." To this I quite agreed. It is quite true, and what every gay woman has told me, and is my philosophy.

But if there should be a row? — "I'll chance it — how am I to know anything about it, she might have done it anywhere, when she goes out. I should swear all was a lie, I should say I never had seen you in my life, and no one shall see you if you come at dark, and only when I tell you."

Next night I was there — my prick had been standing as I walked along, and yet I was nervous. I sent her out for shrub and then Sarah said, "I can't get a word out of her till the light is put out, then she talks fast enough, and asks me what the pleasure of fucking is, and if it hurts. — A girl she knows has made her think it hurts. I have told her that it depends upon whether a girl lets a man do as he likes or resists him. — If a girl don't resist, she won't be hurt. She thinks you such a nice kind man, and wonders a man with such a fine moustache, can call her 'my dear,' and speak to her as you do."

"Shall I get into her to night?" "I would rather be out when you do it, I have told her she'd be better if she'd been poked, and she said she supposed she shouldn't be quite well till she married. — I said she might get poked before that, and her husband know nothing about it."

I asked Sarah before the maiden about her own health, her womb, her courses, and so on. The girl looked at me and at Sarah with the appearance of mental strain, which people partially deaf often have. — "Well my dear, and how are you?" — I then felt her breasts and belly, and as I knew her little ailments, the questions were wise enough. "I must see you with your clothes off." "Go with the doctor," said Sarah. "I have told her you'll want to look at her as you have looked at me." There was such a lot of palaver about the affair, that it crossed my mind I was going to be done.

The girl lighted a candle and went to the bedroom. In the room was a fire. I could scarcely now preserve the gravity of a doctor. — She took off her clothes to her chemise, and a fine little girl she was — I pulled it up, she half resisted, but as if recollecting who I was, stood still.

I asked all the searching medical questions I could. "Lie down, don't be ashamed, I am accustomed to see girls naked — there — so — just so — open your legs a little wider, now put your heel there — that's it, — don't close your thighs when I open the lips — that will do."

There the girl laid on the side of the bed, her thighs distended, one heel up so as to facilitate and keep the legs open, the little thin lips of her vulva gaping, and shewing the pink lining.

I took a candle and saw the orifice which the prick enters, inside it the membrane closing it, excepting down near the bumhole, where was a little opening, that looked as if a little finger would scarcely go thro it. The girl was unmistakably a virgin.

I could scarcely tear myself from her cunt, praised its looks, said what a nice made little lass she was — "And now my dear, tell me, have you ever put your finger up this?" and I touched it.

"No sir," said she faintly. "Are you sure? Tell me the truth, it is no good deceiving a doctor." "No, sir." "Now I know you have," said I, glorying in my baudy treat. "You have tried?" "I tried but it hurts me." "I must try — if it hurts you a little don't mind — it's for your good." — Talking thus, I wetted my little finger with spittle, and pushed it gently through the little orifice and up her cunt, which felt soft and slimy inside. She winced. — "Oh, you hurt me, sir."

Then I turned her bum upwards, and looked at the little cunt from behind, and afterwards saw her naked from head to foot. I laid her on her back, gently rubbed her clitoris with my finger, and asked if she ever did so. — "I fancy you do what so many girls do." — Then I kissed her, told her she was a dear girl, that she would not be better till she had had done to her, what her own mother had had done. I could see her readiness, but had not the cheek to attempt or propose it to her then, which seems funny now, but so it was.

I went back to Sarah in such a state that my resolution left me — I sent the girl out for soda water, and the instant she was out, gushed my sperm into Sarah's quim before my prick was well up it.

When the girl came back she drank shrub. I spoke of her nice limbs, told Sarah of her form, took half a sovereign out of my pocket, told Sarah to buy her boots, and that I felt inclined to give her a new dress. Then on pretence of satisfying myself, took her into the bedroom and again looked at the virgin cunt, pulled out my prick (and didn't she look) and pissed before her. — "You will be better when you let some one use this with you." — She turned away. I don't think she quite heard what I said.

The same things took place between us next time. I asked about the action of the medicine, and familiarised her with talking to me about all the little secrets of her sex. That freedom on subjects usually hidden from each other, paves the way for fucking. Again I saw her little form, from her nascent bubbies to her arsehole — I now put my middle finger thro the hymen and up her cunt — I had cut my nail to prevent my hurting her — but she declared it did hurt badly — I played with the few short hairs which were shewing on her mons, praised her legs, feet, neat boots and stockings — asked if she liked them, and was overwhelmed with grateful replies. — Then I hinted again at giving her a dress, told her she had better not mention about having had a doctor to anyone, and stifling my wants I went into the other room to Sarah.

Sarah said, "Try as soon as you can, for with such a young one now, you never know what will take place. She may be fool enough to tell some one, but she won't if she once gets it done to her — I will then tell her that she will be ruined for life if she mentions it."

Next night Sarah met me out. — Said she, "I will stop out till twelve, make her lushy with shrub if she won't do it without, and then fuck her, but she'll let you. — She is in love with you." — "Didn't the doctor say he would perhaps give me a new frock?" said she to Sarah. — "How could he know I had tried to put my finger up?" — Sarah told her that doctors knew everything about women. — Then I asked her if she had ever seen a man's cock. — Yes her brother's, who showed it her once. He was about fourteen years old, and she used to sleep in the same room with him, and "she had seen it stiff."

"You'll have her — she has had such a talking to. If she hollows, push a pillow over her face and they won't hear underneath — but the lodger overhead might be coming up stairs, tho he scarcely ever comes in till twelve o'clock. — I'll be in the street for him, and come in when he does, we'll come up the stairs together. — If I hear anything I'll make a noise and knock at the door, so don't be frightened — only you'll have had her before then. — Don't be nervous or you won't get a stiff one." — Sarah had heard from me that once or twice when over excited, my prick had refused to do its duty.

"I have nailed a rug over the door inside and put the chest of drawers against it. — We do that generally in winter to keep out the cold, and go thro the little passage between the bed and sitting room" — which was partly true only. There had been a curtain.

"I told her also you only had an old housekeeper, and were inclined to take her to help. — The girl was delighted." Sarah had given her a pill (I had taken her a box of common aperients). "She thinks you will soon bring on her poorliness, and that she will be quite a woman then." — I sometimes wonder if all this preliminary was needful, and if the girl did not know pretty well what she was about, but this is a narrative of facts, and not of opinions.

Altho the maiden had not been a fortnight in the house, she had been as far debauched in mind as she well could be. — To have been told all about fucking, and by a grown woman, to have confessed to that woman, and to a doctor, all she had done with her cunt, to have got money, new boots and stockings and some other things, see the chance of having a place in the house of a doctor, who twice had looked at and felt her cunt, was certainly enough to upset any girl. — It was a fine preparation.

That night she let me in, said her mistress was out and had left no message. "Never mind I will wait." — I sent her out for shrub, and prepared to try my luck, but felt as nervous as if I were going before a judge for murder — I can't understand myself being like this, for it is only at times that I am so.

She had a little shrub. — "Come here dear and tell me about yourself." — I praised her hair and eyes, which were very good. Taking her between my legs I began feeling her breasts and belly, asking her medical questions all the time, then I lifted her clothes and afterwards said, "Let me see your stockings." For an instant only she resisted as a girl might.

"Why? I gave them you — I have seen your little cunt and your little bum, have I not, and must look at them now." — Then I again lifted her clothes, put my hand up, and a finger on her clitoris, and talking all the while, began rubbing it. "Oh Doctor, don't," said she wriggling her little cunt away from me. "Ah, it's pleasure, but nothing like the pleasure you'll have when a man puts his cock up you," said I, feeling that the ice must be broken. My prick was getting so rampageous, that I felt inclined to carry her to the bed, and ravish her, but I went on talking.

In a few minutes more "I *must* look at you." Into the bedroom we went, she took off her clothes, and again I saw her little virgin cunt at the bedside.

However much I may plan an attack on a woman, — there always comes a time when I follow my instincts and not my plan. — When my prick almost feels bursting, and I am overpowered by voluptuousness, I scarcely know what I do, or what course I take. — Then if the woman is not quite ready in her lewedness, and I make a false move, and startle, frighten, or delay, my chance is gone. But if she be lewed, sayings and doings dictated by nature, infallibly win her. There is a strength of will, and a moral force that a man has when he is furious with sexual want, over any woman whose body is tingling with desire for a male, which make him sure of having her.

Up to this time I know all I did, what followed my excited state only leaves the broad incidents clear — I fell kissing her cunt when looking at her, and sitting at the side of the bed. Then I cuddled her, and told all about fucking. — Then on pretext of looking at her once more, got her on to the bed, and placed a pillow so that her bum was on it, experience had taught me that in case of resistance, my prick would have a better chance of entering if her bum was well up. — I got on the bed, pulled out my prick, and said kissing her, "Let me fuck you love, your poorliness will come on then — you'll want no more medicine, and have such pleasure." — "No-hoh, no, sir — I mustn't till I am married — you'll hurt me. — I mustn't, Doctor!"

I cuddled her as she attempted to get up, promising money and a silk dress, that I wouldn't hurt, and that whoever told her it hurt told nonsense. — "No-oh-no," — but she was nestling in my bosom, and my finger was on the little clitoris. — Suddenly she said, "Will you take me to help as a servant?" — I promised. — In another minute she was on her back. I wetted her cunt with spittle, my prick lay against it, and I feared I should spend before I got it up her. I grasped her bum, pressed her, and drove my prick with all my might. — "Oha-oh-oh," she cried, each cry louder than the other as my prick battered her virginity. — Another cry, another shove, and I was spending up her. Soon, on putting my hand down, I found that not above an inch and a half of my prick was in her cunt, and my desire was to keep it there. She begged me to get off, but I lay soothing her. My prick kept stiff. The idea that my spunk was in her, the delight at feeling the little hairless cunt lips enclosing my swollen gristle, nerved it again. I gave the gentlest push, then harder, and it glided up until I felt it could go no further.

What a delicious, slow, prolonged fuck. The little cunt smooth with sperm, but so deliciously tight and compressive, and I had first moistened that little interior, broken that virgin barrier, thoughts which increased inexpressibly my voluptuousness. I recollect all I did, and what passed through my brain during the second operation. There was only one alloy to this pleasure. Without making a noise, she kept crying, and I spent kissing her, her tears running down her face. But I am not sure that these evidences of pain and nervous shock did not add to my enjoyment.

I lay in her long, pulling her closer as my penis kept shrinking. — It was delicious to hear her say that there was no longer pain, but — "I don't know what sort of feeling" — in her cunt. When I thought of the mischief my prick had done, I delighted in using the words cunt, spunk, prick, fuck, and the whole erotic vocabulary, whilst she lay quiet with my prick still in her, listening but making no reply. What a delicious treat for her also.

I cautioned her against moving, till, "Let me wash you, it will prevent soreness, and your husband won't know what I have done to you." Girls at that age have implicit faith in a doctor, indeed I have found that most women have.

Candle in hand I opened her thighs, and saw the results of my pleasure. — A mass of blood-streaked sperm filled the mouth of her prick-hole, smears of blood lay between the cunt lips and on the thighs. On my prick was blood where the stem joins the balls, but small in quantity. Gently I pushed my largest finger up her cunt. She winced. I revelled in feeling it thick and pasty inside. — Soon my prick gave a throb, and with a movement, almost a jump, came from the droop to the stiff. I longed to be up her again, but feared my prick would droop before I did so. "Lay still, my little darling."

She tried to move but too late — "No Doctor H**m**d, you shan't" — I had lain myself on her and grasped her little bum with both hands and pushed with my prick without guiding it. In a few thrusts it found the right channel, and with one hard shove went clean up her. She gave a little cry and then was quiet. Was the distension now giving her pleasure?

I had spent twice, and to have my prick three times up a cunt in half an hour was a trial — I don't recollect in all my life, having done such a thing in the same time more than once or twice. But now I have had nearly thirty years good fucking and am in early middle age. It was one thing to get my prick up, and another to finish the fuck. After the first burning excitement had evaporated in a few sharp shoves, a desire to be quiet seized me. — Obeying it I talked to her, and my precious prick, thinking it had done enough began to dwindle. — I felt ashamed, forgetting that the girl could not know whether I had spent, was spending, or was going to spend. — So for half an hour, without my cock leaving her cunt, it kept shrinking, then swelling at some effort, and so on. Now I pushed my fingers well under her little bum cheeks, and feeling the stem of my prick wet, I put her hand down to feel it. Then asked how her cunt felt. — All this did not keep me to full rigidity for long, yet I never once got my cock quite out of her. — There was no superfluous fat outside it, and her cunt was easily got at, and my firm hold of her little buttocks kept it close up to my prick, and so I managed it.

At length she complained that I was making her "ache dreadful." I thought of rubbing her clitoris, and putting my finger down did so. The girl felt its effects, and so did I — my prick began to feel voluptuous thrills, and as if sperm was in my balls. No doubt the stretching, pushing, and friction of my cock up her little cunt had inflamed her. The rubbing of the clitoris made the sore little cunt hotter. Gently pushing with cock as stiff now as ever, I heard her sigh and saw her eyes close. She was spending — I saw it in her face, felt it by her manner, and by the sensation her cunt suddenly conveyed to my prick — it was the crisis of my night's enjoyment. — Up her cunt rapidly thrusting before she had recovered, I spent in her again.

I got off of her. She lay seemingly exhausted, did all I told her, and let me do all I wanted — I again washed her cunt, gave her more shrub and she laid down, and went fast asleep for a full hour — I sat down gloriously contented.

It would be an hour and a half before Sarah came back. For an hour during which I read, Emma was still asleep. I pulled up her chemise, and saw the top of the little split peeping out between the closed thighs — I frigged my prick. All I had done, all I meant to do passed through my mind, and at last with much effort I spent, and was done for, for that night and no mistake. What a vagary to indulge in. How can I account for that sudden onanistic letch, I who hate masturbation?

I awakened her — her little quim was swollen and of dark color, the outer lips even I fancied were swollen and irritated. I gloried in the jagged opening made of the little hole of three hours previously, but felt sorry at the depression she was in, for I could now scarcely get her to reply. — Kissing her, promising much, and begging her never to tell any one, I left her.

Sarah was outside. I gave her her money and told her all about it. — Said she, — "The little devil spent! — are you sure?" — Sarah doubted it. — She didn't know whether to encourage her to tell, or to ask no questions, but get rid of her soon, say she was deaf, was not strong enough, or something else. Sarah had her pay and wanted to be quit of the business.

But I wanted to fuck, to frig, to lick her, show her my cock, teach her the art of love, to learn her virgin ideas and sensations; so said she must keep her, arrange how she liked about knowing or not knowing, but I must have her again or we should quarrel. —

Sarah against her will agreed — I was positive, peremptory. Sarah was strong in the desire that I should not see the lass again. Perhaps she was quite right, but I had my wishes to gratify, and did not clearly see Sarah's reasons.

On the second night after the cunt rupturing, I met Sarah on her beat. The girl had told her all. Sarah had said she was sorry, but what was done, could not be undone — and it was lucky it was with a wise gentleman like Doctor H**m**d, or bad consequences would come. — She'd be ruined for life if she told any living soul, and if the doctor wanted to do it again, he must. She should turn her out if she thought she'd mention the affair to any one — or allowed any other man even to kiss, or feel her.

I went quietly enough the next night into the bed room with the lass, and had as much difficulty in getting to look at her cunt as before. But I fucked her, and had the delight of seeing her frig my prick, and watch her looks as it swelled. Then I ejaculated the spunk into her. Afterwards I licked her little cunt till she spent, and much trouble I had to make her come that way — I can't understand why I tried to set her to frig herself, which she wouldn't do. — It was a brief honeymoon that and the succeeding nights. — I got her perfect confidence, and this went on nearly every other day for some weeks.

Then I fucked Sarah, and liked her fully developed cunt better than the younger one's. I began to notice that if not very randy, the little one's cunt failed to work up my pleasure, whilst Sarah's big one did. There was indeed but little sympathetic movement in the little one's cunt, and I could only well get my prick two-thirds up her. — At first it delighted me to thrust till she called out, and her, — "Oh don't push so far, sir," — used to fetch my spunk like a shot. — But I grew tired of that, and came to the conclusion, that a good full sized cunt, elastic, fleshy, pulpy, and deep, was the most satisfying to my pego.

Sarah grew tired of keeping the girl for some reason, altho she got two pounds instead of one, each time I saw her. — "The little devil bothers me, she is always asking about you, and about Mr. F**z*r. I have made her sleep on the sofa, for I have found her feeling about my cunt when I awakened. — She thinks of nothing but your coming, bothers me to read your baudy books (I had lent some), and would talk of fucking all day — I am frightened to let her go out. I wish you would let her go." — I had now fucked the lass in every attitude and agreed to it, and told Sarah I would stop away a fortnight.

The girl, I heard afterwards was in tears when she found I did not come. Sarah told her I had gone abroad — I was sorry for the lass, but Sarah had but little pity. — She thought the girl had done very well. — "When she came, she hadn't a rag to her back, now she has more good clothing than me." — I had indeed given the girl lots of good clothes. — "She is set up, and has got a good place as servant, where she will work hard, but what of that. It's better than stopping at home with a drunken father who half starved and ill-treated her. One of his shop mates would have done her business. — Now she can take care of herself, she knows enough."

Her place was at a little grocers' shop in W**d**r Street. — A month afterwards I loitered near the shop curiously, and saw two youths, seventeen or eighteen years old, in it; sons of the woman who kept it I found. Sarah said I was wrong to go near. — "The best thing for you is never to see her again — if any row comes, I'll swear you never were at my lodgings in your life. — No one has seen you come, it has always been dark."

I remarked that the youths would get into her. — "I hope they will, that will shut her mouth. — She won't go long without it being up her, and the sooner she fucks the better," was Sarah's opinion. I never either saw the girl afterwards, nor heard of her.

I don't forget the delight of the girl when her poorliness came on, which it did about a fortnight after I had had her, nor the way she used to burst out into quiet laughter, when she pulled my prick about till stiff, and how she said. — "Oh you do make my legs ache so." All little girls get the leg ache when I lie long between them. — One of my delights was to turn her on her side with her bum towards me, fuck her from behind, and go to sleep so with my prick well in her. It is easier to do it that way with a small bum, than with big buttocks. But pillows must be put under the side of the young ones, to bring their cunts up to a convenient level. Fucking so was one of my delights with Molly, whom Betsy Johnson got for me. At Sarah F**z**'s I never had anything in my pockets to disclose my name. I used to tail the girl whilst Sarah looked on, and have awakened with my tail still in the girl and

Sarah tranquilly working in the room, and singing in a low tone to herself.

But I don't understand Sarah's behaviour in the matter; why she wanted to be out of the house when I broached the girl, and so on. — Other women have however acted in peculiar ways under similar circumstances, and the reasons for the dodges of gay women are only known to themselves. Somehow I think that Sarah's man had something to do with her desire to get rid of the girl, but about him I could glean no information; tho at times I was forbidden to go to her lodgings, because she said *he* was there.

CHAPTER XIII

*The Christmas cattle show. — Mrs. Winifred P****e. — Recognition. — Assignation. — A conversation in a cab. — Talking and groping at a brothel. — Both on heat. — Winifred's marriage night. — The utility of the monthlies. — The husband humbugged. — An explicit account of marital habits. — Her husband's tool and toolings. — A gamahuche. — A lick of a prick. — Our last meeting. — Fifteen minutes' hard ramming. — We part for ever. — About my remaining manuscript.*

This deaf maiden occupied me about two months, and whilst Sarah disposed of her, a bit of luck befell me, which kept me from Sarah longer than I intended. Just then also I was not very free.

I went to the Christmas cattle show, saw a fine looking young woman stare with a surprized look at me, and recognized Winifred. She turned away her head, and laid hold of the arm of a man beside her, who looked like a middle-aged, country, well-to-do tradesman.

I could not keep my eyes from her, cared no more about the cattle, but followed the couple for half an hour at a short distance from them; with curiosity reflecting on what I had been to the lady, and she to me, till my prick stiffened. Every phase of our liaison passed through my mind as I followed the couple, and the reminiscence was delightful.

Soon I noticed her looking stealthily over the shoulder of the man. Her eyes met mine, and she very slightly shook her head. I got closer to them. — On they went, staring hard at the cattle and speaking at times, the man knowing as little of what was going on between me and the woman, as one of the bullocks. — Again her eyes met mine. She was fascinated and at length smiled. I followed on, thinking of her increased height and improved looks, and wondered how the little downy browny-edged cunt looked now after years of growth on it; for it was four years that Christmas since I had seen it.

A strong desire to see it again sprang up in me. I wondered who and what the man was, and if she'd had a male piercer up her since she'd had mine.

I followed watching them for half an hour. All at once he left her and entered the water closet enclosure. She remained, for a second or two, standing still, seemingly looking at the cattle. Then her head turned to see if he was visible, and to see for me. In a second I stood by her side. "For God's sake take care. It's my husband, he won't be gone a minute." "Meet me." "I can't, I dare not — go now." — "Where do you live?" "We are only here for a week, we are at ****," and she told an hotel near a railway station and what her name was. — "You *must* meet me, and I'll be outside the hotel at eight o'clock tonight." "No, he'll be at home then, perhaps he won't at six." "At six then," — and repeating the address and name to myself so as to make no error, I moved away and wrote it down on one of my cards, finishing just as the man reappeared. In half an hour still watching them I saw them leave the building.

Then I thought I wouldn't go to see her, for she might have told me the wrong address and name, yet her eyes looked, as I fancied, full of desire for me. — Was it fancy — was it conceit on my part? — If she's married it's a shame. — Adultery again! — What awful temptations come to me — I won't go — I wonder how her dear pretty cunt looks. How large her bum now is — how like her mother she is. — Thus ran my thoughts, and after resolving that I would not go to meet her — I went.

The hotel was a small but perfectly respectable one, not far from a railway terminus. Punctually she came out. — Following me well away from it, we stopped. "I'm so frightened, my husband might come along, what would he say if he caught me talking with you?" "Get into a cab with me." "Oh, I dare not." — She kept looking up and down the street in a nervous state. "What do you want?" "My love, how can you ask. A chat about old times. Come." "I'm married, really I am, and am so frightened." — There was no time to lose. With a little persuasion she followed me at a distance, and got into a four wheeler. — Ah! those blessed wheeled baudy houses.

For a minute it was nothing but kissing — long long kiss, given and taken. Then volubly she began an account of herself. One of my hands was round her waist, the other in a second was on her cunt. — "Don't now — you must not. — I'll get out else." What a charming scuffle! — "Nonsense, Winny love, haven't I licked it and fucked it?" — Again we kissed, I told my love, in two minutes she was feeling my stiff prick, my fingers were buried between her warm cunt lips, our mouths were together, and tongues meeting. "What a lot of hair's on your cunt, love, now — how your clitoris has grown — how fat your thighs are; my darling let us fuck — get up, and sit on me. I'm dying to spend in you again." — Kiss, kiss. — "No that I won't." "Do — turn your bum round and sit on me, you know you once did it that way on a chair." — All was useless — "I shall spend in your hand then." She left off feeling my prick at once. — "You shan't do that." — I coaxed, but all was of no use. — "If I do want it, I won't let you *now*." "Meet me to-morrow." "I'm frightened." — She couldn't do this or that, but at last arranged to meet me. — "You want fucking I know, Winny." "I'm not going to let you do it tho," were her last words, as she got out of the cab and walked away.

At eleven o'clock the next morning, there was Winifred with a veil on, at the back of L**c**t*r Square, my favorite place of assignation. — Ten minutes after, we were in the A**a in the room with the glasses, where Sarah and I had our baudy gambols. For five minutes we did nothing but kiss, but she'd come for fucking, and had no hesitation about it. To my annoyance there was no fire, and it was a cold foggy day. The woman would light one. — "But there's a good fire in the room up stairs." — Quickly up we went. "Take off your things love I'm dying to see your lovely form, — to kiss that dear quim." — In five minutes we were in bed, my prick up her, in three minutes after with kisses and sighs, with tongues joined, my spunk was gushing up her cunt, and we were spending together in ecstacy.

Laying in her arms, prick wallowing in the mucosity of her delicious cunt, she began telling me about herself, as soon as our silent pleasure was over. — Her narrative was told in snatches, interrupted only by our varied amorous endearments. — "Go on love." — Then she talked on. — "Oh! feel how stiff it still is up you." — "Oh! yes, but take it out and let me wash, I'd better." — Kiss — kiss. — "No, go on telling. What did your sister do?" — On she talked — kiss — kiss. — "How smooth your lovely fat bum is Winny." "Oh it's running out, it will be on my chemise — take it out, do." My prick was dwindling, bringing out with it my libation. Easing my weight, she hitched up her chemise from under her bum, leaving the sheet recipient of our sexual exudations. — I turned on my side and covered her moist gap with my hand, delighted in feeling the overflow. She handled voluptuously my clammy tool. So we lay close together, cuddling, feeling, soothing yet exciting each other's genitals, kissing and tongue sucking, till my prick was erect again. Then our bodies joyously joined each other, and made us one, and we were fucking. Ah that prolonged, delicious, thoughtful exercise, which the second ejaculation requires — In voluptuous thoughts — in intense mental pleasure — in the perfect enjoyment of a woman's charms, I think the second fuck is better than the first.

She slopped and rubbed her cunt dry without hiding the operation — telling her tale all the time — I stirred the fire, we drew chairs to it, and sitting close together, feeling, kissing, and every now and then looking at our machines spent a few minutes. Winifred had no sham regrets, fears, scruples, compunctions; we were lovers as of yore. She'd come for fucking, and forgot every thing else. Soon as we found it would be warmer in bed than by the fire, after at the bedside having looked at her dear, pretty cunt well, into bed we again got, and now both start naked. She'd never been naked in bed with me before, I think.

How we cuddled and kissed. — How our tongues played with each other — how I felt her from top to toe over and over again. Then as she was pressed for time, I mounted her and rubbed my pendant tool between her cunt lips, and frictionized her clitoris with its tip, till stiff. Then I plunged it up her, stroking and resting, now thrusting it hard up her till the sperm began to rise, then waiting, and half withdrawing it to stop the pleasure — talking lasciviously all the time — then resuming the oscillation of my loins and buttocks, till again with cries of ecstasy we died away in each other's arms, and dozed with cunt and prick in loving conjunction. — With what regret we unjoined our bodies.

What a lovely creature she had grown. Now with splendidly shaped limbs, largish thighs, fine buttocks, and one of the prettiest of cunts. The fringe around it was thick, crisp, close and darker, tho still of a chestnut brown, the lips soft and full, the clitoris developed strongly. It had lost its coral hue, and had deepened in colour. How pleased she was to let me see, and do what I liked with it. By the bedside it was cold — so I pulled the sofa to the fire, and laying her on it there, completed my sweet investigations. — She hadn't the slightest hesitation, seemed proud of yielding, made no ridiculous attempts at decency. — Decency between us, between a man and woman who have fucked each other, is really indecency.

Her face was now much like her handsome mother's. Her hair the colour of that on her cunt, but there a shade darker. Her blue eyes had still their sharp expression. They looked softer as we sat feeling each other, yet were sharp even in their lewdest moments, and she got lewed enough, and shivered and kissed me, as she laughed at each baudy word, each amorous trick of my fingers.

When we left, she agreed to meet me again if she could. They were only going to stay in London a few days, for her husband must get back to business. Winifred was supposed by him to be with an *aunt,* whilst she was in the baudy house with *me,* and she went to her aunt's directly she left me.

Her life since she left London may be told in a few lines, altho she talked about it incessantly that day, as well as at our next meeting.

She went with her mother to ****. Her father-in-law seemed from her account, to be a rather superior sort of person for his position. Then she went as a shop woman — but her mother took her away, so that she might better look after her — Lydia just then disclosed where *she* was, said she was married, and offered to keep Winifred, who went to her. She stopped there a few months, and went back to her mother, who had found out that Lydia was not married, tho big with child. The pious lodger did however soon marry her. — Winifred was useful, and her father-in-law now kept her at home, but she was restless and wanted to see the world, but could scarcely get out alone, which so annöyed her, that she said she would go to service again.

The fact evidently was that her mother saw that Winifred wanted fucking badly (tho she had no idea that a prick had already been up her vulva), and kept a tight hand on her. Just then a tradesman in the town offered marriage. He was more than twenty years older than Winifred, but comfortably off. The mother insisted on her accepting him and they were married. She was now pretty comfortable, he was a good sort of man, and rather jealous, but had never found out the absence of her virginity. — "You married him, Winny because you wanted a man." "Perhaps I did a little for that, but I wanted to get away and be my own mistress."

Next day I waited for Winifred who never came. I wrote, risking consequences, and the day following she did. The room was warm, and there was a good fire. I had with me sandwiches and champagne as arranged, for our meeting was at one o'clock (she was an hour behind her time and I'd given her up), after a snack and a glass, I began undressing, and she without any request did the same rapidly. She enjoyed giving me her nudity. We sat on the sofa, at one time with sandwiches in our hands, whilst with the others we felt both prick and cunt, — eat and handled our machines at the same time, both lewed to our back bones.

Scarcely had we finished the sandwiches, before I'd opened her thighs, looked at her cunt, and then recollected what I did to it before I had deflowered her. How rapidly things flash thro my brain. — "Shall I lick it Winny, do you recollect?" "If you like," laughing. "Does your husband do it?" "He has never done it yet." Next minute, kneeling with my backside to the fire which nearly burnt the skin, with her legs over my arms, my hands under her beautiful smooth buttocks, I was licking her lovely split. How sweet it seemed, how stimulating its odour, as my tongue glided over its surface, how short the amusement. In a minute or two, almost as it seemed before I had begun, her thighs and belly were quivering. I could feel the movement of her buttocks, her cunt jogged so gently up and down against my mouth, and with — "Ah — ar — A — har — my love — A — har," her pleasure came, and her cunt rolled out its salt moistures. As I rose she lay back on the sofa with eyes closed, and thighs wide open, the pearly essence running out of the red orifice. Five minutes after we were in bed fucking.

She'd taken my prick in her mouth for a momentary embrace before I put it into her cunt. — She opened her mouth the instant I suggested it, delighted.

With passions calmed, with genitals softened and moisted by pleasure, tranquilly side by side in loving proximity, handling each other with the restless but delicious sensation of lewedness semi-appeased, and awaiting the resurrection of my prick and the hardening of her clitoris, one of the most delicious conversations I ever had with a lovely woman, was then mine. — Winifred was frankness itself, she was always so, it was her nature, just as by nature she was amorous, and inclined to the lascivious preliminaries of sexual conjunction. Had she remained in London alone when her mother left, she would have turned gay from sheer love of the male. Her marriage by satisfying her partially, and cooling the heat of her quim — had as far as I know and believe kept her chaste. — Intrigues are difficult in country towns, which are easy in the immensity of London. She now showed either her liking for me, or her sexual voracity, for certainly she'd have taken more fucking than I could have given her; and perhaps it is as well for me, that the time she could remain was too short to test my virility too much.

In this state of body and of mind, she had a manifest pleasure in telling me all about herself and husband, had no hesitations, no shams. She gave me direct answers to my questions, and expected me to answer with equal frankness, which I certainly did. — Never did a couple explain their sexual habits and conditions as we did. Her frankness was contagious. [I have never since told a woman as much, or been asked as much.]

Her husband stroked her not quite every other night. He didn't play amorously with her at first, nor even look at her cunt much after the first week of marriage. — "I'm stiff, let's have a bit together," was all he usually said, then mounted her. Sometimes he did her twice if she hadn't spent, but didn't like being asked. At times she said she'd not had pleasure when she had, because she wanted it again. — He thought that women who wanted much stroking were beasts. — When he had done her, he turned his rump to her, and fell asleep directly. — We laughed about her marriage night. She'd consulted Lydia, and named a day when her poorliness would be just over, thinking his poking would bring it on again. — She'd noticed that at that period if she frigged herself it returned slightly. It did on her marriage night. She described to me with delight how she writhed, and jerked her bum back, and cried out. "Oh you are hurting me so," as he got into her. — We laughed heartily at it. Poor man had he but known!

"Yes his is as long as yours, and just the same thickness," said she in answer to a question, feeling my prick carefully all the time she spoke, as if to make sure she was right. "But somehow it isn't as nice as when you're doing it." — Then I put my prick up her. — "Ah! I wish you were my husband," she sighed out just before she spent. She declared she'd never had any man but her husband and myself, but had frigged herself pretty often. She'd never been in the family way by me, — was so soon after her marriage, but miscarried — her husband didn't want children. "I think I'm in the family way now." — Then with the only bit of hesitation she had shown, "Well — yes — he did it to me last night." "Say fucked you, Winny." "Fucked me," said she laughing and pleased to say it.

I have had many married women. It is against my principles to have them, but fate is invincible. Some have been amorous enough, have rejoiced in my libidinosity, joined with me in salacity, but most have avoided reference to their husbands; and when I have been curious about their husband's capabilities and sexual vigor, and the size of his prick — have always avoided the subject. — "Don't let us talk of *that.*" — "Oh, it's a shame to ask me." — "Now I won't answer you," — and similar replies I have had at first, and only with difficulty got my curiosity satisfied, and sometimes not at all. But here was Winifred, delighted to talk about it all. The quiet way she felt me before she told me the size of his prick, I shall recollect to my dying day.

Again we met — "I'm so sorry we're going back. — I've asked him to let me stop with my aunt for a week, but he won't." "We could have met every day." "We would," said she. — Such was her liking for me or my prick, that she agreed to meet me again — "if possible, — but I'm sure I can't stay more than a quarter of an hour." — She was ready to run any risk. I had the quarter of an hour. — Dressed and at the bedside I fucked her. In ten minutes afterwards, "I wish I could do it again but can't." She lay expectantly quiet where I had placed her. I frigged an erection, inserted and thrust with energy, but no spunk came. — "I'm coming dear," she gasped out and spent; but I didn't. Then I got furious, and rammed with violence. I could almost hear the slap of my balls against her backside. — "Ah-a — I'm coming again dear."" "My — sperm's coming too love," — and it spurted up her.

In haste we washed. I kissed and licked over the surface of her fresh washed cunt, for I felt madly in lust for her. She kissed my prick, we parted, and I have never seen her since.

It was a most delicious week, a charming interlude in my erotic performances, which are now wholly with professional pleasure-givers. It makes me regret the delights of teaching the art of love, and fucking those who met me for the pleasure of fucking alone, and not for pay. Shall I ever have such chances again?

Much as I have abbreviated and omitted, what a quantity of manuscript still remains. — Alas! a casual look through it, reveals the fact that, like much of that written just before this period of my history, it is prolix and copious in detail. — More so even than that preceding it which I shortened with so much trouble. — It is exuberant, because written for my secret pleasure, and I revelled in the detail as I wrote it, for in doing so I almost had my sexual treats over again. — It mattered not to me whether similar pleasure had been mine before or not, whether the erotic whims and fancies, amorous frolics, voluptuous eccentricities, were identical or not. — I described them as they had occurred at the time, and the pleasure of doing so was nearly the same, even had I done them twenty times, and described them twenty times.

But the woman, the partner in my felicity was frequently fresh and new to me, and I to her; and this newness prevents satiety in sexual frolics. There is always a shade of difference in the manners and behaviour of women in sexual preliminaries, and even in final performance. One woman never kisses or sighs, embraces or fucks, in exactly the same manner as another. The broad features from beginning to ending are the same. A coupling of the genitals finishes it all. But there are delicate shades of difference even in fucking which make the variety so charming, and describing them was ever new and amusing to me, when the charmer was new to me.

Yet on glancing through the remaining manuscript, — now in my mature, if not only years — the repetition seems a little wearisome. — What is to be done — abbreviate or destroy — which? — Abbreviation is laborious, and emasculates — the freshness of the writing is gone — nice shades lost. — But destruction saves all future trouble.

Perhaps entire omission of portions will be best, but that will destroy the continuity. In the narrative in its integrity, it is easy to see how in my youth, content with the simplest forms of sexual pleasure, I have gradually with advancing years and experience, been led to strangely erotic whims and devices, and have had the greatest pleasure in acts, and deeds, and thoughts, which in my ignorant youth would have revolted me. — To omit much is to destroy this continuity of idea and action. — No. It must be abbreviation or total destruction. Abbreviation, or else a full stop here, and nearly twenty years' narrative go to the flames.

Another thing — through the suggestions of women, by pondering over those suggestions — by reading works of erotic philosophers — from pictures, curiosity, and opportunity, — I have once or twice done what I regret, what in fact is almost a remorse to me, tho I really see no harm in it. — What a contradiction this, but thus it is. — Shall I destroy those chapters, erase those parts — or leave them — perhaps (for who knows) for some to cry shame. — To omit them is to sacrifice the narrative, and the illustration it affords to myself of my sexual idiosyncrasy — if such a phrase may be used — I know not what to do with this antagonism of thought and intention.

It must remain — written by *myself* and for *myself*, none probably will ever see it but *myself* — therefore why cheat *myself*? — let it remain.

I wish I had begun this revision earlier, perhaps now I shall never complete it — or complete it only in time to destroy it, before I myself am destroyed. — *Tempus edax rerum.*

END OF THE SEVENTH VOLUME.

MY SECRET LIFE

BOOK EIGHT

'WALTER'

WORDSWORTH CLASSICS

CONTENTS

CHAPTER I

*Sarah's jealousy. — Her ballet posturings. — My postures. — An escape of wind. — Wheelbarrow fashion. — A young lass suggested. — Harriet, sweet sixteen. — Financial arrangements. — Doctor H**m**d again. — Tooth brush and tooth powder. — Virginity doubtful. — Harriet screwed, unscrewed, and opened. — A tight vagina. — Sarah's strange behaviour. — Three in a bed. — Harriet jealous. — Runs away. — The baudy-house with spyhole closed. — On the size of my prick and others. — On the capacity, elasticity, and receptivity of cunts.*

When I went back to Sarah, she was surprized at the length of my absence, and thought she had lost me. I told her, without mentioning who the lady was, of my good fortune. She was spiteful, as gay ladies are when they have missed their man and their money. I expect she had begun to regard me as a regular source of income. She doubted if the lady was really married, nor altered her opinion when I told her I had had the first of the lady. She hoped the lady had not clapped me.

We went to the peep hole and for one or two evenings had various amatory frolics, and then I made a discovery about Sarah.

She had surprised me by the ease with which she posed in difficult, lewed, and odd attitudes that I put her in. — This evening we had been sitting drinking, and she was larkish. I remarked the ease with which she attitudinized. — She laughed and got up. "Look here then." — She threw off her chemise, put up one leg nearly to the level of her shoulder, and placing the tip of the toe against the wall so as to rest it, inclined her body downwards towards the floor with her hand touching it. — It *was* a sight. Her cunt was gaping, showing the broadest red face which a cunt can show without being pulled open by fingers, the dark thick hair shewing all around it, until lost at her bumhole. The thicket in one armpit was quite visible, and all this was seen at a glance. — I went on my knees to look at her split, and put my finger on it in baudy ecstasy.

She stood upright and I begged her to do it again. — "Look, I don't think I can do it now but will try." Throwing up her leg, she caught hold of the toe with her hand, then pulling it higher and higher, she turned round and round on her left foot. It was a quite fresh view of the cuntal territory. The dark fringed lips were now not open, but were slightly squeezed together, yet made prominent. The red stripe was scarcely perceptible but the lips shewed the crimson beginning, and a peep of the arse valley was got. The sight was entrancing, and in a minute hurrying her to the bed, I plugged her cunt. She was in rare lewed mood and soon spent. I had that night pissed against her cunt, and we now both spent together lusciously.

"I am as randy as be damned," said she. "I always am just before my month — fuck me again."

We sat down after our exercise. Said I, "You must have been a dancer." She laughed. — "Did you never see me before you met me in the street?" "Never." "Are you sure?" "I think so." "Did you ever see the play of *** at Covent Garden!" "Yes." "Ah. Then you saw *me*. — I used to dance in it." Then I drew from her that she had been a figurante — but never learnt why she left the theatre. She did not mean to go on again — altho she could if she wished. — "There are reasons, I'm not going to tell if you ask me all night."

In the attitudes then she placed herself again, then danced naked, and postured as the ballet dancers do. — "Come and hold me so, and so — take off your shirt." — I did. — Then she placed me so as to hold her in various attitudes, as men hold female dancers in ballets. — There were we naked before a large glass. — She in attitudes exposing her backside and cunt, — I now with stiff prick holding her. — Sometimes she held by my prick. — Soon after posing in a few attitudes she again got my pego into her cunt, and again afterwards till I was fucked out. — She was hot that night. This was at the baudy house with the glasses.

I went away delighted. — Thought I, some fellows would give no end of money to see her. How often since I have wished as I saw the ballet dancers cocking up this leg, or throwing out that,

that their drawers were away and I could see their quims. — Now it must be wide stretched, now what a sight it would be. — I fucked a ballet girl some years ago as I think I have told, but perhaps that is one of the narratives omitted in order to shorten this history, but that was for the pleasure of fucking thro a cut I made in her tights. I think I have told this but am not sure. She for a minute or two had pirouetted, but I only had with her a momentary amusement. — But now I have a fine limbed woman who can do it all, and will do it when I like — so I thought on.

A night after when I wanted her to posture naked she refused. — We had words, I paid her, and to her astonishment went away without fucking her. Again I met her and asked her. Again she would not, and again away I went. — The third time she said she would posture a little, and so to the A**a we went.

When indoors she refused, was sorry she had ever "shown off so," wondered how she came to be such a fool as to let out about herself. "Champagne and lewedness did it, Sarah." — As she still refused, I put down the money and was going away, when, "Don't go without poking me, I'll do it." — Twenty minutes afterwards, altho sulkily, there she was, one toe against a metal shelf, I naked with cock upright — now looking at her gaping quim, now peeping under her buttocks, now looking at the reflection of our naked bodies in the glasses. I made her throw up her leg and catch the toe, and as with an effort she did so, out slipped a little fart. — "There," said she, "I swear I will never do it again," and she wouldn't that night. — I fucked her and left her in the sulks.

I would not go with her again until she promised, and soon her posturing was part of my evening's amusement. We used to attitudinize before the looking glass, laugh at our postures, and say what money men would give to see us two naked together. — I dare say rich men have induced ballet girls to do as much, but more they could not; and I was fortunate to have had such voluptuous entertainments so cheaply.

Then I fucked her wheelbarrow fashion. I have tried that, I think, with other women but am not sure. It seemed now a novelty. With Sarah's long limbs I could accomplish it well. She put pillows on the floor for her head and arms to rest on. I sat myself at the side of the bed naked. She was naked also, put her legs gradually up on to the bed, one on each side of my haunches, then I held her legs at the proper level. It was a beautiful sight to see her bum gradually coming up. The buttocks' furrow only shewing a little at first, and then the dark hair, thick and curly on the sides of her cunt, coming into sight, and between it the red gap. Then I leaned back for a few seconds in admiration, pulling open the bum cheeks, and burying my finger in the red lane. — Then pressing down my prick, which resisted elastically, being moved out of its perpendicular, I inserted it in her cunt and drove it home, passing my hands under her thighs, shoving and exciting her to the crisis. My senses recovered, I sat down on the bed again, keeping my doodle as close into her cunt as I could, and passing one hand round to her belly felt her clitoris, till my prick came out of its pool, and the lascivious junction was over.

This was very exciting, but as a fuck the position is inferior in pleasure to many attitudes. The man's prick is bent down, the clitoris end of the cunt loses its friction. The woman's posture with both her hands and head down low is fatiguing. If they both spend there is no repose after the emission, and the tranquil, languid pleasure which follows the active ramming, ballocks wagging, bum wriggling, twisting, and after squeezing, is lost.

I had not thought anything more about little unfledged cunts, was satisfied for the time, I suppose, with my past amusement with deaf little Emma. I went then once or twice to Sarah's lodgings. She let me in herself for she didn't always keep a little servant, but had often only a charwoman. — There I made her do a little fantastic fucking, as well as posturing, when the following occurred.

I suppose that having got money by supplying me with a youthful virgin, she wanted another bonus, and became the temptress. She said one night when I met her out and stopped only to have a chat that she'd just got such a nice young maid, would I have her? — My letch for youthful quims was, I suppose, smouldering, and it at once blew up into flame. I asked the price and agreed to pay as before, *if the girl was virgin*. But there was difficulty about the virginity, for the girl was quite sixteen, had had her courses for some time, and had been in service. Sarah thought she was virgin, but knew she couldn't deceive *me* — would I go and see her? She gave an inciting account of her nice looks, and as she was at a charming age, an age at which I had had of late years few, my women having been either younger or much older, I arranged to go and have a look at the girl.

I was to be Doctor H**m**d again, Sarah indeed always now called me Doctor — I went and saw a tall, thin, bright looking, dark eyed, dark haired girl, who looked quite sixteen. Her eyes flashed as she spoke, and I said that I fancied she knew a prick from a rolling pin. — Said Sarah, "I never knew a girl who was sixteen who didn't, girls who have nursed their brothers have seen a prick stiff, even if they haven't stiffened them — but she is worth a poke whether she's had one before or not, tho I believe if she had been poked, that she wouldn't come to me." She had done her best. — "She may never have been poked, even altho she may not give you trouble to get up her." — I made up my mind at once that the girl was not virgin.

Sarah was for my getting it over soon if it was to be done. *She* was not going to hide her being gay from the girl, as she had from the deaf girl at first, had already told her how she got her living, and that a good easy living it was. This girl's name was Harriet. If I wanted to be sure that she was intact, making her drunk and looking was the way. Sarah would help me, but the sooner the better. It was of no use keeping her if I did not want her. — She did not want a good looking girl there. "Afraid of Mr. F**z*r?" Perhaps she was, but that did not matter to me, Sarah said snappishly.

The girl was told I was the doctor to Sarah and I once used to "*Do her over*" (her usual term) — but now tho I came to see her as doctor, I never fucked her, but I talked freely, baudily, and never charged for my medical services, I was an odd but good man.

The girl I found answered perfectly to Sarah's description of her. Her flashing dark eyes had an unusually soft expression in them. A sweet expression of lewedness and voluptuousness, which some girls have just after their first menstruations have settled down to the exact monthly period, leaving them fresh tinted, soft skinned, and ready to receive the love of man. — This struck me to be the case with Harriet, who I think came from one of the outer suburbs of London, but somehow I was never as curious to verify this impression, or to learn anything about her, as I have been about some women.

In a day or two I was again at Sarah's lodgings. — "Do you mind Harriet sitting in this room? There is no fire in the bedroom." "No." I did not. The girl then sat down at needlework, I sent her for brandy and wine, giving her the change. We all drank, and the girl quickly enough. Sarah went into the bedroom. Whilst absent, after joking the girl I pinched her bum. She cried out. Sarah came in. — "What's the matter." "The gentleman's pulling me about." "Lord, I thought he was kicking your arse you make such a noise." The girl opened her mouth wide, stared, and sat down confused. — We laughed. I said I should like to kiss Harriet's and not kick it, I was sure it was as pretty as her face.

Presently I went behind her, putting my hand under her chin, kissed her and noticed then that she had good teeth, but not too clean. "You have a nice set of teeth, but you don't clean them." "My brush is worn out, Sir."

"Let me see your teeth better." She resisted. "Don't be a fool," said Sarah, "let the Doctor see your teeth." When I had done so, "Here," said I. "Go to the chemist, buy a toothbrush and a box of tooth powder as quickly as you can." Off she went — I never could bear any woman with dirty teeth.

I had given her five shillings. She was back in five minutes, and pleased enough — especially when I told her to keep the change. — She opened the box to look inside at its contents standing close by the lamp. I was standing with my rump to the fire smoking. "When that is gone I will give you more — clean your teeth every morning and night, and in a week your mouth will be as sweet as your cunt, just after you have washed it."

The girl dropped the box, spilling the contents over the table —stared at me for a second — turned her back, burst out laughing, checked it, and rushed into the bedroom. Sarah cried out, "Damn you, you careless little beast, you've spoilt my table cloth," and fetched her back. "It's no use minding the Doctor." The girl got up the tooth powder, I threw half a crown to Sarah, saying, "It was my fault, black-cunt, and that will help to clean the cloth."

It's too long to tell all, but I kept up that style of talk, and got the girl to sit by the fire with us, her mistress saying, "Come if he wishes it, he always has his way here." And I talked baudy enough to have turned a clergyman's hair grey. The girl's eyes from shunning at length looked at me, Sarah kept telling her not to mind me — not to be a fool — that she must hear men talk so some day. Perhaps she had already, I thought.

I asked her questions which a medical man might. When she did not reply, Sarah rebuked her. "What can it matter to *him* — you might be ill some day, and want him."

As I got heated by wine and the look of the girl, I promised her money for boots and stockings provided she would let me put them on. "Take the money — don't be such a fool — take it," said Sarah.

I took my leave, saying, "Dark hair, and dark eyes just like Sarah — I wager your cunt hair is dark like Sarah's." The girl blushed and did not reply. "It is black," said Sarah laughing. "I have seen it."

The girl became so quiet that I began to think she had heard such talk before — but her manner afterwards convinced me she was not accustomed to it.

I saw Sarah next night in the street. "We'll make her drunk and look at her cunt tomorrow night," said she. — But we were baulked, for the girl's menstruation came on, and we deferred the job. But I asked the girl all about her courses, as a doctor might. She gave me plain but modest answers. By the time her monthlies were over, she had ceased to evade my questions even when baudy. When Sarah laughed, the girl did so altho uneasily — four or five nights' smutty talk were breaking down her modesty.

Then Sarah told me she had shown her my baudy book and advised me to bring another, and we arranged that when she was tight, Sarah should go out and I should examine her cunt and do what I pleased.

I had taken quite a different liking to this girl from that which I had for the deaf one, who was like a child, and whom I desired because she was so. But Harriet, more than a year older, had made me feel lewed in a different sense. — It was the charm of getting into a very young woman, whose passions were getting roused by nature and quickened by me. — She was not so young as I had wished, but young enough to be a pleasurable novelty. Tho I don't know really what can be called very novel to me in the way of women and the manner of playing with them.

One evening behold me at the house. Wine and brandy and water was had. It was a cold night and we sat facing the fire. —

Baudiness was on, altho we had not planned what to say, but it was to be enough to stimulate the girl's lust to the highest, and after having made her either screwed enough to permit me to do anything with her, I was to look at her virginity, or for it, and fuck it out of her if she had got it as best I might. I did not like this business, tho I consented to it, as I have before in my career.

"Come and sit here," said I to the girl. "It's cold there."— She did, and we were all three in front of the fire, I in the middle. I gave her two glasses of wine without much effect. Sarah winked at me, half filled a tumbler with boiling water and lots of sugar and brandy. It was as strong as the devil but the sweetness disguised it. —"Here Harriet, take a good drop." She gulped it, Sarah and I took a little, then again the girl took large gulps. Soon her eyes brightened, and she giggled in the way girls are often affected, at the beginning of a lush, and before the stupid stage comes on.

Then Sarah raised her own petticoats to her knees, to let the warmth of the fire reach her bum, as the most modest woman will do if by herself, or with her female friends, or husband, present. "Let me see your new stockings and boots," said I, for I had given the money for them. She hesitated. "Shew them to the Doctor." The girl let me raise her petticoats to her knees, showing a thinnish but neat pair of legs.

I praised and stroked them. "Keep the petticoats up like your mistress, you see she likes the fire to get to her cunt." "Oho," said the girl, dropping the clothes. Sarah laughed — "I like to warm my cunt. What do you drop your clothes for, you little fool." I pulled up her clothes again, she let me, and we had more brandy and water. Then I felt Sarah's thighs, then gradually felt the girl's thighs. — "I don't care — *there*," said Sarah in answer to me, and she pulled up her clothes quite to her navel, put one leg up against the chimney-piece and, half turning round in her chair, shewed her cunt. "I like my cunt looked at — like it fucked — you've seen and fucked it many a time, haven't you, Doctor?"

Harriet stared, said "Oho!" and giggled, but resisted me, who was now trying hard to feel her. She was gradually getting screwed, and her resistance grew less as I insisted.

Then Sarah pulled out my prick, I felt Sarah's cunt, got Harriet on to my knees, and felt all about her limbs, and then was a confusion of baudy deeds and baudy talk. Sarah rose, winked at me, said she must go out, and in a minute had gone — I locked the door.

Harriet seated herself in Sarah's arm chair, I dropped on my knees, throwing up her petticoats, and saw that she had slight blackish hair at the bottom of her belly. I pushed between her legs and pulled them round me, and that brought her bum to the edge of the chair, and my prick which I had pulled out just touched her cunt. With a cry she got back, but she being in a sitting position, easily I pulled her to me again, my stiff prick now touching her thighs. She was now laughing a drunken laugh. "Feel my prick," said I, putting down her hand. — "Oh! oh!" said she trying to do so as if delighted. "It's my prick," said I. "Yes," she answered.

"Let me fuck you — come to the bed." "Oh, no! I can't." — "Have you ever been fucked — wouldn't you like it." She giggled, and had just sense enough left not to answer. I had now my hand between her thighs, was fumbling at her cunt, and she did not resist.

Then I got up, sat on a chair, pulled her on to my lap, held her back, and putting my prick in her hand felt her cunt, and kissing her said, "Let me fuck you." I got no answer, but she kissed me, grasping my cock. — Her eyes closed. — Saying "oh — don't sir, — oh don't" — in a thick stammering manner. "Did not you hear what Mrs. F**z*r said." "Oh, yes," and she held my cock so tight that she hurt me. Sarah had not left ten minutes.

I led her to the bedroom and without resistance got her on to the bed. There was a candle left alight. — Partly by gentle force and partly by entreaty, I got up her clothes and separating her legs tried to look at her cunt. She tried to rise and I pushed her back. Her head fell on the pillow. I lugged her to the side — "Don't — don't" — forced apart her legs and pulled open her cunt lips. — Drunk as she was, she resisted enough to make my look uncertain, but I saw that it was an opened split. Passion then vanquished me, I forgot my object in looking, her flesh looked so nice, the slight hair on the pretty little pouters made me beside myself — putting her straight on the bed again, I covered her without resistance, unconsciously she wanted fucking. The next instant my prick was lodged at the entrance.

"Oh you hurt — oh you mustn't — oh pray," was all she said.

I felt I had broken thro nothing, no obstacle had met me, yet I seemed to make but very little way. Thrust after thrust, further I entered yet but slowly. At length I was up it to its top and spending. A tight fit and no mistake if it was not a virginity. — Beyond "Oh! oh! don't" — not very loud, she had given no utterance of pain, and by the time my prick could go no further, and my balls were banging against her buttocks, she was quiet.

I had spent too excitedly, was she or was she not virgin? The thought was working. With prick up her still, I rose on my elbow to look at her and put my hand down to feel her cunt. By the light of the solitary candle, I could see no blood on my fingers. Just then she opened her eyes. "Oh I am so ill — I shall be sick, get away, sir, let me get up," said she in incoherent tones, and began to retch. I pulled out my prick, and with my shirt tail wiped the whole face of her cunt. Then I raised her up and got her a basin, into which she vomited. — "Oh my head, I am so ill." She kept moaning, I got her warm water and made her drink it, which brought up the remainder of the liquor. Then she fell back and fell asleep.

I looked at my shirt tail on which were spots of sperm, but no blood — I doubted if she were a virgin and resolved not to pay Sarah. Looking at her made me lewed again — I lifted her clothes and looked at her cunt, pulling wide apart her thighs, then put my finger up it — never had I felt anything so tight, even as the sperm rolled out round my finger. The little deaf one's cunt was loose by comparison. — Soon I mounted her, then she awakened but let me do what I liked. Again my prick went up inch by inch through her slimy tube, so tight was it, and enjoying it I consummated slowly. Stupid as she was, my prick roused her passions and she spent. She awakened to it, and gasped like a fish out of water.

Indeed I never saw a girl more agitated but in a peculiar way when spending. The majority of young ones are so quiet about it. But this girl's mouth opened, her eyes turned up till nothing but the white was visible, her lips quivered, and the next instant she seemed asleep. She had spent, but scarcely seemed to know it. Sarah just then came in and I told that she was not a virgin and should not be paid virginity price.

"I believe she is virgin, for all that — did you ever have a girl of that age with such a little quim?" "How do you know that," said

I. "I have seen it." "When?" Then came an account of doings which I have heard similarly before, and I believe it is much the way in which the elder female usually proceeds, when she wishes to seduce the younger.

Talking the night before with the girl about fucking, she had excited her by all the means in her power. — The girl, curious and finding her mistress so communicative, asked if it hurt at first, and was told sometimes, but so little as to be a mere imagination. That many women it didn't hurt in slightest degree, and that she could tell by looking at her cunt if it would hurt *her* or not. — That and the offer to show Harriet her own cunt settled the matter. She had shown the girl hers, and had looked at the girl's. Sarah admitted that she had not seen what is usually a virginity, but was nevertheless sure if the girl had been fucked with a prick of the ordinary size her cuntal opening could not be as small as it was. "If you fuck her much, I'll bet her cunt gets much easier."

"You must like looking at cunts." Sarah said she did, at the cunts of girls who had never had it, but — "I did at Harriet's for your sake as well as my own, for I want the money."

But I wouldn't pay but half, with which she was not at all contented. I was in fact angry and under the impression that she had tried to sell me. I liked my girl — there was a genuine freshness about her, yet at times I thought the girl was shamming. Why did Sarah hide her being gay from the first young lass, and ostentatiously proclaim it to this one? I afterwards thought. The game for this one was clearly not the same as for the other. But why when she knew that the hymen was not there, did she not tell me? Because she thought I shouldn't find it out. — "You are a downy card," said Sarah. "For all that I believe that the girl never has had a man put into her, don't let's quarrel, I'll send her away."

I did not want that and said I should have her again. — This conversation took place whilst Harriet was snoring on the bed with two spermatic libations up her. Sarah spiteful about the half fee said she'd wake the girl — was I not going? No, I would hear. Sarah did not seem to wish that. — To the bedroom we went. "To think of that little devil having been fucked," said Sarah, as she looked at her. Shaking Harriet, the girl sat up bewildered — the fume of the liquor still strong in her. "What are you doing on my bed?" said Sarah. Rubbing her eyes — "I don't know — Oh my head — Oh, I'm so ill." "Why, you have made a mess on my bed." "Oh I couldn't help it, I am so ill." "You have been on the bed with the Doctor — he has fucked you, you little bitch." No reply. "Hasn't he fucked you?" No reply. Another shaking, and the girl began to sob. "Hasn't he fucked you?" "I don't know." "You do, your clothes were up. — Hasn't he?" "I think so, but I don't know." "He has, and I will turn you out."

"Oh — Oh — Oh don't — you told me to let him do what he liked — Oh my head." "Yes, but I did not think you'd let him fuck you, at your age you little beast — how often did he do it?" "I don't know," said she blubbering. Then suddenly, "Oh don't hit me, I am going to be sick again" — and she went to the basin and retched.

It seemed cruel work — the tears and pain the poor girl was in. "It's my fault," said I. "Oh here he is," said the girl. "Tell mistress it arn't my fault." Sarah laughed. — "How often has he done it to you?" "I don't know. I was asleep. Oh don't let her turn me away sir, I am so comfortable here." — "I should think you are," said Sarah, "and to let him fuck you." "You told me to let him do anything." "I meant if he wanted to kiss you, and put his hand up your petticoats, and feel you — but who'd have thought of your letting him fuck you, at your age, you little beast." "I could not help it — Oh!" — and she tumbled back on to the bed.

We went into the sitting room, and saying that I meant to have the girl again I departed. The next night I was at Sarah's and, making no bones about the matter, said I wanted Harriet in the bedroom. Said Sarah, "It's funny, you come to see *me*, and yet want my servant, Doctor. — Well if you will, I suppose you must." The girl wouldn't come, so I pulled her gently into the bedroom.

I was thoroughly lewed, she sullen, had taken medicine, and what with that, the night before, and only having slept a drunken sleep, she gave so much trouble when I wished to look at her cunt, that I called in Sarah. — "You little fool," said she — "when a man has fucked you, you may let him do anything — let him see your cunt or anything else," and away she went.

The girl yielded. At the side of the bed, thighs distended, I opened her cunt whilst I held a candle to it.

Her love seat was that of a girl of full sixteen, an age at which I have seen but few. It looked long and delicate but with unusually pouting lips for her age. A strongish clitoris shewed and nymphæ full and thicker than usual. — Clitoris and nymphæ in fact, were much more developed than is usual in girls. (I wonder if that be a sign of a warm temperament.) The channel of coition was unusually small at the mouth, and I fancied looked as if it had been just torn or stretched at its upper part. — Was it that her hymen had only been partially destroyed, or stretched and opened, and had I completed the stretching? — Altho the membrane with a *small* hole was not visible when I first saw it, was there a membrane with a *large* hole? In the excitement of my first look and hurried fuck, I now could not be sure. She had a very full mons or mount with short thick hair but small in quantity on it, close to the top of the nick, and but a little way only down the lips. Altogether tho unusual in appearance, it was a pretty and libidinous looking, exciting cunt. There is a physiognomy in cunts, some are prettier than others, some more exciting to look at than others, tho it is difficult to say what it is in the appearance which excites in one more than in the other.

Tho I couldn't discern signs of hymenal rupture, on my putting two fingers up it she called out. Then lust stirred me to action, and pushing her on to the bed I entered her. Its feel was the same as on the previous night, and she said I hurt her. For about three hours I pulled her cunt about, for in her way she was a novelty. The deaf girl was a full grown child who would talk and fuck but not always spend. This girl was bursting with randiness, her young lusts were on with all their force. She soon took delight in everything I said or did, all was new to her, her lustful sensations were even new to her.

The look of a prick, the feel of its smooth skinned rigidity, its friction and lubricating overflow were all new to her, I believe absolutely new, spite of the absence of a hymen. So she took to all the preliminaries and exercises of love with delight and with the eagerness and ardour of a hot cunted one. I had not been deceived in my first impression about her. She was dying for the juice of the male, restless with lewed sensations, in the springtide of her lust, and under the urging of sexual curiosity — I had just caught her in time, and she with me revelled for weeks in unrestrained lasciviousness. If I had not had her, some one would. The first man who had kissed and fondled her might have felt her cunt, she couldn't have helped letting him; and once felt she would have let him do anything. Her warm nature was commanding her to surrender her person to the male. She was dying for a prick.

I took a fancy with her (I always have some special fancy with each woman) to lay in bed both of us start naked. Thin as she was I somehow liked this — tho why I am unable to say. How give reasons for any letch? There in clean sheets which I made Sarah provide (and indeed bought one new pair) we used to indulge in lewedness. Her slim young form pleased me much, and naked I used to cover her, or put her on the top of myself — fuck her belly to belly, or to bum, till I was satiated. These varied postures test whether the female is a hack or a greenhorn. If accustomed to salacity they fall into them readily, and in a way which cannot hide their knowledge whatever innocence they may allege, whilst the neophytes show an astonishment and quiet delight not easy to imitate and deceive. — "You can't do it so, Doctor." "Yes, we can try — see — there" — was said more than once during my varied performances with Harriet.

I had her frequently for more than two months, and it is certain that the mouth of the vagina, the site of the hymen, got bigger. Whether it stretched or split I can't say — but easier for my prick to enter, it certainly got. Inside it remained a tight sheath to my penis, tho quite elastic, and perhaps large enough for the greatest male cunt stretcher. I incline to think she never had a true hymen, or had broken it early in life, leaving a larger orifice than is usually found before male penetration. — I used to fancy that the mouth of the prick hole had opened gradually more at the top than elsewhere, but cannot pretend to assert that it was so. She told me that when about nine years old, she and another girl, a schoolfellow, used to push their fingers up each other's cunt. At all events I came to the conclusion that a prick had never been up her till she had mine.

Sarah, after I had once or so had Harriet, used to go out leaving us together, first asking me if I wished her to stay. She felt sure of her double pay and wished to make a little more out of doors — I often let her go. If she returned before I had left, she would tell me before Harriet if she had had a man — or two — or none, as the case might be; but she didn't any longer use baudy language before the girl, altho she had done so freely until I had fucked her.

— Then she grew impatient about keeping her. Hadn't I done with her. —"Take her away and keep her, I can't have her here much longer. She won't work, and it won't do to have a charwoman in whilst she is here."

It is one of the charms of life that the pleasures of women never tire. When weary of one, I change and all old pleasures come fresh again. — One woman you may best like to fuck on her belly — another with her bum to your belly, another to grope, then one to frig, then one to gamahuche. It is rarely that the entire round is equally pleasurable with one. — When I change, almost forgotten pleasures revive. So it certainly is with me. — With fresh cunt not only comes fresh courage, but fresh amusements. The variety depends on the difference in the sexual make and tastes of the woman, for all women cannot fuck so well in the same fashions. They also like men, have when their passions are fully evoked their own lascivities and letches. — The man who is well versed in amorous games, is sure to hit on that fashion of fucking which is best suited to both. This is most true of modest women, but in larger degree of gay women. — "Men are fond of variety, I like to see what a new man wants to do with me," said Sarah one night when we were talking.

One night Sarah was in the sitting room, I in bed with Harriet with my finger up the tight little cunt, when I thought I should like to feel Sarah's cunt. — I jumped out of bed and to the astonishment of Harriet brought in Sarah and made her get naked into bed. I laid between them and quickly had a middle finger up each cunt. Then I put my prick into one after the other and probed alternately, comparing size and feel, and discoursing on the effects of age, growth, and fucking combined, in enlarging and stretching a pudenda. However large a cunt it may be, it mostly sufficiently compresses the prick to make it spend. — Few exceptionally large cunted ones I have however known in this particular.

Harriet, who used to nestle up to me and feel my balls incessantly, asking many questions about fucking, and so on, was now quiet altho I did not then notice it. — Soon I thought I would fuck Sarah, and got on to her, she nothing loath. "I think it's time I had a turn," she said, after I had put my prick in her. I wanted to compare, so out I pulled it and got on to the little one, who had turned her bum towards us. When I had a few thrusts up her, then again

I put into Sarah, who was in a mood for pleasure, and we had a very voluptuous fuck. The girl had again turned her rump towards me.

I tried to pull her round — but she resisted, got out of bed, and ran into the other room start naked as she was. — "What's the little devil up to?" — said Sarah, who, also quite naked, followed her. — I went after them and there were we all start naked in the parlour. The girl wouldn't come back and made no reply. Sarah boxed her ears. — I swore. "You've done it to her," said Harriet. "You little bitch what of that," said Sarah. "He has a right, he would do it to me often if he had not seen you, blast you. You'll go out of my house, you shan't keep here." The young one was jealous, which was funny, and it both annoyed and amused me.

Sarah was slightly screwed, let out finely, and it took an hour to get things to rights again. Then in bed I began in Sarah and finished up Harriet, which terminated the night's amusement. I have had before a young girl, who grew ridiculously jealous of her mistress when I fucked her. — It was now late spring and light at nights, which interfered with my going to Sarah's lodgings. Then I went out of town and when I returned the girl was gone — Sarah said she had run away, that she would not work, was always frigging herself, and thought herself as good as her mistress. They had had words and the girl had bolted one night, taking her things with her. — I offered Sarah money to get her back. She said she tried, tho I don't believe she did. I never saw the girl again. — "I'm glad she's gone, for she is in the family way," said Sarah. "I don't believe it." "She is, she'd her courses on just before you had her, and hasn't since." "It's some other man." "None other has had her I'll swear." Had I done the trick again?

Some where about this time I went to the peep hole one day and found it closed. Perhaps as the baud once said to me it had been "blown upon." She may have caused that herself, may have slain the goose with the golden egg. It paid well, we began to find difficulty in getting the room, it was so often engaged. Too many knew of it evidently, and it no doubt was "blown upon."

Its rooms were arranged cleverly in every way, for the purpose of spying the temporary occupants of the back room; who whatever they did, and nearly wherever they placed themselves, could not escape observation, nor the glare of the gas which seemed to concentrate upon them. The partition at the peephole could not have been three quarters of an inch thick, so wide was the range of vision through it over the room. It was, I think, thicker in other parts, but we could hear well usually thro it. The way the hole was bored thro a dark spot in the pattern of the wall paper, the cork which filled the hole was colored to match, the way the pictures on each side could be raised and lowered, were all most cleverly managed. The house in a bye street which had but little traffic of any sort had only noise outside about every five minutes, and excepting then, we heard fairly the talk in the back room. It was not a swell bagnio, tho, and had but five available rooms. [I have since seen an equally well arranged house at Paris, where every word said by the performers could be heard, and everything seen.]

What I saw through the peephole had one special consequence. It satisfied me that my prick was a full sized one, and well beyond the average rather than less. — Out of a hundred which I saw, there were not as far as I could judge twenty larger than mine, and Sarah said there were not ten. I saw one or two Brobdingnagians, perfect battering rams, but the largest of all was the titanic shaft of the man who whacked Sarah's buttocks with it and knocked it hard on the table as well, tho its big plum shaped, swollen head was bare of foreskin, and was carmine with lust. Sarah said his was the largest she had ever seen, and that talking with others of her class who had also seen it, they were all of the same opinion.

But tho for some reason Sarah would not take that titanic, potential machine into her body, and tho I saw some Paphians' handle other Brobdingnagian tools hesitatingly and affect to think them too big, say they would hurt, and so on; they one and all *did* insert them in their cunts, and as it seemed to me with pleasure. I believe there never was a prick so big in any way that a cunt could not take it without pain, and even pleasurably. Its tip might perhaps knock at the portals of the womb too hard for some, but that is all. I have heard women say that the harder those knocks were the more pleasure it gave them. All the talk I have heard of pricks being so large that women could not, or would not, take them up them is sheer nonsense. Several women have told me so. Some said that they loved to see and handle big ones. None said that such stretchers gave them more physical pleasure than those of moderate size. The elasticity and receptivity of a cunt is in fact as wonderful as its constrictive power. The small prick of a boy of thirteen it will tighten round and exhaust, as well as one as big as the spoke of a cartwheel, and it will give pleasure to both equally.

CHAPTER II

Recherché eroticisms. — An outcome of the brothel spyhole. — An abnormal letch. — A man for a month. — Alone with him. — Mutual nervousness. — The ice broken. — Pricks produced. — An exiguous tool. — Unavailing masturbation. — Sarah's participation. — Cuntal incitation. — Prompt rigidity. — Onanistic operation. — Spermatic ejaculation. — Instantaneous copulation. — One on and one off. — A gorged cunt. — Masculine minetting. — A gristly mouthful. — Sucking cum fucking. — After supper. — Sarah's oration. — The end of the orgy.

Then took place the crowning act of my eroticism, the most daring fact of my secret life. An abnormal lust of which I have been ashamed and sorry, and the narrative of which I have nearly destroyed, tho according to my philosophy, there was and is no harm in my acts, for in lust all things are natural and proper to those who like them. There can be no more harm in a man feeling another's prick, nor in a woman feeling another's cunt, than there is in their shaking hands. — At one time or other all have had these sexual handlings of others, yet a dislike to myself about this sexual whim still lingers. Such is the result of early teaching and prejudices.

Twenty-four years had elapsed since my frolics with the first Camille. — Then I had frigged a Frenchman. Then I did the same with the man that big eyed Betsy got me. Then I'd felt the Captain in the dark at Lizzie M***d*n's. Since that I had not touched a male. What I witnessed through the baudy house partition put new inclinations into my head. The handsome pricks which I had seen women play with, the ease with which their doodles were handled, the ready way a girl brought a rebellious prick to stand and spend by coaxing it up in her mouth, etc., raised again desire to feel and play with a prick myself. Other men's seemed different to *me*, and at times I said this to Sarah in some such terms as these. — "I should like for once to feel a man's prick, to see closely his prick standing, see his spunk come out much or little." And so on.

The baudy house sights always terminated in fucking Sarah, and then for a time the desires which arose during my peeping ended abruptly. I talked about them at times when lewed nevertheless with Sarah, who said, "One man's prick stands and spends much like another, play with your own, but if you want, I can get one easily enough, and I'll let him come here for you, if Mr. F**z*r is out of town."

But I thought she meant a fellow who let out his rump and prick, and of that class I had an insufferable dislike and fear. They were I had heard thieves, their pricks used up, and I wanted nothing to do with an anus [at that time, not having found out the pleasure you both take and give by pressing the bumhole of a woman when fucking her] so for some months, altho she described some men as eligible, I would not see them.

At length in the winter she said, "My old woman (a crone who did her charring, and was in fact her servant altho she did not sleep in her rooms) can get a young man about twenty who's not a sod — he is a working man who has been without employment for two months and will be glad of a sovereign." I thought I was going to be sold, but as I had only promised her a sovereign for getting me a man, I came to the conviction that I had really a chance, so arranged that he was to go to her rooms.

But unpleasant notions came. A poor man! he will be dirty and smelling of sweat — be rough — his linen ragged. — To get over that Sarah said, "Give me a sovereign, he shall have a new shirt, and socks, and drawers, I will buy them" — so I gave that money.

The evening came. I felt so nervous and even shocked at myself that I wished I had never undertaken the affair. — It was in vain that I argued with myself, and spite of my conviction that there was no harm in my doing it, when I came to her door I nearly turned back. I had been trying to strengthen my intention by thinking over my former wishes and curiosities, of the various amusements I should have with him, and how much I should learn of the ways of a man, to add to the lot I knew about women. All was useless, I almost trembled at my intention. I entered, saw Sarah. "He is in the bed room — such a nice young man, and quite good looking, I never saw him till I went to buy the things." I said I felt nervous. "That is stupid, but you are not more nervous than he is, he's just said you were evidently not coming and he was glad of it, and would go." Again she assured me that he was all the charwoman had told, a young man out of work, wanting bread, and not a sodomite.

I followed her into the bedroom. Saying, "This is the gentleman," she shut the door and left me with him. He stood up respectfully and looked at me timidly.

He was a fine young man about five feet seven inches high, rather thin looking as if for want of nourishment, with a nice head of curly brown hair, slight short whiskers, no moustache, bright eyes, and good teeth. He was not much like a working man and looked exceedingly clean. "You are the young man?" "Yes sir." "Sit down." Down he sat and I did the same.

Then I could not utter a word more, but felt inclined to say, "There is a sovereign, good night," and to leave him. All the desires, all the intentions, all expectations of amusement with his prick, all the curiosity I had hoped to satisfy for months left me. My only wish was to escape without seeming a fool.

With the exception of the sodomite whom Betsy Johnson had got me, it was the first time I had been by myself in the room with a male for the clear intention of doing everything with his tool that I had a mind to. My brain now had been long excited by anticipation, and wrought up to the highest when this opportunity came, and every occurrence of that evening is as clear in it now as if it were printed there. Altho the exact order of the various tricks I played may not be kept, yet everything I *did* on this first night, all that took place, I narrate in succession, without filling in anything from fancy or imagination. I could even recall the whole of our conversation, but it would fill quires (and I did fill two or three). — I only now give half of it, and that abbreviated.

I sat looking at him for some minutes — I can frig him, thought I — but I don't want to now. — What an ass he will think me. — Why does he not unbutton? — I wonder if he is a bugger — or a thief. — What's *he* thinking about. Is he clean? — How shall I begin — I wish I had not come — I hope he won't know me if he meets me in the street. — Is his prick large? — These thoughts one after another chased rapidly thro my brain, whilst I sat silent, yet at the same time wishing to escape, and he sat looking at the floor.

Then an idea came. "Would you like something to drink?" "If you like, sir." "What?" "Whatever you like, sir." — It was an immense relief to me when I called in Sarah, and told her to get whiskey, hot water, and sugar. — Whilst it was being fetched I went into the sitting room, glad of getting away.

Sarah, in the sitting room, asked, "How do you find him?" — I told her I did not know and was frightened to go on. — "Oh! I would now, as you have had him got for you, then you'll be satisfied." — Again she assured me he was not on the town, and I need not be afraid. The whiskey was got, and behold me again alone with him. I made whiskey and water for myself and him and took some into Sarah. I began to ask him about himself. He was a house decorator in fine work, such work was at its worst just then, being a young hand he had not full employment, had been out of work nearly two months, he had pawned everything excepting what he had on. This all seemed consistent. He told me where he lodged, where he was apprenticed, the master he worked for last, the houses he worked at. "If you are a decorator your hands will be hard, and if you kneel your knees will." "Yes but I have had scarcely anything to do for two months, and but one day's work last week. Look at my nails." — They were stained with something he had used. Then he had had one day's chopping wood which had blistered both his hands, for it was not work he was accustomed to. Blisters I saw. There was evident truth in what he said.

This relieved me, together with the influence of whiskey and water. I got more courage and he seemed more comfortable, but not a word had transpired about our business, and an hour had gone. Then my mind reverted to my object, and I said, "You know what you came for." "Yes sir." He changed white, then red, and began to bite his nails.

My voice quivered as I said, "Unbutton your trowsers then." He hesitated. "Let me see your cock." One of his hands went down slowly, he unbuttoned his trowsers, which gaping, shewed a white shirt. Then never looking at me, he began biting his nails again.

The clean shirt, coupled with his timidity, gave me courage. "Take off your coat and waistcoat." He slowly did so. — I did the same, gulped down a glass of whiskey and water, sat him down by me, and lifting his shirt laid hold of his prick. A thrill of pleasure passed thro me, I slipped my hands under his balls, back again to his prick, pulled the foreskin backwards and forwards, my breath shortening with excitement. He sat still. Suddenly I withdrew my hand with a sense of fear and shame again on me.

"May I make water, sir, I want so badly," said he in a humble way, just like a schoolboy. "Certainly, take off your trowsers first." He looked hard at me, slowly took them and his drawers off, and stood with his shirt on. I took up the pot and put it on the chair (my baudy brain began now to work). "Do it here, and I'll look at your cock."

He came slowly there and stood. "I can't water now — I think it is your standing by me." "You will directly, don't mind me." The whiskey and excitement having made *me* leaky, I pulled out mv tool and pissed in the pot before him.

He laughed uneasily, it was the first sign of amusement he had given. Directly I had finished, I laid hold of his prick and began playing with it, I pulled back the skin and blew on the tip, a sudden whim that made him laugh, and his shyness going off, I holding his prick, he pissed the pot half full — I was delighted and wished he could have kept on pissing for a quarter of an hour.

The ice was now broken, I took off *my* trowsers, and then both with but shirts and socks on, I sat him at the side of the bed and began my investigation of his copulating apparatus.

"I want to frig you," said I. "Yes sir." "Has any man ever frigged you." — No living man had touched his prick since he was a boy, he declared. — Then I began to handle his cock with the ordinary first fucking motion.

I had scarcely frigged a minute before I wanted to feel his balls. Then I turned him with his rump to me, to see how his balls and prick looked hanging down from the back. — Then on to his side, to see how the prick dangled along his thigh. Then I took him to the wash stand and washed his prick, which before that was as clean as a new shilling, but the idea of washing it pleased me. Then laying him down on his back, I recommenced the fascinating amusement of pulling the foreskin backwards and forwards, looking in his face to see how he liked it. — He was as quiet as a lamb, but looked sheepish and uncomfortable.

His prick at first was small, but under my manipulation grew larger, tho never stiff. Several times it got rather so for an instant, and then with the desire to see the spunk come, I began frigging harder; when instead of getting stiffer it got smaller. I tried this with him laying down, sitting up, and standing, but always with the same result — I spoke about it. — He said he could not make it out.

His prick was slightly longer than mine, was beautifully white, and with a pointed tip. I made it the stiffest by gently squeezing it — I had had no desire in my own doodle, but as I made his stiff once when he was lying down, my own prick came to a stand, and following a sudden inspiration I laid myself on to his belly, as if he had been a woman, and our two pricks were between our stomachs close together. I poked mine under his balls, and forced his under my stones, then changing, I turned his bum towards me, and thrusting my cock between his thighs and under his balls to the front, bent his prick down to touch the tip of mine, which was just showing thro his thighs. But his prick got limper and limper, and as I remarked that, it shrivelled up. We had been an hour at this game, and there seemed no chance of his spending. No sign of permanent stiffness or randiness or pleasure. He seemed in fact miserably uncomfortable.

Then he wanted to piss again from nervousness — I held his prick, squeezing it, sometimes stopping the stream, then letting it go on, and satisfying my curiosity. That done, I made a final effort to get a spend out of him, by squeezing, frigging slow, frigging fast. Then I rubbed my hand with soap, and making with spittle an imitation of cunt mucous on it, titillated the tip. "I think I can do it now," said he — but all was useless. "It's no good, I'm very sorry, sir, but I can't, that is a fact. — I don't know how it is."

The last hour had been one of much novelty and delight to me, tho he couldn't spend; but the announcement disappointed me. It came back to my mind that he might be, after all that Sarah had said, but an overfrigged bugger, who could no longer come. For I had heard that men who let themselves out for that work at last got so used up that it was difficult for them to do anything with their own pricks, and that all they could do was to permit men to feel their cocks, whilst they plugged their arse-holes. So I repeated my questions, and he again swore by all that was holy that no man had ever felt him but me; and he added that he was sorry he had come, but the money was a temptation.

I laid him then again on the bed and felt his prick. We finished the whiskey, and I sent for more; and in a whisper told Sarah that there was no spunk in him. She brought in the whiskey herself, and laughed at seeing us two nearly naked on the bed together.

Then I asked him when he had a woman last, if he liked them, how he got them, and so forth. He told me that he liked women very much — sometimes he got them for nothing, and they were servant girls mostly. When at houses if servants were left in them, or even if the family were only for a short time out — young fellows like him often got a put in; or else made love to them, and got them to come out at nights. He warmed up as he told me this, and his prick began to rise, but on my recommencing to masturbate him, it fell down again. He declared that the woman he last had was ten days previously, when he gave her a shilling out of the trifle he had gained, and that he had never spent since. Then he began biting his nails, adding that he hoped I should give him the money, for he could not help not spending, and was desperately badly off — "I have had some bread and cheese, and beer, but I have not tasted meat for six days."

Three hours with him had passed, the frigging seemed useless, but talking about women had brought *my* steam well up, so I began to think of letting him go, and plugging Sarah to finish. "Sarah is a fine woman isn't she? Did you ever have her, or see her naked," I said suddenly, thinking to catch him. — She *was* fine, but he had never seen her in his life, until the day but one previously. — "Would you like to see her naked." Oh! would he not. I knew Sarah would do anything almost, so called her in, told her his cock would not stand, and that we wanted to see her naked. "All right," said she, and began to undress.

He kept his eyes ardently fixed on her as she took off her things — I remarked to him on her charms as she disclosed them. He said "Yes — yes" — in an excited way. Then he ceased answering, but stared at her intently. When her limbs and breasts shewed from her chemise, a voluptuous sigh escaped him, and he put his hand to his prick outside his shirt. Feeling him, I found his prick swelling. "Don't pull off yet Sarah." She ceased taking off her chemise. "Pull off your shirt." Helping him he stood naked with his prick rising. — "Now show us your cunt." Down Sarah lay (after stripping off her chemise) on her back, one arm raised and shewing her dark haired arm pit, her legs apart, and one raised with the heel just under her bum, the black hair of her cunt curling down till shut in by her arse cheeks, the red lined cunt lips slightly gaping. — It was a sight which would have made a dead man's prick stiffen, and mine was stiff at the sight altho I had seen it scores of times. I forgot him then, till turning my head I saw his splendid cockstand. — His eyes were fixed full of desire on her, and he was a model of manly, randy beauty. — "Is not she fine?" said I. "Oh! lovely, beautiful, let me do it," addressing her. "No," said I, "another time perhaps," and I seized his tool with lewed joy.

For an instant he resisted. Sarah said, "Let my friend do it, you came for that." I frigged away, he felt its effects and sighed — I frigged on and felt the big, firm, wrinkled ball bag. A voluptuous shiver ran thro him soon. "Oh! let me feel her — do." "Feel her then." Over he stooped. "Kneel on the bed." Quickly he got there and plunged his finger into her carmine split. Again I grasped his tool and frigged. He cried out, "Oh! I'm coming. — I'm spend — ing" — and a shower of sperm shot out, covering her belly from cunt to navel. I frigged on until every drop had fallen. Then letting go his prick, he sat down on his heels, his eyes shut, his body still palpitating with pleasure and now fingering his still swollen doodle.

The effect on me was violent. Sarah's attitude on her back at all times gave me a cockstand — it had stood whilst frigging him. — There she lay now, a large drop of his spunk on her motte seemed ready to drop down on to her clitoris, higher up on her belly little pools lay. Tearing off my shirt, scarcely knowing what I did, crying out, "Move up higher on the bed" — which he did, I flung myself on her and put my prick up her cunt. — My prick rubbed the spunk drop on her thatch, my belly squeezed the opal pools between us, the idea delighted me — I fucked away, stretched out my hand, grasped his wet prick, for he was now conveniently near me, and fucked quickly to an ecstatic termination.

The greater the preliminary excitement, the more delicious seems the repose after a fuck — the more it is needed, and I had had excitement enough that night. At length I roused myself. My cock did not seem inclined to come out of its lodging. I felt that

I could butter her again without uncunting. So keeping it in, I raised myself and looked at him sitting at the head of the bed, naked and still feeling his prick, which was again as stiff as a ramrod.

"He can spend after all," said I, my prick still up Sarah. — "I told you he was a nice young man." "Should you like to fuck her?" "Just give me the chance." The tale of the soldiers putting into each other's leavings came into my head. "Do it at once." "Lord," said Sarah, "you don't mean that." But I did. "Do it now." — I rose on my knees. — As I took my belly off of Sarah's, they were sticking together with his spunk. It made a loud smacking noise as our bellies separated. — My prick drew out sperm which dropped between her thighs. — As I got off, he got on, and as quickly put up her. The next minute their backsides were in rapid motion.

The second fuck is longer than the first, and I had time to watch their movements. — A man and woman both naked and close to me, were copulating — I could see and feel every movement of their bodies — hear their murmurs and sighs — see their faces. — There stood I with my own prick now stiff again watching them. — My hands roved all over them — I slipped my hand between their bellies — I felt his balls. — Then slipping it under her rump it felt the wet spunk I had left in her cunt, now working out on to the stem of his prick as it went in and out — I got on the bed and rubbed my prick against his buttocks. I shouted out — "Fuck her, — spend in her — spend in my spunk," — and other obscenities I know not what. — I encouraged his pleasure by baudy suggestions. A sigh, a murmuring, told me he was coming. My fingers were on his balls, and I let them go to see his face. He thrust his tongue into Sarah's mouth. — "You are spending, Sarah." — No reply. — Her mouth was open to his tongue, her eyes were closed, her buttocks moving with energy, and the next second but for a few twitchings of his arse, and their heavy breathings, they were like lumps of lifeless flesh. Both had spent. The fancy to do her *after him* came over me — my spunk — his spunk — her spunk — all in her cunt together. I will spend in her again. — The idea of my prick being drowned in these mixed exudations overwhelmed me libidinously. — "I'll do it to you again. — Get off of her." — "Let me wash," said Sarah. — "No." — "I will." — "You shan't. — He was getting off, she attempting to rise, when I pushed her down. — "It's wiser" — I didn't know what she said scarcely. — "No — no — no — I want to put into his spunk." — Her thighs were apart, her cunt hole was blinded, hidden by spunk which lay all over it and filled its orifice. I threw myself on her, my prick slipped up with a squashing noise — I know no other way of describing it. I think I hear it now.

I felt a sense of heavenly satisfaction. Her cunt was so filled that it seemed quite loose, the sperm squeezed out of her and up, until the hair of both our genitals were saturated — I pushed my hand down, and making her lift up one leg, found the sperm lay thick down to her arse hole — I called out, "Your spunk's all over my ballocks," and told all the baudy images which came across my mind. I told him to lay down by the side of us, and made Sarah feel his prick at the same time I did — I felt my pleasure would even now be too short and stopped myself. Sarah with a sigh cried, "Oh — my God — go on," her cunt tightened, she let go his prick and clasped my buttocks to her — I still held his prick, and tried to lengthen my pleasure but could not, her cunt so clipped me. Abandoning myself to her the next instant almost with a scream of pleasure, I was quiet in her arms and fell asleep — and so did she, and so did he — all three on the bed close together.

Awakening, I had rolled off close to Sarah on to my side, my prick laying against her thigh. — She lay on her back asleep, he nearly on his back. All three were nearly naked, myself excepted who had on an under shirt next my skin. — She had silk stockings and black merino boots on. My foreskin had risen up and covered the tip of my prick. In the saucer at the top was spunk which had issued from me after I uncunted. — The lamp was alight. Two candles (they had been short pieces) had burnt out, and the fire had all but expired. The room had been hot all the evening, for there were three of us in it, three lights burning, and the fire. Now it had got cold, and a sensation of chillness was over me.

I got up and looked at the pair. — She a splendid woman, firm and smooth skinned, and of a creamy pink tint — with the dark hair of her cunt in splendid contrast. He a fine young man with white flesh, and with much dark brown hair clustering and curling round his white prick, and throwing his balls into shadow. His prick still large was hanging over his thigh, the slightly red tip half covered by the foreskin pointing towards Sarah, and as if looking at it. Then sexual instinct made me pay attention to her. — She lay there with two libations from me, and one from him in her cunt. I desired to see how it looked and felt it, but was so distracted by my various erotic impulses that I cannot recollect everything accurately. — All I know is that I laid hold of her leg nearest to me, and watching, pulled it slowly so as to leave her legs slightly open. I put my finger down from the beginning of the cleft. It felt thick and sticky, yet but little spunk was to be seen — looking down towards the bum cheeks, I saw the bed patched in half a dozen places with what had run out from her — I thrust my finger up her cunt and she awakened.

She sat up, looked round, rubbed her eyes, said, "it's cold." Then she looked at him. "Why — he's asleep too, have *you* been asleep?" — Then she put her fingers to her cunt too, got off the bed, and on to the pot — looking at me smiling. — "You *are* a baudy devil and no mistake — I don't recollect such a spree since I have been out." "Your cunt's in a jolly state of batter." "It will be all right when it's washed" — and she proceeded to wash, but I stopped her.

He was snoring and had turned on to his back — his prick which seemed large lolled over his thigh. "He's a fine young man and his prick's bigger than yours, and what a bag," said she gently lifting up his prick and shewing his balls. I saw it was very large, as it had seemed to me when I squeezed and felt it before, but then I had been far too excited to notice anything carefully. Now I began to frig him as he lay. "I thought you had done me, for for two hours I could not make his cock stand." "Ah! it was nervousness. — He has never been felt by a man before, some would give ten pounds for such a chance and you are to give him a sovereign." "Do you think he can spend again?" "Yes, see what a lot he spent over me; if he was well fed, that young chap would be good for half a dozen pokes, he's been half starved for two months."

I gently laid hold of his prick, and pulled the skin down. One feel more and it rose to fullish size, and lay half way up his belly. "I thought it would directly you touched it from its look," said she. Said I, "I will frig him," and commenced in the slowest and gentlest manner, scarcely touching it. The stiffening began and the foreskin retired, the tip got rubicund and tumid, an uneasy movement of his thigh and belly began, and muttering in his sleep his hand went to his prick. — I removed mine. Soon his hand dropped by his side again, and he snored and muttered something.

Sarah, who had put on her chemise, then laid hold of his prick and frigged it. — "He can't spend, he's done too much already," said I. "I think he will tho." Then I, jealous of her handling, and lewdly fascinated, resumed the work. — Had he not drunk and eaten heartily, and been very fatigued, he must have awakened, but he didn't. Not spending, I spat on my finger and thumb, and making a moist ring with them, rubbed his prick tip through them. That did it. He muttered, his belly heaved, and out rolled his sperm, as he awakened, saying, "I've had a beastly spending dream, and thought I was fucking *you*." Seeing us laughing he seemed astonished, and was angry when told of our game. We all washed, we men put on shirts, and he got good humoured again.

I had scarcely eaten that day, felt empty and said so — Sarah said *she* was hungry, he that he could eat a donkey, for he'd not had food since the morning — I had never eaten in Sarah's lodgings, for the style didn't suit me, but felt that I must eat now. "Shall I fetch something at once? It's near midnight, and all the shops will be closed." — We had been five hours at our voluptuous gambols, but it did not seem half that time.

I gave Sarah money. She fetched cut beef and ham, bread, cheese, and bottled stout, and also whiskey. — Whilst she was away, he recovered his temper and felt his cock. He said he hated "beastly cheating dreams." "Are you fond of feeling men?" "It's much nicer to fuck a woman," I replied and told him that for many years I had never put finger on a prick but my own.

Spite of dirty knives and a dingy table cloth, we all fell to at the food. — He ate ravenously and told me that the last time he had meat, a mate gave him some of his dinner. I gave him a cigar, we had more whiskey and water, the room was hot again, we sat round the fire with our shirts only on — Sarah was dressed. — He told me again about himself, and soon the conversation drifted into the fucking line. He had lost his modesty and with it much of his respect for me. Instead of only answering and saying "sir" he began to ask me questions. Just as a woman's manner alters towards a man, directly he has once fucked her, so did his alter now that I had frigged him.

I asked if he liked being frigged. — No he did not like — "spending in the air" — did I? "No" — but I did such things at times Then Sarah alluded to his big balls, we both felt them, and such a large bag I have never seen before. He said the boys at school joked him about it. Boys know the sizes of each other's pricks.

I wanted to go on. The novelty was so great that I could not see and feel him enough; circumstances which I did not expect had brought Sarah into the fun, which increased the amusement. I am in the prime of life, and altho never attempting such wonders as some men brag of, can easily do my four fucks in an evening with a fresh woman, and sometimes more, altho then used up a little next day. I had now only spent twice and my prick seemed on fire. Wine, beer, and a full stomach soon heat a young man who has not spent for ten days. I pulled his prick about as we sat round the fire, and it readily swelled. He prayed me to desist, he'd had enough that night, but I had not. So I made Sarah take off her clothes to her chemise, and sit opposite. I sat next him smoking and looking at his prick, and feeling it at intervals.

Often in my youth, my prick has stood before my dinner was finished. A dozen times have I got up and fucked in the middle and finished dinner afterwards. — This meal began to tell on all. Sarah raised her chemise to let the warmth of the fire reach her legs, and showed her silk stockings and red garters. — "What a fine pair you have," said he — and down went his hand to his shirt. I saw a projection, and pulling up his shirt, there was his prick as stiff as ever.

"I'll frig you, and you look at Sarah's legs." He objected, had had enough of *that*, he would sooner fuck Sarah. — I had not brought him to fuck my woman — my letch was for frigging him. — Whilst this talk was going on I held his prick. Sarah showed us one of her thighs and told him to let me do what I liked — I had a stiff one and was dying to let out my sperm. I would frig him, and he should fuck her afterwards. A young man with a standing prick always thinks that there is enough sperm in it for any amount of fucking. — How often I have thought whilst my cock was standing and burning to be in a cunt what wonders I would do, and directly after one coition did nothing more.

I put Sarah on the bed, myself by her, him by the side of us on his back, and upside down; his belly so placed that his prick was near my shoulders, and I could conveniently feel it. His prick was throbbing with lust — I laid on Sarah with prick outside her and began frigging him. He sighed and cried out, "Oh! let me do it to her — do — oho — do." I meant to play with him long, but Sarah was lewed, placed her hand between our bellies and put my prick up her. — Then all went its own way. — If a woman means you to go on fucking when up her you can't help yourself. Without moving their bums, they can grip with their cunt muscles and grind a man's tool so that he *must* ram and rub. I was soon stroking as hard as I could, but holding my head on my right hand resting from the elbow, so as to see his prick which I went on frigging. It was a longer job than before, with all our lewedness and good will, for both of us. At length out came his sperm. At the sight of it out shot mine into Sarah, who responded with her moisture, and all was quiet.

We reposed long, then I got off. "Now you may have her." — Sarah washed. He laid on the bed, and after wiping up his now thin spunk from his belly, began frigging himself up. Sarah laid down by his side and let him feel her clean cunt, but it was useless; and after some violent fisting of his tool, he rose saying, "I'm done up" — and again we all sat down before the fire, smoking and drinking, and talking about fucking, the causes and the consequences thereof.

This talk went on for an hour or so. Sarah said jeeringly to him, "Why don't you have me." — Every ten minutes he frigged his cock uselessly. Then he ate more food. — Sarah went to the watercloset, which was in a yard, and dressed partly to go there, for it was cold. — His prick looked beautiful but lifeless. — My baudiness was getting over and I was tired, but thought then came into my head — a reminiscence of my frolics with French women. But tho I had done everything but one with Sarah, I did not suggest what was in my mind before her — I had a stupid lingering modesty in me. — We were both fuddled and reckless, and Sarah now down stairs. I locked the door, saying, "If you'll promise not to tell her, I will make you stiff enough to have her." He promised. — I laid him on the bed and putting his prick in my mouth began to suck it, first with the skin on, and then gently with the skin off. The smoothness delighted me. I no longer wondered at a French woman, who told me a prick was the nicest thing she ever had in her mouth. I did exactly as it had been done to me as nearly as I recollected; spit out after the first taste, and then went on mouthing, licking, and sucking. It took effect directly. — "Oh! it's as good as a cunt," said he. It was stiffened by the time Sarah came back. I went to the door and unlocked it, he had resumed his seat, then Sarah washed her backside and went back to her seat by the fire. He'd never had his cock sucked before.

We finished the whiskey — it was getting towards one o'clock — Sarah said, "It's time we got to bed — why don't you both stop all night? — it will be cold, for I have no more coals." The lamp was going out, and she went to the next room to fetch candles. When she came back, "If he is going to fuck you, he should begin," said I. "Yes, and I am going to bed whether he does or not." She stripped to her chemise and got into bed. "If you don't have her now, she is not to let you when I am gone, get outside the bed." — Sarah did. — With cock stiff he got on to her in a minute. I saw by a cross twist of his buttocks and a sigh that he was up her — Sarah gave that smooth, easy, wriggling jerk and upwards motion with her buttocks and thighs, which a woman does to complete the engulfment of a doodle — I put my hand under his balls. His prick up to the roots was up her cunt.

Then not a word was spoken. A long stroke ensued, and gradually after hard quick ramming, their last pleasure shewed itself. My randiness increased by watching him, I made him leave her cunt before he had well finished spending and again plunged my prick into her reeking, slippery, slimy vagina. I gloried in feeling their sperm upon me. I was not in the habit of giving Sarah wet kisses, but as I thought, I longed to meet her mouth with mine, and with our tongues joined, and hard thrusts, a pain in my pego, and slight pain in my arse hole, I spent, and Sarah spent. "My God I'm fucked out," said she.

It was three o'clock a.m. — eight or nine hours had I been in one round of excitement — I had frigged him three times and he'd fucked thrice — I had fucked six times — I had fucked in his spunk, and had sucked his prick — Sarah had been fucked quite eight times. How many times I had spent I did not then know, being bewildered with excitement and drink. — As Sarah got up she seemed dazed, sat in a chair, and said, "Damned if ever I had such a night, I'm clean fucked out." Then paying them I left. It was at our next meeting that Sarah said I had fucked her six times. In my abbreviation of the manuscript, I have omitted some of our lascivious exercises, which were in fact but a repetition of what I had done before.

I was thoroughly done up the next day, not only with spending but with excitement. My delight in handling his white prick in repose, half stiff and in complete rigidity, was almost maddening. The delight of watching his prick glide in and out of her cunt was intense. The desire and curiosity of twenty years was being satisfied. My knowledge of copulation and of the penis getting perfected. — Yet I went home in an uncomfortable frame of mind about what I had done with him. There was no one in my home just then to wonder at my being so late, to notice my excitement, or to question me, which was fortunate.

CHAPTER III

Unavailing repentance. — Gemini frolics. — Pricks between bellies. — I on him. — He on me — tip to tip. — Boots and stockings. — A lascivious triad. — Gamahuching all round. — A looking-glass got. — Genital manipulations. — Simultaneous fuckings and friggings. — I fuck, she sucks. — Variations on the same tune. — She on my prick sits. — He her clitoris licks. — Three on our sides together. — Amatory exercises with ropes. — Sarah's pudendal capacity. — An assault of two pegos. — Finger and penis co-operating. — Miscellaneous lascivities. — A scare in the street. — A scare at Sarah's. — A suggestive question. — Desires excited. — Heavy pay for an anus. — Sodomy cum onanism. — Fear, disgust, and hasty retreat.

I went home used up, but excited beyond measure. I could not sleep for thinking of having frigged a man. The smoothness of skin, the loose easy movement of the outer skin over the inner rod, and its whiteness — the gradual change in color of its plum shaped tip from pink to a deep carmine, the shooting out of his sperm, the voluptuous shuddering whilst he fucked Sarah, the saucers which came and went in his arse cheeks when he fucked, all danced before my eyes as I lay in bed, and I saw them as plainly as if the fucking was actually then going on. — Again her distended cunt lips, with the thick spunk oozing, my prick pushing between them with a squash, squeezing the spermatic mixture out on to my balls, and up to her motte, and gumming our hair together, my grip of his stiffened cock as I fucked her the second time; all filled me with an incredibly furious, baudy excitement, making my prick stiffen and throb, spite of my fatigue and preventing my rest.

Then came reflexion. — Had I really frigged a man — still worse — got my own prick wetted with the sperm of another man.

Above all sucked his prick! — An act I had certainly heard of being done by men to each other, yet all but disbelieved, and looked on as a very foul action — yet I had done it, had enjoyed it all. Much as I had done and seen before, I was not quite easy in my mind, spite of my philosophy that any sexual enjoyment is permissible — that our organs of generation are for our own use and pleasure, and that what men and women choose to do together they have a right to do, it concerning no one else. Such are the results of prejudices and false education. It ended in reflecting that I never had intended to do those things, that opportunity had let me unwittingly to do them, and resolving that I would never do it again, I fell asleep.

Next morning at breakfast I thought, "That debauch will never be renewed." After luncheon, "What was the harm after all." Then I began to think I should like to feel him once more, to watch the phenomenon of the spend more coolly and philosophically. — Once more to make him spend, and to watch his prick from its stiffening to its shrinking. To watch his face and see how pleasure affected it. Why should I not bring him and Sarah naked together as I had done and see his prick rise, let him fuck her, and watch as I did last night — surely there is no harm — or not more than in looking at such doings through a spyhole. — The man is clearly not a sodomite, or he would not be so ready to fuck her. He is out of work, and probably is what he says he is. It is a chance which never may come again to me.

I thought of the double fuck without the washing, of the prick in my mouth, and then felt ashamed. — "I must have been screwed and so excited that I did not know what I was about, I shall never do *that* again, and hope he won't tell Sarah." I then took a gallop, determining again to get him. I had slept so badly on the previous night that on my return I laid down. My mind wandered to his prick and what Sarah called his purse. I wondered if his prick was really bigger than mine and wished I had measured it — I wondered if he spent more or less than me, and many other things; and at last came to the conclusion that I ought to be ashamed of myself, and being empty in stomach and fatigued, said, "I have done with that business." — Then I went to my club, had dinner, desire to see him again then came back, and soon I was with Sarah arranging for another meeting.

Said she, "You'd a pretty good night, I declare that if I were to tell some women what we did, they'd only believe part of it. — He wanted to sleep with me." She dare say he would come again willingly, she would go and see — I gave her money to buy him trowsers, cravat, and collars, said that he was to take a bath, and also gave her money to feed him well — Sarah met me out an hour afterwards. He would be there the following night.

She had done all I wished, and the fellow looked as spruce as possible — I was again nervous, and so was he, but a few minutes' conversation put us at ease. — We stripped, and behold us close together, I holding that handsome tool of his. He asked if Sarah was coming, but I did not want her then, and sat with his balls in my hand, for a time thinking of the size and fullness of the scrotum.

Of the sovereign — he told me that he first paid fifteen shillings for rent, and the rest where he owed money — that Sarah had got him good food, — that he had not spent since that last night. "When I thought of it all, I got to want it," said he.

Then I washed his genitals and made a complete and curious examination of his penis and scrotum, and had more complete quiet pleasure crowding in that than on the previous occasion. Before when feeling his prick it did not make me randy — tonight it did. My examination began to tell on him, and when I had pulled the foreskin once or twice up and down, his rod was stiff. Then up stiffened mine. — I began frigging him. — "Now I will look at your sperm as it comes." Suddenly he laid hold of my prick. — "Hullo, don't do that."

He relinquished it begging pardon, saying he did not know what made him do it. — My pulling *his* about seemed quite a proper thing for *me*, for I paid him for it; but directly *he* touched *my* prick, I felt disgusted. — The mind is an odd thing — if a gentleman had felt me, should I have been equally shocked?

This preliminary was soon over, he was on the point of discharge when I stopped, and making him sit down, watched his stiff prick gradually droop, and then I went at him again and so on. If a copious discharge is to be got out of a man, that is the way to do it. — At length after playing so for long, he said he must and would come — so I frigged as fine a spermatic ejaculation as I had had on the first night. It spurted out a yard, quite.

I had intended not to let Sarah appear that night, but feeling his cock had made my cock stand. "I'll frig myself," I said. But I hated spending in that fashion. — After trying to restrain myself till I could do so no longer, I called Sarah. She was dressed. Throwing her on the side of the bed, up went her clothes, and I put up her, he looking on. Up came his prick again at the sight. — He asked to have her, but I wouldn't let him, and handled his tool whilst I fucked her.

I carried out my intentions, frigged him four times, and had no end of amusement with him. — I had a taste that night for rolling over him as if he were a woman, when his cock was stiff, and making mine stiff, and laying the two pricks together. I tried all sorts of ways of making his stand. Sometimes by pulling the skin up and down, sometimes by shaking the top — now by giving it a rude pinch — now by squeezing his balls. I tried every way which I could recollect women had used on me, or I had heard or thought of. There was now no difficulty about it, for his cock kept standing after very small handling; and he had still sperm, tho getting at each discharge less in quantity and thinner. At his fourth discharge all was over, but there were still things which I wished to do with him. One was to put his prick in my mouth. Again I rubbed my lips on its smooth white stem, and kissed it, and all but put it in. — But I never will do that again, thought I to myself.

The amusement however seemed incomplete without Sarah. Again I fucked her, and then let *him* do it to her. That was a very long job and finished the evening, and him.

Afterwards. Each meeting I thought would be the last, yet I had him again. Sarah participated in the amusements regularly. The evening did not seem complete without the two. I was infatuated. — Of course four discharges a night could not be kept up, but I did not see him every night. — But as much spunk as could be got out of him I got, pumping him pretty dry with my fist, and myself as well, but into Sarah's cunt. I now tell only some of my amusements, and as near as may be in the succession in which they took place. They could not all be done on one evening.

My baudy imagination being set to work, all sorts of possibilities came into my head. We soaped well our pricks, and under our balls and arse furrows. Then lying on the top of him, we thrust our pricks under each other's balls, and working in the soapy furrows, both spent on each other's backside. — It was not convenient, our pricks rebelled at being so bent and thrust, but the novelty made up for the inconvenience. — Novelty stimulates desire. — I got much amusement from lying on the top of him, when our pricks were not stiff, and feeling the testicles and two cocks in a bunch together. Sarah, then quite delighted, felt our intermingled genitals. Then I put him on the top and myself beneath, Sarah held a looking glass and candle, so that I could see when on my back two ballocks in a heap together. Sarah was delighted with all my lasciviousness and said she never knew such a baudy man as I was.

One day standing up I soaped both our prick tips and we frigged ourselves. We put the two tips so close that they rubbed together, and we spent against each other's glands.

These lascivious vagaries and delicacies did not suggest themselves all at once. Firstly my delight was to watch his face as he spent, then to see the prick stiff, the sperm shoot, the tremulous shaking of his backside, and to hear his quiet murmurs of pleasure. After I had had enough of that, I betook myself to more fanciful amusements.

Spite of myself, my mind recurred to the feel of his prick when in my mouth, and altho I vowed to myself never to let it go into it again. — Yet why? thought I at length. Have you not licked a cunt? Have you not had the fresh warm piddle squirt against your face from Sarah's cunt? — Have you not savoured the salt liquor which distils from and keeps moist a woman's cunt? Nay. Have you not when moistened till almost running out, by its sweating (so to speak) under the action of your tongue on her clitoris, shoved your tongue up her cunt, and brought it back into your mouth with delight and ecstasy at giving her pleasure? Is the putting into your mouth a prick, dry, clean, and smooth as ivory, worse? — But it's a man's. In her mouth a prick is quite proper. He may lick, tickle, and suck her hole, that's quite natural. But a man's! — No I won't.

For all that, one night whilst feeling it, when he had washed after I'd first frigged him, I again washed it carefully, and laid him on the bed. There hung his prick and his testicles, the tip just covered by the prepuce. As I pulled back the foreskin, I put out my tongue and tickled the top. "Your tongue is on it," said he laughing. — Then I took it in my lips. It was like ivory. I longed to minette with it, and passed the limp, soft, flexible tool entirely into my mouth: not a bit was outside. — It went back towards my gullet and there I held it, till it began to swell. I passed it up and down in my mouth, licked and sucked it, put it out and let it stay till it drooped, then remouthed it, and continued this for a long time. At length his sperm had been so accumulated by the dalliance that he said he could bear it no longer and would frig himself if I did not. I then brought it up to the spending throb, pulled it from my mouth, and finishing with my hand, his spunk shot up. There is nothing like coaxing a prick a long time, for accumulating the spunk in the reservoirs of concupiscence. I'm sure more comes then, than from a hasty frig.

Then I fucked her before him, then sent her out, and again sucked his prick which was in powerful order — I laid him on the bedside in the attitude most convenient to lick a cunt, and so that I might see his face whilst I operated. It is easy in a man's face to see when his ballocks are about to send forth their juices. — A red Indian, they say, can preserve his features when being tortured. I doubt if he could when spending. — A man's face then is rather stupid, nor is that of a woman's, as she is holding tightly to her fucker's backside for the full engulfment of his throbbing cock in her cunt, highly intellectual; but it's much more lovely than that of a man's face.

I offered him money to suck my prick. He would not, and that night's amusement ended. Then much to his delight I began to let him fuck Sarah. Whilst they were doing that trick, I handled his balls, put my hand between their bellies, made them turn over on to their sides and lift their legs in all sorts of ways, so that I might see the movement of the prick and the swell of the lips of her orifice. — I made him fuck her standing up, then on the side of the bed, whilst with a candle I moved round them, satisfying my curiosity. Then I fucked her and made him similarly satisfy himself. He was delighted to grasp my balls whilst my prick was pistoning her. — Modesty and timidity had now left all of us. — Unrestrained libidinous enjoyment was everything to us, each doing the best to stimulate each other's lust. Sarah had become more active, suggestive, and libidinous than we two. She delighted in it.

My libidinosity increased by indulging it. I longed to see ourselves in the various attitudes. — Sarah's table glass was small, and having placed it so as to get a glimpse of ourselves, and finding it unsatisfactory, I bought at a broker's shop, a long, large old-fashioned looking glass in a mahogany frame. We together nailed it up against the wall at the level of the top of the mattress, and so that we could see ourselves from head to foot as we lay. Then our sensual delight was doubled, for as we fucked, or frigged, or sucked, we could look in the glass, and talk about our attitudes.

One night all three highly strung — I was near her, he by her side on the bed. "Oh look at his prick." "Ah! it's not stiff — he'll spend." "Frig it, frig him Sarah." She did. "Are you coming, Jack." "Aha." "Yes — my spunk's coming." "Oh fuck me, fuck me," cried Sarah, or "I'll frig myself." "Stop, Sarah, I'll fuck you," and I put my prick up her. — She grasped my rump with one hand, with the other grasped his prick, and so did I. Both Sarah's and my hand were on it. Sometimes she had the stem, I the scrotum. Just before *we* spent out spurted *his* spunk. Then as we felt it, we poured out our sexual tributes, a spasm of libidinous sympathy fetched us both together.

I began then to pay for his baths, his food, and fine linen so that he came perfect from head to toe. He had no hair on his body, excepting on his prick and armpits, and but little on his face. — What with idleness, good living, and baths, he became as smooth as ivory and as nice to feel as the nicest woman. He got in a fortnight plumper, altho I took so much semen out of him; but he was young and strong. — What pleasure for him! — The only annoyance to me was that his prick, when he got randy and it stood, had a strong smell. — The smell of most cunts I like.

After I had sucked him that night, I never repeated it but once. — Altho we had lost all modesty, I did not like Sarah to see all, until late in the evening when whiskey and baudiness told on me. Whatever we did together, I never lost sight of my principal object, which was to frig him, and see either his tool or his face when he was spending. — When Sarah came in, at first we used to sit round the fire drinking and smoking, all as naked as the weather permitted. Sometimes he told his adventures with servants in the houses where he had worked, she about what men had done. The conversation always was erotic. — Until the spirit moved me to action, I usually sat by him in an easy chair, with his tool in my hand. Sometimes he laid hold of mine. "Look at you two feeling each other's pricks," Sarah would say, with a toss of her head. — "Shew me your split, and see if it will give his cock a rise." — She would show it gaping, and his cock would rise. Perhaps he'd kneel in front of her, fingering her cunt, or licking it, whilst she cocked her leg up to facilitate his work. At times both *his* and *my* fingers were up her cunt at the same time, and fifty other baudy tricks we did.

I had now made Sarah suck my prick, but I disliked still to tell here that I had had *his* prick in my mouth; yet one evening did so. Behold us soon all three on the bed, *she* with *his* prick in *her* mouth, and *he* with *my* prick in *his* mouth. I feeling about *her* cunt and *his* balls, as well as the difficult attitude permitted. Another night we followed it up, by his laying on the bed and she kneeling over him with his prick in her mouth, her backside over his feet, and I at her backside fucking her — I alone could plainly see this in the looking glass, and a most delicious sight it was.

My most satisfactory amusement, I think, was frigging him whilst I fucked her. I used to lay him down so that his prick was well within reach of my hand and in view whilst I did so. At times Sarah laid her head on his chest or his belly, as a pillow, he laying across the bed, and then his prick was just by my shoulder. Then putting my hand up I frigged him. At other times, laying partially on his side with his legs up against the wall at the bed head or near her head, his prick was equally close to me.

Once his tool looked so beautiful that it seduced me entirely — I had again vowed to myself that having had his prick in my mouth and felt it swell within it from flabbiness to a poker, under my lingual pressures, I would never do it again. — But now lying with my prick up Sarah, my left hand under her smooth backside, my right round his prick; my pleasure coming on I could not resist it, and engulfed his stiff cunt-rammer in my mouth. My backside was then oscillating, his hand could just reach my arse and he was feeling my balls. I felt he was near his crisis, withdrew his prick, and at that instant out shot his sperm, just between Sarah's naked breast and mine.

Instantly, for such was the lascivious effect, Sarah and I mingled our mucilages in her cunt. I never had his prick in my mouth afterwards.

He got fond of Sarah and constantly besought me to let him have her. Then after I had frigged him, we would all three sit round the fire. "Shew us your cunt, Sarah?" — She'd open her legs so that the article was visible. I watched his prick, which perhaps hanging down lazily between his thighs immediately at the sight of her gaping cunt would gradually thicken until it looked like a short roll of ivory. Then it rolled on one side as if to get away from the big balls. Then with a throb straightened somewhat, its top still pointing downwards, and the little red tipped orifice beginning to show more out of the foreskin. Then it gave a throbbing knock or jump against his thigh and proudly lifted his head, and with other throbs in succession stood grandly stiff against his belly, and the prepuce gently slid off, leaving uncovered two thirds of a deep crimson knob. Then I would gently pull up and down the skin with a slow motion, pleased at the involuntary action of his prick, caused by the mere look of a dark haired cunt. "Let me fuck her — don't frig me this time, you have frigged me enough. — Oh! do let me put into her." Then I let him feel her cunt, and his lust goaded to the utmost, he would sigh and groan almost and lick her cunt. Then I let him have her, or had her myself and frigged him whilst up her. "And so we passed the pleasant time, as well we could, you know, in the days when we were randy arsed a long time ago."

One night, I sat her on my prick whilst I sat on a chair, her bum against my belly, her cunt outwards. — In a looking glass, my ballocks then almost seemed to hang from the arsehole end of the cunt. He knelt down and licked her clitoris whilst I fucked her. Sarah enjoyed the double action, and spent murmuring her lewed sensations; clutching his head, whilst I held her round her haunches tightly, my fingers on the hairy motte. In that position I could only ram gently up her. When she'd spent, he fell back on the floor and frigged himself looking up at her cunt, my prick still up her, and the sperm running out on to my balls, as my cunt plugger slowly left her.

I was slim and supple as an eel. I would on the bed put into Sarah, and then we would both turn on to our sides belly to belly, keeping our privates coupled. Sarah would throw over me her uppermost leg, so as to open her bum furrow, and he laid on his side with his belly close to her rump, thrusting his prick forwards. — The tip would just touch the end of her slit, which was nearest to her bum hole; rub in the furrow, and touch the bottom of my prick as it lay engulfed in her. Then we all began fucking together. I ramming up her, he rubbing his prick up against our coupled genitals, which he had bedewed with saliva. We never hid our pleasures —

I would cry out when coming — Sarah would murmur her pleasure, and he the same. The three voices blended whatever baudy, stimulating words fell from us. "Oh! fuck — cunt — spunk — oh — I am coming — I'm spending — spunk — ballocks — aha — ahre" — I spent up her, he against her furrow and the stem of my prick, or over my balls, or against her arsehole or thigh. If the rubbing against our flesh didn't fetch his sperm, he brought himself to a crisis with his hand, and at the last moment put his prick against her flesh and spent somewhere.

One night as he was tailing Sarah, I felt his hard, wrinkled, full, large scrotum, and slipping my fingers further up, let his stiff lubricated shaft slip through my fingers as it worked up and down her cunt. Then reversing my hand so that his prick rubbed against the back of it, I slowly glided the middle finger up her cunt. "What are you doing," said she.— "Feeling up." — She said no more, the lasciviousness of the act pleased her and him, the whole length of my finger was up her side by side with his prick, whilst he was fucking. His prick glided over my wet finger as they spent together. I had already fucked her, was cool and collected, and noticed the tightening of her cunt as she spent, in a way I never had in any woman; for clear observation of the muscular action of a woman's cunt, at the supreme moment of spending, is impossible; tho my prick is conscious of its constriction.

I did that more than once. Sarah's, altho one of the most delightfully compressive cunts, was undoubtedly largish. — Once she allowed us to try to get both pricks up her together, but we could not manage it.

[It is difficult, even with two very rigid tools to do *that*, for I and another man have tried it since with a woman. But such is the distensibility of a cunt that I'm sure it *will* take two pricks at once.]

Then we reversed our position, and I pushed from behind and spent against *his* balls, whilst he fucked *her*. I liked to vary my pleasures, and when away thought of what I had done, and arranged variations of the fun for our next meeting.

[What whims and caprices lust generates! I have often thought how absurd the following part of my narrative seems, but the deed didn't seem at all absurd to me then.]

Bringing both pricks into use at the same time pleased me much, the difficulty was that our legs got in the way. After thinking how to obviate this, I put a big hook in the ceiling, and a rope hanging from it with loops at the bottom. Into a loop Sarah put her upper foot, and that slung her leg out of the way. Sometimes he put his foot so. Such ingenious devices voluptuous pleasures led me to. They have seemed ridiculous since, but delighted us all immensely at the time.

Afterwards I put up a second hook and rope, at such distance apart that Sarah could easily put through them her legs up to her knees, and she laid for ten minutes at a time with her legs in the air so distended that her cunt gaped wide. We saw her cunt and anus peeping out from under it. — When in that position I fucked her. Before that we men stood and admired her exposure, feeling each other's pricks, and in the looking glass admiring ourselves in the baudy postures.

I made *him* another time fuck her whilst her legs were slung up, and as soon as his prick was out I investigated her cunt and saw his sperm in it. I find now nothing objectionable in semen — that essence of love.

Whilst I fucked her in that position, I once made him kneel over her with his backside towards me and his prick in her mouth. Then I recollect for the first time that I noticed his anus.

Soon after I had him, I took a fancy to see him in silk stockings. He put on a pair of Sarah's, which so pleased me that I bought him a pair, and a pair of kid boots. I never had him afterwards without them. When on the top of Sarah, with legs together in silks and boots alike, altho the male leg is different from the female, I could scarcely tell which was which, from heels to rumps. But the split and the spindle shewed the difference in the sexes.

Once I made Sarah lay on the top of me and do the fucking, whilst he squatted on her back. So placed I frigged him. Some of his sperm came on to Sarah's hair and made her angry. Sarah didn't mind being spent over anywhere excepting her head. Some of his spunk fell on my face, and I did not like it.

During one period of this erotic frenzy, being as it happened by myself in town alone, I was there nearly every night. My curiosity was insatiable. I would sit on a footstool with my head between his legs, and ear resting against his ballocks — I made the two stand up belly to belly touching, whilst I laid down between their legs and looked up at their genitals, sat with my face against his balls, and his prick up against my nose, whilst Sarah delicately tickled *my* prick with her mouth. I pissed against the tip of his prick, and in brief did every fantastic, erotic, frigging, feeling, tickling, skinning, coaxing, sucking tricks to his rod and balls that I thought of, and always with delight. At last always seeing the tip get redder, the rod stiffen, and the gruelly sperm jet out of it.

Sarah said, — "You've ruined that chap. He can now get work and won't." — I had then seen all I wanted, and also felt offended with his familiarity; told her I would not see him again, and then he would go to work. "He won't, I am sure." — But I kept away, and whilst doing so recuperated, for I'd knocked myself up a little with this lascivious excitement. I saw one day somebody like him in the streets, which frightened me, although I had never allowed him to see me with my hat on. When I wrote to Sarah and she met me at a house, she said he was sad at not seeing me, and she had told him I was out of town. — "Have you ever buggered him?" she asked suddenly. The question revolted me, such intention had never once entered my head, had never even occurred to me.

Two or three days after I was again alone in town, and awakened with such lewedness that had my grandmother been in bed with me, I believe I should have gruelled the old lady's quim. Tossing about, and resisting frigging myself, the baudy amusements had with him and Sarah kept running through my mind; and altho I had vowed to myself never to see him again, the desire to do so became overwhelming, and I wrote to Sarah to get him.

The evening came, and how strange! I felt part of my old nervousness. — He put on his silks and boots, which Sarah kept. — At the sight of his white flesh, and roly poly pendant, mine stood upright. We stripped. I pressed his belly against mine, grasping him round his buttocks (he was smooth as a woman), and his prick rose proudly at once.

I handled his prick, pleased with the soft feel of the loose skin. — "Fetch me, or I'll frig myself, I shall spend a pail full" — I wetted both our pricks and bellies with soap and water, then putting him on his back on the bed, mounted him. Our pegos were pressed between our bellies, and grasping each other's rumps, and shoving our pricks about as well as we could, the heat and friction drew both our spunks, and we lay quiet till our tools shrunk down over our balls, forming a heap of testicles and pricks.

Then came a dislike to him and disgust with myself that I often had felt recently. But it vanished directly, I felt lewed again and when I felt his cock. It was stiff soon. As he finished washing it he turned round, and I saw it thick and swollen. Just then Sarah rushed in and prayed me to go. "Do, oh do pray, or there will be a great row — for God's sake go." She was much agitated, I had never seen her so before. "You must — you shall go, — or I shall be half ruined." Yielding, I went as quickly as I could, and he did after me, I heard.

Next night I saw her out, and could get no explanation about her agitation; but she told me I could not go to the house for a week or ten days.

What gave me about that time such hot fits of lust it is not easy to say, but I was in full rut. At times a fellow's prick stands much more than at others, sometimes it is idleness, sometimes stimulating food, sometimes strength. For some days before I saw him again my prick stood constantly, I was again alone in town, and why I did not ease it by fucking don't recollect — Sarah I could not see any where, and I did nothing but think how I would frig him, and tail her, when we met.

When at length we met, he told me he had not spent since I'd made him. Laughing, Sarah said, "The beggar wanted to have me, but I wouldn't let him." Perhaps a lie — I touched his cock which sprang up stiffly at once. He stripped, and his red tipped, white stemmed sperm spouter would have fascinated any woman — I undressed, my cock stiff as his, and libidinous frolics began.

"Have you buggered him" — Sarah's question came suddenly into my mind as I handled his throbbing prick, his rigid piercer. "Fetch me, frig me, then *you* fuck Sarah and let *me* fuck her after — go on — I'll frig myself — I must spend" — said he, and began frigging.

I stopped him. I put him in various attitudes and looked at his naked rigidity — feeling it, kissing it, glorying in my power — with my own prick upright. Both were wanting the pleasure sorely, yet I dallied and my brain whirled with strange desire, fear, dislike, yet with intention. Then I placed him bending over the bed — his bum towards me, his head towards the looking glass — I stood back to look. There were his white buttocks and large womanly white thighs, his legs in silk, his feet in feminine boots. — No one could have imagined him a man, so round, smooth, white, and womanly was his entire backside and form. It was only looking further off that I missed the pouting hairy lips, and saw a big round stone bag which shewed the male. His prick was invisible, stiff against his belly.

I closed on him, put my hand round and gave his prick a frig — his bum was against my belly. — "Fetch me — oho — make haste, I'm bursting" — looking down I saw his bumhole and the desire whirled thro my brain like lightning. Without pausing or thinking, I felt his prick from under his balls, and whilst he almost shivered with desire — "Oh! make haste, fetch me" — I put both hands round him, feeling his balls with one, his prick with the other; and my own stiff prick I pressed under his ballocks, saying, "Let me put my prick up your bum."

"That I won't," said he disengaging himself and turning round, "that I won't."

Furiously I said, "Let me — I'll give you ten pounds." "Oh no." "I will give you all I have" — and going to my trowsers I took out my purse, and turned into my hands all the gold I had — it was, I think, more than ten pounds.

"Oh no, I can't, it will hurt," said he, eying the money. "It won't." "It will. When I was apprenticed, a boy told me a man did it to him, and it hurt him awful."

I don't know what I replied — but believe I repeated that it would not hurt, that it was well known that people did it, and as I talked I handled his prick with one hand, with the other holding the gold.

"It *will* hurt — I'm frightened, but will you give me ten pounds really?"

I swore it, talked about that of which I knew nothing — that I had heard it was pleasure to the man whose arsehole was plugged — that once done they liked nothing so much afterwards. His prick, which had dwindled under fear, again stiffened as I frigged, he ceased talking and breathed hard, saying, "I'm coming." — I stopped at once.

"Let me." "I don't think you can, it seems impossible — if you hurt me will you pull it out?" "Yes yes, I will."

He turned to the bed again and kneeled, but he was too high — I pulled him off — then it was too low. Again on the bed and I pulled his bum to the level of my prick, I locked the door, I trembled, we whispered. I slabbered my prick and his hole with spittle. His prick was still stiff. There was the small round hole — the balls beneath — the white thighs. — I closed on him half mad, holding him round one thigh. I pointed my prick — my brain whirled — I wished not to do what I was doing, but some ungovernable impulse drove me on. Sarah's words rang in my ears. I heard them as if then spoken. My rod with one or two lunges buried itself up him, and passing both hands round his belly I held him to me, grasping both his prick and balls tightly. He gave a loud moan. "Ohoo I shall faint," he cried. "Ho, pull it out."

It's in — don't move or I won't pay you, or something of that sort — I said, holding myself tight up to him. "Ohooo, leave go, you're hurting my balls so" — I suppose I *was* handling them roughly — but his bum kept close to my belly.

I recollect nothing more distinctly. A fierce, bloody minded baudiness possessed me, a determination to do it — to ascertain if it was a pleasure — I would have wrung his prick off sooner than have withdrawn for him, and yet felt a disgust at myself. Drawing once slightly back, I saw my prick half out of his tube, then forcing it back, it spent up him. I shouted out loudly and baudily (Sarah told me), but I was unconscious of that. She was in her sitting room.

I came to myself — how long afterwards I cannot say. — All seemed a dream, but I was bending over him — pulling his backside still towards me. — My prick still stiff and up him. "Does it hurt now." "Not so much."

His prick was quite large but not quite stiff. A strong grip with my hand stiffened it, I frigged hard, the spunk was ready and boiling, for he had been up to spending point half a dozen times. My prick, still encased, was beginning to stiffen more. — He cried — "I am coming, I am coming" — his bum jogged and trembled — his arsehole tightened — my prick slipped out — and he sank on the bed spending over the counterpane — I stood frigging him still.

He spent a perfect pool of sperm on the bed. The maddening thought of what I had done made me wish to do it again. I forgot all my sensations — I have no idea of them now — I knew I had spent, that's all. "Let me do it again." "That I won't for any money," said he turning round.

Then I frigged myself and frigged him at the same time furiously. Fast as hands could move did mine glide up and down the pricks. Pushing him down with his arse on the sperm on the counterpane, I finished him as he lay, and I spent over his prick. balls, and belly. In ten minutes our double spend was over.

Immediately I had an ineffable disgust at him and myself — a terrible fear — a loathing — I could scarcely be in the room with him — could have kicked him. He said, "You've made me bleed." At that I nearly vomited — "I must make haste," said I looking at my watch, "I forgot it was so late. — I must go." All my desire was to get away as quickly as possible. I left after paying him, and making him swear, and swearing myself, that no living person should know of the act.

Yet a few days after I wrote the narrative of this blind, mad, erotic act; an act utterly unpremeditated, and the perpetration of which as I now think of it seems most extraordinary. One in which I had no pleasure — have no recollection of physical pleasure — and which only dwells in my mind with disgust, tho it is against my philosophy even to think I had done wrong.

CHAPTER IV

*Sodomitically complaisant Paphians. — Conversations on sodomy with Sarah. — I suggest. — She refuses. — Mutual incitements.— Mutual consents. — Trials and failures.— Successful at last. — Her sensations. — Effects on her bum hole. — Another trial suggested. — I decline. — A lewed evening. — Fucking, minetting, and masturbating. — Candle and fundament. — A railway carriage on a frosty day. — An old love acquaintance. — Fanny G***d*n. — Amatory advances. — I threaten onanism. — Cushions on the floor. — We on the cushions.*

I must have been, indeed was, in an almost wild state of mind that night. When I got clear of the street, I saw some gay women, chaffed, and asked them how their arseholes were. My mind ran on anus and nothing else. — A beautiful legged French woman — it was a muddy night — lifted her petticoats and showed nice legs — I went home with her, and turning her bum towards me, looked at her arsehole and asked if *she'd* been *buggered.* She was angry. Then I found I had not money enough to pay her, and we had a row. — I went to one of my clubs, borrowed, went home with another woman, pulled her about, looked at *her* sphincter, and asked if *she'd* been *buggered.* — "No." I offered three pounds to her to let me. I might try, but she thought it impossible. Her bum was towards me, her hole very brown — and the mere fact of her permitting it so disgusted me that I paid the price of a fuck and left *her* directly — I went home yet with another woman, whom I fucked dog fashion, pulling open her buttocks and looking at her bumhole as well as I could, whilst shoving up her. Then I went to my own home, thinking of buggery, and wondering what the sensation was like — for I had no defined notion of it left, such was the state of mad excitement in which I had performed the act. Then I fell asleep.

The next night I saw Sarah in the streets and avoided her, and for a week or so. Then I met her and took her to **** St. for amusement — I never mentioned him, and told her not to do so. At a second meeting the same. But she, — "Aren't you going to see ***? He's every day with me bothering, asking what he is to do, what he's done to offend you. He cries about you almost."

I said that I never meant to see him again, and was sick, sorry, and sad about the affair. — So she told him, I believe, that I had gone abroad. From that day to this I have never set eyes on him, and avoided enquiring about him till once long after. Then Sarah told me that after having spent all his money and pawned his clothes, he had gone to work at painting again.

I cannot describe the effect these frolics had on me. Spite of myself I could think of nothing else. — This is the more remarkable because until the few last years I could not bear the look of an anus, and when I fucked dog fashion, I rarely looked at the lady's bum hole. — Now all was anus — anus — nothing but anus. The incidents flashed across my mind repeatedly, and altho the recollection of the thing sickened and even revolted me — altho I felt disgusted with myself — still I desired to try again, to know what the pleasure was — for of that I seemed to know nothing — had not the slightest idea — all was blank.

One night I took woman after woman to a house — and after looking at their cunts, suggested that the other entrance would suit me better. I was unsuccessful at first, and felt abashed, yet persisted. — At length I had a tall dark French woman, and began by fucking her dog fashion — then pulled apart her bum cheeks, and said I should like to put into her bum hole. — "You must give me another sovereign then," said she quickly. — Out came my prick. "Wait a minute," said she. Going to a closet and returning with cold cream, she began to anoint my prick with it, and then anointed her own bum hole — turned round — and the next minute guided my prick there herself.

I refused, left directly, and took a disgust at her; but thought I had had an instructive two sovereigns' worth.

Next night an English woman consented freely, and instantly I paid her and left, my curiosity satisfied. My fancy then turned to

Sarah. I thought of our conversations, of the attempt with our fingers, and soon took to fucking her with her backside towards me, and looking at the round orifice when doing so. At length I made the proposal to her, and she said she'd see me in hell first.

The conversation then had a bumhole ramming tendency — I told her what I had tried with the Devonshire woman in my extreme youth, but never about the man. We sat and talked, then lay down and talked about it, till she — "I have a good mind to try." "Do, and if it hurts I'll never do it again." "Did it seem to hurt the woman you did it to?" I told her I could not tell, that it seemed like a dream years, years before. "Try it — I want to try with *you* whom I know, and if we don't like it, we won't repeat it, I half wish to know what it is like," said she.

She came and leant over the side of the bed. I think I see her now — with her bum projecting, the dark haired, full lipped cunt pushing out between her thighs. She was tall, her bum exactly at a level for the work, everything was convenient. "Now if it hurts, promise not to go on." She straddled her legs apart conveniently. With one hand holding open the bum cheeks to see, and with my heart beating, I guided my prick. It began to droop and as fast as I write this, it shrivelled up.

I frigged it stiff, again and again — but the instant the tip touched the brown hole, it shrank. I thrust it up her cunt till almost ready to spend, then pulled it out, and again tried. Down it drooped. Then she sucked it stiff, and again presenting her mark, I again essayed. It was equally useless. All but finishing a fuck in her cunt, to stiffen it for a last trial, I pulled it out and pushed towards the brown circle, when my discreditable prick spent over her rump, and I was unable again to stiffen it, altho I tried my fingers, her fingers, her cunt, and her lips.

I had promised her five pounds if I effected the delicate entry, and she thought I ought to pay it. I did not, and paid fucking price for I had now made up my mind to do it, and when I make up my mind to a thing, like it to come off. — "I have had a stiff prick from merely thinking about your bum hole, and now I fail. When can I try again? — I don't think my prick likes the color."

Next night I went to the spot she usually was to be found at **** and off to the A**a we went. My pego almost lifted me off the ground — I had a pot of cold cream. Hastily we undressed, and turning her buttocks towards me I greased her hole. Then *she* funked it, and turned round. She had been thinking it over and would rather not, altho wishing to try the sensation, she said.

Refusing her invitation to fuck, or be sucked, I buttoned up in a temper to go away. — "The other night I seemed to wish it, but now I fear it, but come and try — give me your word that if I cry out, you will pull it out."

I got a stiff stander of the first order, a little more cream on her hole, a little on my piercer. I gave a push and entered. — "Oho — I can't bear it — take it out — take it out." I drove it up to its limits, pushing her close to the bed — grasping her like a vice — and fucking violently, spent — I had barely done so, when her sphincter tightened round my knob, hurting and ejecting it. She staggered to a sofa and laid down. I threw myself on the bed exhausted with excitement, for again I felt almost mad.

Said Sarah, "Well — I have not a hole left now that a prick can get up that has not been spent in. I would not have believed it but I've done it at last." She washed her anus, I my tool, then we sat and talked.

She said the first sensation was painful, and after that it was a strange sensation, half pain half pleasure. As before — I knew I had been up it and spent, but as to comparing the sensations of the two orifices I could not. — I couldn't realize how I had done it — and didn't recollect any sensation at all. I felt again surprised and shocked with myself, and that's all. This of course was foolish, but my narrative is true.

I took a dislike to Sarah for permitting it and for a time avoided her. When we next met, she told me she was all right. "There is nothing in it after all — I've heard several women say so, you may do it again if you wish, I'd like to try again now without fear." But I didn't wish, I had had enough of the fantasy.

Indeed I liked to think of what I'd done less and less — felt angry with myself. — Spite of my philosophy my act revolted me. But Sarah often referred to it, at first hinted that she'd like to try again, then openly asked me to do it, and was surprised that I refused. "Ask Mr. F**z*r," said I — meaning her husband. "No, I'll never be a whore to him," she replied [singular life, and notions.]

Sarah now with me never disguised her wants, her lusts, or

sensations. — Perhaps the feeling that she need not sham and lie to me was a luxury to her. "You'd better not have me to-night." Or — "I don't want it to-night." Or "I'm just ready to spend, for I've not had a bit of cock I liked for three days, and Mr. F's away" — were phrases, or like those which I often heard. She didn't hesitate to say she should like to be bum-fucked again. "Just to try if there *is* any real pleasure in it. —I wonder *you* don't, as you say you don't even recollect *any* pleasure in spending." But I wouldn't, and never did try.

About three weeks afterwards I went to her lodgings. — She had been out that evening before I called. She said, "I wanted both a man and money, I'm randy be damned to night, and have not fucked for three days — give it me, old man" — and she pulled my prick out of my trowsers. — She had been drinking. I had taken wine with me to her, and when she had drunk two or three glasses, she began talking about her bum hole. "Come, don't be stupid, put it in there, it's my birthday — Mary **** told me that her man often does to her, and both like it. Do it, bugger me and I'll frig myself when you're in." — So she talked and incited me again to open her rectum. I refused resolutely, and didn't like her persistence.

I fucked her soon afterwards. — She sucked my prick as I laid on the bed. She put her finger up my rectum whilst sucking. Immediately after, she threw herself on the bed by the side of me and frigged herself. "I'm damned randy to night," said she. I raised myself and looked at her whilst she was masturbating, and thrust my finger up her cunt to please her more. In the middle of these operations, she stopped, went to a closet, and got out a wax candle. "If you won't bugger me, push this up," said she — threw herself on the bed, and again began masturbating. — Smitten with the novelty, I did as she asked; pushed it about five inches up, and watched her whilst with distended, quivering limbs and sighs she finished her pleasure, the candle up her arsehole.

"If there's a woman who knows more, or has done more than I have, I am damned," said she, "and you — you — of all the baudy beggars in London, I think you are the baudiest." — She did not mind what she now said or did with me.

Thinking of her expressed wishes, and the times when the young man and I used to be laying naked by the side of her, I regretted that we could not give her the double poking simultaneously in her arsehole and cunt, which perhaps we might have accomplished. I never had that delight. — She said she would try to find some one we could all trust, to try it together, but she did not.

Soon after I saw but little of her, yet for a time only fucked *her.* She began again to incite me in the other direction. "Put your thumb up a bit, Doctor, I want to spend, and that fetches me," I did it perhaps once or twice or so, whilst she frigged herself, but disliked it, tho I did it to please her.

Whilst I absented myself from Sarah, and tried to forget my frolics with the man, I was at about ten o'clock one clear, very cold, frosty morning at the terminus of the G. W. Railway and going to visit a friend at S***d*n. — The train was just ready to start, when a lady in a splendid sealskin and other furs, whom I had but slightly noticed as I walked up and down the platform, met me full face, gave a slight smile, and stopped. — "Don't you know me?" "Why it's Fanny G***d*n" — and I recognized an old Paphian acquaintance, whose lovely body I had lain in several times, and whom I last saw at the ball given at G***t P***l**d S^{t}, on the night when I went home with Lizzie M***d*n to B****t*n S****e, and when captain Blank tailed her in the dark on the bed, with me and Nellie ***** in the room.

"Going to *****?" "Yes." "So am I." — She had a seat in a carriage where there was no one else. — "Let's ride together." "Very well, but no nonsense mind." I called the guard, who was hustling the people into the carriages, and got my rug out of my compartment into hers. "Keep this compartment for me and I'll give you five shillings." "Will if I can, Sir." — The next minute, Fanny and I were alone in the carriage of an express train known [then] for its rapidity, and which would not stop for nearly an hour.

The instant the train had well started, Fanny and I were kissing. — "Why, it's six years nearly since we slept together." — Pleasant talk of about that period we began. Where was Polly **** and Mary ****? Jane so and so was dead, and so on. Fanny herself was now M^{rs} *****, had left off gay life three years — they thought she was married to ***** — he had taken her as his wife to his mother and sister, and she believed would really marry her. She was true to him. He a good fellow, and with plenty of money since his brother's death. — "Now leave off." "You can't look me in the face and swear that no other man than he has had you for three years?" "That I can" — looking at me as she said it. "You fib," said I kissing her. She returned the kiss — "I always liked you, how strange we should meet here," said she.

Fanny was sumptuously dressed and looked thoroughly respectable and rich. She had got stouter. "Yes, nearly a stone heavier." "Let me feel." "No — now — no nonsense — talk as much as you like." "Well! let me feel outside" — and I began by pinching and prodding her in all directions. Then I put one hand thro the sealskin jacket. "Your breasts are twice as large, and I expect hang a wee bit." "No, that they don't" — was the angry reply. — Then I kissed Fanny again, and all this hadn't, I'm sure, occupied five minutes, for the reminiscence had warmed both me and her. The first kiss made my gland tingle, and now I had an erection of the first order. Then as I kissed, I thrust my tongue against her lips. — "My God, how I want you. I wish I hadn't got into the carriage with you, for I shall have to frig myself." "Oh you beast," said Fanny laughing. "You always were such a talker." We talked on with our faces close together. — How delighted she got, at what I recalled of our free loves and free lovers. As I kissed her now, she threw one arm round my neck. "Ah! what larks those were," said she.

A very few minutes more talk, and I suggested poking. — "No." She was indignant at the proposal, she had vowed to be true and meant it. Every fellow she met who had once known her seemed now to want her more than ever. We went on talking and kissing, our legs were close together under my rug, warm thighs were against warm thighs. — "Oh! you naughty woman, you unkind creature, I must take my thighs away from yours, it makes me think of the time when I lay naked between them." — She laughed. My lewedness was affecting her voluptuously. Frost now covered the carriage windows, so that we couldn't see out of them. I pushed my hand up her clothes and got it on to her knee, spite of her. She had drawers on, and I couldn't feel her flesh.

"Why have you drawers on, I never knew you to wear them before?" — "To keep my legs warm, of course." "To keep hands from your cunt, Fanny." — She laughed, I still tried on feeling. —

"Now don't—I won't let you."—But something in her manner told me I had made her lewed, she was so soft in her voice—I well nigh bursting, and wildly erotic, pushed away the rug, pulled open my travelling cloak, and rapidly out came my prick in magnificent erection, red tipped and throbbing.—"If you won't let me, Fanny, I'll frig myself, I can bear it no longer—I must spend—let me put one hand on your cunt whilst I do it, and fancy I'm again up the lovely warm slit." I began the friction with my hand, tho I really didn't mean doing it; but can't say how I might have finished had she been obdurate.

More than once, the threat of frigging myself, coupled with the exhibition of my machine in enticing order, has made a woman yield to me.—Women know well the delight which the gristly, horny rammer gives them, of the soothing pleasure when it sheds its balmy mucilage in their cunts. They cannot bear to see the soft, pearly, viscous fluid spilt on the ground, when nature is saying to them warmly, "The proper place for that is between your thighs." It was so with Fanny.—The sight of it thrilled her, the movement of my hand up and down the stem annoyed her. Hurriedly and angrily even, she pulled my hand away from it.—"Don't be a beast, Walter (she'd not forgotten my name), how can I?—I don't like risking it—I'm very happy with ****,—suppose he found it out.—Now leave off—you'll get a woman easily at ****—leave off."

"Let me only feel you." "No." But with a slight struggle in a minute my fingers were well between the lips of a soft, satiny, fat-feeling, very moist division between her thighs; the palm rubbed in a strong crisp bush. My finger settled on her clitoris and rubbed it gently, our mouths met, kissing and moistening each other. She laid hold of my prick with her gloved hand, and it throbbed violently at the soft touch, and a delicious silence ensued, whilst our tongues played with each other. Then rapidly I threw myself on my knees. Lust had overcome her and she yielded—I threw up her petticoats, saw her handsome legs and large thighs, covered tho with the drawers all but a little bit high up, where they were naked, and the creamy flesh on either side shewed—mere creamy lines, between which peeped the dark brown thicket. The smell of the female came overpoweringly up my nostrils, whilst I kissed, and kissed, and tickled the red button at the top of the delicious aperture, which my tongue could scarcely reach from that posture. Yet it was enough. — "Oho — aha — I shall spend if you do that." My God! The ineffable delight of that minute or two, whilst my hand sought with difficulty every part of her nudity, whilst my tongue tasted the sexual salinity, and my nostrils revelled in cuntal aroma!

"Ar-ha! ar-ha! leave off now — do it properly then." She sobbed out. — Up I arose. "Take off your bonnet, love." — It was quickly done. — "Now your cushion." In a minute all six seat cushions were on the floor, two were soon covered by my travelling cloak and her sealskin, in a second her head was on that, her lovely form on the other cushions. — On her back, her thighs opened wide invitingly, for her red center cleft was now yearning, her feet disappeared under the seats. What a lovely form it was, tho so much covered! How beautifully shaped her legs looked in thick, double woven, red silk stockings, and white drawers above. But they alas hid her complete beauties — I quickly pulled them aside, and then the large ivory buttocks partly shewed. The hairy gates of her elysium opened, I saw the road. How close it looked low down by the furrow, which the lovely buttocks formed behind it. "Come on, fuck me," said Fanny — now with reckless lust, and just as the train entered a tunnel with a crash, her belly and mine met, our bodies were one, our tongues joined, and as the train emerged into light, an ecstatic gush of sperm filled her cunt to overflowing, and we lay revelling in our conjunction — till she — "Lend me your handkerchief if you can get at it, it will make me so uncomfortable if it gets on my drawers." — I rose up, for a moment looked at the lubricious rivulet which began to flow, then wiped the channel myself. She sat up smiling. Throwing our wrappers over us and replacing two of the cushions, we began to converse. — "It was lovely, I haven't poked for a week." "Nor I for ten days, for Harry's been away hunting." "No wonder your cunt was full."

"Ah!" said Fanny, "I've broken my vow, you've made me do what a dozen have tried and couldn't. You're a dangerous devil. — The baudiest devil — I never heard such a lewed tongue."

Then she got up, and for a few minutes we talked, putting our furs and our coats over us, for it was cold. — "Leave the cushions there, we'll do it again presently." Fanny only laughed. We again talked on of past times and kissed. Soon — her glove off now — she handled my prick. I felt her adhesive division. "Now, is not a change nice, Fanny." "Yes, but I didn't mean to let you, I swear I didn't." In a quarter of an hour we enjoyed each other again on those cushions, and again my pocket handkerchief was put into requisition. — For all that, a bed is pleasanter than a shaking, jostling, oscillating railway carriage, going forty-five miles an hour.

The train stopped at my destination. Lowering the carriage window, I saw my luggage being put out. "You get out here," said she. Turning round at her, she looked so lovely that I closed the window. — "No. I'll go on with you." "Don't be foolish." — But I had a hotter fit of lust on me than I'd had for a long time. — I'd been without a poke for a few days, and all the lust of my youth, and all its recklessness, seemed on me, as I looked at the lovely face of this woman, whom I had twice fucked within the hour — I felt desire to have her again, had some vague notion that if I could alight with her, I could get her to some house and see all the naked beauties of her body, for she had filled out to the voluptuous complete form, which a well fed, well fucked woman of eight and twenty or thirty does: yet I had only *felt* all this — could see but little of it, so muffled up was she in winter clothing. "I'll fuck you again before we part." And when saying that, the train rolled on.

Now the train stopped more frequently and we needed caution, for some one might get in, spite of the guard who had shown himself at the station when I dropped the window. "It's no good your getting out with me and I hope you won't. Mother will be there, and I don't want her to see me with you; promise you won't speak to me on the platform, or I won't let you again." — She was going to see her parents. Her lover had gone to the country in hopes of open weather for hunting. Seeing that I could not get her in the way I wanted, nor at all unless I promised — for two fucks had cooled her quim a bit — I promised.

I could not manage to fuck her now, tho we sat kissing, feeling, and stimulating each other till we were within about an hour of the station at which she would alight. — "Damned if I can. — Turn round and show me your lovely bum." "I shan't." Then I felt again all about her bum and thighs, then with much trouble got a bit of her dress undone, so that I could half feel her bosom. But this was cold work and all in vain. — My prick was thick and full, but not stiff. — Then I told her of my gambols with the lady coming home from Aldershot, and at length she knelt down on the cushions, my cloak and hers together making a pillow for her head — I pulled aside the drawers, saw a superb bum, and the dark haired pouters dividing it, kissed it all over, pressed my prick between the lips in a half limp state, and it stiffened directly the red tip felt the presence of the red mouth, and with throbs swelled to full size. I banged it up against her womb and began fucking. Her vagina was deliciously lubricious, smooth, soft, yet clinging to my glans as a randy cunt does when the male sperm lays in it. And after a delicious long exercise, resting and recommencing at intervals, till at last with quick thrusts and wriggles I spent, whilst her cunt tightened and spent with me.

We reached **** and both got out — I saw her leave with a common looking old woman, paid my extra fare, took a return ticket to S***d*n, and in an hour was on my road there. — It was a most delicious three hours I had spent with her, three hours of pure love, for it was in no way mercenary. — What a treat for us both. She said so as she gave me a parting kiss, and outside my trowsers squeezed my ballocks in a gentle lewed way, and added, "You're the loveliest fucker, don't tell anyone."

Fanny G***d*n was a lovely, hazel eyed, dark haired, and darkish skinned creature. She had one of those lovely heads of hair, thro which you can see clear to the roots, and the flesh. Each hair grew to full length, without any of those short straggling finer hairs, which in some women seem to hinder the growth of the stronger and make the hair look ragged. She was a voluptuous creature when I first had her, and of fine form. Her form now seemed perfect, tho I could see but little of it — I have never met her since, nor sought to do so. — Such meetings are delicious, and might not be so if repeated often with the same woman.

CHAPTER V

*Two years back. — Harriet's lust. — At a B***s**s lapunar. — Cunt inspections. — The way ladies go up stairs. — A large clitoris. — Flat fuckers. — Gay ladies' letches. — A stercoraceous letch. — A fat Jewess. — A larger prick needed. — Libidinous attitudes tried. — A brown bum valley. — Age guessed by it. — A piddle in a basin. — A game at sixty-nine. — Choked by cunt. — Cunt soaping and washing. — A flaxen haired, plump Dutch wench. — The two cunts meeting. — Why did I select a big fat woman? — Another lapunar and other whores. — My habit of questioning women. — My lascivious questions. — A year later on. — At B***s**s. — At a lapunar. — A woman selected. — My indifference. — Her dislike. — The chemise on fire. — Gratitude, lust, and voracious fucking. — The ocean crossed. —Negro and Negress copulating.— Her cunt and his prick. — I frig him. — A white woman's opinion of a Negro. — About Negroes' pricks.*

I find that, by a blunder, manuscript which ought to have been dealt with before has been omitted, and I must go back to that year in the spring of which I had the lithe, amorous, and lascivious Harriet. It makes my prick stiff and my frame thrill now, as I think of her lubricious, yet tight sheath and the voluptuous ecstacy with which she spent. My own pleasure is always largely increased when I give pleasure to the sweet creature I am enjoying. — I know the difference between the sham and overdone signs of pleasure which whores feign and that of the woman whose cunt is yearning for a prick and semen, and who sighs gently with a sweet voluptuous tremor, as my prick enters her. — Harriet was one of those — I guess that her sexual passion increased as she grew older, and it will take a good man to satisfy her cunny. No wonder she frigged herself when I was away, and perhaps ran off so that she might get well fucked again.

I was some times that year abroad, and not being much by my self was fairly chaste. — Yet I amused myself occasionally with Paphians, who lodged in flocks in the licensed temples of Venus — I had at times for inspection six or eight of these venal fuckstresses on the same night. I have done this before in earlier years when on the continent, as I think I have told, tho possibly that part of my manuscript may have been burnt with others relating similar fugitive adventures. There were one or two amusing episodes that summer. One with a very big, splendid, fat creature of Jewish type of face, and another with one who but for me might have been killed.

I was in the month of *** at B***s**s, a well known town to me, and where as told I have had many amorous frolics. — At dusk I went to the lapunar, No. * in ***** Street. — It was the hour when the women are just got up and dressed for the evening, and before much fucking had begun. — I went at that hour purposely. — "The price of the house is ***** francs," said I. "No," said the abbess of the unchaste nunnery. "It is ****" and she named exactly double the tariff of the charmers, for she saw I was a foreigner. I rose to go, denying it. "You've been here before?" asked she, seeing that she might lose custom. "Yes, many times." "Très bien donc, restez."

Then I told her I meant to inspect the charms of many, have two at a time to see their hidden beauties but not to fuck; that the ladies would have only the tariff, excepting she who received my final adoration, and who would have her *douceur*; that none need come unless they liked that arrangement. The abbess went out, rang a bell, and soon I heard the rustle of silks and the soft shuffle of feet. Opening the door, I heard the abbess saying something about my being "*drôle*" and the women laughing. — Then in trooped a dozen. "Have you told the ladies?" "Yes, Sir." "Come with me then," and I selected two who pleased me.

We left the room together. "Montez, mes chères." On they went. "Pull your clothes up above your rumps as you mount, and go not too fast." — A pair of naked, broad backsides went up in front of me, whilst I following, looked at their handsome limbs, peeping for the shadow of the hairy valley between their thighs. The girls laughing.

Soon in the bed room I had the ladies naked on the bed, thighs apart, clefts opening. I felt and kissed their flesh all over. — This one had much hair, that one less. — One was hairy to her buttocks, the other smooth and almost hairless to her anus. One cunt with small clitoris, the other with a protuberant. — "Ah! ma chère, vous aimez les femmes." "Hé — Heé — Hé — mais oui, pourquoi pas." Finishing with them. "Au revoir — send me up that tall blonde, and the girl with the biggest clitoris in the house." Away they went, saying I was "*un drôle*" and directly after the two women whom I had commanded appeared.— "Non, non, monsieur, not in that room, that is Miss **** room, you must come into ours. — She may get engaged and want her room." Into the room of the tall blonde I went, saw a fair haired cunt, and by its side a dark haired cunt, out of which jutted a clitoris as big as a well sucked nipple, one of the largest I ever saw, with flags falling down from it till hidden by the outer lips. — "You fuck women with that, ma belle." "Jamais, jamais donc — I love men not women." "Why not? — if you like women, all is fair and proper in love. — That is my motto." — But she persisted in her love for men alone.

Then I had the troupe of Paphians sent up to me for further selection, and had another couple, and then another. — Said I, "Jeannette, she with the large clitoris, rubs cunts with you doesn't she? — Tell, and I'll have a bottle of champagne. You stop and I'll fuck you." I sent the other away. I was wrought up with the sight and the smell of so much cunt and female loveliness, and had selected my Venus. "Stop the night with me." "How much?" She told me the tariff, and saying I would stop, champagne was brought and a cake. My Venus began at once to enjoy herself, I drank but little, she much. I sat seeing her eat and drink; and stifling my lust, amused myself by watching and studying so to speak the woman. — More and more I can do that now. I like to sit looking at them, hearing them, encouraging them to talk on, scarcely speaking myself, but thinking and contrasting them mentally with other women I have had.

Two thirds of the bottle had gone, when my Venus, unasked, suddenly rose, and pulling her chemise half way up her thighs began to dance a Spanish dance. — "La — La — La — Lala — Lalala — Lala" — sang she. "I can dance — look." "Pull your chemise higher up and show your motte." "Non — non — that will spoil it."

Dropping her chemise she sat herself on my knee, put one arm round my neck and kissed me, with the other took my pego out of my trowsers. "Aha — it's stiff — let's fuck." "You've been fucked before?" "Not since yesterday — fuck me — but I shall piss." "No, wait" — I held the basin for the operation, watching the lips open, the stream issue, and then on to the bed with her. I had well nigh forgotten the big clitoris till feeling hers. — "Jeannette has a large clitoris, she rubs cunts with the women, doesn't she." A laugh. "Yes." "Sometimes with you?" "With us all, we have all had her for a caprice." "She likes then women?" "She likes all — men and women. — She's been buggered and fucked at the same moment by two men — she is proud of it." "Une vraie cochonne." "There are three women who like her — I'm not one, but we all have done it with her." — My lass was screwed.

The wine and talk, and perhaps a fancy for the man who had seen eight other women's cunts and had selected *hers* for fucking or perhaps a sudden sting of lust, a recurrence of her daily desires [for gay women have lewed moments, enjoy fucking as much as other women. With them a spend daily is a necessity, and I believe they always spend once daily if not twice], now made her grasp, and squeeze, and frig my prick, kissing me lustfully all the time. — The next minute I was between her thighs, the hair of our mottes entwining, my prick moving in and out and probing her cunt to its utmost depths. — Then we died away in each other's arms, and lay tranquilly coupled in spermy slobber, till the prick left her. She washed out the sperm, and again we sat and talked, and both smoked.

I talked about the other women's cunts. My caprice in seeing so many amused her. I must be rich, she thought. Men had strange whims. Nothing surprised her. — There was a gentleman came there, who laid down on the floor, and one of the girls whom he *loved*, and whom he always wrote to the day before, to tell her to hold herself in readiness, then sat over him, and bogged in his mouth. She swore it was true. He always gave her a hundred francs for this stercoraceous amusement. — [I didn't believe it, but now after more knowledge of male whims, think it likely enough to be true. — There is no oddity, no bestiality, no sanguinary deeds that are not pleasurable to the lust of men — each has his letch if he likes women at all — so have women.]

After another poke we parted, for I did not stop the night, tho I paid her the price of one. — No doubt she was just as well if not better pleased with my absence than with my company. It left her free to get others, and more money.

A few nights after I was there again and repeated my amusement. I think I must have seen all the cunts in that establishment, and one or two of them twice, including her with the big clitoris. — [Tho I didn't think much about tribadism then. — I was beginning to think more about it, and its reality came more strongly to me a few years later on, as I grew older, and I grew still more curious about the ways of women with women, and the voluptuous pleasures they could get without the aid of a man.]

A month later we were again in the same city, and this time I sought a neighbouring, large, handsome lapunar. — It was not much more expensive than the other (they are all state regulated, and the price not high). I selected a very tall, big, stout woman, who had one of the loveliest faces I ever saw, but of a Jewish type. She had dark hair and eyes, and a porcelain complexion. She said she was twenty-four, but I believe her to have been thirty-four, and certainly she weighed seventeen stone. — For all that she skipped up stairs quite briskly, and jumped on to the bed in her nudity quite lightly. She had a fully developed, fat cunt, and masses of thick, crisp, dark hair, half way to her navel. She didn't look ugly with it tho. I don't now like a woman with so much hair about her cunt (I once did) so choose them thinner and younger; yet this woman's ensemble pleased me much for a quarter of an hour.

Her size made me desire to place her so as to see such a fresh handsome bulk in various attitudes. — I have always studied naked women artistically. It has added to my pleasure in every day life, for as I see a woman stooping, sitting, kneeling, going up and down stairs, or cleaning door steps — or in any other attitude (dressed I mean) — I know how her cunt would look in such attitude could I see her naked — I think of her cunt and that adds to my pleasure wherever I am. I know how in the ballets, the cunts of the ballerinas would look if their drawers were away, for have I not seen Sarah F**z*r's cunt naked in all such attitudes. — Thus does my artistic, anatomical, and sexual knowledge add to the pleasure of my life. — Did I not in my youth see my adored Sarah Mavis in a few voluptuous poses.

I brought this woman then into various attitudes. When kneeling with her huge white bum towards me, "You're thirty I'll swear," said I. "I'm not, what makes you think so?" "Hair is all round your cunt, and nearly round your cul, and the bum valley is brown. In all women when approaching thirty, that furrow from bum bone to bum hole gets a brown hue." She laughed but denied the thirty.

Then I tried fucking, first with her big buttocks towards me, but they got in my way. I almost needed two inches more prick. Altho I got an insertion, I couldn't probe her nicely. — Then I tried her at the bed side, laying her on her back, whilst I held her thighs. But her cunt seemed large and did not satisfy my pego. — Then I got on to her belly, but could scarcely with my hands reach far round her hips, and grew displeased with myself and with her, and my prick began to shrink. Afterwards I tried her again and again in all postures, but it was useless, and I left off without spending in her, after quite an hour's trial. — Was it her fat — or the looseness of her cunt — or was I nervous — or did I not like her — I cannot say which — I couldn't fuck her tho she was a splendid creature. I felt much annoyed with myself.

The lady began to be tired of me, saying I had occupied her a long time — I admitted it. Telling her I should give her a double fee, that contented her; and to stimulate her I had champagne. — After a time she wanted to piss, so I put her on the bed with a basin under her buttocks, and distending further with my fingers the already open lips of her quim, witnessed the golden stream. It was the largest pair of buttocks I think I have ever seen squatting over a basin, and as I held it, her cunt looked vast, yet pleased me much. I no longer had desire, and did not stiffen spite of the ballock stirring spectacle.

Said she, "Shall I gamahuche you?" That she did — first standing at the bed side, and then leaning over me, with her big backside, reflected in the glass of her wardrobe, and the gaping dark haired cunt in reach of my fingers. — It felt outside big enough to have put my head up. — The lingual exercise took effect, I rose to full manhood, and then turning her into a proper attitude on her back mounted her. But I couldn't fuck her.

Then again came my sudden impulse of lust, a desire to view the beauties of my Venus in all parts, in every position — now the belly, then the buttocks — desire to change her pose incessantly.

"Show me your arse, let me see your lovely buttocks and cunt.—Lay over me, make sixty-nine."—"Yes, but I am heavy," said she, mounting the bed. The next minute she was covering me, half kneeling, half lying over me, my head between her large white thighs, her cunt a few inches above my head, the tip of my pego in her mouth. I again felt the delicate titillation of her tongue, and the smooth rub of lips and palate, as it went further into her handsome mouth. My hands roved restlessly over her ivory backside, my eyes now revelled in the brown furrow; at one end the wrinkled bum hole; lower, the red gap with its hairy fringe, looking large enough to have taken my hand up it (but the externals of a cunt are often deceiving as to size of the vagina. The face of the cunt looks very large in a big stout woman, but I have felt a comfortable tightness when up them).

The sight, the feel, the gentle suction, perhaps with the aroma, for she was sweet, took effect. My prick slowly stiffened, voluptuous thrills ran through me, fresh desires arose.—"Put your bum lower, let me gamahuche *you*."—Adjusting herself hastily as if she liked it, with thighs still wider apart, cunt gaping more, it came slowly down to my face the inner lips touching me, the prick hole on me.—Ten minutes before I would not have touched that large hairy vulva with my lips. It was in size and look the very last that I should have taken for a gamahuche.—Now it pleased me, its very size pleased now, as I thought of giving *her* pleasure, not myself. My God! what a mouthful. As I thought of giving this big creature sexual delight, my prick stiffened and throbbed, my tongue touched her clitoris, and rapidly slid to and fro on it. Lower sank her cunt, and then my mouth was full of it instead of my tongue touching her clitoris only, now it slid over a large smooth surface.—The change stimulated my lust. What more rapid than the agility of a tongue agitated by lust. She sucked my prick, its whole length was in her mouth. I was coming—my sperm ready to rise—I clasped her big buttocks tightly, my tongue went like lightning over her cunt, I felt an agitation in her backside, heard a murmur. With her thighs round my ears I could hear no more. Her cunt slid rapidly backwards and forwards over my mouth and face, her clitoris nestled in my lips, my nose went completely up her cunt, my face was almost buried in her cunt, when she shuddered and sank heavily and tranquilly on to me, her cunt covering me from the cheek to cheek, from chin to nose. I could not breathe for it. — She had spent, was silent, and motionless.

At that instant I became conscious that my own pleasure had ceased. I heaved my arse up, but my prick was in the cold tho I felt her hand round it, but she had ceased minetting me. "Go on, go on," I cried — disengaging my mouth from her cunt. "Why don't you suck me?" In her own pleasure she had forgotten mine. At my cry she resumed her work. For an instant the current of my semen had stopped, but quickly pleasure came on, and I drowned her mouth with my libation. She sank on the bed, half on her side but still partly laying on me, with a napkin to her mouth — and I with eyes closed, thrust my fingers up her moist cunt, whilst she gently pressed my empty penis.

"You've spent," said I getting up. "Yes — why, you've been pulling it about for an hour." "You like minette?" "I'd sooner have a man, and be what you call *fooked* — n'est-ce pas? But if a man plays minette nicely I can't help having pleasure." With that she washed her cunt. Seeing the great white buttocks over the basin gave me another letch. Making her remain in her micturating attitude, I soaped her cunt well and washed it myself. — A soapy cunt feels very nice to the hand as it is passed broadly over it to and fro gently, and hers was a deliciously soft handful, from bumhole to clitoris, under its saponaceous surface; and I delighted in soaping my own prick and testicles with the hand and the soap which had come off her quim.

Lust in its impulses is with me now, more sudden and curious than ever — I had had almost a dislike to this big Jewess (for Jewess I am sure she was tho she denied it) when I failed to get into her dog fashion (*en levrette* she called it) my prick refused to stand well afterwards, and only her gamahuching brought me up. Yet now I wanted to fuck again, and my prick without solicitation was rigid. I put it into her cunt then withdrew it. "Get me the smallest girl in the house, and with fair hair." She went out, and returned with a plump little Dutch girl with hair like flax. I laid the Jewess on top of her. She quite hid her. Then I laid the Dutch girl between the Jewess' thighs. Then she gamahuched the big dark woman into ecstasy, and whilst she was still licking her cunt, kneeling on the bed to do it. — I kneeling at her backside, penetrated the flaxen haired cunt, and spent rapturously in it. Then I bid them adieu. [I did not incite them to flat fucking, tho I saw between their open thighs the different colored cunt wigs together. It surprises me now that I did not. I seemed to have been aroused fully to such spectacles at a somewhat later period of my life.]

When I came to write about this amorous fun, I wondered why I had taken a big woman like the Jewess. I have had enough big, fully matured ones, intended to have no more, and my taste now runs in another direction. Yet I selected her — I cannot account for these sudden letches which upset all my intentions.

It was my letch for the time, I was in the vein for cunt inspection and the night following went to another lapunar, not of the highest class. I had not much want for female aid or conjunction, but an overwhelming, insatiable desire to see all that the women had hidden of their bodies, to compare and note differences, and ask every one of them questions about their sexual tastes, sensations, and habits. I have done that for many many years, have asked scores of times on first acquaintance, expecting more frequently lies than the truth, yet still I asked. — It is delightful in itself to put the lascivious questions, searching for the most hidden thoughts, feelings, and deeds of these lovely creatures. — When I have known a woman or girl a short time, I have nearly always got their confidence, and then over a bottle of wine, when its generous influence has been felt, I have but little doubt that I got in the main truthful replies.

Long before this period I prepared a set of questions, of which I knew the order pretty well by heart, through repetition. — At about this time I bethought me of additional questions about tribadism, of cunt to cunt rubbing, or as it is called flat fucking; but to which amusement it is only of recent years that I gave attention, or that these feminine games gave me much sensual pleasure to think about, or had roused my curiosity. — From hundreds of answers to these questions, coupled with my own experience in facts, I think I have as good a knowledge of the sexual tastes and habits of men and women as most; excepting old baudy priests, who know all through confession. — The replies of many of the females, particularly of the young ones, I know already have been given in various parts of this history.

I have had many servants. All had been poor, and in their

youth had nursed their brothers if they had any. Many had been nursemaids when they left their homes. — Some were nursemaids when I fucked them. They enjoyed my talk on sexualities. It is one of the additional pleasures which servant girls, and women who are not gay, give me. — It adds to the physical pleasure which they always *give* and always *have* with me, for a servant if she will take money, and gifts (and all women will, for that is my experience) have met me, and surrendered to me, for the pleasure of fucking, and not for money.

As before said (often perhaps — I forget) I always got the confidence and liking of gay women when I visited them regularly. They at times like reminiscences of lust and of their precocious experience, and will often talk freely when there are one or two together, and are a little known to each other. [Two gay ladies of late have often met me together in baudy companionship.] Then over a bottle of champagne or two, they generally will exchange confidences, answer my questions, and tell the truth to each other and to me, tho I have found some manifest liars even when their tongues were loosened by liquor. These were principally the leading questions, which I have put to hundreds, the first mainly to the quite young and youngish, the more searching to females of all ages. — The first twenty or thereabouts I have always asked servants and young girls and nursemaids.

At what age does a little boy's cock get stiff? When do you think a boy first feels pleasure in its stiffness?

At what early age do you think a boy can spend?

Did you ever make a boy's cock stiff?

Did you ever frig a boy till he spent and what was the age of the youngest you made spend?

Did he spend quickly? did it spurt out? was his spunk thick or thin? was there much of it?

How old was the youngest boy, who wanted to put his hands up your clothes, or was curious about your sex or your cunt?

At what age did you know what fucking was?

At what age did you first know that you had a womb, and that children came out thro cunts?

How old were you when you first felt randy?

How old when you first frigged yourself?
How old when you were first fucked?
Did you spend at the first fuck, or if not did you feel any pleasure at all?
Did your first fuck hurt you much, and did you bleed much?
How long was your cunt sore afterwards?
When during a month do you feel most lewed, before or after your monthlies, or whilst they are on?
Does your clitoris get stiffer when you frig yourself, or you feel lewed?
Did you ever frig a girl? What age was the youngest girl you have frigged?
Do many girls frig each other?
Are there any girls after twelve years of age who don't frig themselves?
If girls want the pleasure, do any restrain themselves from frigging?
At what time of day or night do they generally frig themselves?
How often have you ever frigged yourself in twenty-four hours?
Did you ever lick another girl's cunt?
Did another girl ever lick *your* cunt?
Which do you like best, fucking, or frigging yourself, or being frigged, or having your cunt licked till you spend?
Do you like licking a girl's cunt?
Do you like being licked by a man or a woman?

The further questions to the fully experienced women in the *Ars Amoris,* were:

Do you like sucking a man's prick, and have you sucked one?
Do you like the feel of a prick in your mouth best when it's stiff, or when it's limp?
Do you mind or like his spending in your mouth?
Which do you like best — fucking or being gamahuched?
Which do you like best, a man or woman to gamahuche you?
Do you like gamahuching a nice woman?
Do you like a finger up your cunt when you are gamahuched, or up your bum hole?

Do you *generally* spend with men, or with a man who is new to you and fucks you for the first time?
Do you like fucking as much as you did when you were seventeen?
Do you like being dildoed?
Which gives you most pleasure, being gamahuched, frigged, or dildoed, or fucked?
Did you ever suck a man's cock while you were being gamahuched?
Does flat fucking give you much, and prolonged pleasure?
Are you longer before you spend that way than when being fucked?
Do the two women flat fucking usually spend at the same time?
Does your cunt feel as satisfied after flat fucking as it does after a man has fucked and spent his sperm in you?
Did you ever see a man buggering another, or one sucking another's prick?
Did you ever swallow a man's sperm?
How does sperm taste?
Does sperm seem a nasty fluid to you?
Were you ever buggered and do you like it?

These are leading questions. The replies suggest others. — The answers given to them by *many* women will, coupled with a man's own wide experience and observation of women, leave him but very little to learn about them; and enable him to form sound opinions about their sexual tastes and habits, and the phenomena accompanying their lust and spending, as well as about the habits and tastes of men.

Now I go back to the regular order of my history, as it followed after my erotic gambols with a man at Sarah's lodgings.

Again I was at B***s*ls and went to a well known lapunar, tho not the one where a year previously I had had eight women of a night to inspect; nor that where I had the big Jewess, and the flaxen hair cunted Dutch girl. — I was with a tallish, rather slim woman, with legs and thighs and backside disproportionately large to her arms and breasts. I was not much enamoured of her when I had her in the room, and did not at first attempt to inspect her charms nor did I think she was much pleased with me. Gay women have their likes and dislikes like other people, and some of them show their indifference (once in Italy at N*p**s, I recollect a lovely little girl about sixteen years old refusing to let me have her, saying, "I don't like you and you shan't," — and she left the room). This girl didn't like me, I'm sure. "Mon Dieu! haven't you seen enough," said she, when tardily and without speaking I began my inspection. Her manner quite chilled me, my pego did not stand, but anticipating its rise in time, I began asking her one or two of the questions I usually do of gay women, whom I have seen for the first time. — I was not inclined to talk much, but to sit looking at her and thinking about her — I have been much like that during the last few years with gay women.

It was a night of summer. The woman stood with a very fine chemise on, made of such exceedingly slight, thin, gauzy material that I could plainly see through it her entire form, and the dark hair of her motte. — She was close to the window which had white muslin curtains touching the floor. "May I smoke," said she. "Certainly." She struck a match of some sort and lighted a cigarette — I was sitting a couple of yards from her, talking.

Suddenly I saw flame at the bottom of the curtain and her chemise on fire. — With a rapidity and presence of mind which I scarcely gave myself credit for, I jumped up, crying "You're on fire — pull your chemise off." — With one hand with a violent tug I tore down the curtain, with the other clutched her chemise and tore it off. She had started with terror at my cry, and my closing on her; then aware of her danger, shrieked and dropped her chemise. Within half a minute or less I had stamped out the flame. About two feet of the bottom of the muslin window curtain had been burnt, and nine inches of one edge of her chemise. The thin tindery stuff in another second would have been in flames up to her waist. I had saved her certainly pain and perhaps serious injury, for her back was to the curtains, and she would have been enveloped in flame before she had found it out.

Standing still start naked, terror struck for a few seconds looking at the dirty half blackened stuffs. She then turned round, put her arms round me, hugged me and kissed me passionately for a minute or two, saying, "My God — you've saved my life. — My God, I should have been burnt. — Ah! how good. Have you burnt your hand? — Ah, my God, you've saved my life." — Kissing me at each word almost. "How did it happen? — My God, what good fortune and the door was locked. — We might both have been burnt." With difficulty I got away from her embraces, so great was her gratitude. A moment after. "Ah! come — mon chéri — baisez-moi — fuck me — do — I want you so. — I'm dying for it — you've saved my life. — Ah! fuck me, fuck me." She kissed me, closing on me again, thrust her tongue into my mouth, pulled out my prick for me, knelt, kissed it, took it in her mouth like a luxury; again got up and holding my prick with one hand, with the other round my neck pulled me towards the bed. — "Ah my love, — my darling — fuck me — you've saved my life."

I didn't need further incitement, but stripping myself mounted her. She never ceased her kisses when my body was joined to hers. "My love, my darling — fuck — I'm spending — ah your prick — your spunk's in me. — Ah — my — God — sperm — foutre." Tongue caressing tongue in that sweet liquidity, reminding us of the liquifying of our genitals, stopped further utterance; and if ever a woman enjoyed a man she did, and so did I her.

Then for three or four hours, we worshiped Venus — the revulsion after the terror seemed to have filled both her and me with lust, hers stimulated mine. — As fast as she could stiffen me by kiss and fingers and tongue, she did, and we fucked. She wouldn't let me go. "Ah! don't leave — make love again. — Wait for me — don't spend." — Away she ran after one copulation with unwashed cunt, and I thought some necessity of nature had called her away. No. She had run to tell the other women in the house. Some came up in their voluptuous half nudity. — "Look, I was standing here, etc., etc., etc. and Monsieur did this, etc., etc., etc." She narrated the occurrence over and over again to the women, and to the abbess, who came also up to see. The girls looked admiringly at me — I was a hero — and think some would have liked to have had me, for women love a bold man. — The idea of force enchants them. It is that which makes the soldiers the female conquerors.

Fucked out, with tool dwindled to a bit of skin, I left. — Three days after I had her again. She was still as grateful and full of desire for me — and singularly enough I for her. "Spend. Ah God! I could spend with you for ever. And when I first saw you I didn't know what to think of you, thought you'd the clap or some ailment, so odd were you. — I wished you hadn't chosen me." She told me all about the house, and the women, her real name, place of birth, and parents. "Oh don't spend in my mouth, tho I'll do anything you like — but fuck me — I like you to spend in me." — The next day I left the city and never saw her afterwards. This incident was altogether due to throwing on the floor a lucifer, after she had lighted her cigarette.

A few weeks after I crossed the ocean, no matter where to. — If any one had before I left Europe told me I would touch another man's tool, I would have sworn that I would not. — But I did — curiosity alone was the cause of it.

During the time I was the other side of the ocean (I must for reasons give not much account of my doings there, they were written but I have destroyed most of the narrative) was where there were many coloured people, and then this incident occurred.

I went to a gay house one day, and was with a white woman, when through talking I took a fancy for a black one. — A Negress was fetched for me, and a very finely formed creature she was. The hair of her cunt was thick, short, and closely curled, like the hair on a male Negro's head, but was shorter, and not quite so fuzzy perhaps. It was scrubby to the feel, there was plenty of it, and a couple of crabs would have made a nest there, where they could have reared a family, and defied anything but chemical solutions. Her clitoris and inner lips were smallish and of a very dark mulberry red, and the effect was ugly; but her prick hole was a lightish pink inside the lips, and like white women's in most respects. She spoke broken English.

The white woman was American. We fell to talking about black men, whose pricks I had heard were very big and long; and getting curious, I expressed a desire to see one and to see a Negro poke a Negress. The two women consulted for a minute, the Negress went away, and in half an hour brought back a Negro — a fine young man and well dressed. I had rather feared some bully, or a trick would be played on me, but the white woman assured me whilst the Negress was away that it was all right. That if he would come, which she wasn't sure of, he was quite a respectable man, and very fond of the black woman, who would fetch him. *He* would do anything to stroke *her*, but *she* didn't like *him*. At the request of the white I had ordered liquor of some sort, which they all drank when we were together. I did not.

He came in evidently abashed, grinned and chuckled, and showed teeth like snow, but was a little hesitating about showing his doodle. I didn't even like to ask him, for I felt very nervous as usual. — The white woman pulled it out for him. It was limp, but big, and I think it must have hung down five inches or more in its quiescent state. After a time I laid hold of it, for I see no harm in that now. Why should not a man feel another prick, if the two agree? — Then it got a trifle smaller. The white woman helped to pull off his trowsers, and tucked up a shirt made of a linen with big stripes all over it, and I found he had a large ball bag. He stood jabbering and chuckling whilst the woman showed him off. Then the white woman felt it. The man said, "I no fuckar Sar," and shook his head. The black woman who was dressed then stripped and showed her cunt well, and the Negro's cock gave two or three sharp jerks and swelled up in a moment to double the length and size. But it stood out nearly straight from his belly instead of nearly up against it. Then he moved quickly towards the Negress and laid hold of her.

He began playing with the Negress' cunt. "Fuck this white lady," said I. He grinned. — She would not let him, she declared. "Fuck your friend then, and get on the bed." "No, no" said she. "Yars, yars," said he, pulling her. — I promised her more money to let him, which had the desired effect. Before commencing, she laid hold of his tool, shook it, and pulled the foreskin up and down, — said she, "Look, Sar — look. — Nigger man hab dam big cock, Sar, — more big cock than white man cock, Sar." Then she let him fuck her, and I was amused at seeing his big tool, moving in and out of her dark cunt like a piston, and I handled his dark balls whilst he fucked.

The white woman watched them with me till they'd finished, and said, "Aren't you going to fuck me." — Leaving him spent and silent on the top of the Negress, both reposing after their exercise she having spent seemingly, I went into an adjacent room with her and tailed her. She was either hot arsed that day, or I had pleased her, or the spectacle of the two Negroes copulating had excited her, for she wanted me to tail her again almost directly, which I could not do. I sent out for some liquor, which I could drink as well as she. She was a handsome woman, and it gave me pleasure to sit and talk to her, every now and then feeling her cunt, and looking at her as she sat in various nude attitudes. — She had never seen two blacks fucking before, she told me, saying, "Don't they look like beasts." She had been fucked by a black man once but only out of curiosity. She had seen many niggers' pricks. They all had very large pricks, and were fond of exposing them on the sly to white women, whether *they* wanted to see them or not. Their bodies smelt so that she couldn't bear them, particularly that very Negro, who if he met her in the street followed her about, begging her to let him have her, and actually with tears at times rolling down his cheeks. — He was a waiter, and fond of the black woman but not she of him. It was in the hopes of fucking one or both of them, which had got him there. So we talked on. — Again she said, "Don't they look like beasts when doing it." "If they do they've made you lewed." Seeing others fucking always made her lewed, she replied. — Then having heard all she knew, or could tell about the procreating machines of the Negro race, both male and female, we fucked again. — An hour had run away in this pleasing, instructive conversation. Then we went back to the black couple.

I now quite overcame my foolish nervousness, and again handled his great dark tool and pendants; curiously amused at its dark skinned stem, and its contrast with its tip, red like that of a white man's, but perhaps of a little darker red, it was I'm sure nine inches long when it stood. There may be pricks as long as that in white men, but I never saw but one that looked so, tho I've seen many. It was scarcely thick in proportion, tho thick enough. Then I wondered if his sperm was the same as a white man's, and promised him money if he'd let me frig him, he'd only fucked once he said. At first he refused, but persuaded by the Negress he let me, and I frigged him till he spent over the Negress' belly and cunt. She lay at the side of the bed shewing her cunt, whilst the masturbating operation went on. His sperm was like a white man's.

She wiped off his semen, washed her cunt, and for a little time his tool hung down. — Directly he had spent I had quite a revulsion of feeling, neither cared about looking at him, nor his tool, paid him and the woman, and was going away when the Negress ask me if I was not going to see him again tail her. — That again stirred my lewedness, so I waited an hour or more, when she handled his tool, till it stiffened again. — She went to the bed, the Negro following her. He placed her at the side of the bed, and began gamahuching her quite spontaneously, neither having been asked to do so by me, nor by either of the women. — I couldn't resist again feeling his big stiff prick for a minute whilst he gamahuched, for it soon grew stiff again. Then he mounted her, and they fucked like any other mortals; and such are the likes and dislikes which seize me that I couldn't bear now to look at her cunt, when his great black tool had flopped out of it after he had spent. At a glance there still seemed lots of sperm, tho it was his third spend. She washed her cunt, he his prick, I sent out for more strong liquor which the three drank. I did not touch it. We sat a long time. He with his long drooping tool visible, and the Negress quite naked. Our talk was all about white and black pricks, and cunts, and the nigger then asked me to show him my prick which I refused to do, for which I thought myself a fool when I began to write this.

I had been altogether something like three hours at this curiously varied and exciting amusement and was going away, when I thought I'd like a parting look at his big machine. The white woman lifted up his shirt unasked (for he had put it on) and held it for me to see. — It seemed to amuse her very much to show it to me. Then she tucked up his shirt round his waist, the Negress handled his tool, and I asked her to make it stiff if she could. She succeeded. He stood up quite proud of it, each woman then put a hand round it, and at the same time, I also grasped it. The tip was then just showing inside my fist, so it must have been nine inches long, to have lain with three hands at the same time round the stem. It is difficult to guess the length of anything, and that's the way how I came to think it full nine inches long.

I paid the Negress and left the room with my white one who excited me to more amorous exercises. As I was going away after paying my white one, — "I'll just have a look at blackie's cunt again," said I, "if she's there." "I expect she's gone out," said Whitey. But opening the door, there was the nigger on the top of her, ramming away so furiously that the bed shook violently, and both were chattering, gasping, and snorting in such a way as I never heard a man and woman before or since when fucking. They were five minutes at it I should think whilst we stood looking. At last they spent, his prick came out wet and limp, and then I left. I had not paid him anything excepting for frigging him. I rather think as was told me that he came for the poke. — But I don't know how they divided my money. I gave it all to the Negress.

A few days after I had that black woman together with the white one, and put my prick first into one, then the other, to see if my prick noticed any difference. I spent in the nigger but didn't like her. — She told me in broken English all about "Big Negro man" — and it was what the white woman had told me before. She let him do what he liked that day, because feeling my white prick had made her randy, she said. "Me likes white man — not black."

It is the only time I ever felt a black man's tool, or saw a Negro and Negress copulate, but I saw some of their long pricks afterwards in a pendant state, at a bathing place, and also at places where some working in water exposed themselves. It gave me no amusement to do so that I can recollect. All their pricks were I think when tranquil and pendant much longer than those of Englishmen, whose pricks in every condition I have seen many.

What struck me as most peculiar was that his prick, when stiff and hard, did not stand so upright as a white man's does, but seemed to stick out more horizontally from his belly. — Both women said that all black men's tools did. I wonder why. Perhaps it's their length and weight, which makes them bend forward. Negresses' cunts should be deep to take such long procreators up them. I wonder if they are so.

CHAPTER VI

Sarah suggests a juvenile. — My indifference. — She impecunious. — My fears. — She allays them. — I consent. — Fair haired Lizzie. — "Don't call me aunt." — Smitten. — Sarah advises Lizzie. — Advises me. — Sarah stroked. — Lizzie peeps. — Lewed frolics. — Stockings and boots again. — Sarah in bed with Lizzie, stockings put on and legs felt. — Garters and cunt. — A silk dress bait. — Hooked. — Pudenda exhibited. — Simultaneous masturbations and gamahuching. — My sudden letch. — Lizzie a witness.

Sometime after and in the spring, I went to Sarah's lodgings. Most of my erotic frolics there had taken place in the months in which it was dark at half past five or six. Sarah asked point blank, "Would you like another young one." My letch for young ones was satisfied, and I said I did not care about it. — When next I saw her she reverted to the subject. If she *were* virgin I would not mind, I replied. Sarah would try. — Then I thought of the cost. I could only give ten pounds, and must see the young lady's cunt before I fucked her. Sarah refused angrily and the subject again dropped. — Afterwards meeting her on her beat one night, we had a chat. She spoke of the trouble of finding the proper sort of lass, and so on. — Was it not worth fifteen pounds? "Perhaps," but she was to recollect that every time I saw those little ladies' cunts after their first fucking, I paid two sovereigns, that they cost money besides, and were very expensive.

Sarah was hard up and asked me to give her a sovereign, which I freely did, and don't recollect her ever asking me for money before. She remarked that I did not see her so much as formerly (which was true, for I kept to my home and also because I had been abroad). She missed me much, she said. A night or two after

I met her, and she said she would try to get a girl for ten pounds, hoping if I was pleased I would make it more. She asked me to give her another pound. "I think I know of one — but must go to fetch her if I get her." She refused explanation and I gave the sovereign.

A week or two passed away, and I had no women gay or strange, for it was the London season and all of us were in town. Then I met Sarah in the street, and went to a baudy house with her. "I wonder I have not seen you. I have got one, come as soon as you can and see if you'll have her. — She's a nice girl fifteen years old — quite fair, quite light haired, blue eyes, and oh! so plump." "I can't bear fair haired girls." Which was true. "What does the colour matter, you can't expect all you want for ten pounds, and you never said anything about colour. I am sure she is a virgin."

"Have you been feeling and looking? You like a young girl to sleep with." Sarah laughed, said a young girl amused her, but, "If you don't like her, give me another sovereign and she shall go back, but you won't have such a chance again, and she has neither father or mother." At last I arranged to go, but said I hated light hair, and certainly wouldn't have her unless I saw a virginity.

Sarah was annoyed — "I've taken the trouble, but give me another pound to get rid of her." She should know better another time. Then not caring about the girl from her description, I gave her the pound. She took it saying, "I must try to make something out of her." — She was sulky, and would not play any lascivious pranks with me, was in a hurry, must make money, she was hard up — she always stopped three times as long with me as with any one else, she said. "Where are your silk stockings?" I asked. "Pawned." She owed rent and couldn't starve.

Perhaps I would go and see her, I said. "The sooner the better," — for she was not going to be fooled. In such a sulky nasty temper, I had never seen her before. I didn't like parting so, so took her into a public, and gave her grog. — There we talked about the virgin, and the subject grew more interesting to me.

I should not have such a chance again, had she not been hard up she would not have taken the trouble, but she'd known me a long time, and had never asked me for a present. — She might have expected I would have given her a flimsy now that she was in trouble, and now I only offered her ten pounds, when before I'd given her fifteen. No I shouldn't see the girl, for something had just come into her head — I'd had the offer, and now some one else should. I blazed up directly I thought some other man would have her, I couldn't bear it, and said I'd have her. The more I said I would, the more she said I shouldn't. — But it ended in my promising to pay handsomely, if the girl was virgin and prepossessing.

"How about shewing her cunt?" Sarah would arrange. Drink would not do, for she couldn't bear the taste of spirits. "If you like her, you must not mind money. — She hasn't a rag to her back — give her clothes — I have told her friends I will get her a situation, and they think I'm married — I'll soon tell her I am a gay woman, and we will have as with Harriet baudy larks before her. I'll talk her into it. — You say you're a doctor, you act that well, and it will all come right. — She calls me her aunt, but I am not." — "But if she gets riotous." "She can't read or write, and doesn't know the name of my street or any part of London, what can she do? — She could only run away." "Suppose she went to a policeman." "I should say I'd turned her out for stealing." Good, kind aunt. [If she were her aunt which I sometimes thought, altho I never knew.]

I was to go at the girl at once, for Sarah must get money somehow. — I was before the girl to begin with Sarah all imaginable lasciviousness. — I got so excited talking about it that I said, "I'll have her." I'll have her, yet I didn't seem to care much about the affair. She will be no fuck worth spending money for. A little hairless cunt, tho a novelty, is not a great one to *me*. I hate door mat colour haired girls, and fifteen pounds will be thirty-five soon. But as I'd now given my word I would see the girl, and give Sarah three pounds and cut the affair if I didn't like her. — Thus I thought. But a little cock stiffening came on and I thought — "quite light, flaxen hair; but has she any on her motte? — it's long since I saw a very light haired *virgin* grummit" — and pondering on the various coloured quim hedges I have fucked, found myself at Sarah's door the next night.

The street door was usually ajar, but on that night I had to ring — I heard a clattering of feet and the door opened. "Mrs. F**z*r within?" "Yes, sir." There stood a girl, whom I could barely see in the faint light of a small candle, placed somewhere up the stairs. — Her feet made a row. — A clumsy country bitch, thought

I, as I entered the room. But in a second, my cock stood at the sight of the maiden with the clumping boots.

She was very tall for her age, with a beautiful, light coloured hair, large bright blue eyes, and a pink fresh complexion — plump as if she had lived on the fat of the land, and with the strong healthy look which some peasant girls get on bacon and potatoes, and which a town girl of her class, fed on steaks and mutton, rarely gets. I should have guessed her turned sixteen, but for a young look in her eyes. — She wore deep black, and short petticoats, and had a perfectly modest look although she stared at me; turning away her eyes when mine met hers, and colouring up strongly. Well she might, for Sarah had already given her baudy instruction, had told her that I was one of the gentlemen who fucked her, but the only one that did so at her home — was a doctor and knew all about girls at sight. — A night's sleeping with Sarah, who moreover had, I expect, well tickled her little cunt for her, was enough to make the girl stare at me.

I never liked females with quite light hair on either their heads or tails. Now my first thought was, what is the colour of her cunt fringe, is it short or long, thick or thin, or is there any? — I felt in a desperate state of lewedness. "Who is this?" "A country girl who is to be my maid." "What is her name?" "Lizzie." "Come here and give me a kiss" — her eyes opened wide. "Give the doctor a kiss." "I shan't."

"Give me a kiss and here's half a crown." "I shan't." "Don't" — and putting the money in my pocket I turned to Sarah and talked. — Then laying hold of the girl suddenly, I snatched kiss after kiss whilst she struggled. — "There, I have had my kisses for nothing," said I. The girl smoothed her hair, and her face was scarlet, but she didn't seem so much offended. A kiss from a gentleman is always gratifying to that class. "Here is the half crown." She never looked at me, but advised by Sarah and holding out her hand, she took it.

I turned to Sarah. We were then both facing the girl who had sat down and was working — (the other little servants had always been kept working). "How is your cunt, Sarah, black as ever?" and I put my hand up her clothes. "Let's feel it, Sally."

Lizzie looked up — then with a start stood up. "Oh my — oh! — aunt!" said she, and sat down again. Sarah took no notice of her.

"All right, my cunt's as tight as ever, Doctor. Hoh, look there, — look — your prick will come through your trowsers." I felt Sarah's quim, and whilst my hand was moving over her belly, she unbuttoned my trowsers and pulled out my prick. "Oh isn't it stiff, what's made you so lewed all in a minute?"

"Thinking of Lizzie's cunt, I suppose. I've been longing to put my prick up her from the minute I saw her."

"Oh Doctor you *are* a man." Lizzie, whose head had bent more and more closely over her work, but whose eyes I could see had been glancing at my doodle and my doings, dropped her work and went out of the room.

"We have scared her, we are going too fast." She went after her, told the girl not to mind, it was my way, and the way of many men. — Soon back she came to the room with Sarah.

I sent her out for liquor, and gave her the change. — I am an old stager — money will open every female's legs. — She wouldn't drink. Then I sent her out for wine which she said she had never heard of. Tasting it, she spat it out. As she got the change a second time, she looked at Sarah and hesitated. "It's for you, the Doctor is always kind." The girl smiled sweetly as she took it and thanked me.

I wondered at the length of time the girl had been gone. — Sarah said she had changed her public house. Other girls had gone to one close by, which was also known to her former charwoman, so she thought it safer to send Lizzie to the adjoining street, and had that morning shewn her the way. I was now dying for the girl. — "Unless I first see her cunt I won't pay virgin price." "Have patience for a day or two, and give her clothes. — She is like the rest of the girls mad for fine dress. — If she sees what *we* do, it will break her in, but we mustn't go too fast, tho I want the money bad enough God knows." — For some time past I had thought Mr. F*** (her man) and Sarah were not one, so put the question. — Sarah angrily told me to mind my own business. "He's more likely to *take* than to *give* me money now, but that's my affair."

There was no chance of the lass yet, so thought I'd have Sarah, asked her to the big sofa, laid her down there, and chaffing baudily pulled her clothes up above her knees. — There sat the girl working, and glancing every moment at us. — Sarah told her to pour out a glass of wine and bring it to me. Whilst doing so, I pulled Sarah's petticoats up to her navel, she had disposed her limbs so as to show her cunt off to advantage, but in a sham modest manner.—"Oh! no Doctor, I can't before Lizzie," and she made a movement of putting her clothes down.

"Oh my, Surr, doan't," said the girl springing forwards and trying to pull the clothes down. She spoke in a country dialect. "Oi —moi—Surr, doan't—it's a shame, it be."

I pulled them up again. Sarah never succeeded nor intended to succeed in hiding her cunt. I pulled out my prick saying I'd fuck her. The girl desisted, saying, "Oh moi,—well Surr—Surely—Oh! well"—looking alternately at Sarah's belly and at my prick. "I can't before Liz, for she will be wanting it done to *her*—come to the bed." I walked to her bedroom leaving Sarah in the sitting room.

She did not come directly so I called to her. She came, then began to strip, and whispered, "I have told her if she never saw a man poke a woman to come to the door and peep at us." The door was left ajar—two candles she put on a wash stand so as to show a strong light. When stripped, Sarah placed herself so as to expose her cunt.—I felt it, titillated it, opened it, and held the light to it. She felt my prick, kissed it, fondled it, and put it into her mouth. I put her on the top of me, and she put my prick up her cunt. There was her backside and my balls beneath it, within five feet of a pair of candles, and a pair of young eyes were a few feet off.—We put ourselves into other baudy attitudes and at length fucked (I on the top), with noisy demonstrations of pleasure. It added to my pleasure to know the lass was looking, and believe it did to Sarah's. [I have since more fully experienced with a lady the increased voluptuousness of knowing we were looked at during our embraces.]

"She's seen—I saw the door move," said Sarah. "If she doesn't frig herself tonight, she has not got a clitoris or a spend in her." "I bet you'll frig her, Sally." "I mean." "You like doing it I know." "I like teaching a young one, some one must."

We went back to the parlour. There the girl sat demurely but nervously at work. Before, she had looked me full in the eyes, but now when I spoke she coloured up, looked down, and seemed in a state of confusion.—There was a guilty consciousness about her, a concupiscent modesty which charmed—her confusion delighted me — I admired her face more than ever as she blushed, and as I thought that her little eyes had been within a few feet of my prick, when fucking Sarah, I could have pulled her on to the sofa and ravished her there and then; so much did I desire her.

I recollected that nearly all the young girls I have had liked shrub; so she fetched some, tasted it, and spit *that* out — I asked what she liked, named fifty liquors and among them cider. Yes, she liked cider. That piss making liquor I knew wouldn't answer. What was it she drank for dinner. "Beer sometimes sir, but mostly I drinks water." "Did she like beer." "No." "You don't like anything." "Yes I do sir, I likes good ale." — Ale — I thought little or no chance of making her mussy on that. "Do you like it bitter." "No Surr, I likes it sweet, what they sells in bottles, I had some on my birthday."

Sarah and I talked smuttily again, then the girl bent over her work more closely, — "Let's look at your legs again, Sally." She was now sitting in the easy chair. Without a word, she pulled up her clothes to her knees. "You want another pair of silks," and I slipped my hand higher up. — The girl from time to time was glancing at us, but in a nervous, agitated manner. I saw that she couldn't sit still, whereas she had been so calm at first. — Was her little cunt heated?

I went to her, "You have got four shillings — give me a kiss and I'll give you another." "No." "Let him," said Sarah. "Get money when you can, that's my motto." Tho she slightly resisted me I took half a dozen. — "That's right," said Sarah.

"How much have you got now." The girl took the money out of her pocket, counted it, and smiling said, "Five shillings." — She had a lovely smile as she told me and then looked into her open hand admiringly at the money. "Did you ever have so much at once before?" "Never." "What shall you do with it?" She looked at Sarah, then at me, then at the money. — "I think I shall buy a pair of gloves." We both laughed at that, and she looked annoyed. "Why gloves?" "Cause I ain't never had a pair." I knew a girl who had exactly the same desire, but don't recollect if I have told about her or not.

I told her to pour me out a glass of wine, and when she was close by Sarah, I asked, "Has she got nice fat legs?" — "Oh so nice, she is nicely made." "Let's see, and I'll give her a nice pair of new boots." "There's a bit of luck," said Sarah — I laid hold of the girl and began gently to raise her clothes. "Don't be a fool, let him, and he will give you a pair of boots." The girl resisted, but I could see half way up her legs. "Yes I will, and a nice pair, if she lets me see her legs now, and put the boots on when she has them."

The girl's resistance grew less, tho she kept struggling and saying, "No, — oh my — I can't," and so on. — But Sarah pulled her on to her lap, and with one arm round her slender waist lifted the clothes with the other. — There were the nice little legs exposed, between the legs of Sarah equally exposed. — How could the girl resist, when her mistress' clothes were nearly up to her belly?

The girl's legs were proportionally fatter than her body — many country girls are so thro walking. — I admired them and smoothed her limbs down, praising them, and saying that I should like to see them in better stockings. She flattered, now stood quite still. She gartered below knee. Winking at Sarah, suddenly I put one hand higher up, and my fingers just on to her cunt. — She got clear off and burst into tears. — How delicious was that feel of her cunt, altho on the outside only, and but for a second. The first feel of a fresh girl is exquisite in its novelty, and what luscious thoughts *she* has afterwards about it.

Sarah angrily. — "It's too bad, doctor, why you have only seen her tonight — I am quite jealous." She caressed the girl. "I can't help it, look here" — and out I pulled my cock. "You lustful beggar." "Lizzie makes me so, I'd give her a silk dress to look at her cunt as I look at yours, and other things as well if she'd let me fuck her." "Hish! Hish!" said Sarah in a modest way, but laughing. The girl's eyes opened wide, looking at my prick and at me. Her ears seemed to move as I repeated my offer. Then she went untold out of the room.

"Don't go further tonight," said Sarah. I supposed she was right and did not, but the little devil had fetched my lust up awfully — so I laid Sarah then and there down on the sofa, and whilst I was fucking, Lizzie opened the door, but quickly retired and held the door ajar and peeped, so Sarah told me.

I gave Sarah money to buy the boots. It was understood that I was to put them on — Lizzie showed me down stairs. Sarah gave us injunctions to be quiet, for there were strange lodgers below. She held a candle over the banisters when the door was opened. — "Give me your hand," said I in a whisper, "and here's another shilling." "Now your hand again." She gave it, and I put it on to my prick which was not stiff. "Oh sir," she cried and pulled it away. Then into the street I went laughing. — The girl knew it was my prick, she had touched it altho she could not see it. I had made rapid progress.

Next day, Sarah told me she had questioned her about the money and the girl counted it. — She would buy two pairs of gloves. Then the boots and stockings. She wished it was the day to go to buy them. "Mind he is to put them on." "Does he mean that? Then he'll see my legs." "He saw every thing last night. Didn't he?" "Oh! my, yes." "And he put his fingers on your cunt, didn't he?" "Oh, my, yes." Said Lizzie after a while, "But I won't let him put on the garters." "Then he won't give them you." "But they will be of no use to him." "He will burn them sooner than let you have them." "Then I must, I suppose." "Of course, ain't you lucky to get them? I never knew such luck — he seems to take quite a fancy to you, he'll give you other things if you don't make a fuss; let him do what he likes if you get money."

Thinking of Sarah's doings, said Liz, — "Do you often do like that" (fucking). "Nearly every night." "You don't seem to mind it." "I love it, and no girl knows what pleasure is till a prick has been up her cunt — did you see his prick, Liz." "Oh, yes — don't it hurt?" "Never, you can't tell what pleasure is till you try. Soon *you'll* fuck, Lizzie." — All this Sarah narrated to me with very much gratification, evidently she liked teaching the young ones.

Then I got out of Sarah with a little hesitation that she'd felt Lizzie's cunt, but I never knew until later that she had done more; that she had cuddled her, just to show her how men got on to women — had put her on the top, and had had a game of flat fucking, to Sarah's delight no doubt, but of the pleasure that Lizzie had helped her to, the girl was profoundly ignorant, even when she told me about it at a later day.

After having talked over all the girl had seen and heard, Lizzie said, "Did you hear what he said about a dress." "No," said Sarah altho she had. "What?" "He said he'd give me a dress." "Oh, so he did." "Did he mean it?" "He always does what he says." — Sarah was soon going to sleep when the girl remarked, "He said a silk dress, that costs a lot of money. Do you think he meant *that*?" "Oh, certainly, but did he not say you must let him do something?" "Yes."

"What?" The girl was silent. "What?" "Let him look at my thing — Ah! he's dirty." "All men like to look at girls' things — you let him." — "That I won't." "Just as you like, did you see him look at mine?" "Oh my, yes." "Do you like silk?" "Oh my, yes, it's so shiny. I used to stand outside the church and look at the ladies, and knew I would never have silk." "You can if you don't make a fuss about shewing your cunt."

At day light the girl awakened Sarah, and her first words were, "Are the shops open early, when will you take me to buy the boots?" "Not for hours, besides unless you promise me to let him put them on, it's of no use buying them, I can't offend him" — and Sarah went to sleep again.

Later on — "Shall you buy the boots before breakfast?" "Of course not. Shall you let him?" "*You* don't seem to think it any harm?" "*Harm*! you must be a *fool*." "Well, I will if you'll be in the room." "He mayn't like it." The boots and stockings were bought.

The girl's freshness had stirred my lust to its depths. — The gift of boots and stockings was I knew a sure beginning. I have done the same a dozen times with women successfully. A poor girl can't refuse them even with my conditions. — Then their legs once shown and handled, the second feeling and handling seems nothing — I knew well also the use of handsome garters — I began my baudy acquaintance with several girls by the aid of garters. I now bought a blazing red silk pair with large gilt buckles. — "She'll let you, but if she cries leave off, she is awfully timid, and anxious to get the dress, but her fears unsettle her. — The silk dress is the fetch, she'd like it without showing you her cunt, but it will settle her, she'll shew it."

The girl came in. Sarah again pulled up her own clothes to her garters, and then to her cunt, pulled up her stockings and tied her garters as an example. Then turning to Lizzie, I said, "Where are your stockings and boots? I'll put them on." The girl coloured up and hesitated. "Fetch them," said Sarah. The girl brought them, they were in a bundle. A kiss she resisted but little, another and another kiss followed. Sarah remarked, "You make me quite jealous, Doctor." — "Let me put them on." Lizzie looked at me, then at Sarah, then sat down on the sofa and tucking her clothes between her legs, began to pull off her clumping boots.

I brought the lamp near, and helped to pull off her boots and old darned blue stockings. Her feet were washed and white, and I kissed and praised them. — Her garters were tied low down. I pushed on the new stocking, till at her knee, there she resisted. — "No, sir, oh no — I ties my garters there, always below my knees" — (many poor girls do). "How can a pretty leg look well, with garters there." "I won't let you higher." "Well you don't make a fool of me again," and with a sudden pull, I drew the stocking clean off her leg, and put it on the table. "If you don't let me I'll burn them."

Tears rose to her eyes. She looked at Sarah, but Sarah said not a word. — "Let me garter them higher." Again I began putting on the stocking, and this time half way up her thighs. Then, I put on the old garter and gave a kiss on her naked thigh. Then the same with the other leg.

I put on the boot, and hugged the neat little leg, knelt in front of her, pushing the boot on so to speak, and with such force that she fell back on the sofa, and I had a glimpse up her thighs — one leg was complete. "Let me see that leg now. — No higher, I must see well above the garter." How handsome the little leg now looked compared with it in clod hoppers and woollen stockings. At each succeeding act, the girl in her delight let me do more. She giggled with vanity. — There was the other boot. "Oh make haste," said she [it was the Louise of my youth over again, excepting that Louise was half groggy and twenty years old, this one sober and fifteen — but how alike in vanity].

I had stiffened. "Look what your dear little legs have done" — and out I pulled my cock. "Oh sir, oh do put the other boot on, let *me* put it on myself." — They are all alike.

She took no heed of my prick, her sole desire was to get the boots quickly on — I gave it her, sitting back on my heels on the floor, and contemplating as she tugged and tugged it on and then buttoned it shewing to her knees heedlessly now in her vanity.

She asked her mistress when both were on to see them. Sarah said they looked charming. — The girl, having now got them on, would only lift her clothes to her knees — said Sarah — "Do what you promised — he must see above the stockings." — Pulling out the garters, I said, "I'll give you these." — How the girl's eyes glistened. "And let me see higher, I shall feel your little thighs whilst I clasp these pretty garters round them, or I won't give them you."

She sat down, never seemed to notice my prick, which I still kept out to affect her imagination and satisfy my own lust. It was so delightful to keep my prick under the eyes of the pretty young creature. — She eyed only the garters. — "Let him," said Sarah — I dropped on my knees, pushed up the petticoats, undid an old garter and clasped the new one round her thigh; then suddenly seizing both legs, I pulled her forward, hoisted high up her legs as she fell back, and pushing my head under her clothes, my nose came on to her motte, and the moisture of her cunt was on my lips. — I kissed and kissed it and slipped my hands up under her bum, she cried out loudly, Sarah laughing. "Oh, Doctor, you shouldn't unless she lets you." It was a comedy.

"I have kissed her cunt, and will give her a silk dress to let me *look* at it as I do at yours." — "Give *me* a silk dress and you may fuck mine for a month," said Sarah.

She had still only one garter on. "Let me put on the other." She looked at it sulkily. "I shan't — there."

I dangled it before her eyes chaffing her. "It's a dear little cunt, is the hair the colour of your head, tell me? There's hair on it, isn't there. Tell me." — She silent, kept looking at the garter. The play and chaff was exquisitely voluptuous to me.

Again approaching her she ran close to Sarah. "Oh don't — don't let him, aunt." — "I'm not your aunt, don't call me so again, if you do again I'll" — and there she stopped, and immediately changed to a coaxing tone. "Let him, what's the use of one garter." But she would not, so I gave the other garter to Sarah. "Show us your cunt, Sarah, and let's fuck it." Up went Sarah's clothes, and after a little dalliance we went into the bed room and I fucked her. — The door again was left ajar to let the girl peep, and she did. Then I gave Liz the other garter.

"You shall walk out in the boots," said I when I was back in the sitting room, my lust appeased. — I sent her out for ale, but could not get her to drink any. — She had forgiven what I had done. It was amusing to see her every now and then looking down at her feet. She no longer resisted kisses, but show her legs and stockings again she would not. Sarah at times lifted the girl's clothes and shewed them to me. — "You are getting on fast," said Sarah, when I had sent the girl out again for soda water. "I can see she likes your kissing. I wish you'd had her, for those girls in the rooms below are always about the stairs, and I think listening" — (alluding to a family which had taken rooms below hers). "I shall complain to the landlord, he always objected to lodgers with more than one child."

Next night I could not go there. Sarah met me in the street. The silk dress the girl had spoken about, but never about the conditions. — Sarah reminded her. "He really did mean he would give it me, didn't he?" "Yes, but he was to look at your cunt." "I can't — can I?" — it came to at last. "You can, nobody will know, I don't see harm." "But would he give me a dress for that?" An hour afterwards, — "Black silk isn't pretty is it, I am in black," — "I wear black," said Sarah, "you needn't, no one here knows you." The girl was already demoralized — the conversation heard, the sights seen would have upset any virgin. Then night and day was a woman with all her harlot's cunning, whetting the girl's appetite for sexual pleasure, stimulating her lust and vanity, and showing her how she could get voluptuous enjoyments and fine dress together, without work — many women like doing this to young ones, I know.

I saw some pretty cheap silks, and bought a dress, black with little yellow dots on it — I saw Scotch ale stores written up, so bought two big bottles of strong sweet Scotch ale.

Putting all into a handbag, at night I went there, told Sarah, who advised trying the effect that night, that the dress would do it. Lizzie had been so talked to about the folly of refusing such a simple thing as shewing her cunt that the girl had laughed herself at last at her weakness. Yet she had not said she would consent.

Sarah's behaviour, I noticed, was so different from that to the two other girls she had got me. — She half bullied those — this one she led on, so that she asked Sarah what she should do; and Sarah, always at first telling her to do as she liked, ended by advising her to submit.

Instead of giving the girl the change this night I put it into my pocket, and she looked disappointed. — Sarah left the room and I took Lizzie in my arms as I sat on a chair. — "Don't, Sir, doan't," said she, but now quietly, and she took kisses kindly. — "How do you like your boots." "Oh very much." "Let me see them, sit on my knee." — She did, I lifted at first the clothes a little, then higher, then up went my hand to her garter. — "No doan't, sir." — But I pulled her closer to me, and pushing the hand up on to her naked bum, held her quite close to me by it.

"Oh doan't — oh Missus." "Don't make a noise, love, let me feel your dear little bum, now. There, it won't hurt and I'll give you half a crown. I won't move my hand, I won't try to feel your cunt."

She wriggled, but I kept my hand on her bum — a smooth, firm, plump one. "Here's the money — but you shan't have it if you don't stand still." — She quieted. "You're very rude, Sir." My hand kept roving over the deliciously smooth flesh — I could scarcely prevent myself from slipping it round to her motte, but had given my word so did not. — "Here's Missus coming, let me go." "Let me see your sweet little cunt, there is a darling — and I will give you a silk dress." "Oh no, oh let me go."

Sarah kept out of the room, knowing that just then I should get on better by myself. I told Liz to call her. "She says she won't be long, but she must do something to a dress to night," said the girl returning.

Then I reminded her I had seen her legs, had kissed her cunt, that she had seen my cock — I pulled it out and went up to her trying to make her feel it. Saying, "I can't bear this," she bolted to her mistress' room, I after her.

"Lizzie's been feeling my prick," said I. "Oh, Sir — I ain't." Sarah laughed. "Why didn't you?" and coming to me and catching hold of my tool, Sarah gave it a shake. "I like the feel of it, but don't feel it, if you don't like. — Doctor, can't you get girls enough to feel your prick." "Oh plenty, but I long to have Lizzie's little hand round it."

"I have some Scotch ale for Liz," said Sarah. "Isn't it kind of him to think of you." — The girl smiled, the ale was delicious, she liked it and soon had drunk a tumbler full. We all had some. Another bottle was opened — another tumbler, the girl gulped down a third glass. "No thankee, Sir — it's oop in my head, and with moore I'll be mopsy," — nothing induced her. "Oh no, I'm getting wusser." The ale had done much, had made her laugh and excitable, but how far it acted on her cunt and lust, I don't know. After kissing, pinching her bum, and looking at her garters which she now allowed, Sarah winking, brought in the lamp, lighted two candles, and then, "I have a silk dress for you." Her hands and arms flew out as she said, "No, oh," and when I produced it she clapped her hands and danced with joy. — "For me — for me? Hoh."

"Yes, if you let me feel and see your cunt." Her face fell, looking at the silk all the while. "I told you the doctor always did what he said — don't cry, you needn't if you don't like," said Sarah.

The girl with eyes fixed on the silk, rubbed a dirty rim round her eyes into which tears came. "I wish you would give *me* the silk, you might look at my cunt, and fuck it for a month." "Let's look at yours then." — Sarah flung herself back on the bed, pulled up her clothes, and opened wide her thighs. — The girl laughed now at that exhibition, she'd been shocked three nights before.

"That's what I want *you* to do, my little darling, if you won't, I'll give the silk to some one else." — I began to fold it up, it had been spread over the bed, and then to put it into my bag.

"Don't take it away," said Sarah. "Liz would look beautiful in it — perhaps she'll let you. — Don't you lose it." And she went close to the girl, who made an impatient gesture but never spoke. She whispered something to her — but the girl still stood mute, reflecting.

"Doctor — go and have a smoke, but leave it here — it is so beautiful — I am sure she won't lose such a chance, it must be worth five pounds." "It's worth more, but I must go soon" — and I went into the sitting room and lighted a cigar. But soon Sarah called me, she had persuaded her, had made her wash her cunt, and put on a clean chemise. "She will let you," said she.

The girl was standing with her back to the bed — the candles and lamp were on the wash-hand stand fronting her, her eyes were downcast. I put my hand up her clothes, and felt the slightest quantity of hair on her motte. "Lie back, darling, open your legs." I lifted her up and pushed her backwards on the bed. — "Oh don't — I won't if you go, aunt — stay with me," said the girl to Sarah who was leaving the room.

Sarah sat by the side of *her* on the bed. "Lay down then — there — so — there." — The girl fell back again unresisting.

I threw up her chemise, pulled wide apart her thighs. Sarah had undressed, placed one arm over her, laying by her side on the bed in her chemise, exhorting her. "Let him. — How I wish I was going to have that dress." Wincing but yielding the girl lay quiet —

I pushed up one thigh and held it so. Cunt, belly, and bum came well into view. — My lips kissed every part. Rapturously my fingers distended the little red division till it looked almost as broad as it was long — I knelt holding the candle. Again and again I opened and let the lips close, in such a state of voluptuous excitement that I could scarcely believe my eyes. There was an unmistakable virginity, set in as pretty a plump, smooth, frame of fleshy white and pink and indications of a coming fringe as ever man set eyes on.

I moved away a few feet putting down the candle. "Has he done," said she. — "Be quiet," said Sarah, who winked and nodded at me. — I went as I often do at such sights backwards and forwards — now seeing it near, now from afar, until I thought I'd ravish her. Sarah guessed my intentions, my eye meant mischief, and shook her head. She was frightened of a noise and the family below. "Those girls are there," said she hurriedly and anxiously. So I dropped on my knees, again stretched open the little lips, kissing and inhaling the aroma of the pretty coral orifice. Then covering it with my mouth I began gamahuching.

She had laid quite quiet and perhaps lewedly gratified, listening to my praises and exclamations of delight when pulling her little cunt about, but as my tongue titillated it — "Oh! what's he adoin' of." — She moved. "Lie still, he's not hurting you," said Sarah, putting her arm closer over her, and keeping one leg apart from the other. "Oh, he's alickin' it — doan't — it's dirty — oho — ahar." "It will soon be nice, Liz — lay quiet dear," said Sarah. — Lizzie's last "Aha" had the sigh of pleasure mingling with it. Now she laid tranquil whilst in libidinous delight my tongue roved rapidly over the lovely little split. — Can I make her spend? One cunt was not enough. Whilst with my head between the young thighs, I could just see Sarah's thighs and dark haired motte (for she had lifted her chemise) and that her middle finger was between them. In an instant, passing my left hand over Lizzie's right leg which Sarah held, I buried my fingers in Sarah's cunt, and went on gamahuching Lizzie. Sarah was frigging herself gently, the spectacle had roused her lust.

Then passion ran its course and maddening lustful wishes chased each other through my brain. — I strove to follow each erotic inspiration. To gamahuche Liz. — Frig Sarah. — Fuck Liz — Frig myself. — Fuck Sarah — Suck her cunt. Each desire came in its turn — I wanted to do them all at once, but each before I could gratify it was chased away by another. — On I went licking Liz, holding her bum and left thigh with my right hand, my left hand fingers now buried deep up Sarah's cunt. Liz sighed, her backside slightly moved. She will spend, the little darling. On I sucked and licked, licked and sucked — I got up to frig myself, fell on my knees again, fascinated with the look of the two cunts and gamahuched on, and felt Sarah's cunt. — All was silent. The sound of my tongue slopping and slipping over Liz's cunt alone was audible. The little darling's bum moved restlessly, then like lightning my tongue moved over her clitoris. A twist of her thighs, a slight shiver of belly, a slight heave up of backside, soft, almost inaudible murmurs of pleasure told me her pleasure was coming. Sarah, slightly rising and looking at me, said, "She's spending." "Ahar — o, har — no, arhar," murmured Liz almost inaudibly, her belly shivered, her left thigh closed gently on me for an instant. "Aha — ahar" — a flush of salt moisture met my tongue. The sweet little lass had spent.

I rose up instantly. She lay with eyes closed, one leg now hanging down, the other held by Sarah — the pretty cunt was covered with moisture and slightly open, showing the coral gash. My prick was bursting. — Opening the lips more with my left hand, with my right I frigged myself, the tip almost touching her cunt. There lay Sarah frigging herself and staring at me. — "Hold open her cunt." — Sarah put her fingers on Lizzie's cunt lips, frigging herself at the same time. — Then quickly out gushed my sperm on to Lizzie's vulva. The opaque masses, and the thinnish transparent gum covered it and Sarah's fingers as well; and I dropped down on a chair close at hand, and looked at the luscious picture before me, still twiddling my prick gently and voluptuously, bringing out the last drops of sperm from it.

Whilst so, Sarah's fingers had covered Lizzie's cunt, both of whose legs now hung down. — She frigged the girl with her left hand and her own cunt with her right hand. — "Ahar — my God — spunk — spunk," she cried as her thighs for a moment quivered a little, and then dropped down lifelessly. — We two had frigged ourselves. Lizzie had spent under my gamahuching. — All were voluptuously satisfied and tranquil, silent as the grave.

Liz had spent — my spunk had jetted on to her little vulva —

Sarah had finished her frig — all had spent nearly simultaneously. Now all three were in voluptuous repose. Motionless, excepting Sarah's fingers which still played gently on Lizzie's cunt, both the women's eyes were closed, both their legs hanging down, side by side.

As I contemplated them lying there, thighs and bellies naked, cunts showing, a violent letch for Sarah suddenly sprang up — I rose. "I'll fuck you, Sarah." "No," said she opening her eyes. But I pressed my belly against hers, hoisted up her thighs, and rubbed my half limp tool against her cunt. "No, no," said she laughing. — But my prick had risen somewhat, stimulated by the lascivious frolics — I lunged it — it swelled — it stiffened — and before it had quite risen, I hit the mark, squeezed it in, and buried it to its roots in her cunt. — "No, no, not before the girl," said she. I suppose it was a sham, but I'd got her tight, her thighs high up, my prick stiff in her. "Oh aunt," said Liz getting off the bed and standing, her eyes fixed on Sarah's belly. Sarah said no more but abandoned herself to me. — Ah! long long hard strokes I gave, but keeping tight hold of her, Sarah's cunt soon heated by my thrusts helped me, and in ecstatic pleasure we finished our fuck, Lizzie silent and looking on. An unexpected deliciously voluptuous termination. What an unpremeditated, sudden letch, how many of my lewed delights have sprung suddenly upon me — and what complete sensuous gratification such sudden letches gives me.

CHAPTER VII

"The dress is mine." — How to get it made up. — Sarah's advice. — Sarah's greed. — Change withheld. — The girl's disappointment. — Shilling seductions. — A maker promised. — Conditions of payment. — A strange cunt in the dark. — Funking and bolting. — A broken bottle. — Who was she? — Sarah's device. — Three in a bed. — An assault resisted. — Between thighs. — Virginity ruptured. — Baudy blasphemy. — A sore cunt. — Sanguinary proofs. — Second entry and first pleasure. — Three hours' felicity. — On the divine nature of human genitals. — The sanctity of copulation. — Phallic statues. — Wisdom, worship, and reverence. — I leave my shirt.

As my dripping doodle left her cunt, Sarah rose. The silk was on the pillow. Lizzie turned her head. — "The silk is yours," said I. She scrambled up and took it in her arms. "It's mine isn't it? — how beautiful. — Oh how soft." She put it down suddenly. "Hoh! he's hurt me — he has done something to me." Fear on her face and looking at Sarah. — "I'm wet, I'm bleeding. — Ohoo." Turning her back she put her hand up her chemise and felt her cunt. — Sarah laughed, pulled up Lizzie's chemise and looked. "It's nothing but his licking you, and his spunk — I told you what came out from men's pricks — wash it — never mind the doctor, you won't mind him now."

Down the girl sat and washed her quim. There are not many virgins have had a man's sperm on their cunts, without having had a prick inside it, but she had. — "It's made me want another poke," said Sarah. The girl stood looking at the silk, opened it, folded it up, put her lips to it, forgot her cunt, and took no notice of any one. Then she pulled a piece in front of her, turned round, and looking at Sarah, said as if the idea had only just struck her, "But how am I to get it made up?"

"I'll pay for it if you let me fuck you," I replied. She turned her back to me and said to Sarah, "Can't *you* cut it out?" "No." Silently the girl again and reflectingly stood looking at the silk.

"It's mine, ain't it?" said she at length. "Of course." "I'll put it in my box may I?" "Of course." "It's beautiful, I can make it up if you cut it out." "I can't cut out my own." "What am I to do," said Lizzie, looking quite dismayed. "Get more money, then have a dress maker." "I have only got eight shillings." — Then the girl turned again and looked at the dress — she had never looked at me, so absorbed was she in her acquisition. Giving a sigh as she wrapped it up in paper, she pulled a small box from under the bed — took a key from her pocket — unlocked it, put the silk in, locked it again, turned round, looked first at me and then at Sarah over and over again. "It ain't no use till it's made" — and with a sigh went into the sitting room. My prick was still hanging out as she passed me.

Sarah closed the door and laughed. "She will let you have her, if she can't get money to make that dress up — it won't be long first."

I was wild with desire, for her cunt almost lipless, and of light pink tint, between her white thighs, and with but a suspicion of hair on the motte, had made me lewed beyond all description — I wanted to get into her at once. Sarah said I might try. "But it will be useless, and you've spent twice — wait a day, she'll be wild to get it made up, and if she can't she will let you fuck her — but I am frightened of those damned girls on the stairs."

Then Sarah begged me to let her have five pounds, she was so hard up — I let her have it. I had made her presents every night for my entertainment, so she was making money — I was sure there was something wrong between her and her man — or some one.

In the parlour the girl was sitting thinking. We had more ale — I sent her out for soda water. Then we talked about her. — "Some men if they had such a chance would give fifty pounds," said Sarah. "You don't know any one who would or you wouldn't have got her for me. — She'll cost me a good deal yet before I get into her." "You will have her soon, don't give her the change next time."

Lizzie brought the soda water, and her face grew dull as I

put the change into my pocket. Unobserved she left the room — Sarah noticed it. "I'll bet she is at the silk." She went thro the passage into the bedroom, and came back. "Come softly." Going to the door I saw the girl looking at the silk, which she had spread out on the bed, in silent admiration of it, and soon she came back to the sitting room looking quite glum.

I toyed with her, promised a shilling to shew me her garters. — She let me and took the shilling — I'd give her another shilling to feel her bum. "No, I won't." But my hand was on it almost before she'd refused — and letting it rest there, she grabbed the second shilling. "Another just to feel that little cunt I have licked to night." "Oh no." The legs close, the bum goes back, but I feel it. — "Oh no now, Surr." Her resistance ceases, my hand roves over the smooth belly, scratches in the moss, rubs the top of her split, and a shilling does it — money, omnipotent money!

It was but five days since I saw her first. Had she any clear idea that I had frigged out my spunk on to her cunt? [I knew later on that she hadn't.] Modesty was going — lewed notions had come — pride of dress sprung up — and when I said, "If you'll let me fuck you I'll make your dress up, and give you a bonnet and parasol," I had said enough to keep her awake till she saw me again. — Sarah told her again that night that the pleasure of a prick up her cunt was greater than she'd had when I licked it. It's the old old story, the old old way.

Next night taking ale with me I rang the second floor bell as I thought, for the door was closed, but in error rang that of the first or third floor. The door opened, a short female stood in the dark. Putting down the bag as she shut the door, I put one hand up her clothes and pulling her to me kissed her. As my lips met hers, my hand touched a well haired cunt. It was all done in half a second. The girl or woman, which ever it was, screamed loudly and ran to the stairs. I snatched up my bag and opening the door bolted — whilst she, as I afterwards heard, ran up the stairs yelling. It was a pitch dark night and she'd no candle luckily, but that class never go to the door with a candle. The instant I felt the hair of the cunt, I knew it was a mistake and not Lizzie. I did not go back that night, and wondered what had been the result of my assault.

I dropped a line to Sarah, who met me out next night very late, as I went home from a dinner; and told her what had happened.

She had heard a woman hollow but that was all she knew. She thought it was a lodger quarrelling, and afterwards that it was one of the girls of the family she so much objected to. — We talked over their ages, and came to the conclusion that none of them had cunts fledged like the one I had felt. She called out "Mother," I had thought. I knocked my bag hard against the door as I ran off, and broke a bottle of ale — Sarah had wondered at my not arriving.

This affair made us uncomfortable, and Sarah anxious for me to finish. The girl was wild about the dress. Sarah said that the best thing was to get into bed with her. They'd both go to bed early next night. She was to get up and let me in if the street door was shut, and go to bed again — I was then to get into bed with them.

The street door was open, and after waiting a minute in the passage, in fear lest the other female should appear, I went up and knocked at Sarah's door. "Who's that?" "It's I" — Sarah opened it. "Who'd have thought of seeing you, we are both in bed." She retreated to the bed room and got into bed again, Lizzie was in bed by her side. "Who'd have expected you to be in bed at this time. — I'll get into bed with you." "There is lots of room," said she, and it really was a very large bed.

"What have you got in the bag?" "Ale, but you can't drink ale." "I can." "I was going to send for wine." "I can go," said the girl. She saw, I fancy, the change in her pocket. — "It's of no use making you get up, so we will drink ale, go and get the corkscrew." The girl hesitated. "Go — your night gown is clean," said Sarah. She fetched it, leaving us in the dark for the moment. "Get into bed and do her — if she won't let you, I'll hold her — don't give her a minute to think about it. — We've been talking about fucking the last hour, and she will do anything to get the dress made up," said Sarah hurriedly.

The girl brought the corkscrew, and really looked lovely in her night dress. — "Come to bed," said Sarah. "Piddle before you get in, Liz," said I. "She's just piddled." "Do you dry your cunt after piddling." "Oho," said Liz as she got into bed. I took a chair to the bedside, opened the bottle, and they both had ale whilst we talked baudiness. "Have you got your dress made?" "No sir, it will cost such a lot." "I'll pay for it, and give you a new bonnet and parasol as well, if you let me." Her face was a study. She looked partly bewildered, partly delighted. Then her face grew blank, and she laid down silently.

"Let me see your cunt again and I'll give you half a crown." I had made up my mind now to do her, but it suspiciously occurred to me that since I had seen her quim she might have been fucked by some one — her virginity sold to some one else by Sarah — "I won't." "You little fool," said Sarah, "when he has seen it and licked it. — You don't want your dress I suppose." — The girl who was lying on her back turned to Sarah. "I don't like letting him."

"Let him, he's already seen it," and she pulled down the bed clothes. There was her pretty round white rump towards me — Sarah gave her a gentle push and she lay on her back, and her night clothes Sarah pulled up. "Look, Doctor." The girl did not resist or speak. I seized the candle, Sarah pulled open the girl's thighs, and I opened the delicate little split, and saw that it looked just as it had before, but her position was not favourable for inspection. I kissed it rapturously and told her how I loved her. I licked her little clitoris with difficulty, she broke away, and in doing so, knocked the candle out of my hand and we were in darkness — Sarah swore, got out, lighted the candle, and got into bed again.

"What are you going to do, Doctor?" "Going to bed." "What a lark. It will be a close fit." "I mean to sleep here." Rapidly undressing and naked, I got in to bed next to Liz, and in the twinkling of an eye was cuddling her. Oh, the delight of that delicate little naked form touching my flesh everywhere. "Go away now — you shan't," she said as I squeezed up to her. But her efforts were useless. I had lifted her smock, and her naked body was against mine every where. She got closer to Sarah. — That only made more room for me. Her bum was against my belly, my prick against her bum valley. What a delicious position. — My hand reaching over her haunch felt her little nick. She restless and denying me, Sarah advising, "Let him, — don't be a fool."

I could not get at her well, so drew back and forced my hand under her bum and between her thighs. — "Oh! he's a hurting me. Oh — do — not, — don't let him, Missus — don't." — My hand then went to her front, then again to her back, and then roved all over her from neck to knees. Closer and closer she got to Sarah — I laid hold of her little hand, and pulling it back on to my prick, kept it there. Sarah spoke about fucking. The girl now lay silent — her hand was firmly held by mine around my prick, she now unconscious to all but sexual wants I expect. No wonder. Her clitoris had been well previously rubbed by Sarah, Scotch ale and lewed talk had warmed her. She was in a mood which Sarah knew better than I, who only knew my own want, but felt by instinct that she would resist no longer. — Then Sarah sat up. "You two are better without me — you will be love-making in a minute and fucking." So saying she stepped over us and quitted the room.

"Don't go," cried the girl clutching at Sarah's chemise. I threw my hand round her — my leg over her — my body following pressed her back, and before Sarah had well left the room, she was on her back and I on her belly.

I was so lewed by abstinence, so full of sperm, which was almost boiling in my ballocks that I feared I should spend before I had her — Sarah told me all afterwards for she listened. — I was on the girl's belly, her legs were closed, mine outside. "Open your legs, dear — let me put my prick in — when you know what pleasure fucking is, you'll want it night and day." — I promised dresses, theatres, even to keep her, and everything else, but she kept her legs closed. It is doubtful if she recollected what I said, for she never told me of many promises afterwards. She was now under the spell of the prick — lewedness and curiosity well filled her, she wanted the prick but feared it, and when she didn't think of *that*, she thought only of her new dress made up. What mixed sensations.

The strongest woman cannot keep her legs closed against the man's knees when he is well on top of her and his arms round her. *His* legs are sure to open *hers*. — With one knee I forced her legs apart, the other knee followed, and I was between hers. "Oh — don't you" — my prick went between her thighs as my belly closed on hers and struck blindly anywhere outside her cunt.

It was a heavenly moment when I thought that my prick would go where never prick had gone yet. Pressing heavily on her, I felt for the slit and lodged the tip of my prick there — Ram — Ram — Ram. — "Oho get off." I was coming, and thought I could not be on the right line, so put down my hand and pushing it brutally on to her cunt hurt her, and she cried aloud. — Sarah outside at the room door called out, "Don't make that row." My prick was now well lodged in the middle, and with all the force and weight of my thighs, arse, and belly, I thrust; and as I was told by Sarah for I don't recollect it, blaspheming like a trooper. "Cunt — ballocks — spunk — fuck you — c — c — cunt." I had done it and spent as soon as my prick entered. She moaned as my hot prick got right up her. Coming to myself, there stood Sarah in her chemise watching us. — She had come in when the girl cried out, and saw and heard the consummation.

It is a heavenly sensation to recover from the pleasure, and assure yourself of the journey you have made up a fresh girl — I seemed to awake in Elysium. — "Do you like it?" — I heard a rattle. It was Sarah piddling. Keeping the girl tight to me I fell asleep — Sarah had gone back into the parlour.

I awakened very soon. She had barely moved. I felt her cunt, my fingers were smeared with blood and semen. I pulled down the bed clothes and saw her chemise was bloody — I recollect scarcely any girl of her age who bled so much. — She was exhausted, and took another glass of ale. Sarah, whom I called, came in, winked at me, and we scarcely spoke for half an hour. I felt Liz all over but couldn't get a word out of her, until asking if she did not want to piddle, she said she did. I have noticed that a woman always pisses a lot soon after her defloration.

"Piddle, my darling, never mind me." She got out, and on to the pot, put her head against the side of the bed and moaned. Leaning on my elbow looking at her in voluptuous contemplation, and twiddling my prick up to readiness for another turn. "Come to bed," I said — she didn't. — How I gloried at the sight of the red on her chemise. "You *will* have my dress made up, won't you." "Yes darling." "You said you'd give me a bonnet." "So I will." "You said a parasol." "So I will." "I am so glad." — She stooped down and opened her trunk under the bed. — "Oh, isn't it beautiful," said she taking out the silk. I will go and show it to Missus." — Off she went to Sarah with it.

They came back together. What vanity at such a moment! She'd forgotten all about fucking. "Come to bed." "No." She was sore. Sarah told her to wash her cunt, and she did, after a sort of command in which Sarah joined, I looked at the orifice my prick had made. The difference of half an hour in her sexual organ delighted me. The bleeding split, I would that I could have photographed it, but it is photographed on my brain. — Her cunt looked inflamed and it delighted me to hear her say it felt burning hot. Said Sarah, "You'll want to fuck again directly." — The very idea of hurting her delighted me — the blood on her chemise made my cock stiffen. "Look at my prick, this is what burst thro your cunt." She looked long and fixedly at it.

She got into bed, but would not let me do it. Sarah, saying she was tired, got into bed telling Liz she'd have pleasure the next time, but the girl refused saying, "It's too big." — She kept asking what sort of parasol it would be, and the colour of her bonnet. At last I could not contain myself. Wetting my finger well, I felt up her little cunt forcibly, for persuasion was of no use. Sarah, on feeling my stiff stander, said, "Let the doctor." She wouldn't. "Then I'll fuck Sarah." Said Sarah, "I'm dying for it." I got over Liz but did not mean that, and when passing dropped on to her, forcing open her legs with my knees.

"O doant'ee, Sir, you'll hurt me," she cried so loudly, that Sarah, "Be quiet for God sake, they'll hear you all over the house." — Then she was silent. I laying in tranquil voluptuousness on her, my pego now not quite ready, dangling against the lovely little gap, and gradually swelling up to its duty. Then gently feeling the smooth and bleeding surface, and wetting it with spittle (for she'd washed away my sperm from its outside) I softly inserted my prick, and with gentle pushes sought the innermost depths of her cunt — "Ohoo — Ohoo — Ohoo." — She moaned, and that was all. With my stiff prick thus sheathed deeply in her dear little ravished bleeding cunny, I lay tranquilly without moving, letting her feel the stretch, the heat, the tingle which the contact of the male tool gives the female receptacle; and awaiting its reciprocally sensual tightening and grip on mine.

Soon her cunt constricted — that involuntary tightening — Ah! that I could taste the voluptuousness which the woman feels when her cunt closes thus round the prick. — A second's pause, again a clip, then another move of my prick, another squeeze of her cunt. "Ah-ar — ahar," she sighed quietly, and I knew that the divine pleasure was stealing through her senses. Gently I probed on, pulling it out slowly to its tip, then slowly pushing it up again. "Arhar" — "ahrr," sighed Lizzie. Then I pushed hard. — "Oh don't." Gently again I probed. "Isn't fucking lovely, Liz?" "Ahrr — Ahrr — oho ahrr." "She likes it," said Sarah whom I had forgotten. — Now with baudy instinct, out went a hand to Sarah's hairy quim. She was frigging herself. Again Lizzie's buttocks had my double clasp, her cunt felt wetter — my prick glided more easily, I kissed her — I lunged, then faster, harder, faster. "Aha," she sighed and her limbs moved sympathetically. Sarah frigged herself vigorously. Sighing out "Fuck her — shove your prick up her — make her spend — isn't it nice, Liz? — Oh — prick — spunk —ballocks," sighed Sarah in her ecstacy. — "Aha — ahaa a," and Lizzie's sighs came sharp and quick, and nature made her writhe and wriggle her sweet little belly and bum, as now quicker I moved my prick up and down in her, throbbing to emit its sperm.

Then nestling it close up to her womb, with gentle thrusts hitting its portals, out spurted the impregnating, life giving, creative fluid of my testicles. Out from my swollen, turgid pego gushed my blood's essence — my sperm — my seed. Thick and copiously it gushed out, whilst in loving unison with my precious flood came Lizzie's vaginal juices, issuing from every pore, from every duct of her lovely sheath. Our sexual essences mingled in her cunt, whilst still my prick drove gently to and fro in it, midst mutual spasms of ecstatic pleasure, and murmurs of delight in the throes of fucking — in joys which those of Paradise cannot excel. — Oh! Divine function of nature! You O man to inject the precious life giving sperm into the cunt. — You O woman to receive, absorb the lubricious liquid of the prick, and fructify it in your womb.

Yet this divine function, this coupling of the man and woman in the supremest ecstacy of mind and body. This sexual conjunction, this fucking, which is the foundation and the stay of love between the sexes. This act which may form and give life to a sentient being, to a being with a soul, to one partaking of the ethereal life — of the Divine essence. This act which by the law of nature may create in God's own image a being with a soul to be hereafter by him either blessed or damned in all eternity. This act of mighty power and eternal endowments is called foul, bestial, abominable! It may not be mentioned or talked about. — Yea, even when the law has sanctioned it, and the Priest has blest it, it may not be even hinted at in public! Nor may the sexual organs, those blessed implements of coition with which the pleasure is got, and the act is done, be named or alluded to. — Age after age has wasted its thoughts in inventing words to refer to the act and its organs which shall puzzle and perplex as to their meaning, but which are called for the time decent, under the false notion that the penis and pudenda are indecent, filthy things. Yet thoughts about the use of these organs or the sensations they afford are ever present to the senses, and a delight to both sexes in health. The hopes of earthly happiness are mainly derived from them, and without their function life is worthless. — Yet this grave inevitable necessity of life is thought obscene!

Has the creator made this necessity of our existence foul and obscene? Is it not to blaspheme him to say that it is so?

We who know so little of the beginning or the end of all things instead of calling the sexual organs and their conjunction foul and obscene should rather sing loud paeans in praise of them, for they are emblems of the Creator, and fucking is obedience to his laws, and is worship of him.

Then in that big bed, in that Paphian's chamber all was quiet. — Sarah on her back with eyes closed, her lust satisfied by her own hand. — Lizzie in sleepy voluptuous lassitude, with spermatized, bleeding, lubricated cunt, and the spermatizer still laying within its juicy folds. All her pain was over — only the soft pleasure from her semenalized absorbent organ was stealing through her senses. The languor of the spasm of pleasure was on her. Was she thinking of my prick, as I was of her cunt, as I lay over and up her, my prick softening, lulled in the seminal bath of our joint making? What libidinous, voluptuous recollections, thoughts, and wishes steal through *my* brain at such moments as this, and why not through the brain of Lizzie. — Man and woman are joint participants in the sexual pleasure, and in the voluptuous thoughts which are the cause and consequence. Such minutes are paradise in life, are heaven before life has left us.

After an hour's repose — not sleep but repose idly lying between the two women. Now feeling one cunt, now the other, both cunts moist with recent pleasure. Now looking at, now feeling the still bleeding quim of Liz, now feeling Sarah's hirsute full sized gap, and after Sarah had looked at Liz's — and Liz had looked at Sarah's cunt — and we had kissed all round voluptuously, and we had talked of fucking incessantly, and Liz had felt my prick, and I had gently frigged her to incipient pleasure, and Sarah had done a little frigging to the girl, and had titillated her own cunt as well, I mounted and fucked Lizzie again. Again the sweet lass mingled her genital juices with mine, in now a long voluptuous fucking, whilst Sarah with louder ejaculations of lust than before again spent with the aid of her fingers; rubbing my backside, feeling my balls, fingering my bum hole with one hand, whilst with the other she brought herself to sexual ecstacy.

Then after an hour's repose, with some effort I fucked again, and arose from the warm, steaming, blood and sperm splashed couch. It was late. Finding my shirt covered with sperm and blood, I left it to be washed there, and went home without one. — I was alone in my house then, and for a week could do what I liked without its being noticed, and I slept delighted, and rejoicing in my evening, and the little cunt I had deflorated.

CHAPTER VIII

Lizzie's form and cunt. — Our next meeting. — Sarah frigs Lizzie. — The second gamahuche. — "Whatever is it." — The dress made up. — A dog fashion poke. — A stercoraceous furrow. — My disgust. — Lizzie's relations and antecedents. — About little boys' cocks. — Sarah's impecuniosity. — Lizzie's disclosures. — Sarah's Lesbian tastes. — "I don't like her thinging me." — A lapunar reminiscence. — A flat fucking baud. — Lizzie on Sarah. — Sarah's admissions. — Sarah drinks. — A flat fucking exhibition. — Lizzie's sexual ignorance. — A masturbating essay. — "It spits."

Lizzie had the loveliest form, from head to foot she was perfect as a girl. Wonderfully plump and formed for her age, her breasts tho nascent were firm and fullish, and her skin was like satin. — Her buttocks were solid and as large as many a girl's at seventeen. Her cunt had plump roly-poly little lips and would become, I should say, *pouters* if she became thin, but they swelled out from such a plump motte, such flesh between the lips and the thighs, that there is no chance of that I think — I never saw a more exquisite youthful cunt. — It was like that of most young girls of a coral tint. She had a fully developed clitoris. It didn't look at all ugly, but showed slightly between the lips even when her thighs were closed. Slight inner labia joined it, which died away soon into the general surface of the vulva. — There was just sufficient hair on her motte to make it feel mossy. — It was of a bright flaxen tint, somewhat darker than the hair on her head, which was light, but of an indescribably beautiful bright tone.

It was a lovely cunt to gamahuche, and I did that often enough to her. Clitoris and labia seemed to meet my tongue so deliciously, that I often paused, giving my tongue rest, whilst I gently nibbled the gristly nubbly projection. — I wonder if Sarah was attracted by the look of Lizzie's cunt.

The night but one following, Sarah was angry at having stayed at home awaiting me the night before without seeing me. — Lizzie had got her bonnet and parasol. — The dress had not come home, and she walked about the room with petticoats only on, the parasol held up over her bonnet. Her delight and vanity was almost idiotic.

"Come into the bed room." — She hesitated. — "Go to the doctor, he may do anything — he'll only do it again." — Into the room the girl came. As I put my hands up her clothes, she dropped the parasol with modest instinct. — I kissed her. "Oh, my bonnet — don't now, you'll hurt it." — Bonnet and parasol I soon put out of the way.

It was a charming evening, the lacerated ragged edged hymen looked heavenly. I think I see it now, and she was such a little lovely made lass — I looked her over from the hair of her head to her toe nails. Cunt even bum hole came in for its share. Sarah had made her scrupulously clean. — She didn't spend when I poked, and lay as most quite young girls do without attempt to wash her cunt after the fuck. It suited me, for I like now a girl beside me with her cunt full of my sperm. No young girls wash it until they are taught, no married woman does after fucking, no woman after copulation naturally does. All when in bed turn their bums to you with spunk in their cunts trickling out. They never think of soap and water. — Lizzie lay so, I fucked her twice but she did not spend; young girls are so different in this respect.

Sarah, who had gone out after seeing me with the girl, came home. — "He's done you over twice, ain't you lucky." — "Not spent? — have you washed?" — "No." — "Get out and wash, always — I do," said the knowing old card. — (She didn't tho) I said I did not wish it. — "She'll spend if she do the next time," said Sarah. The girl washed and got into the bed again, Sarah squeezed herself into the bed, and the little one lay in the middle. It was late.

We talked of fucking — Lizzie then said that she'd never had before such a sensation as the first night when I licked her. If true, her first pleasure had been under my tongue or she lied awfully. That amorous lingual friction had fetched her. — After a time we had brandy and water, and Liz Scotch ale, for I had brought it with me as before.

All in bed again. — My cock seemed to have emptied itself for the night. Sarah put her hands across Liz to feel me. "It will be up soon," said she. Then her hand went on to Lizzie's cunt. — I removed her hand and took its place and business on myself. Then Sarah frigged me a little, and then put Lizzie to do it.

My cock soon swelled. — As much of my finger as I could cram up Lizzie's little quim had been probing that orifice in all directions for some time. — "Feel her well up and about," said Sarah, beginning again to frig the girl, "gamahuche her, doctor."

I moved on to my knees and began licking her little cunt — holding her arse with one hand, and stretching out the other which went into Sarah's black thicket. — "She likes it, doctor." — The girl's bum began to wriggle — a sign and enough — The next instant I covered her, and my prick was up her. A few thrusts and wriggles. — "Ahaa," sobbed she, delicately. — "Oh! whatever is it — oh — h — ha — ha." — The sweet child had spent. — Putting out my hand as I felt my pleasure coming, I found Sarah frigging herself, which seems now quite her custom. She'd been fucked that night, but had no pleasure she said frankly. — Turning to Liz she gave the girl a kiss and burst into laughter. — "Aha, what is it. Aha," said she, imitating the girl's manner and exclamation as pleasure had overtaken her. Afterwards when in a funny mood we would say, — "Aha whatever is it — you know what it is now Liz." The girl declared she never uttered the words, and no doubt she was unconscious that she did. — They were the funniest I ever heard a female say just before spending.

She spent with me regularly the next night. — The more she fucked the better she fucked, and the better she drew me. — She became voluptuous in the extreme, and took as much pleasure in the various lascivious excitements as I did. It was as delightful to her to be taught, as it was to me to teach her.

The dress came home, and she looked lovely in it. I took a fancy to fuck her in it, but the chance of rumpling it gave her much grief. She couldn't understand why I wanted to spoil a nice dress. — She was nice and clean in her habits, and put away her clothes with great care. — This made me like having her extremely. But I must abbreviate, and only tell of novelties which marked my acquaintance with her.

I stroked her the next time dog fashion. — "What! do it that way, that's funny." "Yes dear, just as you've seen dogs do it." "That's like beasts then and you shan't," — but I would. — The bed was too low and she was too short to let me get conveniently up that tight little cunt in that fashion. — So I put the pillows in a heap on the bed, and stood her legs on a couple of hassocks fetched from the sitting room. — My pleasure was to have her in that posture, and at the bed side in her silk dress. — Up went the dress over her bum and I drove my prick between her cunt's lips with such a thrust, that she called out — drawing back to indulge my eyes with the luxury of seeing — I saw what? — Out it came. "You dirty little devil your bum's dirty." — Up shrivelled my doodle at once.

The girl turned round and began to cry. I began to reflect whether I was unkind or not. — There she sat, looking a perfect little lady in her silk dress — I thought how I had enjoyed her the night before — had enjoyed her even that night — a little water will wash all away. But I felt so annoyed that I could have boxed her ears — I had no patience to talk or even look at her, was disgusted, and angrily determining never to see her again, went away leaving her sobbing and calling out. — "Oh don't go — don't, oh don't, — I was in such a hurry to come up, I was at the privy when you came — oho — oho — oho," she sobbed.

I could not forget, and it must have been a week before a grand stiff stander admonished me that a cunt was an useful article, and that in the sweetest woman it is only an inch or so from her arsehole. Then my mind recurred to the fresh, velvety skinned, plump little Liz. I forgot the dirtiness and went again.

Sarah told me that the girl had fretted so, that she had never left her alone. — It was my own fault, had the girl washed after my first fuck she'd have washed her bum. — The girl could scarcely look at me and cried. — "I thought you'd never come again." "I knew he would." "You like poking her too much to keep away long" (to me).

My swelling cunt stretcher made me forget all for the minute — I watched her strip. — How nice she looked as she drew garment off after garment, and each girlish beauty came into view. I was soon in bed with her.

Directly I had consummated, the nasty recollection returned, and it did so at times afterwards. At length I forgot it for the little girl was scrupulously and naturally clean in everything.

The violence of desire for her being over, and having fucked myself out, and also fucked, frigged, and gamahuched her into similar condition, I saw her less frequently. — Sarah did not get money by her and that was *her* regret, the girl missed my doodle and that was *her* regret. — I rarely now gave her money; but set her up in all sorts of clothing. Sarah never talked all this time of getting rid of the girl as she had of the others.

I tried to get out of Lizzie who she was, and where she came from, and as usual altogether failed. It is the difficulty with most of the girls. Every thing else I learnt — I tried to pump her at critical moments, when with finger on her clitoris, or when her hand was round my prick, or when lewed with each other, her heart would naturally open to me, but she said she dare not, she was frightened of Sarah. — But little by little a bit of her history leaked out, and I think that she was an only child of a widowed mother, and living almost in want. — Liz seemed never to have worked in the fields. She spoke with a provincial dialect which she soon began to lose. She never seemed to have mixed with any of her own sex, excepting on Sundays, nor to have played with boys; and she was surprizingly ignorant of baudiness. She understood mangling and washing, and was a beautiful needle woman. She said she could milk, bake, make butter, and sausages. Her mother did mangling, and she helped to earn their living at needle work. I think she was the illegitimate child of a gentleman who allowed her mother a small stipend, and that she was a relation of Sarah's. — She told me her mother had brown hair. — Was she like Sarah I asked. — The girl was going to answer, then she looked hard at me for a minute and replied. — "No" — I believe Sarah was her aunt.

She knew that boys' cocks stood. — She and another girl had made a boy's about five years old stand "she was a nuss gal." The boy was quite quiet while the "nuss gal" made it stiff, — "Can you do that (fuck) as often as you like?" was one of her earliest questions to me. "And won't nothen coom out till it be stiff?" — I know now from the questions I have put to many young lasses, that they all feel little boys' cocks, and delight in making them stiff. — Instinct teaches them to do so.

Sarah, who I am sure had then lost her man, and was more and more impecunious, used to come home early, often ill tempered and low spirited. Unasked she then would get into bed with us. — She was kind in an extraordinary degree to Lizzie, would kiss her when laying by the side of her, and always ask how often I had fucked (generally now but twice.) — Sarah's fingers were always on the little one's cunt. — She laughed when I found them there, and then used to push her hand over Lizzie and catch hold of my prick. — In those attitudes we went on talking till I fucked again. Sometimes Sarah used to feel Lizzie whilst I was fucking her, and frig herself at the same time. She made no secret about it now. — "I must do something; I don't often spend with a man, and like frigging while you are doing Liz."

Previously I had somehow formed the opinion that Sarah liked feeling the cunts of young ones, but thought nothing much about it. One day she was slightly screwed, and got into bed, just as I got out to piddle, then pulling every thing up and showing all her parts she said. — "I'm getting stout doctor aren't I?" — I felt her bum and belly and just opened her cunt lips. — "I want a fuck so, give me one." — "I'll try after I have had Liz again." — Sarah turned round and clutching Liz, lifted her on to her belly, began to kiss her passionately, twisted her limbs over her, and wriggling her belly up to her so that their cunts were close together, moved as if fucking. — Liz tried to get away. "Don't now, don't." After a few heaves Sarah let her go, laughing, turned her rump towards us and frigged herself.

I thought of this a good deal, and it increased my desire for knowledge. This form of sexual voluptuousness amongst women now haunted me. I question Liz about Sarah's behaviour in bed with her, for she always now slept with her, and no man was ever there. — It was not as formerly when Sarah said, "You mustn't come for three days," and so on. I found that Sarah had a letch for frigging herself, and *that* with the young one seemed her solace in the absent pleasure with the male. Her taste for the man it may be was diminishing. She had done this almost from the first day Liz came to London. Then I guessed that Sarah did something more. — I asked questions, and threatening not to see Liz any more if she did not tell me the truth. She disclosed that Sarah pulled the girl on the top of her, and pressing clitoris to clitoris rubbed them together, till Sarah at least had the full enjoyment of that voluptuous friction. — It was flat fucking, tribadism, the amusement of girls at boarding schools and convents, and perhaps harems [and often as I know since, of some harlots].

"Don't tell her," said Liz. — "She has made me promise not, and says you'd hate me if you knew of it — you won't hate me will you? I don't like her *thinging* me — I don't like her wet thing *in* mine." "Is it not nice?" "It be a little nice sometimes, but I don't like thinging like that." — I promised to keep Lizzie's secret.

"You call it thinging, why?" "Cos her thing be gin my thing," said the girl laughing, — "it be like two snails." I roared with laughter at such an illustrative remark, and never heard flat fucking called *thinging* before or since. [I have since heard a funny term for it tho.]

Then I began to think about flat fucking, and recollected what in my youth Fred had said, and what I had been told by Camille of women rubbing their cunts together, that I had seen two French women doing it (for my amusement, as I thought, and simply to show me how by placing themselves like a man and woman in copulation, they could close their cunts on each other). One woman I recollected had a strongly developed clitoris and I had not liked it. But I did not believe in women having pleasure that way, and the baudy sight had passed from my mind. Nor had any clear idea of the truth even arisen in my mind, when I saw two servants on each other in the bath room at my cousin's school, or Gabrielle on Violette.

I had heard since of women flat fucking, and suddenly recollected a row at a brothel, in which the amusement had been referred to.

When I spent my first fortune, I took after longish continence, to visiting harlots who let me have them for five shillings, and would let a man do almost any thing. One night I went to see a woman and arrived just as she was having a row with a woman who was about forty-five years old. My girl came into the room with me, but unable to contain herself, left me; and I opening the door, heard her and another lodger bullying the woman for getting quite young a girl into her bed. "You old cat, you dirty slimy cunted old bitch. — I'll tell them all." She came back into the room with me and slammed the door. She was slightly screwed and noisy. "The old bitch gets Mary who's not fourteen years old into bed with her. — It's the little servant here — and pulls her about — Polly ***** caught her at it, and the girl said she did."

"Why does the girl let her?" "Oh she's a dirty little bitch too." "Well, I pull *you* about and you *me*." "Oh that is quite different." Perhaps the woman was jealous, or was it whores' morality? I told her I saw no harm in two women doing what they liked to do.

I had never given the subject much thought, but now began to think of the way women could bring their organs together for mutual pleasure, and of various tricks that way which I had seen women perform, but the subject never seems to have interested me fully till now. Then I got some medical books and some French books, and under Lesbos, Tribade &c. and some other words, got the key to the full mysteries of Sappho and the Lesbians, which added a mite more to my knowledge and admiration of the wonders of the article called cunt.

My promise of secrecy I kept, but often looked at Sarah and longed to question her on this subject, I began to talk about quim to quim friction — flat fucking — and explained the word *tribadism*, which word Sarah had never heard — I let her know that I thought no harm in women rubbing their cunts together, or gamahuching each other; and Sarah at once, I thought, got more free in her manifestations towards the girl.

Sarah was much more often screwed now than previously, just as if she were in trouble. One night she came in when we were in bed, for she did not now always stop in for me, and laid down besides us. "Get on the top of her Liz," said I just to see how far I could go in that direction. "I like to see you on top of her like a man fucking her."

Liz refused — Sarah gave her a kiss and laughed, put one leg out and her arms round her, and rolling on to her back, pulled Liz right on to the top of her, kissing all the time.

"She looks as if she were fucking you," said I, "put your cunts together, pull off your chemises, let's see you both naked." — I assisted in pulling them off. — Liz said, "No, no," and resisted slightly. But Sarah heaved up her thighs round the girl and grasped her little arse. "Be quiet Liz," said I, "do it with her."

Sarah suddenly seemed quite screwed, her eyes looked wild with lust, she held tight on to the girl — heaved up her legs, and put her heels round Lizzie's calves — I threw myself on the bed. — Widening open a little Lizzie's thighs, I could see Sarah's black haired cunt below, meeting the mossy cunt of the damsel — I put my fingers there, begged Lizzie who was restive to be quiet, incited Sarah to get her cunt as close to the girl's as she could, and they were soon so close that I got two fingers up Sarah's cunt, and the thumb of the same hand touched Lizzie's, tho with difficulty.

Then baudiness reigned supreme. I was delighted. "Rub your cunts together," said I after a minute's fingering. "We can't." — "Try, rub your cunts together and I will give you a sovereign." "What do you mean?" She was still holding the girl in her arms. "Oh! how modest, *you* know all — did *you* never have pleasure with a woman by flat fucking her? rub away at Liz, hold her quite tight — squeeze your quim up to hers, teach her, she'd like to know every thing, and a man can't teach her that," said I now wild with lust.

Sarah kissed Lizzie without ceasing, it was one long unbroken sound of osculation, and began heaving her buttocks and wriggling, but I saw she was shamming. — "I am not going to give you a sovereign to be humbugged," said I and putting my hand down between both their thighs, I pushed two of my fingers into Sarah's cunt again.

My fingers seemed to stir Sarah's lewedness. Wriggling and kissing Lizzie passionately, she said, "Never mind him, let me darling — do." — The girl told by me to let Sarah do what she liked lay quiet, the little one's legs were held by Sarah's big legs, and she wriggled and fucked whilst I kept my fingers at work in her cunt as well as I could. There lay the big woman clinging to Liz, twisting and writhing, wriggling and sighing, kissing the girl with passion, thrusting out her tongue, and almost burying her fingers between the girl's buttocks. It was a very long embrace, and neither of them took heed of me now. — Liz was obedient, Sarah's eyes were closed except at intervals. Instinctively at last, Lizzie grasped Sarah's haunches. With a sigh. — "Oh — do it — darling — ah — ai — aha." — Sarah relaxed her hold and was quiet. I knew well from the look of her face, from that changing of colour when she spent that she had spent now; the whiteness had spread over it which was an unfailing evidence.

The lasciviety of the scene, the intense enjoyment of Sarah

urged me on — I now lusted for Sarah. — "Get off, Liz — is your cunt wet? is Sarah's wet? I'll fuck you, Sally." Sarah opened her eyes and looked at me remarking "That bugger knows every thing." Then lifting her thighs she again began squeezing Lizzie and rubbing against her. "I'll fuck you, Sally." She took no notice but writhed as hard as she could embracing the girl. "I've only begun," said she. "She's a darling." — Randy to madness I pulled Lizzie off, and the next instant was up Sarah's cunt. — Lizzie laid by the side — on to her little cunt went my fingers, feeling, groping the little most slippery article, till I emitted what sperm was left in me up Sarah's vagina. Then Sarah with my libation in her, clutched Liz like a fury, and got her between her thighs. In vain she struggled, the big woman held her fast, their cunts met, and Sarah had her Sapphic delight, screeching out, so that the lodgers below would have heard enough had they been listening. But Sarah in her maddening pleasure forgot all about them then. She was groggy.

After that night I talked with Sarah about her liking for the girl, and about flat fucking. Sarah neither then screwed nor lewed, avoided the subject, said she had only done it for a lark and had no letch for anything of the sort, but preferred a prick to any other kind of solace for her cunt. On other occasions I told Sarah all I had read and knew — that I thought no worse of a woman for having a woman, than I did of a man for frigging a man. "Your cunt's your own, and if two cunts agree to frictionize each other, it is a perfectly legitimate pleasure." Little by little she admitted much — but considering that I had spent in and on her in every way possible for nearly four years, I had difficulty in getting her to admit her liking for flat fucking Liz. — She never did quite admit it. — She had done it once or twice she said, when screwed but had no taste for it. She liked a good, thick, stiff prick up her. Freely brandy and watering Sarah one night and dosing Liz with Scotch ale, I got a repetition of the Lesbian game, and completed the evening by fucking both the females.

It was long before I could make Liz believe that my prick wouldn't stand as often as I wanted. — "How do it come out when it knocks in me so." — Her language in describing anything erotic was most peculiar and amusing — I let her frig me once, and see the ejaculation of my sperm. — She frigged clumsily as all young girls and many women do, and I had to guide her hand. — "Look it's coming — aha! look quite close." I was full that night, and my sperm shot up on to her face. I had intended that it should. The anticipation of it jetting on to her pretty features had delighted me. — She let go my prick. — "It spits," said she, "it's hit me — you made it do it on purpose — it's dirty." "My love, sperm is never dirty." — She laid hold of my dwindling organ retracting the skin, and more sperm fell from it. She dropped my doodle again. — "I thought it was going to spit again." — I told her it never spit unless it was stiff. She would afterwards look at my cock when stiff, and give it one or two clumsy frigs, but never finished me, and frigging was not to my taste except under unusual erotic excitement, yet I did it occasionally.

CHAPTER IX

Cuntal contrasts. — Feminine friggings. — Cuntal trials. — Pleasure-giving capabilities of different pudenda. — Baudy lessons to Liz. — Double gamahuching. — Liz gamahuches me. — A mouthful. — Micturating oddities. — The cunt funnel. — Bum slappings and fustigations. — The organs ministering to sexual pleasures. — Aunts and nieces. — Young virginities sold. — Fornication philosophy of the poor. — Absence. — Four months later. — Both on the pavé. — "She would *turn out." — Sarah's efforts and kindness. — They disappear suddenly. — Fruitless enquiries.*

I had much pleasure with Sarah and Liz together, the contrast between them was so great. Sarah beyond the usual height of women, with a dark and well haired cunt, laying side by side naked with the little one whose cunt was all but bare, was a beautiful sight. Sarah obeyed me implicitly and made the little one do so. — "Open your thighs — open your cunts," and both were distended. — Then Sarah frigged the girl, then the girl frigged Sarah, and both operations I began to notice pleased Sarah as much as me. When I had roused my passions fully, I put into one or the other of these charmers for a finish, but the little one generally had my Priapean offering.

I did with them what I find I often do when I have two females together — I wonder if all men do the same, if not, what enjoyment they miss — I delighted to put first into one, pull out my prick, and then put into the other, return to the first and so on. I did that with the other two girls whom Sarah once got me. — After my first spermatic ejaculation and my lust was subdued; at my second trial, cooler than both in lust and brain, I could judge of the different qualities or fitting of the cunts, could notice the different feelings which my prick experienced in them. Certainly there is a difference in the sensation on the prick between the fully formed cunt of a woman of twenty-five, and that of a girl of fifteen — tho towards the finish of the delightful exercise within them I could not perceive much; the all pervading pleasure then drowning judgment. Most cunts, if deep enough, feel the same when the prick swells and throbs in its intensity, as the sperm rises up through it. Nevertheless there have been many cunts in which my prick did not feel its fullest enjoyment, even in the height of the pleasure; and even as the sperm throbbed out, I was conscious of a certain unfitness, and of incomplete pleasure. There was the delight of initiating this pretty lass into the art of love, as well as in giving in her sexual gratification, apart from the enjoyment I had in doing what I liked with her sweet fresh body, which in itself was an intense satisfaction which made me almost love her. — Sarah at first hesitated at every suggestion to let the girl participate in our recherché pleasures, but yielded. — I made Liz solicit her. It pleased me to think that the young one was desirous of helping in the satisfaction of my letches, it was like the pleasure of making her say baudy words. One by one, things I had done with Sarah, Sarah, Liz, and I then did together to our mutual gratification. The diary of my erotic enjoyment is complete and copious in particulars about these two. Writing it, and afterwards reading it has given me the solitary pleasure so often told of. I find even a chapter on the subject of that pleasure, but it will be destroyed. This is only to be a narrative of facts.

Sarah had given me the fullest gratification with her mouth. I have gradually begun to appreciate this variety of prick friction and wanted her to do it before Liz, to instruct the girl. It would please me to see the girl looking on. That Sarah held out against long. — One night I said — "Ask your *aunt* to take my prick in her mouth." "Do, Aunt," said the girl trapped into saying "aunt." — "I'm not your aunt," said Sarah fiercely, and nothing would persuade her to do it. — Then I fucked Liz whilst Sarah went out man hunting. — My letch was the stronger thro Sarah's refusal, and I told Liz that she'd often put it in her mouth, and that I'd spent there. "Oh you, ain't you story." — I affirmed it, said that some women loved doing it, and talked so nicely that Liz longed to do it. — But "No, but I will if Mrs. F**z**r will."

I left when Sarah had not returned, and knowing her usual promenade went there, met her, and asked her to gamahuche me the next night. As she refused, I said I shouldn't go for a week. She knew I would do what I said, and repenting of her obstinacy promised. Getting exacting now I insisted on full pleasure. — "I'll never let Liz see *that*." — It delighted me to think and suggest my letches, standing and combatting Sarah's objections at the corner of a street, men and women passing and looking at us.

When a letch lays hold of me I can think of nothing till I have gratified it, but could not this one until two or three nights afterwards. — Then I took good sweet champagne there, for I had now found that sweet drink tempted Liz the most. — We all nearly stripped whilst drinking it. Then I laid on the bed, Sarah sucked my prick, and afterwards Liz did the same. Liz was quite serious about it, and evidently liked it in her mouth. She laughingly said so — I did not spend, it was but a preliminary. — Then it was for the first time before Liz that I gratified Sarah with a complete gamahuche. Sarah gave way to her passions openly, sighed, talked baudy, felt Liz's quim with one hand, and clutched my head with the other during the operation.

Then I laid on the bed, Liz kneeling over me with my head between her thighs. — I took the whole of her dear, sweet, coral, fresh washed little split in my mouth and gamahuched *her*. — She could not see Sarah, who at the same moment began to gamahuche *me*. — Then for some minutes all was luscious tranquillity. As Liz and I felt our increasing pleasure, I clutched Lizzie's little buttocks harder whilst my tongue played over her cunt, and Sarah's long tongue played round the tip of my prick, now tickling the frenum, now the little orifice, now taking it fully into her mouth where it rubbed over palate and tongue. So we deliciously played with each other for a time, Sarah pausing when my backside would not keep quiet with coming pleasure, and I, when I felt the wriggling of Liz's backside and belly, ceasing to lick, giving tongues, cunt, and prick a minute's repose, and letting the excess of our pleasure subside for a time.

Then my spermatic reservoirs refused to retain their balmy liquid longer, the lascivious play of Sarah's mouth overcame desire for further dalliance, and Liz's little cunt titillated by my tongue to lewed frenzy, agitated itself over my mouth, whilst my tongue responding fixed on her clitoris and licked wildly. On a sudden her cunt clung to my mouth with pressure whilst it moved, and a salt effusion spread over it, her backside quivered in my hands and she sighed softly. I oscillated my rump, my prick seemed on fire, and, almost bursting in a cunt, and something more than a cunt, and shot out a torrent of soft mucilaginous sperm into Sarah's mouth. She never relinquished my prick till every drop was drained out of my testicles, and my pleasure slowly subsided, mixed with a slight pain at the last suction. This time certainly Sarah enjoyed her work. She had got more and more lewed during my long acquaintance with her. She loved her meretricious trade and I am sure, altho she says she doesn't like it, that she really enjoys the feel of my prick in her mouth. Directly she had done, she began feeling her own cunt, and shortly afterwards I gamahuched her.

This double gamahuching pleases me much. I certainly like my penis so frictionized in a nice, smooth, cherry lipped mouth, more than I used, and the lick of a delicate little hairless cunt like Liz's is a deliciously erotic tit-bit. I had this amusement again and again on other nights. — Liz (unless Sarah has told her) knows not that her mistress has taken my libation into her mouth, for she has a napkin at hand which ultimately receives it. Now I longed for Liz to gamahuche me completely, for the girl had hitherto only taken me into her mouth for a minute, or so. With a little encouragement she said she'd do it longer, for she little knew my intention. — Sarah then knelt on the bed and I fingered her cunt, whilst Liz operated on my penis. — Her pretty, cherry lipped sweet little mouth seemed scarcely large enough to take my pego, yet in it went. — "Go on darling put it further in." "Oh! ain't it stiff," said she, taking it from her mouth and looking admiringly at it. "Yes, lick the red tip. — Yes, so — now put it in — suck it, love." "Shall I make it spit," and she began clumsily to frig it, after she'd again taken it out. Frigging is not learnt in a day, and Lizzie can't do it nicely at all.

I didn't wish that. — "You shall make it spend, so presently, go on sucking it now dear." — On she went — the crisis was fast coming. — "Go on Lizzie darling, go quicker. — Further in your mouth, dear." — She obeyed, she was now fascinated with the amusement. "Arha — go on — aha." — My pleasure was complete, and before she was aware of it I had filled her mouth with my love essence. — Then she rushed to the chamber pot. — "Oh, you're a nasty doctor." Sarah laughed. — "You've done more than me, Liz." — The girl was a little angry, but in a minute or two, laughed about it. Between man and woman no form of lust, or game of sensual satisfaction is really displeasing. The one sex always likes giving pleasure to the other. Every form, device, or manner of amatory amusement, played with every part of the person, is proper. — Prick, cunt, arsehole, armpits, breasts, mouth, all can minister to sexual pleasure. — Both sexes in time find that out, and enjoy them all.

Other forms of erotic pleasure took their turn. One night I fucked Sarah to let Liz see the come-and-go of a prick in a cunt. I had fucked Liz and then gamahuched her, and Sarah had frigged herself. We had all drunk a lot, and it was pleasure to see each other piss. I was intensely ruttish that night. — I again set Sarah to gamahuche me, whilst I gamahuched Liz kneeling over me. It was, as I had already spent twice, a long business to bring out my sperm, for I am not as young as I was; and the lass was not so ready with *her* pleasure, but she spent long before I did. I find that having my prick sucked is certainly a most luxurious way of finishing an evening when nearly fucked out; there is no labor excepting for the gamahucher. It is a sabyritic way of finishing an evening.

Then I had a return of my micturating letches which seemed to please Sarah, the more so and I think mainly so, as I made Lizzie participate. I streamed against her little quim, and she streamed over my prick, but the letch did not last long and terminated by this erotic whim.

In a shop window I saw some china funnels, such as are used by chemists. The idea struck me at once, being then lewed, and walking along with lascivious combinations working in my brain. I bought one of which the neck was perhaps as large as a small sized prick. "Sally I want to fill your cunt with my piddle through this funnel." Sarah refused, then examined it, she was not going to have *that* put into her. Then she laughed, then joked, and by the time she'd had a little grog, wondered how it would feel, and at last said it would be a lark to try the funnel.

Putting pillows under her head and shoulders, she resting really only on her neck, head and blade bones, she hoisted herself up, and her back almost vertically against the bed, and so that her cunt was nearly horizontal. Gently I inserted the funnel in it, stopping when she told me. Full four inches were well imbedded in its folds. Then I pissed freely into the trumpet end of the funnel, seeing the water rise gradually in it, whilst, not a drop escaped from her vagina. At length she laughed, that moved her cunt, until a small quantity rose out by the side of the funnel. It was one of the most singular whims I ever gratified, but what pleasure it gave to all three of us. There was but one way of relieving her from her position, which soon became painful — I withdrew the funnel, and the saline contents ran over her belly and buttocks. She was start naked, and the piddle only spoiled the pillow cover, which she stripped off instantly when she had got upright. What infinite variety of pleasures a cunt can give to men and women with erotic fancies. Sarah enjoyed this lark immensely. — She kept the funnel. Did she show it to other men and women, and tell? I'll bet she did.

Lizzie, as said, was present with her "Ohoo moi" and was delighted with the exhibition. She was now present at all our baudy rollockings. Sarah was getting her into high training for harlotry. She denied *that,* when I remarked it, and talked of getting Liz a situation so soon as I wished no more of her. — The little fair haired beauty however had pretty well learnt what the profession of Venus was, for she had witnessed all my whims with Sarah, and had performed many of the same tricks with *me.* I used to sit feeling both their cunts at the same time. Sarah would lie down and we would look at her cunt, afterwards Sarah and I at Lizzie's. So when I said two or three nights after, that I'd like to put the funnel up Lizzie's cunt, Sarah laughed, and the girl only said, "It will hurt me."

"Why it's not nearly so thick and big as the doctor's prick," said Sarah taking the funnel out of a cupboard. The little lass prepared to put herself in the attitude, but this time instead of against the bed, against Sarah, who, naked, held up the girl's legs, and brought the little cunt into the horizontal position. Then I inserted the funnel nearly as far as it had gone up Sarah, and in that little cunt it seemed to go up just as easily. The dilatability of a cunt is truly wonderful. — Then I quite filled the funnel with my golden stream. — "Nobody would believe it if I tell any one," said Lizzie. Sarah looked astounded. — "Tell any one? — You little fool, you'd get yourself and all of us imprisoned if any one was told of the fun we have here, have you told any of the people in the house?" — The girl said she hadn't, but looked confused and much as if she had, for she now talked, I found, to some other girls in the house. — A woman's a born gossip, she can't keep her tongue still. A secret worries her, and it would not at all surprise me if Liz has told another girl. — She had got to be quite proud of her sexual knowledge, and one day in our tête-à-tête said, "Some gals doesn't know nothing about a doin it as we does." — How did she know *that* unless she'd asked girls?

Nothing pleased me more than putting the two females side by side naked on the bed, kneeling with their buttocks towards me. Then the big handsome hemispheres of Sarah, which always looked larger in that position than in any other, contrasted beautifully with the small but dazzlingly white bum cheeks of Lizzie; whilst the contrast between the dark haired pouters between Sarah's thighs, and the little semi-hairless lips, yet flaxen hue of the split, was cock stiffening. Then I used to slap them alternately, then kiss their backsides, then their cunts, then slap and kiss again till tired, or until I fucked one of them. Sometimes I licked Liz's cunt in that attitude, whilst I felt or contemplated the dark haired pudendal charms of the big neglected one, and sometimes fucked her.

After a time when Sarah treated Liz just as she would another harlot, I took pleasure in making the little one slap Sarah's buttocks. Sometimes we both slapped them together till they were red and tingled. Then Liz slapped them whilst I fucked Sarah, she laying over me, Sarah said it made her lewed. — Certainly she seemed to encourage the girl to slap her, and bore the blows with great tranquillity, but I didn't believe then that she had physical pleasure. — I smacked Lizzie's white little bum, but she didn't like it.

At that time with all my knowledge, I was singularly ignorant of the effects of flagellation, of the heat, lust, and physical enjoyment, that may be generated by judicious bum whacking, flogging, and birching. Perhaps this smacking of Sarah's buttocks was a lewed instinct of mine, leading me up to the higher knowledge of the sexual mysteries, and of the impulse given by the generative organs to the brain, and the entire human frame. I now know they are always at work, and are the great source and actuating principle of human existence, and perhaps of all animal life.—The prick and cunt are the prime motors of humanity, the food but heats and stirs them to action.

Tho Lizzie ceased to call Sarah "Aunt"—she let slip that title occasionally, and I should not be surprised if she were really entitled to that appellation. In my youth, the smallest and youngest girl (and still the youngest I yet have had) called the female she was with "aunt."—Another girl, if not two, whose names I just now forget, but of whom I have told called their mistress' "aunt," and I fancy that, many aunts among the humbler classes make a little money out of their nieces' virginities. — They know well that at about fourteen years of age, girls escape their care, will play with boys and youths, and are pretty sure to be broached before they are sixteen. Aunts often think that a gentleman may as well have the broaching of a little cunt and pay for it, as a coster lad have it for nothing.—Indeed I believe that to be a philosophical way of looking at it, common to a large number of the poor people in all countries.—Camille (the first), fetched and sold to me her sister Louise.—Other girls have got their young female relations for me, and liked doing it, liked the pimping. —The poor, and wisely, and right in their simplicity of nature, see no harm in copulation as those better off profess to do (but whether they really see harm is another question).—A girl is not among nine-tenths of the population morally damaged by a little illicit fucking, as she is among those who look upon a hymen as a prize and guarantee, in the woman they seek as a wife.

All said—the female who keeps her cunt hymenized and under seal amongst the well-to-do-classes, only does so that she may get a higher price for it, either in money or position. She sometimes never attains either, and mostly has to wait long for it, wait for years, and frigs herself during her waiting, languishing for want of a prick and spermatic lubrication, which is health giving to a female.—A poorer girl has earlier the prick up her, and every day, perhaps, has the intense pleasures of fucking, and all the varied amatory enjoyments which a man is pretty sure to give her in all sorts of ways.—Thus the happinesses of life are pretty evenly distributed.—Perhaps the woman who follows her sexual instincts, and who is thus the most natural, has the best of it. Fucking is the greatest pleasure of life, and the woman who delays getting it for years, loses much. The woman who waits till she is twenty-six before she is fucked, loses ten years' pleasure, compared with one who has a prick up her at sixteen, and regularly afterwards.

I began at last to be weary of the girl, and at the same time got anxious about her. She, like all others, wanted to go out and show her fine clothes. — It was of no use opposing it, and Sarah took her out. But the clothes were showy and Sarah, being a night bird and only wearing black silk, the girl looked very bright, and men came after the girl, so that they both took to wearing veils. — Said I, "She will go gay." "Not if I can help it — I like her too well, I'll work for her," Sarah replied.

Then I advised Sarah taking her back to the country — Sarah said that the girl would not go, and moreover, that it was impossible. The girl soon after seemed hurt for I did not see her or poke her as much. — Circumstances were in fact changing with me and I could not get to see her, tho I wished — Sarah said she told the girl to frig herself if she was randy, and I know frigged her herself. "That will keep her from wanting fucking for a bit, but she'll be longing for the right thing in her cunt." — After having had Liz about five months, I was obliged to go abroad. — Sarah was to try to get her into some situation, but where she could watch her — I left enough money to keep the girl four months.

I was away four months. The first night I was back in England I went to P***l**d P***e and met Sarah whom I knew a mile off. I asked her to come to the A**a. — Shall I bring *her*, said she laughing. — By her side stood a girl with a veil on. — I looked. — "Don't you know her?" The girl raised her veil and laughed quite a peal. It was Lizzie.

"You have made her a whore, it's a damned shame," said I angrily. — "I haven't, let's go to the A**a," and there we all went.

"It's extraordinary to meet *you*, for it's the first night I have brought her out. — Look, her things are fresh, the bonnet and dress you gave her are not suitable for the season (for it was the end of autumn) — see her boots, her stockings, her garters and all — all quite fresh." "What have I done that you did not come to see me," Lizzie whimpered.

Said Sarah, "We must live, I put her to a business, but she would not stop ten hours a day in a workshop in a close room. Then I put her at *** and she would not stop there. She would come out, and she'll make ten times as much by my help as she would by herself. — I did not want it, and have been kind to her, haven't I Liz? — I will keep her with pleasure," Sarah went on, "but she won't stop at home without me." — Liz, whilst this was going on, was sitting on my knee, my fingers were on her little sweet cunny, but for a minute only, for quickly we all got on to the bed. — Sarah unasked. — She had her old letch on, and frigged herself whilst I fucked the little one again and again.

The girl had grown an inch, was plumper, had more hair on her little quim, which was more enticing than ever, and was a lovely little creature altogether. I was sorry to think that she would turn out gay, and believed that that was really the first night she was out for the purpose. — A man had already accosted her and the lass had refused him. — Sarah told her that gay life was gay life and money money. — If she meant to get a living that way, she mustn't play the fool, but take any one who'd pay handsomely.

"I wouldn't," said Liz, tossing her head. — "He was an ugly little old man with a white beard and I could not a bear the sight of him — a little old man."

How the girl enjoyed her fucking — and what a lovely cunt she had. — How I enjoyed *her*, but circumstances were too strong for me, it was impossible for me to see her much — I made her promise not to be gay, and agreed to give Sarah three pounds a week for her, whilst I was in England. — Next night I saw them at the lodgings. — Sarah said she didn't mind working for the girl, her letch for her she now admitted, but the girl wouldn't be moped up. — She *would* go out, so what was Sarah to do. The end was clear, that she was to be a gay woman.

For another month or so I had her, then again went abroad, leaving twenty pounds for the girl to live on while I was away. — On my return it was well on in winter. — I went to the old haunts — Sarah was not visible — to her lodgings and she had left, and no one knew where she had gone. — I went to baudy houses and there they had missed her. — One old woman looked queerly at me, and said she did not know such a woman, altho any one who had seen Sarah twice must have recollected her. — "Why I have paid you for rooms with Miss F**z*r dozens of times." — Then the woman admitted she knew her and me, but had missed her some time. — "I thought," said the woman, "you was after her for something." She took me to be a detective I think at first.

Said I, "She used a little time ago to be with a young fair haired girl, where is *she*?" "Oh yes, but I've not seen the girl neither — there was some sort of a row about her — but there," said she, stopping short, "I don't know anything about either — there." — I gave her ten shillings to tell me all she knew, she took it, and said she knew nothing more.

I asked two or three gay women whom I had seen talking to Sarah. — They knew nothing. — One I took to a house, hoping to get some information. — She said Sarah was a bad one she believed — I never saw or heard of either Sarah or Lizzie again.

My impression is that some one was after Sarah on account of Liz, and that they both fled from London — I feel sure Sarah had no wish for her to be gay, but Liz had learned to like the red knobbed flesh stick far better than another woman's cunt, and I dare say is merrily fucking about somewhere now, and I hope is happy.

So finished my acquaintance with Sarah F**z*r who, with her substitutes, had mainly amused me for something like four years. I did not however see her usually more than twice a week to have her, and sometime two or three weeks elapsed without my doing so. — At times I was abroad, or away from town for far longer periods, and at other times I was virtuous and at home. — But there were often occasions when I was alone in town, and free to dispose of myself and my sperm. — It was at those opportunities that I had my rutting fits, and notably so when I had the man.

[The adventure which follows is singular in its way — for I had, as narrated, an Irish woman some time since, with the same vanity which marks this one. I have however had English women who vaunted their own beauties.]

CHAPTER X

A light-haired Irish bitch. — Foul-tongued and hot-arsed. — Recondite expressions. — "D'ye loike me." — Her bolt from Dublin. — Baggage detained. — A suspicious tale. — My regrets at losing Sarah. — Camille revisited. — Her brothel venture. — About sodomites and catamites. — Buggers' sphincters. — Her friend's catamitic tastes. — Sodomy cum gamahuche. — Lolotte the young Belgian. — On the qualities of different cunts. — Lolotte's gamahuche. — Reflexions on the change in my erotic tastes. — An artist in lewedness. — French, fat, white-skinned, red-haired and thirty-five. — Refined ministrations. — Anal fingering. — A sphincter dilated. — Lingual delicacies. — Kid gloves and cold cream. — The curious chair. — Erotic suggestions. — Dildo buggery. — A second harlot — two pleasures at once. — Anus and pudenda in simultaneous action.

[For continuity of the narrative about Sarah F**z*r, the following little incident was omitted from its proper place. — It occurred about a year before Sarah disappeared. The date on the manuscript proves that. I don't think I ever told Sarah of it.]

I was going along Coventry St. on a muddy evening, and saw a lovely pair of feet and ankles supporting a well grown body — it was a liberal display of leg in silk — looking at the female as I passed, she winked in the lustful whorish way which a woman does when thoroughly lewed at the moment, and looks at a man invitingly. It is my theory that *she* communicates at once some lewedness to *him*. — I don't mean the lewed look of a woman who incites you only to get money, but when she's really randy and wants a male, wants to be fucked badly. — This woman did so, and at once I reciprocated her lust. She followed me up a side street.

— "You've a fine leg," said I beginning. — With strong Irish brogue which I can't imitate in writing, nor indeed any way, she said, "Sure and there isn't a foiner in all the town, won't your cock stand for shure if you see a little higher," and she pulled up her clothes to her knees in the dark street. — I can't bear Irish women, having found them liars and thieves, and did not like her manner. — "Com long." "No, I'm poor and can't to night, but here is a glass of wine for you." "Och! to the Divil with the cash — shure and we won't quarrel about that — com — shure an I loike the looks of you — I'm close by — com." I followed her and she went at such a pace, as if either the police were after her, or that she was frightened of shitting herself. We entered a house and a comfortable room with a good fire. — A large trunk was on the floor. — Said she, "Shure and I've not been here an hour and not unpacked — I've been a week coming from Dublin — It's God's truth, may I go to the biggest hell if I've been fucked for a week." — All this rapidly in answer to my questions, and some without my questions. — Then she pulled out my prick. — "It's not stiff — wait a second and it'll be stiff enough, damned if I don't feel as if I'd forgotten what a man is," and in a violent hurry, she tore off her things till she was start-naked, boots and stockings excepted, apostrophizing her parts from time to time. — "There's a pair of thighs — haven't I a foine shape — not a foiner by Jasus, and there, feel my bubbs — look at my small waist — and with such a large rump." — By that time she was naked whilst I had only taken my hat off. — Then she grabbed at my prick again (she had pulled it out), then threw herself at the edge of the bed, and opening her thighs, "Put it up me darling bhoy, fuck me chunt — look at the hair on it, it's foine shure, ah! I envy the pleasure yer prick will have in it me bhoy — fuck — com on — fuck." — The slut was hot cunted. — boiling with lust — in full rut unmistakably.

I didn't like her manner, speech, or colour, but altho shortish, a more superb form, more lovely white flesh, never was offered to my embraces — I put my prick at once into her glowing cunt, and directly it was well lodged in its folds, she burst out into such a torrent of baudy words, such obscenity, such ribald screeching, as I never heard before or since from a woman in copulation; tho I have known some gay ladies, when their pleasure was on, pretty frank about it, and have taught a few who were not gay to be warm in their exclamations of pleasure. Of late years I interlard my endearments with lewed words and wishes, it adds much to my enjoyment mentally, for fucking is the sublimest mental as well as physical pleasure. "Aha," she began, "aha — oho — fuck it well — begorra your prick's red hot — it's big. — Ahaa — sure me chunt's as hot as hell — fuck — fuck hard — piss out your boiling spunk into my bloody chunt — sure that will cool me chunt. — Aha God! aha fuck hard yer bugger. — Aha, Holy Virgin my bloody spendings are coming. — Aha — a lovely prick — stiff — push it hard up me chunt — fuck — split me hot chunt into me randy arsehole. — Fuck em both — ahar — fuck — fuck — now — now. — Aha, I'm coming — spend — spunk — fuck — cunt — ballocks. — Aha — arseholes — ahra — my spunks — ahaa — ahaa." She was silent, her thighs quiet. She'd spent ere I had half fucked her, for her fierce baudiness and outrageous obscenity at first seemed to stop my pleasure. — It made me think for the instant that she was mad.

I went on thrusting, my lust getting stronger as her lewed words wrought clouds of meretricious images in my brain, when after a short silence, with a sudden effort she uncunted me, and struggling up pushed me away saying. — "Sure and I just wanted a fuck — I hope I'll die a fucking." — Is she mad or drunk I thought?—But excepting for her excitability, libidinosity, and blasphemous obscenity, she seemed sober enough. She smiled as angrily I cried, "Lie down and let me finish," shut her eyes without answering, and seemed to be feeling her clitoris, sitting at the edge of the bed where I stood swearing, my prick standing stiff in front of me.

"Let me finish fucking, what the Devil are you about," and I clutched her as she rose from the bed, but she escaped me. My passion was roused well by the probing I'd had in her cunt. — "Wait a bit me bhoy, thin and shure I'll be after spending agin, by the Holy Mother you're a lovely fucker, you've learned a bit in your time, many's the chunts you've cooled begorra. — No — No — wait a bit and I'll be spending agin with yer." "Humbug you didn't spend, you lie." "Didn't I spend? shure and I did, it's God's truth — look." On the side of the bed she laid down and opened her thighs wide. — "There me bhoy — I'd just have drowned yer prick in me chunt, if ye'd kept it in a minit longer." — Her cunt was wet enough, it had wetted my piercer and my balls before she'd ejected it, and plenty of pearly moisture was just inside, ready to run out as she separated her cunt lips to show me. Suddenly down went her legs, she walked quickly about the room, gave her box a kick, and with both hands slapped her buttocks several times loudly. — "Dam it, lay down and let me fuck you, you bitch," I cried in a rage. — She laughed and continued slapping her backside.

In a minute or so, she laid hold of my prick which had a little drooped. — "It's a fine hot poker, sure and it is — com on then," and she laid down on the bed side again. — I inserted my pego, which stiffened up as its tip touched her lubricated cunt — I drove it up hard, and soon her baudy words recommenced. — "Aha — that's it — aha — my arse and chunt are all in one shure — split them with your pego. — Aha. Shove your bloody prick up into my womb — Aha — what a lovely peg — Aha — your spunk a comin — don't — stop — wait for me — I'll spend — Aha — fuck, fuck aha — God if ye'd two pricks ye'd have one in my chunt and one up my arse hole wouldn't ye? — Aha, my bloody hot sphunks comin. — Ahar spunk — spend in my bloody chunt. Ah Jasus — fuck me — now — ahaa — ahaa — prick — ballocks — bugger — aha — aa." I cannot imitate her manner or brogue, it is impossible; nor give accurately her extraordinary quaint, baudy, and blasphemous expressions — I never heard such issue from the mouth of a harlot, but have between some drunken Irish women slanging each other in St. Giles, and also in the lowest quarters of Liverpool.

Tho I disliked her lewed imprecations they now stirred my lust extraordinarily. She kept me up to her as I leant over her, gently working her quim and buttocks. "Kiss me love — don't pull it out — there shure and I'll stiffen it again in me chunt, if your ballocks are close up to me. — Can't you *fuck* just — haven't I spent? the spunks squeezing out. — Begorra ye've spent thick, and lots, and hot, ye spalpeen. — Don't pull it out me darlin — kiss me — you've not kissed me, look what foine teeth I have. — Shove your tongue into my mouth. — Oh keep your prick up me hot chunt — put your finger up my arsehole when you fuck again." "No." "Whoy, whoy won't you? (as I refused) Don't then me darlin. — Don't you never do so when yer fucking? Oh ye spalpeen ye do — I love it, love both me holes full — chunt and arse hole. —

There now it's out — whoy didn't ye keep it up me hot chunt." — Thus she went on as nearly as written without stopping, all being said, and acted with surprizing energy whilst still she was holding me tightly to her, as I bent over her standing at the side of the bed, without uttering more than a word or two in reply to her, and, standing wondering, amused and almost silent.

It slipped out, the copulation was broken. "Take off your clothes and come on to the bed and lie down wid me, and we'll fuck agin ye spalpeen in foive minutes — we will, be Jasus. Look at me chunt — look at your spunk — it's wet — it is — ain't your spunk thick," said she examining her finger after a feel. — I didn't like that, yet she had made me lewed. She had accompanied words with deeds, and as quickly as she had spoken, she had turned herself in all attitudes — on to her belly, then buttocks, had opened her thighs, threw her legs quite high up in the air, and other antics just as before, showed me her armpits and teeth, and pulled the cunt wide open to show the libation overflowing from it — all unasked by me; and interlarding her acts, with expressions of strong desire for me.

I now fully excited, stood pulling off my clothes rapidly, and dropping them on the floor by the side of me, silent, unable to resist the fascination of her carnalities and take my eyes off of her. — "Oh look at your spunk in my chunt" said she again. — "Shure and I'm longing for more of it — many a chunt you've filled I'll swear — ain't my breasts beautiful? you shall spend between them some day. — Make haste me darlin — if you don't I'll frig me — I will by Jasus, I'm mad to have it up me agin — come." Then we got on to the bed.

I covered her, I rubbed my tool outside in the overflowing sperm, and was in a few minutes spending with her, with my tongue in her mouth and trying to perforate her bum hole with my finger. After she had shouted out, "Fill me chunt — fuck it — ballocks it well — bugger. — Now. — Shove harder. — I'm spending — ahrr — arsehole." — "Dams and bloodies" in endless combinations she cried, and it had such an effect on me, that I cried out baudy words with her. Never in my life have I heard such a woman. The words from her struck me as abominably foul and obscene, tho some of the words have not, when sweeter, loving women have murmured them with me in our sensual paroxysms — and yet the Irish bitch excited me.

This fuck quieted her — seemed to subdue her — I still laid on her, she still sucking my tongue, or wetting her lips with her spittle, rubbing them on mine, holding my head with one hand, pressing it towards hers, and rubbing her other rapidly, quite rapidly up and down my back and buttocks, as far as her hand would reach; as if she couldn't feel enough of me. — "By me soul and you fuck beautiful — beautiful be Jasus," said she at last. "Sure an we'll do it agin, — a rale man and you are shure. Do you loike me? — your hair's sticking to me chunt." — Smack squash — and moving her cunt a little back, our mottes unjoined, and the glutinous exudations which adhered to our fleshy prominences where they had met so closely made that expressive noise as our genitals partly separated, as she moved her belly when my prick was dwindling out of her split.

Her quick movements, and the fanciful but foul things she said, had so heated me, so libidinously excited me, that I scarcely knew what I was about. "Yes," I replied, "let's look at your cunt." — I had scarcely seen it in my emotion. — "Look my bhoy" — I rose on my knees, she relinquishing my rump, and I looked. "Your hair's the same color as on your head." "Yes, and are my armpits." — She threw up her arms. — "Don't you like the colour?" — I said — "yes" — but I didn't. — It was a peculiar, sandy red color. — I never before saw an Irish woman with that coloured hair, and told her that most Irish had dark hair. "Shure I'm true emerald." She was, as said, very beautifully formed, and had marvellously white flesh. — I threw up her legs, and saw from her heels to her buttocks. — "I'm beautiful made shure and I am, arnt I?" said she, putting her hands round her thighs to keep her legs up.

I looked and gloated. There was her cunt almost foaming with pearly mucilage. — "Lie down me darlin," — and I did. — She laid hold of my prick and frigged it. — "Oh put it in me — do then." — I'll just take a dale of it tonight — I'm wild just. — A bhoy like you will just make her happy — whoy — I've not slept for two nights, I've left one of my boxes at Birmingham — I ran away — I'd no money — I would not stay to be ill thraited — but the first money I get I'll be after it — I pawned me watch to pay my week's lodgings here this very day, sure and I hadn't enough money to pay me cabman. Pay down the first week says the landlady, or it's no good yer laving your box here. — Wait a minute, ma'am, where's a pawnbroker's? and me and me box and the carman went to pawn me watch."

"You've been drinking," I said, thinking at last that it must be so. — Not she. "By the Holy Mother. — Divil a drap — you're a queer chap, don't you loike me? — now you don't loike me — I'll wash my chunt and you'll like it better." She was twiddling my cock then, but left off, jumped off the bed like lightning, and began washing — I washed my appendages also, and was going to dress. "Shure and yer not going to lave me yet, shure and you shan't till ye've don it agin." "I can't again," said I. — She gave me a rapid push, which sent me on to a chair with such force was it given, and kneeling down began to suck my prick. — "Sure and I'll make it stiff in a jiffey. What a lovely prick, and my first in London — Oh Jesus may it bring me luck — and I haven't had a fuck for a week. By the Holy Virgin I'll have another fuck." Sucking hard, and jerking out these sentences at short intervals with much intensity, and with that and her baudy talk, she in time made me stiff, put it into her cunt herself impatiently, and I gave her another libation. She rattled out the same lascivious cries but less energetically, and I noticed that tho she talked lewedly when we were not in action, that her most outrageous, unrestrained exclamations, were only uttered when she was fucking.

She began again telling her history of running away from Dublin. — "I'd been murdered shure had I staid, it's God's truth I tell ye, and I pawned me watch to pay the lodgings here and me cab." — Then she wanted to treat me to whiskey and water. — What would I have. — Then she mounted me as I lay tired on my back, kissing me, and rubbing her cunt on to my flabby cock, I could not stop her. — She talked the foulest baudiness, and said her poorliness was just coming on. — Wasn't it unlucky, just as she'd come so poor and wanted to get some friends. — She loved a man about her. "Sure God," she did, but hadn't had one for a week, she'd had enough to do to dodge them and get away. "Hide and seek and fucking don't go together." But she was safe now she was in London — I got now curious and tried to learn something more, but she shut up at once. — In her lewed excitement it was pleasure to gabble on and let out a bit of her story, but the cunning jealous secrecy of a harlot returned. — Her fear of being detected, of telling too much, shut her mouth. — I thought, and had no doubt, she'd run away from Ireland to get clear of some scrape.

I couldn't get away from the woman, she sent for whiskey and I drank with her. She frigged and sucked me stiff again, and I fucked her spite of myself — listening — disliking — yet excited. — When fucked out I left. — "Another kiss," said she following me to the door of her room, and pushing her tongue in my mouth. "Feel my cunt again for luck." — I did, promising at her earnest entreaty to see her again. "Never mind the cash me darlin — I loike your fucking — sure and ye'll bring me luck," said she as we parted.

I set myself afterwards to repeat what the woman shrieked out in her sexual ecstasy, for she was thoroughly enjoying me, and the sayings and baudy utterances rang in my ears — I did not like them, but kept repeating them to myself, laughing at them even — I went with another woman a day or two after, and as my pleasure increased when my body was joined to hers, I shouted out some of the salacities — it stimulated me. — "Oh ain't you a going on," said she. — "Say fuck, ballocks." — "I shan't" — then — "oh don't make such a noise, or they will hear you up stairs." — But I would. — That giving way to lascivious utterances helped my fatigued ballocks very much. — I'd been with some woman who was out and out baudy, I told this to this woman. I had no reason for hiding it, and told her all. — "A dirty beast," said she. — Some women are naturally baudy and lewed in talk, others are not. — As among harlots so among ladies. I have known some whom I never could induce to use love words frankly — others soon revelled in them.

I saw the Irish woman once or twice in Coventry Street afterwards, but got out of her way. — She always pulled her petticoats up as high as she dared to show her lovely limbs and walked very rapidly. Tho I did not like her, for all that I went home with her once again. She kissed me in the street when I spoke to her, and talked so loudly, that passers-by stared at us — so calling her a fool, I turned away and went up a side street. — She came to me and then I followed her home. — There she again baudied and shrieked out when fucking, the most original salacities and obscenities, and spent with me, and then frigged me up and sucked me to her heart's content; telling me how she had got on, and what a man did to her, and what he had given her, how she meant still to get her trunk from Birmingham. She hadn't yet. — Altogether she went on almost like an erotic maniac and I was glad when I got away.

I saw her once or twice in the streets afterwards, but she did not see me; then I lost sight of her. I don't think that altogether she was about the West End a month — I must have seen her had she been about longer. I have never met such a foul tongued woman in my life before, she must have been bred and born amongst the lowest. — I haven't told a tenth part of her original erotic sayings, and combinations of baudiness and blasphemy. It seemed to me that when her sensual pleasure came on, that she scarcely knew what she said; that every baudy and blasphemous word she'd ever heard, came struggling up together to describe and emphasize the pleasure she felt in her cunt. — I told her of it. — She said it was my fault, and that she didn't cry out so with other men, it was the intense pleasure I gave. "I'll swallow your spunk and drink your piss if you like," said she. I didn't believe a word she said.

[Once since, at a French brothel, I found an Irish woman, who certainly was more highly obscene than her sisters there. One French woman said she was the greatest "Cochonne" in the house, and all the women were afraid of her.

[The disappearance of Sarah was a great loss to me as I recollect well. She was a quiet woman and handsome, her form good, her cunt gave me the fullest and most complete pleasure, she indulged my lewedness, and when intimacy was established took herself the greatest pleasure in lascivieties with me. — She procured me virgins whom she delighted in fingering, and with two of them in flatfucking, and a man who jointly amused us. In occasional orgies at brothels, she several times got me other free and easy harlots, but about which orgies I have destroyed the manuscript, as I did with the women only what I have done with others. — Her lodgings I could mostly go to, and believe I was the only man who did, and I missed the means of indulging my tastes in those quiet rooms with a willing ministress to them. — Moreover she was not always plaguing me for money — asking me to pay this, or to lend her to pay that — which is the common habit and trick of harlots from high to low — I felt at sea when Sarah was gone, and recollect that for a month or so I was chaste.]

Then I sought Camille — I had seen her thrice only I find whilst I had known Sarah F**z*r, and had some difficulty in finding her out. — She was not so young, but was splendidly preserved. Tho fatter, her soft skin, soft voice and quiet laugh, in brief all her good qualities were unchanged, and I rushed my eager pego into her still delicious cunt, and clasped her exquisitely soft backside with the delight of former days. She had been away from England two years or so, having saved money, with which in her native country she had either bought or set up a licensed house for whoring. It had not succeeded, she had lost all, and had come back here to harlotry. — She cried as she told me about her losses, then began to smoke a cigarette (formerly she did not smoke). She smiled and said it was fate, that there was always water or charcoal to be had when she was old or tired of life. — She was seemingly not so well off as formerly, but said she had a good clientele mostly of married men who paid well, and didn't stop long. She did not go into the street much, for her friends expected always to find her at home. I spent two or three hours delightfully with her talking over old times. — It was no use disguising her age from me, and one other Monsieur who also knew her when she first came to London, the only two, she said; but she took off a few years to new friends when they asked her age. She now spoke excellent English. [Fifteen years later she was alive, and as nice as ever in manner — but she was old and poor, and very often I assisted her.]

Much as I liked, I didn't keep to Camille. I went there when I wanted a quiet chat and information about sexualities (not that I wanted much of that). I find a memorandum of a talk with her, about the effect that continued buggering had upon the arseholes of the buggerees. She thought it detrimental to them ultimately, and had heard so, but the men were reticent on the subject. — About tastes for that abnormal amusement — that there were decidedly those men who enjoyed being operated on — catamites by taste, by nature perhaps; she thought owing to some anatomical difference, or sexual infirmity.

One evening being unusually communicative, she told that she had a friend who came to her rooms at times, and she procured a man to bugger him. When he had had that operation performed, his prick would stand, and he could fuck her and spend.—Nothing else that could be done had that effect; masturbation, suction, flagellation all were useless.—Altho sometimes he shagged Camille after the irritation of his fundament had produced an erection, he preferred being frigged whilst the other man was coupled with him.—It was "vilaine, cochonnerie la plus sale," she said.—"Mais que voulez vous."—"He pay me sometime five—ten pounds sometime.—When I came back to England, he buy me half my furniture.—He send Bordeaux, I cannot such buy—you shall taste. He is good for me and I do what he likes."—Then she fetched a bottle of splendid Château Margaux which he had given her. She had a case of it.—Camille never drank spirits, and didn't care so much about champagne.—I used to take her Claret at times, it was what she habitually drank at her meals.

Then I told her what I had done with the man. She would not at first believe it.—"Fi donc—pas vrai—un beau garçon comme vous."—But she added, "It was curiosity, it is not your taste—bien sur—yet why not if you like—it is for you and him to decide, it concern no one else."

Then I asked her to get me a youngish virgin.—No it was not possible, but a very nice young woman she would try to find. Sixteen and not more than seventeen was named by me as the limit of age.—Aha! I was like the rest she observed, she dare say she could find such.—"Mind Camille—I can tell nearly her age by the quantity of hair on her cunt, by its look, and by the look and feel of her breasts.—No deceit," and I left her laughing.—"Ah polisson, I shall try."

Soon afterwards she told me she should soon have the girl I liked, a young Belgian expected to arrive daily. She had been seduced, was a governess, and could no longer stop in her town. She had never been gay, but was coming to London to try her fortune at fucking. She was in fact brought here by a procuress as Camille admitted.

Anticipation made me restless. I called every day to enquire, and at length had the neophyte in whoring.—She was dressed in black silk, handsome but quiet, and rose like a lady when Camille introduced her—I hadn't believed about her being a governess nor the other accounts of her, thinking it was only said to enhance the price, for I had agreed to pay more than the usual fee for the freshness of the article; but found that she closely answered the description given of her. — Camille helped her to undress, and Lolotte (the name she went by) had black silk stockings on, and bright gold garters, three quarters of an inch broad; she had dressed or had been dressed tho quite quietly, yet on the road to her cunt dressed so as to stimulate male salacity.

I think now with delight still, of my voluptuous feelings as I got my hand between her partially closed thighs, felt the slight thicket of her hairy motte, and gently running my fingers over her clitoris slipped them down to the mouth of the temple of love, whilst she sat passively tho seemingly upset a little, involuntarily closing her thighs and trying to stop my hand, whilst Camille looked on smiling.

"Lay hold of my prick," said I in English forgetting that she could not speak a word of my language. Camille laughed and repeated it in French. Gently she put her hand down and grasped it. — Kissing her, holding her round the waist, her hand on my prick, my hand on cunt I pulled her back anglewise on the sofa on which we were sitting, and gluing my lips to hers I burrowed my fingers up her tight little cunt. Thus we reclined in voluptuous silence, she holding my tool, I gently frigging her. — Releasing her, "Let me see you quite naked." She refused. — But at once I pulled her chemise off roughly, and there she stood in her nudity, and a sweet nakedness it was.

She was well grown, beautifully formed, but thinnish, sylphlike; and had solid pretty breasts tho each was but a handful. From the small quantity of crisp curly hair on her cunt, the little lips, and its general look, I guess she was the age she said, not quite seventeen, and she'd been fucked for the first time, not quite a year. — Her hair was very dark brown, nearly but not quite black, her eyes dark hazel. Her face was however decidedly plain tho pleasing. The sight, and the rapturous feel of her naked charms, in a minute made me rampant with desire, I threw off my shirt and jersey, and pressed my naked body to hers, my stiffened prick was squeezed between our bellies as I clasped her to me, and Camille laughed aloud as I drew the girl into the bedroom. She mounted the bed at my request with hesitation and without speaking. I got on to her, titillated her cunt for a minute, then my prick throbbing and nodding, impatient for its enjoyment, urged me to put it into her pretty, pouting, sexual treasure. At the first thrust her whole body thrilled deliciously with pleasure. — What a charm it is to feel that a woman enjoys the prick. Soon our sighs and murmurs mingled, and her cunt was filled for the first time with an Englishman's sperm. Camille entered the bedroom as we were lying tranquilly in each other's arms, squeezing our genitals together, enjoying the mucilaginous bath of sperm in her cunt, whilst our lips and tongues played together, and mingled our salivas. "Elle est charmante, is she not?" said she. — "Leave us alone, Camille." She seemed in my way then. Away she went laughing. — "Ah polisson — c'est un beau garçon, n'est ce pas, Lolotte?"

Then was the delight of inspecting, investigating with eye and finger, that pretty, red faced gap, now almost hidden by my libation, but I liked its lubricious feel. — Then she washed it, and then I had my first good look at the odoriferous parting. Its aroma was delicious and prick stimulating — it was what I have told, the smell and look roused my prick at once, again we embraced, and both spent ecstatically. Her cunt seemed to fit my prick to perfection, her enjoyment seemed quietly intense. She'd only arrived that morning from Ostend, the journey, change, and excitement had perhaps stirred her lust, journeys do; but there was another cause; she had not been fucked for three months, her lover having been sent abroad she said. I saw no reason to doubt this, tho it may not have been true, but certainly she was dying for a fuck; and after our ablutions, and we laid cosily side by side on the bed again, the feel of my cunt stretcher was I'm sure as great a treat to *her,* as the feel of her tight little cock easer was to *me.* I fucked her four times, and always she poured out her salt pearly juices, to mix with my glutinous libation in her pretty cunt. She was delicious.

In our talk during the intervals of action on a subsequent day, and when we had a little champagne together, she told me that excepting on the night when she lost her virginity, she'd never been fucked more than once in any day. She and her lover had no chance, they could only copulate in the house or grounds. She was nearly always with the children, and all their poking was done quickly and on the sly. — How like it was to the frolics in my extreme youth, when I had difficulty in getting a clear five minutes, and used to shag our servants everywhere; garden, summer house, watercloset, in the hall, and on the staircase, in every imaginable out of the way place and time. — How hurriedly we fucked too, the pleasure hastened and diminished by fear of its being stopped. — Her love making was done under similar difficulties, indeed greater.

Lolotte I found had nice ladylike manners, and to have had that (which out of a thousand Cyprians whom I have stroked I have rarely found) a good education. — Her hand writing was beautiful. I quite believe she was a governess. The son of her employer, a young man about twenty years old first stroked her, it's too long here to tell how. She got *enceinte*, delayed it too long, then in trying to bring on her courses made herself very ill, which led to the discovery. — Her tale seemed coherent and probable enough, for such things occur daily. — Certainly she was no gay woman on the night I first had her. A dozen indications proved *that* to an old experienced *roué* like me. Camille said so, tho she knew only I suppose what the procuress told her.

I took a huge fancy to Lolotte. There was some quality in her cunt which made my animal enjoyment in her excessive. — Those who say that all women are the same in the dark, are utterly ignorant or deficient in sensibility. — Some women's cunts are exquisite to me, and some are not. — Once a cunt has given me that exquisitely voluptuous, complete delight, it always does so; just as a cunt which gives me but mediocre pleasure, which seems at my first fuck deficient somehow or somewhere, and is wanting undefinably in fitness to my penis, it always remains the same, whether I fuck it burning with passion, and with ballocks boiling over with sperm, or whether with the greater deliberation, which but slight sexual desire at the moment enables me to exercise. — Poke, probe, push, wriggle, rest it, or insinuate my prick into Lolotte's cunt anywhere, or anyhow, it always seemed to fit my sensitive pego, and so I lusted for her much, but alas was unable for reasons then existing to see her very often. — Her pleasures were so complete and affected me so, that when fucking others, I generally thought of Lolotte's cunt, even for a long period after I lost her.

Camille would not tell me where to find Lolotte. "I'll always get her for you." Neither would Lolotte tell me where I could find her. I never saw her in Paphian haunts, nor among the foreign colony of Paphians, [of whom there are now thirty for every one who was in London when I had my first French woman. (Camille)]. At intervals therefore I had her at Camille's rooms, for about three months. She soon learnt the libidinous manners of her calling.— I noticed the gradual change from her modest ways, from her frank lust in meeting my ardors, to Paphian professional modes of exciting me.—She no doubt was well instructed, but nature was also her instructress, for she was a warm, hot cunted, vigorous, juicy one.—She liked the male pendant, and certainly she always and to the last, spent with me. As my glowing prick buried itself in the innermost recesses of her moist, aromatic gap, and when it squirted the hot sperm into her, the way she clasped me to her, and murmured softly her pleasure, and her cunt flushed out its salt juices, and when the violent paroxysms were passed and the pleasure subsiding, the way she clasped me still, and nestled her pretty cunt up to my belly, enjoying the cram and gorge of my still thick prick, and the sperm as it lay balmy within her till the latest moment, was most exquisitely voluptuous, and showed her sexual lust, and, I really think, her liking for my embraces.

Then occurred a most libidinous incident with a red haired French woman, now to be narrated. It had the effect of making me wish Lolotte to do the same to me. I had hitherto simply fucked her in one or two attitudes. I called on Camille with the letch on me.—She told me she thought that the girl had left the country, however she got her for me that very evening. My letch was strong on me.—"Faites la minette, gamahuche me, suck my prick," said I, using all three terms to ensure my being understood. "Ah my God no." —"Yes," she had been asked, but—"jamais, jamais"—it ended by soft devices, by Camille's exhortations [as similar refusals since have with others], in her kneeling over me, with her genteel little backside, and pretty pink lipped, curly haired split, within six inches of my eyes, whilst her mouth gently took first the tip, and then all my prick into it. And then the aroma of her cunt and its surroundings excited me.—I smelt, I kissed it, inserted my finger, and then with my tongue played over the surface of the lips. Then my tongue plunged through the delicate red split, and then up the avenue.—At that last voluptuous moment, when the desire to have fingers, tongue, prick, all of my body in the woman, to join my body in its entirety to hers, to incorporate my body and soul with hers by her cunt, it was invincible. Then she ceased her lingual exercise, whilst my tongue reaching further forward sought her clitoris, playing rapidly on it, till a gentle oscillation, and quivering of her backside told of her discharge. The next instant my libation entered her pretty mouth, and both were satisfied.

The next time I asked Camille to get Lolotte for me, she could not. — A rich Belgian had taken her away and would marry her. Camille had thought she would never be gay long, and I was fortunate to have had her. — How true this was I don't know, but Camille all my life I found to be reliable, which is rare in a courtezan. I never saw or heard of the Belgian Lolotte afterwards.

[A paragraph of my original manuscript, without abbreviation or correction, and just as it was then written is retained here. — It is a clue to my mental condition at that date, and a good introduction to the episode which follows. — An explanation of my tastes.]

My tastes seem for some time past to have been much changed, to be gradually inclining to abnormal pleasures. — Have I seen and done enough with — am I getting tired of common place sensualities — am I on the road to a sensual abyss? — Lustful suggestions come to me more frequently from strumpets, or so it seems to me. — Do *they*, or do I — take more heed of them than formerly? Pleasures which in my youth I doubted as possible, the whisper of which passed by me like the idle wind, others which I did not like even to hear of, I now think about. The tongue and the mouth more frequently minister to my sensuous joys. — Do I really like that or not? My imagination well exercised in sexual pleasures, now suggests strange forms of fornication. — I find women willing to gratify them, nay more — have evident delight with myself in doing so, when I have suggested them. Whether those fancies are indulged in with other men, or others of their own sex, and this not for lucre only, it evidently is to gratify themselves as well as me that they do them.

My lasciviousness has increased by practice and women are similarly influenced. — Is it during the last few years, years which I vowed to consecrate to fidelity, that I have thus changed, or have these tastes been growing on me since puberty? A voluptuous offer from a fair woman, I feel now that I can scarcely resist. — Where will this end, in good or evil?

My knowledge of male and female in sexual matters, in their procreative instincts and sexual vagaries, how large it seems. — Yet there still seems a field of pleasure, of enquiry yet unexplored before me. Shall I yield and gratify it? My former hesitations seem nearly gone, boldly and without hesitation, I now ask women for the satisfaction of letches, letches relatively abnormal. — Perhaps all beyond plain belly to belly copulation may be called abnormal sexual pleasures. Much that is done every hour, every minute by male with female is abnormal. But to what does this lead? — What will be the outcome to this wider range of erotic desires. — Good or evil? — Shall I struggle against it or yield? — Have I not struggled before, struggled against my philosophy, and with what result? — my narrative answers me.

Going along R*g**t St. one night a French woman accosted me. — She would give me such pleasure she promised, pattering on, and walking by my side when she found I did not refuse her advances. She answered my lewed questions readily, as I put them out of sheer fun and curiosity, for I had no intention at the moment of accompanying her. — Yes, give me pleasure such as I had never tasted, — any I liked. — She had nice rooms, — warm, baudy pictures and books. — "Ah oui, vous pouvez m'enculer," if it were my taste and would pay, or she would get me a youth, a boy — "Un beau garçon — charmant — sixteen years old no more." — He would bugger me if I liked, for his prick was nice and small — yes, she had seen it, for he had buggered a friend of hers in her lodgings, she had seen him do it, so she knew all about him. Amused with her, pleased with her small soft voice which reminded me of Camille's, a voice so different from the harsh raw voices of most French Paphians, that having an hour or two to spare, I went out of curiosity only to the apartments of the woman.

She had nice rooms, and a selection of thoroughly good, coloured, cock rousing lithographs of fornication. Soon I had looked thro them and sat looking at *her* undressing, for she was the better worth looking at. — She undressed with great deliberation, talking about masturbation, gamahuching, fucking and sodomy, in as quiet a way as if talking about her dress. In these particulars she reminded me of Camille. She said she was twenty-eight. I am sure she was at least thirty-five, was a well known woman, fleshy, solid, smooth, but square built, and not graceful. In flesh white as snow, with two huge firm hemispheres on her chest. Her hair was dark red (a colour I dislike) her backside big, marbly, and white; her motte and cunt, covered with a thick mass of hair of a darker red. Strange to say it was this very colour, which now I think of it, somehow added to the reasons of my going home with her. It was curiosity — a change. She had silk stockings and boots fitting her to perfection of course. French gay ladies always have them, even if they are almost starving. They know the effect of a nice appearance in those extremities which lead up to the cunt.

I turned her about naked, opened her cunt, placed her big white buttocks towards me, saw thick hair round her arsehole, and its true brown tint on the furrow. Then I told her I knew she was older than she said. She laughed heartily when I mentioned the various indications of her age. What was I going to do? — Was she in a hurry? "Ah no." "Gamahuche me — suck my prick, and let me spend in your mouth." "Oh certainly." — She had stripped to her skin I may add without having been asked. She knew she was worth looking at.

I partly took my clothes off. — "Ah no, take them all off like me, pleasure should always be taken properly." — So I stripped to my shirt. — "Non — non — naked like me." — So I stripped entirely. It was a hot night. — Then she sponged round my cock, its tip, and my balls, and anus, most carefully. "Do you like your trou de cul licked?"— "Yes," I replied, tho I didn't recollect the sensation, nor even if it has been ever done to me, tho I think it has. — "I will do it so nicely you shall feel," said she. — Then she washed her cunt. — "Do you like washing a woman's cunt?" "Sometimes." "Wash mine," said she as if she liked the idea of that. — So I soaped and rubbed it. — When dry, she lighted some more candles, arranged a large cheval glass at the proper angle (she knew exactly where to put it). Then getting on to the bed. — "Voila," said she. — All was done without hurry scurry, it was a tranquil, refined preparation for lascivities.

Tho delighted with the movements of the white fleshed woman, my cock was not stiff. I was amused, a voluptuous feeling stole over me, the sort of feeling I sometimes experience an hour or two after one or two fucks — a feeling as if I needed rest, tho still lewedly inclined — the languid, creeping, half satisfied randiness one has, when laying by the side of a sweet woman whom I have fucked an hour before, and in whose cunt the spunk is still lying. — She took my prick and balls with an easy grasp in an unusually big hand, but it was plump, very smooth, and white. My cock began gently to swell as her hand slipped down under my balls, and I felt her finger pressing my bum hole with a soft, twiddling, insinuating pressure. — Then she closed my legs, and kneeling over me and sitting backwards on her heels, she took my prick and rubbed it gently against her clitoris, which stood well out from her cunt lips now opened by her attitude. — Then she laid entirely over me, taking off her weight with her hands, and gently rubbed her whole body over mine; her breast rubbed my nipples, her belly lightly glided over mine, the hair of her motte tickled my prick. — It was an infinitely delicate, amorous play, quietly exciting. — "Ah," said she, "Your pillow is not right, put your head there," and she moved it. — "There now you can see everything in the glass — there."

I let her do exactly what she liked, without telling her anything. — Then she stood by the bedside, and kissed me all over from head to feet. At length she buried her mouth in the thicket of my motte, and lifting my prick and opening my thighs, kissed, licked my balls and gradually along my prick, but avoiding the tip. The titillation of her tongue roused my dormant lust, and up swelled my pego to a noble fucking size. She smiled, and now taking it in her mouth, delicately licked the tip, and then engulfed it to the very roots. I felt it down her throat, and it totally disappeared. — It was delicious. — Out it soon came flaming, burning and crimson tipped, her saliva running down it and trickling on to my balls. — Then she desisted and let it go, after giving it a gentle squeeze. "Suck me, go on, let me spend, get on me so that I can see your cunt." "Don't be in such a hurry for the pleasure," said she laying down by me, letting me feel her all over but leaving my prick alone. — No, I should *not* spend yet. — "C'est trop vite, soyez tranquille."

She talked then about other things so as to distract my attention from my penis, and its lust somewhat subsided. — Then getting off, and bringing me to the side of the bed, with legs hanging on to the floor, she told me to hold my legs up high. I obeyed her in everything. — I had suggested and asked her for nothing hitherto, excepting to suck me, to gamahuche me. When my thighs were up in the air, she gently pulled aside my bum cheeks, and began licking my anus. Every now and then she left off, gave just the tip of my prick a little delicate suck, and then went back to my anus. Her tongue seemed to enter it, a tickling sensation and a voluptuous pleasure spread right up my fundament, and there was a baudy sensation up it which got mixed with the lewedness which came from my prick and my balls. — Again she began gamahuching whilst I lay speechless, tranquilly enjoying the voluptuous treat. — "Aha — what are you doing? Aha." A new sensation came over me, I felt my anus opening and stretching under a gentle twiddling pressure, her middle finger was up my fundament, and she was gently buggering with it whilst gamahuching me. I trembled now with lewed sensations, I could only see her head at the bottom of my belly, gently moving up and down, her backside and ample naked body was reflected in the glass, and so on for a minute.

But I wanted to feel her flesh, that desire to feel the flesh of the other sex, which every male and female has when about to spend, came on me strongly — I cried. — "Aha let me move — let me feel you — let me see your cunt." She rose from her knees, and standing bent forward still sucking me, but now with her thighs straddling open, and I could see her red haired, full lipped cunt, reflected in the glass. It looked as big as a cow's but it pleased me. Then still unsatisfied I made her cease, I got lengthwise on the bed, and she changing her position so as to stand sideways, sucked me whilst I felt her buttocks, rubbing my hand over them, and rapidly thrust my fingers between them, on to her cunt, that cunt which filled my fingers with soft flesh and crisp red hair. — "Ahaa. — I'm spending, fuck, cunt, spunk." Just as my sperm began to rise, she left off spite of my entreaties, and laid hold of my hands to stop me from finishing my enjoyment by a frig, which involuntarily I attempted. — "No, no, not yet — prolong your pleasure, don't be in such a hurry." — She was an artiste, an accomplished artiste in gamahuching.

After a pause she recommenced. This time kneeling over me, her ample white rump and thick lipped, hairy gap, within a few inches of my face. She put two pillows under my bum, to throw it up from the bed and let her suck me more conveniently. — "Ah ma chere, you hurt me," I cried — but my pain gave way to an agreeable sensation. She had introduced her middle finger which was unusually thick and long, much further up my bum than before, and was poking about gently in my fundament. I felt as if my arse was stretching but without pain — then as if a hot fart was struggling to come out, and mixed with these sensations, a strange thrilling pleasure in the part. A desire to treat her the same rushed thro my brain. I pulled open her buttocks and thrust my fingers up her cunt. — For an instant she ceased gamahuching. "Put your finger up my cu, cher," said she and resumed her work. God knows whether I did or not, I can't say, I can't recollect for I was nearly wild, — I felt certainly all about her, in every place my hand could reach. I was mad to discharge my sperm which she kept me artfully from spending, till nature would retain it no longer, and with a scream of pleasure, out throbbed my hot seminal mucilage, gushing spasmodically into her mouth, and I lay senseless. The towel at hand got rid of the libation, and when I had recovered from the intensity of the spasms of pleasure, she was still gently sucking my tool, giving me a prolonged lingering voluptuousness for some minutes. Then she got up, rinsed her mouth with eau-de-Cologne and water, and said, "Have I not given you pleasure, cher?" — Indeed she had — never did I get before such prolonged, such varied pleasure, as this French artiste in sexualities gave me with finger and mouth, by a single ejaculation of my semen.

The prolongation of my excitement, fatigued me I think as much as a couple of fucks. I was temporarily annihilated. She carefully washed my prick and bum hole again, and sprinkled eau-de-Cologne on me. She held my prick when I pissed, then washed the tip and gave it a gentle mouthing afterwards, and advising me to rest, she laid down by my side, talking all about the pleasures. Then she reversed herself, after getting off to shift the position of the lights on the table, and asked me to look at her private beauties, as if I had not seen them enough — wasn't her cunt tight for a big woman, hadn't she a pretty clitoris? "Feel it dear — oh you make me want it when you touch it — frig me *cher*," and whilst complying and feeling her all about, every now and then she again took my flabby doodle into her mouth, and gave it a gentle suck, and again pierced my bum hole with her finger after wetting it, and I let her do it. Then laying by my side, again she took hold of my fingers to frig herself with them. — Gradually so were my senses excited by her acts and words, that a desire to have her gamahuching me again crept over me, as well as to have my bum hole plugged. — It was only curiosity, but I had a strange feeling there which her finger had left, a lewed irritation there, and I put my finger down to feel if it was open. — "Do you like to be buggered?" said she — I said I never had, and never meant, but, "Yes I liked your finger there." — I couldn't help saying that. — "You must pay for a pair of white kid gloves, and I will put it over my finger, and cover it with cold cream, and you shall be so pleased." — "Not to-night," said I astonished. — "Ah yes, pourquoi pas, you have much spunk in you yet — look at your preeke, it is bigger — why you not bouggare me with you finger when I feel you — shall me get gloves?" She spoke thus in broken English generally, but sometimes in French.

In voluptuous lassitude, almost against my will I consented. She got from a drawer a new pair of white kid gloves and a pot of cold cream; those things ready, she went thro the preliminaries as before. My prick, balls, and bum hole were licked and tongue tickled all over with much deliberation, and with curious delicacy of tongue, till I grew restless with lust and my backside wriggled. Then putting a lump of grease on my anus, she put on a glove, covered the middle finger with grease, pushed it slowly up me and took my prick in her mouth. She moved her finger about my fundament, making me feel as before as if I was farting a hot wind. One of her feet was now on the floor, her other upon to the bed by the side of me, and I could as I lay see in the glass the back of her naked body and her movements. Near my chest was her belly, buttocks and her thick lipped, red haired cunt between them. With outstretched hand I felt her cunt from bum hole to clitoris. Slowly she moved her head up and down, conveying a fucking motion and feeling to my pego, prolonging and intensifying my enjoyment exactly as before, but even more deliberately, till now almost with a scream of lewed words I spent again in her mouth. I had immense enjoyment in her mouth, and paying her (quite satisfied) a double fee, I left her.

I went to see her again soon after, solely, as well as I can analyze my reasons and intentions, to find out whether I really liked my bum hole plugged with her finger or not: for my sensations had been so mixed, so complicated, that I couldn't make up my mind on the point. I gave her that night champagne, and so she got still warmer to the work. It seemed, and I really believe, that she delighted in the exercise. After my first ejaculation, she got my pego to rise again, and then asked me if I would fuck her. "A nice tight cunt," she said. — But I did not satisfy her, tho I had verified by my finger that her cunt had the quality she claimed for it.

Then came suggestions. Had I ever done *this or that*? I had done many things that she suggested. Then she got to acts a little out of the common-recherché lusts. — Had I buggered or been buggered? I might bugger her if I liked, for she liked me, and liked the sensation of a man's prick up her "cu," liked her cunt licked or frigged, when her fundament had the pego up it. There was a charming girl who did it to her. — "When you're being buggered?" said I, "impossible." — "No it is not impossible, look," — and she showed what appeared to be a prie-dieu chair, but low backed, large, wide seated, immensely heavy, its back inclining slightly, and most extraordinary in its build. A chair of rough make, and I believe made for the purpose. "It is just the height," said she kneeling to prove it. I stood up at her back and applied my prick to her bum valley to test that. — The chair was open in the back, and then to verify her statement, I knelt in front of her, as she was kneeling on the chair with thighs apart in buggeree posture, and found that I could with a little pushing forward of my head, touch her cunt with my lips, I could have licked her clitoris. She declared that when buggered, her young female friend licked her quim in that way. Would I come again and she would fetch her friend, and then whilst I fucked her friend, she would finger bugger me. — Or her friend should gamahuche *her* thro the back of the chair, whilst I buggered her, or fucked her, which ever I pleased but she preferred being buggered and licked. — Or a nice *garçon* with a lovely prick should come to me and I could bugger him — or be buggered by him, or I could suck him. So we talked on, and she raised a number of curious desires in me by these suggestions of variety. I did not tail her as she asked, but had another pair of white gloves and its greased finger up my bum again, refusing a dildo which she now offered for the first time, and again spent in her mouth and quitted her well satisfied.

A week elapsed. What am I coming to? Her manifold, quaintly lascivious suggestions burthened my mind whenever a lewed sensation passed through my brain, whenever a lewed sensation coursed through my pego, and again I sought her. It was mainly to be frigged by a hand covered with white kid gloves, *that* was now my letch. She kept I found now white kid gloves in her drawers, no doubt using them thus which was quite her speciality. She at first frigged me with her gloved hand for a time, then greased the entire glove, to let me feel the difference in the friction between the dry and the greased. Really whether greased or not greased, a kid gloved hand makes a delectable masturbator. I would not spend that way. When ready to ejaculate bethinking me of her suggestions, and all sorts of baudy desires floating through my brain, "Get the woman who licks you," I cried, and I thought of fucking my masturbatress from behind whilst her clitoris was licked from before by the satellite.

She feared the woman was not within or might be engaged, but would send. In a quarter of an hour during which I varied our libidinous tricks, she came. She was a French, dark eyed, dark haired woman, seemingly not more than eighteen or nineteen.— Champagne was got to stir our energies, and then we set to work. I saw the young woman's cunt, and when I was quite stiff, and after both women had had my prick in their mouths, and one had licked my balls whilst the other was licking the tip; to the chair we went.—With thighs wide apart the red haired one knelt on it, and the little dark one kneeling on a pillow in front prepared for minetting.—Her tongue reached the other's clitoris, and I made her for a second lick it to let me see that it *could* be done.— "Come bugger me," said the red haired one, and putting her hand back, she pulled apart her buttocks showing the brown valley, and the aperture of Sodom.

"You won't! ah yes, you must, I shall spend when you spend in my cu."—It seemed from her pertinacity in demanding it, as if she really desired it, and was disappointed at my steady refusal. I tried to fuck her from behind, but could not get my prick well into her, her bum was so big; and when she lifted her backside and jutted it out, her friend could not well lick her clitoris, so we ceased trying for the minute.

Then said I (it had been her own suggestion on a previous night), "I'll dildo your arsehole whilst she licks your cunt." "Tres bien, but you must then give me another sovereign."—I agreed. From another drawer came two or three dildoes. Selecting a little one which she greased carefully, and instructing me how to use it, I pressed it through the corrugated aperture, and slowly soon it disappeared up her fundament. I pushed it gently up and down, the little one licked her cunt, the licks sounded and nothing else in our excited silence, till the red haired one wriggled her bum and belly, cried out she was spending, and urged me to move the dildo which in watching the two I had for the moment ceased doing, but had left sticking in her rump. I recommenced, she urged the young one be quicker. "Lick lower" she cried, and with a real or well acted spasm of pleasure, all was over. I removed the dildo from its sheath, she for a minute or two leaned over the chair with eyes closed, and the other went on silently licking the clitoris.

I had not yet spent, had restrained myself, moving about with my pego like a brass rod, but was now almost spending without hand or cunt to help me, so excited was I by the spectacle. Speaking in French, "Get up, I'll kiss *you*," to the younger one. — On to the bed she sprang and opened her red gap. With a look, a feel, and a sniff at it I mounted her, and in a second my pego was up her black haired cunt. The red haired one without delay and unasked, inserted her finger in my rectum, I felt the sphincter stretch, and with libidinous images flashing through my brain, in baudy ecstasy I ejaculated my semen, and died away; the lady's cunt clipping and spending with me. "Mon Dieu what a lot of spunk," said she as I got off of her. — I looked and there was. — The red haired one looked admiringly. "My God! a river," said she.

Within half an hour I was ready again, either one or other of the women had handled my genitals all the time, and I had exhausted the poses I could think of placing them in. Then I put the little one on my prick as I sat on a chair, clasping one breast, and feeling her motte at the same time. The red haired strumpet seemingly pleased, knelt down and licked the clitoris of my fuckstress, whilst with almost imperceptable joggings of her cunt, and heaving of my bum, we fucked. The gentle friction, the deep plugging soon told, and we spent. Then tranquilly sitting on me still, my prick shrinking satisfied from her cunt, whilst I felt her clitoris, and our spermy mixtures running out on to my balls, we rested a while. — Red hair sat on the floor naked and silently contemplating us. — Out flopped my doodle, ending our conjunction, and washing genitals all round began.

I'd had a couple of pleasures but was not satisfied, the women had so excited me. — We talked for a time, then I knelt over the head of the red haired one at her request, whilst she laid on her back and gamahuched *me* and she masturbated *herself*. She made me stiff and lewed, tho I had not wished *that,* and did not utilize the erection, having reasons for not fatiguing myself then too much sexually. — When her pleasure was over I laid down, she carefully with sponge and towel washed the grease off my thighs and bum, and I left.

That extraordinary chair keeps recurring to my mind. Its design, weight, size and general ugliness, makes it certain that it must have been made for the special object, which she told me it was used for. Did the woman I wonder travel about with it when she moved, or was it part of the furniture of the house?

I never went near the glove woman again, nor do I recollect seeing her. I had satisfied my curiosity, and did not wish my bum hole opened any more. — But cock's suction begins more and more to please me. — Several times I have refused to let a pretty mouth finish when proffered that pleasure, not having wished beyond putting it into the mouth of a woman I liked. That truly is a lovely endearment before putting it up the sweet one's cunt. Is the taste now gradually coming to me? I begin to find it delightful, when I do not stiffen readily, to make women put my tool in their mouths even if not to consummate there. — Suction by a pretty mouth is not such a bad amusement when a man's fatigued. [Nelly L**l*e a year or two afterwards, often got my second spend that way — her cunt did duty for the first.]

[These eccentric letches appear henceforth to have given me pleasure more in a degree, and more frequently I gave way to cries of lust when in the height of my pleasure. Formerly I had been mostly quiet, or only used words of endearment to my lovely partner; of late frantic libidinosity has seized me at times, and more rapidly than words can express them, flash though my brain visions of what I have done — of what I should like to do — and the words of lust as they escape me, add to my pleasure, and to those of some of my partners who join their cries to mine. I incite them to use them.]

CHAPTER XI

*Change in style in writing this narrative. — Reckless amours. — Nelly L**l*e and Sophy S***h. — Neophyte harlots. — A first night out. — Madame S***k*n*us. — Cuntal contrasts. — A lascivious evening. — Their antecedents and future. — Nelly's face, form, and quim. — Voluptuous complacency. — Her after life. — My tastes for being gamahuched. — Externals of sodomites. — Fantastic male lascivieties. — Champagne and sperm. — Dildo and arse-hole. — Birching tried on me. — Policemen's forbearance. — One in plain clothes. — Nelly's illness and my aid. — Sophy's face, figure, and colour. — Her sliggery pudenda. — Vulgarity and voice. — Married, mother, and widowed. — Harlotting resumed. — Drunken and degraded. — Love in her armpits.*

[It is evident now, altho it did not occur to me at the time when week by week, or day by day, I wrote these narratives, that of late years I had a growing habit of giving opinions on, and reasons for my amorous, erotic exploits. — This certainly was not the case in the early part of this history. — I suppose the change was the result of experience, and reflexion on that experience, which made me write those opinions. They were doubtless involuntary, they came in the natural course of the incidents, and writing them at the time pleased me as much as describing the events. These opinions and reflexions are an index to my mental state at *that* time, and it would be well to retain them all. The need for excision and abbreviation is however inexorable, and few can be kept. The desires which sprang up, the thoughts or experiences which led to them, if preludes to my amorous deeds, will however be retained, where not of too great length.

[Not having been found out in my promiscuous amusements with women, and the ailments of Venus not having attacked me,

I became bold, and did openly hazardous things, which a few years ago I should have never attempted. I longed for women who had never sold their charms, and made advances to some who seemed open to them, some who were as critically placed as I was, and more so, for to them it might have been utter ruin. — With two or three, I had brief amours which we both enjoyed intensely. The pleasure of eating stolen honey is great, and hazardous, illicit fucking, is the finest of honey. Danger and risks no doubt give its charms to such liaisons, but fucking with eyes and ears open at my time of life, was after all not so pleasurable as fucking with a tranquil mind.

[Altho strong sexually, I thought that at my time of life that the strength could not last long, and seemed to desire to lose no opportunity in indulging with the sex, fearing that indifference which sometimes comes with the abatement of virile force. So when I got the chance I had many charming transient amours. Circumstances indeed a little later on favoured me in these, and gave me opportunities of indulging with less risk than before, but what led to those facilities must not be disclosed. Many of my fugitive amours did not exceed the acquaintance of a night or two — nor did I wish them to last — nor perhaps did my female friends. Mostly they were commonplace, and I only tell of those in which was some unusual incident, tho with my habit then, as now inveterate, I duly recorded in my manuscript each amorous adventure.

[The next twenty or thirty pages relate to two young harlots named Nelly L**l*e and Sophy S***h—. I occasionally visited Nelly for many years, the other rarely, tho for as long a time or nearly so. — My libidinous amusement with them were all of the ordinary kind, which I have practised with hundreds of the frail sisterhood, and with many who were not frail in a financial sense. They were as usual, described by me at length in my original manuscript, but the repetition of salacious tricks seems tedious now, so I have carefully weeded out, arranged in some order, condensed, abbreviated this part of my narrative, to about one fifth of its original length; leaving only certain episodes worth retaining for their variety, which I shall put in their chronologcal order nearly.]

Going along L**c**t*r Square one evening I saw a shortish female in front of me. She had short petticoats (worn then), Balmoral boots, a small foot, and shapely calf.—The movement of haunches and legs told me she had the class of form I loved; I can tell by the pose of the foot, and the swing of the bum, what sort of thighs and rump are moving underneath petticoats—I passed and looked at her. She had a quite young, modest face, white and pink complexion, dark eyes, and looked healthy, fresh and enticing. I stopped, turned, and she passed *me*. She is modest I thought.—Bah! what does modesty do here by itself at eight o'clock p.m.?—So I accosted her, wondering at her steady bum swing which looked twenty-one at least, whilst her face looked but seventeen or thereabouts.

"May I go home with you?" "Yes if you like," and she looked back. "Where do you live?"—"I live at—oh I forget, but it's just over there." "Go on and I'll follow."—She hesitated, but turned back.—Up came another female, taller, with flaxen hair, and a nearly white face.—"The gentleman wants to know where we live, what's the name of the street?" "Tibble, Tickle, Tish, or something like it I forget, but I know the way."—Then both laughed heartily.—"Well go on," I said (for we had stopped), "I only want this lady and not you."—I never like talking long to gay women in the streets. "It's Pickle Street," said my selected one, laughing. "Cross over."—Both crossed, I following, when a short, sallow, Jewish looking woman there stopped them.—"What is it my dear," said she. "The gentleman wants to know the name of the street." "Oh, it's T***f***d Street, sair—I will shows the vay," and off she walked rapidly with the girls, I following at a little distance behind them. It was the baud who was giving them their first lesson in street walking, and following them in view.

She opened the door with a latch key—"I only want this dark haired girl," said I, "and I'm only going to give her a sovereign." "Vel, vel, go in, sair."—I went in and upstairs to two handsomely furnished rooms—a lamp was already lighted, and she lit two candles, the girls stood still, silent, and staring at me, I stood thinking—I hate making these arrangements with second or third parties—a baud, and a couple of whores are a match for the Devil.

"I only want this lady," I repeated, "and can only give her a sovereign." "Oh you must give her two sovereigns—it's her first night in London, she's never been out before. Oh she *must* have two sovereigns." "No." "Vel dare is no harm done, sair, you see vat nice young ladies they be, and these handsome rooms but if you won't, you won't — vel go out again my dears." — It was all very civilly said. — No bullying. — She blew out the two candles, not a word had either girl spoken and she opened the door. Said the woman as I moved towards the door, "I can't let her for luck's sake start like that, I brought em both to London the day before yesterday, they've never seen London streets till an hour ago." I paused — I had noticed in the street the girl Nelly staring about in a strange way, instead of cock hunting with the steady glances of a regular strumpet — besides the girl looked so very fresh and so modest, that my prick was standing, and I felt a violent lust for her. — "Well let her stay, I'll give it her, but if I have her another night I can only give a sovereign." — "All right, sair." "But I shall stop a long time." "You may stop as long as you likes, mayn't he Nelly?" "I don't care," said the girl.

The old woman relighted the candles. — "Have Sophy too," said she. I never liked fair haired women. — "No." "Do — it's *her* first night as well — don't make them jealous of each other, they're friends now. — Do, and I needn't go out again tonight." — That struck me as so funny that I laughed. "When you see em both quite naked together, you vil say you never see sich fine gals." "I won't be naked," said one, I don't recollect which. — "Now my dearee, you must please gentlemens if you vants to make friends — Didn't I tell ye now — didn't I tell ye — I'm not a going to keep yer — you've got to keep yourself." Then turning to me, "They will be all right when she knows you, sair; have Sophy, do — she's as white as snow, her thighs and body is, and she is formed beautiful, and her hair's the same color *there*, one's black and the other yaller," and the old woman winked at me again with a leer. The contrast was extreme — "black cunt, flaxen cunt" — thought I. "Well, let her stay too — but I'm not going to pay *you*." — "Oh! all rights, all rights, sair, you can stop all night vith dem. I knows a gentlemans vhen I speak vid him, all rights, sair, my name is S***k*n*us, and I've been here five year, I'm a dressmaker, sair." (I had some idea that I was going to be bilked. "Now my dearees mind vot I as tell you, and I'm sure he'll be a friend to you both," and nodding her head at the girls she went out. I bolted the door. She was a German woman I found, perhaps Jewish, but who had been some time in England, actually worked with a sister at dressmaking, and let her upper floors to quiet gay women, and had now by some chance got these two young women, to introduce to the *pavé* of London.

"Take off your things, my darlings."—The girls giggling and whispering to each other began slowly to do so; it was perfectly clear that they'd not yet undressed as Paphians before a man for pay. Gradually two pairs of splendid calves and lovely white breasts appeared. "Off with your chemises." "I shan't," said one, and the other did not obey.—I pulled them both to me, putting my hands on to their fat backsides, and kissed their large white breasts alternately. I hitched up the chemises of both at the same time whilst they struggled a bit, and saw fine round thighs on both; nearly black hair on one cunt, almost invisible hair on the other. "My prick's so stiff," said I, and getting up I stripped to my shirt, pulled it up to my waist, and showed a red headed magnificent erection.

Both burst into laughter, which astonished me. I pulled dark haired Nelly on to one thigh as I sat down, and began feeling her cunt. Flaxen haired Sophy sat down on a low stool opposite us, holding her cheeks and her chin with her hands, whilst her elbows rested on her thighs, like an old Irish woman sitting on a door step. A vulgar, low look the girl had, yet she was of a most uncommon peculiar style of face, certainly handsome, yet of a class I didn't like. Then I noticed that she had white eye lashes, and very light eyebrows, and for the moment she reminded me of an albino, who to me is very ugly.

Now I talked baudy. "Show me your cunt," to Nelly, who had been feeling my prick.—"Ho! ain't he rude," said she giggling and looking at Sophy.—"Do." "Shan't."—I lifted her chemise to her armpits suddenly. She struggled and cried out, "No, no."—I got vexed and swore, for I hate a struggle with a sham modest whore, and hadn't quite arrived at the belief that it was her first night's harlotry.—"Isn't she a fool Sophy?" "She knows best," was the reply made in a coarse, raw, nasty voice.—I had not heard her speak before. I let Nell go.—"Let's feel *your* cunt," said I dragging up Sophy from the stool.—She offered no resistance. Her cunt was reeking wet as my fingers went between the lips, and she opened her thighs to let my fingers up. I pulled up her chemise, her cunt seemed nearly hairless, there was hair, but the color was so light, and it was so small in quantity, that it scarcely showed. Her thighs and belly were as white as milk, her form exquisite. — Nelly rearranged her tumbled hair, for in a small struggle with her it had fallen, came close up to us and said to Sophy, "You seem to like it." "I don't mind much, he's a nice chap," croaked Sophy. [Nelly, I found in after years, was jealous of any woman being noticed before her — even when she had brought the woman herself to me for fucking.] Nelly was jealous now of Sophy's pleasing me by her willingness.

Darkish haired quims were always my delight, so I took hold of Nelly again. Sophy dropping again on the stool not much higher than a chamber pot, looking on stupidly and pulling down her short chemise over her knees as if to hide them. I titillated Nelly's clitoris, made her feel my balls and prick, and lavished obscenity and kisses, till she wriggled her rump voluptuously. I had stirred her lust. She wanted fucking, it was time for emptying my testicles, so I threw her on the side of the bed. — "No, no, let me get on to the bed properly." — I wouldn't, opened her thighs violently, leant over her, and drove my prick up her fat little cunt, till my balls banged against her arse. Feeling the prick up her, she laid still, for pleasure told on her at the first thrust of my pego. I began to look at her quim as I pushed my tool in and out. Then she kept pushing her chemise down. — "I'll slit your chemise up if you do that," said I irritated. — Sophy came up and looked on, for Nelly then ceased hiding her charms, and, I saw, soon had voluptuous sensations; and from the involuntary motion of her belly, the opening of her mouth, the staring look of her eyes, saw that they were getting strong. Soon she gave a voluptuous sigh and I fetched her juices out, as I squirted a shower of sperm up her.

I was in full blood, my prick stood well up her after I had spent, and I bent over her quiet for a time, then rose, gradually pulling my prick partly out of its mucous bath. — "When were you last fucked?" said I. — For a second she lay quiet as if in her pleasure still, at last, "Two months ago," said she. Sophie chuckled, "Ave yer done it Nell with him, ave yer?" said she. — No reply. — "Have yer now? — now I knows yer have, and yer said, yer wouldn't with the chaps." — Nell never replied, seeming to be still enjoying the last sensations of the fuck. "She's spent a cup full," said I drawing my prick quite out. — "Look — it's not all mine."

Briskly Nell closed her thighs and pulled her chemise over her reeking cunt, from which a rivulet of thick pearly sperm began to run, and she sat up.

"Do you like seeing your friend fucked?" "Never seed it afore," said Sophy, sitting down again on the stool and tugging down her short chemise. "Well, *you've* been fucked." "Why of coorse." "You've seen yourself fucked in a looking glass." "That I ain't, there warn't never a glass in the room at all — I never war in a place afore with a man and woman a doin it. — Never with none but my own chap."

"Wash Nell," said I, whilst I was doing so. "When you're gone." "Gone my dear? I'm going to stop hours." — Nellie washed. — I turned to Sophy and grasped her sliggery cunt. — "Shall *we* fuck?" "If yer like." Her cunt was on fire and reeking, as I laid her on the side of the bed. — What a treat the light flaxen haired motte was by contrast, I had not expected such enjoyment from it. I got my prick in her, but the fucking was much longer, and I fetched her before I came myself. Nelly now looked on curiously, it was her turn. — "You've done it with him Sophy." "And so did you." Then both laughed. Getting off the bed, down went Sophy on to the stool again. "You'll wet your chemise Sophy." "Don't care." — But up she got, wiped her cunt outside with a towel, and threw it down on the floor in a low manner.

There was a freshness in manner, and modesty in both of them, and they had manifestly an enjoyment in my fucking, which made me think now that the old woman had spoken the truth. I had thought it all sham. — Neither had ever tasted champagne I found, so ordered some, telling the woman to get it at ***** a well known place for food and wine [then]. Madame S***k*n**s fetched it and I gave her a glass. — Was I pleased with the young ladies? — Yes and had fucked both. — "They won't wash their cunts properly," said I joking. "*I have,*" said Nelly — "Sophy has wiped hers." "Oh Miss Sophy, you knows what I have tell you." — We had gone into the sitting room which opened with folding doors to the bed room, and the flaxen motted one now washed her cunt properly. We all drank champagne, the old woman left, I ordered another bottle, and soon both girls were quite groggy.

Then they let out their histories. Many times after I heard both, and they never varied. — Certainly it was their first harlotting night, and most likely neither had been fucked for weeks as they said. I warmed them well up with lewed talk, one held my prick, the other the pot when I pissed. It delights me to make fresh women do those little services. I laid them side by side lengthwise on the bed, and then one on the top of the other. The liquor and talk had made them randy. We all stripped quite, and putting the cheval glass to see in it, I fucked one whilst I fingered the other. Then we had more wine, and the girls began to quarrel, which I have often found to occur when I have had two women together and they got lushy.

It really was because I had fucked flaxen motte twice, and Nelly was jealous. I'd fucked Sophy I can't tell why, for I always liked a dark haired cunt, and Nelly's was dark. — I fancy it was that I found Sophy's the nicest of the two cunts, and have since thought so [I sometimes think now that her cunt was the most delicious my prick ever went into] but I never could bear the girl, tho scores of times I have thought of nothing but her cunt, when I have been stroking Nelly and others. I recollect all this clearly because the evening was a memorable one. They now both blabbed and told me all about themselves but the name of the village they came from. — No, they wouldn't tell that. "Don't you recollect that some one fetched me that night, Nelly?" "Yes." "Father said he'd throw him bloody soon into the canal if he came home again with me." "Poor Bet, he never kept her child." "Yes and he made me sleep with him that night." — So that sort of talk ran on, telling me bits of their history as I questioned them, and interrupting and correcting, and helping each other in their tales, both talking sometimes at once. Then we all three turned on to the bed again. I treated the dark haired cunt, and fucked each girl quite twice before the evening was out. When we parted I promised to see them the next day.

[This was their history. Nelly mainly made me her confidant after I helped to keep her during an illness at a future day. Both had been caught fucking without a license. — Sophy by a man of her own class caught in a field by *her* father, who stuck a scythe into her swain's rump. — Nelly was surprized in bed with a gentleman who had promised to marry her, and *her* father turned her out of doors. — The swains neglected the girls — both had family way sensations in their bellies, and were helped out of the difficulty by a local dressmaker. — Madame S***k*n*us, a German Jewess and dressmaker, knew the village one, who advised the girls to go to London with Madame S***k*n*us. They knew they were going to be gay, tho it was not said so. Uncomfortable at their village, off they ran, and that was their first night in their career of harlotry when I had them. — Both afterwards liked gay life, but neither rose to eminence. — Nell for some years led a comfortable life of indolence, as long as she kept to S***k*n*us. Sophy sank to the lowest depths, was always drunk, nearly naked, and would take men home for a glass of gin.]

Nelly was short, beautifully formed and plump, had good legs, small feet, thick ankles, and large bum. — Her skin was a very dark cream color, her hair nearly black, her eyes a very dark hazel, with a heavy expression in them much like that of a cow's. It was a half sulky look. She had thick eye-brows and large mouth but was really handsome. In after years she was often taken for a French woman by men. The hair on her motte was about the thickest I ever saw on an English woman's, tho at first there was not much of it. The flesh of the motte could not be seen thro it, and just over the clitoris it formed a thick little clump almost hard, it curled so. Her armpits were thick with hair even at that age. (She was barely seventeen.) She had hair on her cunt, she said, at twelve. Ten years afterwards when I saw her, it was half up to her navel, but it never grew round her buttocks or arsehole. Her cunt was large at seventeen, and some years afterwards was very large. — I could then put a large dildo and two fingers up it at the same time easily, yet she had even then a wonderfully fine cuntal grip on the prick, it was such a fat cunt inside. She had a beautifully steady walk, like a Spanish woman's, looked quiet, and was proud of walking out dressed simply in good black silk, and being taken for a modest woman. — She was relatively modest, when first I had her. In a week I'd taught her much, and modesty was lost. She said she had had more poking in the first fortnight she had come to town than she had had altogether from *her* young man, who had never tailed her more than about a dozen times in all. Her cunt then had all the signs of recent rupture. — In after years she was the most complacent creature, and did with me every thing excepting bum fucking. Once when I pressed her to let me do that she nearly yielded, but it was out of kindness. —

I was only joking, and but asked as a test. She got me three young virgins, two of whom I poked, a dozen other women, and two men to frig or bugger if I liked — I did not like the latter work. She gradually got poor and ill, and disappeared. Her last stay was in one room. An old gentleman up whose arse she used to put a dildo whilst she sucked his cock, she said, then nearly kept her; he was seventy-six years old, yet could spend under that fundamental and labial irritation.

She early made friends among a good class of married men, and was always at home in the afternoon, dressed usually in a blue satin dressing gown, and nice silk stockings and boots. Her foot was beautiful. She for years rarely went out at night or to public amusements, but passed her time in idling, feeding, dressing, reading newspapers and novels. She said she lost money when she went out at night before ten, so if she went out it was usually very late. She was a very safe woman. Once during what I think was a bad clap, tho she would not say so, and once thro a long illness, I paid her lodgings and some other friend paid for her food. She was on both occasions in the same house (Madame S***k*n*us). She never let me poke her if she had the slightest taint of her poorliness. She was a wonderful frigger. — Her masturbation was most delicate and fetching (some women never can frig), and afterwards she gamahuched equal to any French woman — I have gone to her with my prick as limp as a rag, yet never went away without a spending. She had a wonderful way of pushing my machine if limp into her roomy cunt, and saying "lay still." — Without movement on my part, and no perceptible movement to her buttocks, she stiffened me by the compression of her cunt — her gripping cunt seemed to suck my prick up into it. When about thirty years old she began to paint. At rare intervals then I used to talk to her only, and to tip her when I met her, and for years sent her a sovereign at Christmas.

Before I lost sight of her, she used to say that when first out, scarcely any man wanted more than to poke her, but then that half the men wanted to be gamahuched, and some wanted to bugger. She did not allow that, but got them ladies who did. She looked on at the operation at times, and halved the fee paid for their complaisance.

She explained to me the habits of the male sodomites (she

had studied and hated them), the way to know them, and how to treat them. It was curious, but I never learned to know them by sight, and never wanted.—To the last of her career so far as I know it, and when she barely had a gown to cover her, she managed to get silk stockings, and tho flabby in her breasts, and with a smaller and flabby bum, never lost the shapely legs. Her heart went wrong, she got dirty, and then I saw her no more.

She rarely drank, tho I have made her tight several times by sipping warm brandy and water with her. With a good fire in the room, her clothes up to her navel, legs so placed that I could see her cunt, we talked and she told me strange baudy fads she had known men to have. One young man, after laying her down with thighs distended and open cunt, used to frig himself into a tumbler of champagne and then drink it, swallowing his own sperm. Another made her run a pin into his balls. One brought small peas, and pushed them down his urethra. — He came with his bladder full—and then pissed out the peas against her cunt, or her arsehole, or her breasts. She flogged some men till they spent, and other erotic whimsies. Many men she said liked a dildo up their arseholes whilst they fucked, or were frigged, or gamahuched. One man only fucked a woman when she had a dildo up her bum; a lady friend she fetched for that purpose. He greased the dildo and put it up the lady's arsehole. It was used for no one else and she showed it me. "That dildo's my old friend's," said she showing another and larger.

"I don't like it, but do everything excepting bugger, it pleases them and amuses me. If I did not some other would—I should lose friends." Camille has said the same.—She only once let me see her on the sly with a male friend. I looked thro a key hole at them copulating. Once she got a man to fuck her whilst I looked on, and I frigged him afterwards. He was a big fine man, and said he was a carpenter. Once she began to birch me, the only time I ever tried it, but the pain was too great and I made her desist. Twice she played at flat cocks with a female before me, and on one occasion a baudy tipsy night we had, with a second woman.

She used to fuck and spend in a quiet way, never swore, nor raised her voice, nor seemed angry, nor used baudy language unless asked, and chuckled it out then in a quiet voice. She never got into police rows. How she squared the police I don't know. I asked her if she let the constables tail her—"No"—but an Inspector used to have her. He was a married man and came in plain clothes. She never was "run in" that I heard of, when they ran in fifty women a night from the Haymarket and its vicinity.

During one illness I helped to keep her, and meeting then Sophy by chance, went home with her. She was at enmity with Nelly and said Nelly had had a miscarriage, and the father of the child was a labourer.—Nelly afterwards admitted a miscarriage. When she had been launched a few months she got cautious as whores do, and told me nothing; then came her illness, and after as said, she became as communicative as at first. When I was in love with Jessie C**t*s I did not see Nelly for a year or more. I shan't forget her joy when she saw me again.

Sophy, with the exception of the young lass Kitty with the yellow hair and motte, whom I had in my early manhood, was the only light haired Paphian I ever had more than a few times, rarely more than once. She was full grown tho only seventeen, her hair was like light flax, her eyelashes white.—She was exquisitely made, had the loveliest breasts, and from the nape of her neck to the sole of her feet was as white as snow. Her features were good, her eyes blue and yet she looked like a fool and when she laughed was like an idiot.—Her laugh was a vulgar, idiotic, coarse, offensive chuckle, she opened her mouth quite wide (it was large with splendid teeth), and she rolled her head about from side to side.—Her hands were coarse. She had slight hollows in her bum cheeks at first, in a few months they were dimples, and she must have put on a stone in weight in the time.—Never was there a woman who handled better all over than she, she was delicious to touch, an exquisite piece of flesh.

She had, when first I had her, scarcely any hair on her cunt; as I threw up her chemise I thought she had none.—But it lay close, and made the lips of the cunt look a little darker than the surrounding flesh, nothing more. The clitoris and nymphæ were a delicate pink like a girl's of twelve. The prick hole was small, and also had the look of recent breakage. I've broken thro a good lot of hymens, and know the look pretty well.

Of all the women I ever had, none had so soft, so voluptuous a cunt.—It was quite tight and small, but nothing ever equalled its smoothness. Satin, polished steel, ivory, oiled marble, never equalled its delicious softness to the feel of fingers or prick. It was always moist like any other cunt, tho not sticky or sloppy, but had an exquisite lubriciousness, indescribably as if it was full of spunk just fucked into it. I have made her syringe it out before me, and a minute afterwards it felt just the same. She was a splendid fuckee. Nelly was nice but one of the quietest, and always when fucking seemed suppressing herself; Sophy shivered, quivered but not noisily, and heaved gently, her cunt went clip, clip, suck, suck, in a wonderful way towards her crisis, and then with a gentle heave of her belly and arse, she seemed as if she wished to get my whole body up her, and with a "Ahaa — my dear man — aha, aha," she subsided. She was full of juice, would often spend twice to my once, and we made a fine display on the towel under her bum when my prick left her. Before the first week of our acquaintance was out, she gave way to her passions with me. She liked me, and used to patter out in her ugly, hoarse, coarse, vulgar voice, baudy words, and coarse but loving expressions. — Nelly watching us used then to say, "Sophy — what are you at?" — but it did not stop her. Never have I had more completely voluptuous fucking as far as mere cunt was concerned, but that was all; I was sick of the sight of her directly our bodies unjoined.

I saw both girls daily for nearly a fortnight, and Sophy had my seminal libations more frequently than Nelly — but I could not talk to her, her language was indescribably common and coarse, and whether eating, drinking, speaking, washing or even pissing, her vulgarity and idiocy were intolerable. — She was a cunt of superlative voluptuousness, a magnificent bit of fucking flesh, but nothing more. Tho straight as an arrow, her walk was between a totter and a roll. I could, at a later day, see her flashy, vulgar bonnet bobbing about in the distance wherever she was. She looked, even with good clothes on, the lowest Moll. Sometimes for all that I had a letch for her when I caught sight of her, and for a quarter of an hour to handle her fine flesh, to finger and plunge my prick up her indescribably smooth, luscious cunt, laying on her start naked before putting into her even, was exquisite. — But my liking went the instant my sperm was in her, and I got away as rapidly as I could, resisting usually her seductions of fingers and mouth to reanimate my tool, for she'd never let me go till I had tailed her twice if she could prevent it. She was very fond of fucking by me.

For a year or two (and in after years she returned), she was in the same house with Nelly and Madame S***k*n*us, who dressed and looked after her. There she did well. Then she went to live by herself having quarrelled with Nelly, and I saw nothing of her for a few years. — Nelly then told me one day that she had married an artisan, who was then dying, had two children by him, that they'd lived respectably and she quietly, but that now having pawned everything to keep them, she was going on to the streets again to live. They literally had nothing in their room but a bed, chair, table and piss pot, and would have starved, if Nelly had not sent them food for some time. She could afford that no longer, but she was keeping one child whom she brought upstairs to show me. — It was flaxen haired, like Sophy.

I sent for Sophy, who came. She had nothing on but a cloak and a gown, I pulled up her clothes to see. It was cold weather, there was a fire in the room, she went out, and in half an hour came in washed with a chemise and stockings on lent by Nelly. She'd still her lovely firm and white flesh, but was thinner. She told me her troubles, we had gin which soon got well into her head, then I got her on to my knee, felt her all over and titillated her cunt. When she had had a drink and her sobbing was over, and so soon as she felt pleasure, she rapidly undid my trowsers and grabbed my balls. — "Oh! I ain't been fucked for these three months, the last time my man did it, it nearly killed him and he don't want it now." I questioned her. — "Aye, I do frig myself — he likes me to, and he did use to frig me himself until he got too ill, poor man — let's do it."

I told Nelly to go out, being unable occasionally somewhere about that time (a peculiarity I don't think I have mentioned), to poke with another woman in the room, and was taken suddenly so now. Nelly always liked to be present when I shagged a woman she had brought me, perhaps to see what money passed — perhaps because she liked to see the fucking just as Sarah F**z*r did, and to frig herself whilst looking on. Women have baudy fancies and letches like men. — Nelly went out looking sulky.

Never did a woman enjoy a poking more. "Oh! I ain't had a

fuck for three months — not one damned fuck; frigging ain't fucking my dear — is it? — shove harder — I'm coming." — She'd lost of course all modesty, if she ever had any, but she must have been reared like a pig. — The first fortnight after she came to town, Nell used to say, "Do it — put it in, — up my thing," — and so on. Sophy would say "fuck — cunt — prick," to express herself, within a few days of her coming to London. When we were all three together, she would sit looking at the fire quietly, and suddenly say to herself aloud as if thinking "fuck" — I recollect her brushing her hair at the glass, when Nell and I were sitting down, and when in her vulgar way and harsh croaking voice she broke out singing, "Fuck, fuck, fucky, oh fuck, fuck, fuck — fuck her and fuck him, and fuck, fuck, fuck." "Shut up you beast," said Nell throwing her slipper at her. — She only laughed and turning round, — "I shan't, — I like saying it — what does it matter? — fuckee and fucking and fuck, fuck, fuck."

"Keep it in and do it again to us. I ain't been fucked for three months so help me God." — I tried but couldn't — and rolling off from her and leaving her quim free, she frigged herself, squeezing my sticky, limp tool, hard with the other hand — I washed, pissed and then she gamahuched me till stiff, and again I had her. In an hour she frigged herself again, sucking my cock at the same time unasked, indeed against my wish. She was in rut after her abstinence.

Her husband, and soon after, one child died, and after a time, the second. Then she became a fearful drunkard, the lowest of the low. She never forsook the neighbourhood of *****. About two years after this time I had a letch for her, Nelly fetched her, and she then was screwed. Soon after that, seeing her in the street, I went home with her to an awful hole. — I fucked her dog fashion there, not liking the bed.

When I pulled out my prick she was asleep and snoring. I pushed her up on to the bed whilst she was crying "Sharnt — sharnt — fuck then," and then snorted. I looked at her form as she lay, it was plump, white, and beautiful, and she had now plenty of sandy, yellowish hair on her cunt. I pushed the money under the pillow and left her asleep. Some days after, I made Nelly fetch her for me. — She did so much against her will, but I had my letch. — "Lord God! it was you who left the money was it?" said she with her idiotic grin. "Damned if I knowed who I'd had." — She rather gloried in her drunkenness, and told stories of what happened to her when quite drunk. Once when "bloody screwed," she went home with a man, and when she awoke, found a saveloy up her cunt — "damned if she knew who put the bloody bit o pork there." — At last Nelly refused to fetch her for me, for she did not speak to her she said, as she was always drunk, had been locked up for it, and lived with a pick-pocket, — I've seen her since staggering in the streets, and she always grinned as if she knew me, but never accosted me. She reminded me, in manner, much of a woman named Irish Kate whom I had nearly thirty years ago. Kate was deliciously beautiful both in face and form, but such a low vulgar beast.

I did to this fair haired, butter cunted idiot, what I never did but with two other women as far as I can recollect. [One was Jessie C**t*s.] I forget the other, and the manuscript has been burnt I suppose, but she had dark hair and was poorly, which was the reason why I took my pleasure by fucking in her armpit. [I have done it since tho with a sweet lascivious creature in the fullness of her youth, beauty and lust.]

This was after Sophy had lost her husband, and had turned gay again, and I'd fucked her, and this day had her again. She was just a little fresh. — "Damned if ever I've had a prick in my armpits," said she. I had a special soap with me for I had thought out the letch, soaped her left armpit till in a thick lather, and then mixed it with spittle. She put down her fat white arm, and I fucked between it and her breast from the back. She began to frig herself whilst I did it. — In a glass in front of us, I could see my prick tip appearing and disappearing as I thrust. "Fuck, fuck," she cried as her thighs began to move, and she spent frigging, as out spouted my sperm, and some of it, past her armpit fell on one of her thighs. I then stood with prick in the armpit leaning over her, she with her head back against me in silent ecstasy, eyes shut, and fingers on her clitoris.

"You haven't spent," said I. "Haven't I? feel my cunt, look at it," — I did. — "Do it again." I tried, worked away willingly, shoving whilst she helped me by squeezing my prick to her, but it was no go — for me. — She however recommended frigging herself, my spunk still lay on one thigh, and in the middle of her frig, she put her finger and thumb to it, took the sperm up, put it on to her clitoris and completed her frig with delight when she had got my sperm there. — Oh, how imagination helps sexual pleasure.

"Don't tell Nelly." "Why you fool, you will be the first to tell *her* or any one else." When with Nelly, and she'd had a little liquor, she invariably began to tell what this man did, how that man fucked, — how much she got — whom she had had — "I didn't have a cove last night, so had a bloody good frig before I went to sleep." — Nelly could not stop her. Flaxen head *would* tell of the men she had last, and what they did, and whether she'd spent with them or not, and so on. — "He fucked nice he did, I didn't mean to do it — but I gave up." — That was her style of talk, those her very words on one occasion, when she narrated what she'd done the previous night.

CHAPTER XII

Sophy's lubricious vagina.—My sensitive propagator.—Need for mucilaginous cunts.—In another man's semen.—Sophy's vocabulary.—Her love of the scrotum.—Pissing bouts with Nell, and Sophy.—Both with kid.—Nelly later on.—My procuress.—Miscellaneous and many Paphian peripatetic whores.—Martha.—A female life-guard.—Two little ones on a hot day.—In a cab.—Carry and Sally.—Feeling and felt.—Half-sitting fornication.—Carry in a bedroom.—"Who first fucked you?"—Sally's home experiences.—Brother Jack's onanism.—A trio at mutual exhibitions.—Jack and the pail of water.—Carry cum Jack at 6:30 a.m.—Luck of a lad of fifteen.—Jack's fraternal intentions.—Sally's sisterly anticipations of Jack.

This idiotic, semi-albino faced, wench's cunt, by the perfection of surface and fit, alone attracted me to her. I used to tell Nelly of it. I made Nelly at times anoint my tool with cold cream and unguents, and once poured oil in her cunt and then fucked her, extolling all the time the delicious lubricity of Sophy's light fringed slit, and much to Nelly's jealous annoyance. One day when she had been about two years harlotting, and knew most things erotic, I imagine, she said to me when eulogizing what I called Sophy's *sliggery* cunt (where I got the term I know not),—"You'd like to poke in another man's spunk," and she laughed. "You dirty little bitch, do you think I'd be such a beast?" "I don't see that it is beastly, some men do it"—and after a pause—"at least I've heard so."

Soon after and about this time, my penis seems again to have got the intense sensitiveness of my youth. I began to think of having plunged my procreator into the leavings of Captain Blank in

Liz M***d*n's and Nelly ***'s cunts, and what they said about it, and of similar episodes, and to wonder if any man had a taste for "buttered buns" — I seemed vaguely to recollect that the cunts of the women when thus lubricated had seemed very delicious to me, but attributed that to the fullness of my spermatic reservoirs, coupled with the lovely elasticity, and natural slipperiness of their cunts, and not to anything which Captain Blank had left there. I thought fucking after a man, a dirty trick, yet my prick stood at times, at the idea of its having been in the same sheath directly after another. This at times began now to occur to me when fucking Nelly L**l*e. What a number of pricks have been where my prick is, and what does that matter I thought, then began even to like the idea, and then to wonder if the enjoyment was increased by quickly entering a cunt after another man's journey there. Nearly all my life, as told, I had a most sensitive gland. — As my prick entered the sexual treasures of the dear creatures, I could tell if they had been recently washed out, or had used astringents. At one period I would not let a woman wash her split before I fucked her, unless I suspected that she'd recently had a male. Then after I had had a clap, I made them always wash scrupulously, but paid penance in the diminished enjoyment I had in pistoning, till the natural lubriciousness of their cunts returned under the soft friction and incitement of my prick. At times after their ablution, I covered my prick with saliva, and made them treat similarly their love temples, and sometimes made them moisten my prick tip in their mouths, so as to simulate the natural mucilaginous surface of their cunts, a condition which kind nature mostly leaves a cunt in, to be ready at all times and seasons to receive and gratify "John Thomas," the procreator, propagator, poker, pego, penis, of the male.

Somewhere about this time, the acute sensitiveness of my gland returned, and even increased, and a cunt in copulation without its natural viscosity, at first almost gave me pain. I used my saliva for lubrication copiously, and if I could wait, and the lady would let me (Cyprians often don't like to be frigged or excited too much at first, and object to a prolonged clitorisation), I would rub and titillate her button till I felt the internal effusion of her cunt was sufficient. Then I embraced her with the energy and enjoyment which is the proper compliment that the prick pays to the cunt, and which the man owes to the woman who permits him. Sophy had a cunt with this perfect viscosity, that exquisite lubricity.

Sophy had a vocabulary picked up in the slums and fields I guess. — She was one of the few women I have known who liked playing with my balls better than my prick; hundreds of women whom I have had never touched my testicles, all liked to play with the stem and prepuce. — Sophy would handle my balls gently at first, then squeeze one stone, then the other, then hold the bag in her fist, and left the rod alone. Her language also had a ballocky tone. — "Let's feel your balls — how's your bolly?" When I began to appreciate more fully the pleasure which a nice pair of lips gave my prick, Sophy took to gamahuching with delight, but always held my balls in her hand when my prick was in her mouth. — She would lick my balls, smell them, kiss them all over. She was in fact fond of the balls. — A hard, well wrinkled scrotum made her eyes shine with delight, "Your bally's full to night I know," she'd say.

Of course I had a micturating bout with these two girls. One night I took a large mackintosh and spread it on the floor before the fire, then we took off the sheets from the bed to dry ourselves with, I laid down on my back, Nelly mounted me, and putting my prick up her began slowly fucking; Sophy start naked and straddling her legs over Nelly's arse, when we began to get lively in our movements, she half squatted and pissed on to Nelly's bum furrow which I pulled open with both hands. The hot stream came rattling down the furrow and thence on to my balls, making a pond under my arse. — In the midst of the splashing Nelly and I spent.

Some time after — it was a lushing night and I had taken them wine. — When drink had filled the girls' bladders, I mounted Nelly's belly. Sophy at first said she would not piss, it was her turn to fuck, but at length let fly her stream towards my arsehole. Afterwards I indulged Sophy with a bit of cock. How we laughed as we rubbed each other dry. — That night Nell, tho she tried, could not piss over Sophy, as *she* topped me. Sophy was a wonderful hand at the work, she could hold her cunt lips open and direct her stream like a fireman, in which she resembled another gay lady already told of — I have seen some women unable to do this, and piss quite wildly.

The next night I had them, we all stripped. Nell laid on the floor on her back, I pushed under her rump a foot stool, then straddling over her I pulled up her legs and held them wide open, my arse was turned towards her face, my ballocks hanging almost over it, her cunt about a foot off the ground. — With her fingers she distended her orifice widely, then Sophy in baudy delight coming close up and slightly squatting, thighs wide apart and holding her cunt open, pissed a perfect cataract on to Nelly's cunt. She hit it as neatly as if she had sent it out of a squirt. Then we put Sophy on *her* back, she held her legs as high up as she could, and Nelly and I pissed at the same time on to her quim. Then on the bed, we fucked all three together. — Later, both girls pissed together over my prick as I lay on the floor, and I fucked again. We made such a mess that Madame S*k*s was angry, but I paid for washing and tipped besides, so all passed off pleasantly. — This was all done in the early days of their harlotry. — It was the pleasure of teaching, of initiating them into the amusements obtainable from their cunts, which gratified me. Their gratification was excessive. We made an awful noise when about it, but there were no other women in the house. Madame S***k*n*us occupied the ground floor, the girls the two upper floors, the only servant was in the floor above.

A month after I first met this couple, Nelly said, "You've got me in the family way." "And me too," said Sophy. "It's other men." — Both were sure it was I, and that both were got so in the first week. They always afterwards declared that it was so. Sophy thought it was the very first time I'd fucked her. That poor woman afterwards was always getting in the family way. Nelly, in after years, used to say she never had enjoyed fucking in her life in the way she did the first week with me, and that she was dead sure I'd got her with child within the first day or so.

"Hasn't Nell a dark haired cunt?" said I to Sophy one day when I had them. "Yes, I like black better than my colour." — She had never seen Nell's cunt excepting outside. — Why should she? — It was like her own warn't it? — "Nor you, Sophy's?" — "No," said Nell. — I made them at once look at each other's cunts, and put their fingers on each other's and frig — I had jolly larks with them in the first days, and didn't I astonish them with the tales I told about sods, and flat-fucking — cow-fucking — dog-frigging

— and cock-sucking or gamahuching — cunt-licking, and so forth. — They were both wonderfully green when they came to London; plain fucking and frigging was the extent of their knowledge.

To go back, for I have narrated much which occurred through several years afterwards, I had now supplied the loss of Sarah F**z*r, and knew where to go always for a quiet baudy evening, and could get every want gratified. — For two years I had a complete return of the virility of my youth, I renewed acquaintance with my old friend Camille, had again a strong letch for letting women piss on my hand whilst I felt their cunts in the streets, and one night in L**c**t*r Street, must have had twenty do so. — A few times I saw a lovely made woman who was a *pose plastique*, had her with her tights on, and fucked her thro a hole I cut in them. I fucked also a cheap woman in the Park, and wonder I did not get clapped, but Nelly's rooms were my resting place, whenever I felt weary or worried, or cared not about the trouble of getting pleasures elsewhere; tho later on I did not see her for months, and once, a year or more elapsed between my visits.

I saw Nelly mostly when I wanted a chat and comfortable rooms to sit and talk baudy in, and smoke till a poke terminated the evening. I reverted to my habits of getting peripatetic whores, whose gait, face, or allures struck my fancy. I went, tho but occasionally, to the A*g**e, to C**m***e, and other resorts of soiled doves, and had one or two old stagers whom I had tailed ten years and more previously. I called on Camille occasionally and gave her a cunt basting, and one or two other old acquaintances as well. These fugitive amours were all narrated at the time, but this must suffice for an account of the whole group — I must abbreviate.

Two or three years after, I made Nelly procure me other women, and very willingly she undertook the task. A vicious looking, dark eyed, shortish woman named Martha, said to be married, was one; and I think she was a hot arsed one for she took to my fucking *con amore*. — There was a big, stern looking woman whom I named my "Life-guard blue" — on account of a masculine, stern look she had. I soon had done with her, for altho I had her three or four times, she never would let me see her cunt, nor even feel it much or well. What was the cause, what the matter with her, I can't imagine. Something certainly was wrong in that spicy nook. Nelly declared she did not know, but had heard that she never would let men see her pudenda. I suppose she was ashamed of it. The last time at Nelly's I said to this "she life guard," "I'm not going to have you unless you let me see your cunt properly." She wouldn't, she would sooner leave. — "Well go then." She went, and I didn't pay her. Nelly had her monthlies on.

Some of my doings with both of those Cyprians will be told in their place.

At mid-day on a very hot day, tho towards the end of the summer of this year, I was walking along one of the main highways which lead to the suburbs of London, and was at a spot at some distance from the centre, when I passed two young girls who were sauntering idly along. The taller of the two had her arm round the others' neck, and looked not sixteen, the other perhaps a year younger. They were dressed poorly like the children of artisans. The taller was nibbling a piece of hay, which I saw her pull out of a truss on the pavement by a corn chandler's shop, and staring about her idly and rudely. I was voluptuously inclined that morning, was thinking of the charms of youthful cunts, and gave a loving glance and winked at the taller as I passed them. She returned the glance saucily yet half shyly, and instinct told me at once that if the girl had not had a prick up her cunt, she knew pretty well what a cock and a cunt did when they met. The idea fired my lust.

After passing them I stopped and looked back. They had stopped, and the tall one was looking back, but seeing me stopping they immediately resumed their sauntering. I should like to fuck her thought I, for she has such bright eyes, and turning I followed them quickly, and as I again passed them said aloud, "I'd give a shilling each to kiss you two pretty girls." Again I caught the tall one's saucy inviting eye. When I had gone ahead some distance, I returned and met them face to face again. They were half looking in at a shop window, half in my direction. Encouraged, I stopped at the shop, and looking at the window and askant only at them, so as to avoid attracting notice, said, "Come and have a ride in a cab with me." Immediately the tall one said, "I don't mind." The other only stared at me. The taller one then whispered something to her.

I stood without further noticing them, waiting for a four wheel cab to pass, nor they noticing me. At length one came by, I hailed

her, I put my mouth to her ear and whispered, "You little devil, you know you've had a prick in your cunt, let me fuck you." "I ain't," and she giggled. — I went on whispering about fucking. "What's he a telling yer?" said Sally, who seemed curious at the whispering. — "I'm telling her I'll give you a shilling to feel your cunt." "Shan't," said Sally. "Feel my prick then." "Feel it, it won't bite yer," said her friend. The girl refused. — "Have you ever felt a man's cock?" "No," said she, boldly and positively. "Oh yer lie — yer have — you've twice felt Jack's." — Sally made no reply, was shut up, and looked stupid.

In a little time Sally, by my continued requests, and at the advice of Carry, got her shilling, and not only felt my cock, but let me feel her bum. I had Carry on one side, and Sally on the other, both standing up with their backs to the doors of the cab, both feeling my standard whilst I was feeling their little backsides.

It was delightful to handle their buttocks, but I wanted further satisfaction. "Show me your cunt Carry and I'll give you another shilling." She wouldn't, she should be seen, but that at length was arranged. Sally stood looking out of one cab window, whilst I with a little resistance threw up the other's petticoats as she sat on the seat opposite to me, and disclosed soiled underlinen, and stockings dirty enough to have shocked my prick if it had had eyes. — But it hadn't, and stood stiffer than ever, when a very little triangular bit of flossy brown shewed at the bottom of the girl's belly. To get a better view I seized hold of her legs, and pulling them up, tilted her back. She kept laughing but asking me to leave off. Then Sally turned her head and seeing my game, uttered a solemn, — "Hoh! ain't he agoing on."

I had my look and wanted another feel, so got Carry on to my knees again and my finger on her cunt, whispering that I'd give her half a crown to fuck her. — "Oh no," — she couldn't. — "She'll tell perhaps, and the people will see us when passing." — But she sat feeling my cock, longing for it to be up her, whilst I rubbed at her clitoris till she wriggled her bum. "You rub this till you get pleasure don't you?" "Sometimes," said the slut laughing. "Oh don't — leave off."

Again I tried it on with Sally, and at length succeeded in feeling her little cunt whilst she kept her legs closed, but nothing induced her to let me look, and as she got noisy — "No I shan't then, I don't care if *she* do — *I* shan't, then — leave off" — I desisted.

"Take us back," said Carry suddenly. "If mother goes out afore I get there, I shan't get nothing to eat — and she'll row me tonight when she comes in." — She was very much in earnest. — "Let me fuck you then, and I'll go back at once." — We were just then at a spot where there was very little traffic. She refused. Sally might tell — I refused to go back and increased my offer.

At length, promising another shilling to Sally to keep standing and looking out of the window, I pushed my legs well forward to the front seat, and between Carry's thighs, who was standing up in front of me. She was almost too short, her cunt was a small mark to hit, but the little bitch was in heat, and earnestly and silently aided my efforts. My prick was in such a state that it would have pierced a board, and directly it got its tip on her split, with a heave up of my arse, it was fixed as tightly up her cunt as if she'd been pegged. Then I clasped her little buttocks and fairly lifted her off the floor, she came forward, her arms round my neck, her face near mine, and I began fucking with short thrusts; my prick never moved more than an inch backwards and forwards, the position would not enable long strokes, but it was enough. — "Do you like it Carry?" "Y-hes," she whispered. "It's up your cunt." "Y-hes — a-har." "Are you coming?" "Aha — Y-hes — soon," and then with delicious short wriggling movements we both spent, and Carry's head fell over my left shoulder.

I thought my pego would never withdraw, and in meretricious thoughts was content to leave it in its soft luscious compress, holding her still round her small backside close to me. She lay with head on my shoulder, silent, tranquil, enjoying the gentle dilation that my prick still gave her cunt, when floating, dwindling slowly in abundant sperm — in the soft mucilaginous bath we had made together in her temple of love — her feet still scarcely touching the cab floor, her cunt squeezing more and more down on to my ballocks, as she felt the rod slowly receding from her. — Sally looked round. — "You'll lose your shilling if you don't look out," said I just recovering from my pleasure as I noticed her. — The girl then stared steadily out of the window but Carry was roused, I let go her backside, and slowly she sat back on the seat opposite as we uncoupled, looking at me with quite a luscious smile, a smile of delight and gratitude for the voluptuous treat I had given her. Then her eyes settled on my moist pego hanging its head over my balls, for I had still lascivious delight in letting it hang out for her to see, my knees still between her legs as she sat, her petticoats dropping over them could fall no further. Thus for a minute smiling at each other, we sat.

Time was pressing, I covered up my ballocks and sat up, she dropped her petticoats, Sally turned round and sat beside her, staring first at me, then at her companion. The little slut knew, I'm sure, what we had been up to, but never spoke a word as she took my shilling. I told cabby to drive back, and was glad of air, for the sun was beating down, and the cab like an oven, as I had closed both windows to diminish the area thro which people passing could see.

I took Carry on my lap, felt that gluey little quim, kissed her, and kept up a conversation in whispers, much to the annoyance of the other, who every now and then kept jealously asking what it was all about. — I offered her a sovereign, if she would bring Sally out that night, and induce her to let me fuck her. — She'd try but feared she couldn't. "I knows who will do it to *her* tho." — Her own mother often stopped *her* (Carry) going out of a night, but if she'd had a drop she'd be sure to let her go. — Sally's mother wouldn't let Sally. They lodged in the same house, but she would try. — Soon after I got out, paid the cabman, and told him where to set the girls down.

The evening came, I somehow had made up my mind that I should fuck the virgin Sally — if she were virgin — for I couldn't get her to let me feel her closely enough to verify that. I was disappointed. At a little past seven o'clock at the appointed place, Carry appeared alone. Sally's mother wouldn't let her daughter out. "I think she'd a let yer do it to her if she'd come, she told me she would." — Carry went with me willingly to a house, and I stripped her. — She had put on clean stockings and chemise, I had told her to do so when in the cab in the morning. — "Shall I fuck you," said I. "Yes do," she replied quickly.

I mounted the little lass, and gloried in the sweet little pouting, half fledged sheath I fucked when I felt the little lass was having as much pleasure as a grown woman. She was revelling with me in copulation, sighing her voluptuous sighs in that sweetly quiet way which girls do, till they learn to break out into the lewed exclamations of delight, which many do as they grow older. — Then after she'd wiped her cunt outside, and our passions were subdued for a time, we talked.

At first she was reserved, then open, and for an hour I questioned *her* much, and she *me* a little. What sweet confidences between a girl of sixteen and a man not far from fifty. The difference in age gave our conversation an additional charm. It was semi-paternal, yet all about fucking. — Of the hour's talk, all worth telling may be soon told.

She had never been in a baudy house before, and had only been fucked two months. Her father died some months ago, her mother was a charwoman and drank. Carry had been a short time a nursemaid, and now did work at home, she did all the cleaning in their two rooms, looked after another sister, and worked with her needle. — She and her mother quarrelled. "Now who fucked you first?" — a young man she knew — "quite a young man" — that's all I could then learn. Sally and her mother lived in the room below, her father was a chair maker, but was a blackguard, sometimes disappeared for a month or two, and her mother got their living principally, and *she* often was drunk. There was a brother nearly sixteen years old and a younger sister, and all three slept in the same bed, and in the same room as their mother and father.

Sally knew all about fucking tho she denied all, and was so demure in the cab. She had seen her brother's cock and felt it, and he had seen Sally's cunt. — "His cock is a good big one too." "Then you've seen it." — Carry didn't deny that. The brother one night tried to do it to his sister "And she'll let him one day I knows, tho she says she won't." Little by little, I got out that these two youngsters had one day frigged the lad, and he'd seen both their cunts. He was a shop boy at a grocer's.

Suddenly a light dawned upon me from some remark she made. "It's her brother who fucked you first." — She broke out into laughter, and denied it. — But I insisted, and at last she admitted it.

Carry had to fetch pails of water upstairs, and the lad used kindly to do it for her — one morning her mother had gone out to work at six o'clock, when the lad knocked at the door as he was going to his work, and asked if he should fetch her a pail full. She accepted and he fetched it. She instead of getting up when her mother left went to bed again, and was in her chemise. He wanted to bring the water in. — "No put it down outside." He said he'd throw the water away. So she let him in, he put down the pail, then began kissing her, she'd already seen his prick, and his spunk, he'd seen her cunt, and a few minutes afterwards, that lucky lad's prick was in her virgin niche, her hymen was but a bleeding split, his sperm was sticking his balls on to her buttocks. — She was in for fucking after that. — When once a female's tasted the sugar stick, it's not long before she gets another taste.

Since then whenever Jack got the opportunity he fucked her, and she let him willingly. — "Why shouldn't I now." She'd never had another man. — But Jack was a blackguard, for tho he'd promised to tell no one — had "took his Bible oath" he wouldn't if I'd let him, he had told a shopman where he was working, and the shopman came after her and told her. But she hadn't and did not mean to let the shopman, she couldn't bear him — and I was the only one except Jack, who had done it to her.

She didn't think Jack had told his sister, but he'd said he meant to fuck his sister, and Carry felt sure she'd let him some day when his mother was out. "She knows all about doing it bless yer. — Why she's seen her father and mother adoing it often, and has seen her father's prick."

That was the history got in an hour's talking, whilst feeling and finger stinking, and by that time my pego being in admirable condition and she delighted at its size and look. — "Oh yes, it's much bigger than Jack's," — took it up her notch again, and again I wetted its little soft interior with my sperm, and she spent charmingly in my arms, kissing me.

I was in love with the little lass, and fucked her once more, but she was in a hurry to get home, her mother would knock her about if she found her out of nights, and unless drunk her mother usually kept at home. She hoped her "mother would be out on the screw." — Couldn't I be where I first met them in the day, then perhaps Sally would go to a house, and let me have her. I couldn't well do that soon, but arranged to be that day week at the same spot and hour if Carry would. She agreed but never came, and I never saw her more.

CHAPTER XIII

*The Great Eastern. — Our first meeting. — Her form, size, and history. — Bottled ale. — A lightweight on the top. — The landlady's daughter Betsy. — Virginity inspected. — Maternal cant. — Two backsides to the front. — Da capo. — A treat for Betsy. — A spend on a bum. — A bid for a virginity. — The G E disappears. — Nelly L**l*e's help. — Friend Martha. — Her skinny, bare-cunted niece. — A vigorous evening. — Virginity taken. — A trap escaped. — The bare-cunted one again. — A shindy at a brothel.*

I didn't of course keep to Nelly L**l*e, and some years after I knew her, on one afternoon about five p.m. in daylight, saw an enormously tall fat woman in C*v**t*y Street. She half stopped and smiled, as if on a sudden she recollected me, I seemed also to recollect *her*. What a backside, what a cunt she must have, thought I. — Ten minutes later I was in her bed room. —In ten minutes more my balls were banging against the largest arse they ever touched, and few balls have touched such a large one unless against hers. It was the belly of the "Great Eastern," and I was lying up a cunt which at the first glance looked as big as a horse collar, but which clipped me and fetched my sperm out of my ballocks very nicely.

Some years before this, I was passing thro J***s Street on one cold night, when between the H**m**k*t and O*e*d*n Street — then filled with gay lodgings &c. — I saw an exceedingly tall, fine woman standing still at the edge of the kerb, and thought her a quiet woman waiting for some one. Something induced me to return. Still she stood there and looked at me full, but without smile, sign, or gesture. — She is waiting to piss on the quiet I then thought, — the women often did there, I have seen six at a time

— and delighted at the chance of seeing a woman piddling, which always gives me pleasure. I turned back again, and now she was standing in the gutter. She'll squat down directly thought I, slackened my pace, and at O*e*d*n Street corner looked round, and saw that she was looking after me. I returned then and spoke to her. "It's a fine night." "Yes sir, but very cold standing here." "Let's go home together," said I, feeling on sure ground. "You can't go to my place." "Where you like." "Anywhere *you* like, sir, I've only come to London yesterday." "Let's go here," and we went to the corner house. "I thought it was a queer house," said she, "I've been watching it for half an hour." — She had been standing there all that time and no man had accosted her, tho they had stared at her, she told me.

She sat down and looked all about the room, and without taking notice of me. I thrust my hand up her clothes, and fingers between her cunt lips. — She put her hands down to push them away — then as if recollecting, she let me do what I liked and sat looking at me. I felt all about her backside and quim with both hands, then impatiently got up and told her to undress. She did so slowly and hesitatingly. — We were both soon in our last linens, I threw up her chemise, saw one of the most magnificent sights of full sized female form, our bellies met, my cock entered her cunt, she felt its probing at once and deliciously, and we spent together quickly. — Both wanted a fuck, and she more than I did.

When she had washed her cunt, I made her strip completely and had a full look at her beauties. She was quite six feet high, had chestnut coloured hair, lovely soft dark hazel eyes, chestnut coloured cunt thatch and armpits, was big, fleshy, almost heavy, from neck to ankle. Yet she was a grand woman, was beautifully formed, indeed a lovely voluptuous figure. Her cunt was heavy lipped, fat motted, and looked large outside, yet was as tight as a girl's inside. She examined my prick curiously, and when I had felt and seen her all over (we had scarcely spoken) with one consent we turned on to the bed and fucked again. Then she put on her chemise, sat down in front of the fire and stared at it silently. I asked her what she was thinking of, twice without a reply. — Then she turned her head to me and said, "I'm a whore at last." — She smiled faintly but was dull and depressed, so I sent for a bottle of sherry and biscuits. She drank it very quickly as if to get up her spirits.

"Let's chat," and we did so long, sitting by the fire. — A knock at the door came. — "Shall you be long," said a voice. We had heard an incessant tramping whilst we were talking. "Be damned," said I, "I'll pay for the room twice." We chatted on, I put her on to my knee for a second, so that I might twiddle her quim as we talked. It adds to the charm of a chat to feel a nice cunt, and the women all like it, but I could not bear her weight. I heard her history, which I didn't believe, but heard fully afterwards from her, and in a year or two from a man who knew her well early in life, and it was substantially true as far as her married status, and lapse into infidelity went.

She was wife of a sergeant in the ** regiment which was ordered off somewhere. Whilst she remained at W**c***t*r, a livery stable keeper — I knew his name well — got into her. — Her husband on his return found it out and turned her off. — The stable keeper kept her two or three years, then they quarrelled and she came to London to turn harlot. — She had been in London two days when I met her, and had then nothing of the harlot either in manner or dress. — We adjoined to the bed after our talk, and fingered each other's privates till we fucked again, and having got her address, with the understanding that it was only to enable me to write to her, we parted.

I got her the next day at a favorite baudy house, for her size, fleshiness, freshness and fucking, roused my salacity; and saw her several times afterwards, and then having fucked her well, was satisfied. She soon disappeared from London, and now I saw her again after the interval of about ten years. — She now weighed twenty stone I'm sure. [I have had a taller woman since, but never such a big heavy one.] — Her arse when kneeling on the bed, with its long slit and hairy pouters was overhelming, I could only get two-thirds of my prick in that way, her buttocks prevented more entry. She was easy enough to fuck when on the top of her, was a fleshy bed to lay on, and still a tightish cunted one tho it looked so big outside — a horse collar.

We talked over our first meeting and well she recollected it, and that she'd not cheek to speak to me that night. She said many men had passed looking at her, and she could not accost them. — "Didn't I like you, I'd not then had a fuck for weeks." — She had been kept, and had been whoring alternately since I'd first had her, and that was all I could learn, certainly she had not been in London during that time. — "Let *me* fuck *you,*" said she after I had visited her two or three times. — "You'll crush me." "You shan't feel my weight," — and it was true. She did it so to me afterwards once or twice, but I preferred topping her. She was an economical punk, for I only gave her each visit a sovereign, and was still very handsome in face tho somewhat bloated, which shewed up strongly in day light. She did not care about going out too much in day time, for every one turned round to look after her, and good men did not like to be seen following her home, and as she had a good number of *"visiting friends,"* she mostly kept at home unless hard up. — She was always drinking bottled ale or stout, as if she wanted to make herself fatter, which seemed funny. — From her size she had got to be nick-named "The Great Eastern." [A big steamboat at that date.]

I visited her at intervals whenever her size gave me a letch. I was curious in examining her person. The first thing, when seated in her room, was to ask me for bottled ale. — The daughter of the landlady, a buxom and very handsome lass a little over fifteen years old, brought it in. — I took a letch for her, it was a year or two since I had seen an unfledged cunt, and a burning desire to see hers came over me, and I offered the Eastern money to help me. — It was impossible she said. — "But," said I, "I only want to see her cunt and virginity, a thoroughly good look at it mind, I won't do more than open the lips." — My letch increased and I bid from two up to five sovereigns to see it — "Not a mere glimpse, but a good look of some minutes, mind that."

Under one aspect, that of a mother's morality, this is one of the almost incredible events of my career, but it is as true as gospel. The house was kept by a carpenter and his wife, who lived in the ground floor and kitchens. On the first floor was the Great Eastern (a gay woman), and above were working people quite respectable. The woman of the house had three or four children, and at this time was suckling one, — the father I never saw that I know of, he was nearly always out in the day time. With this twenty-stone whore the mother associated freely, and the children were always in her room, the strapping eldest girl included. I have seen the mother nursing the baby there. — The mother seemed quite a hard working, respectable woman, and all the children were clean and neatly dressed. But the mother talked about fucking almost like a gay woman — the Great Eastern told me — and she always told the Great Eastern when her husband had fucked her, and how often he did it.

I didn't think there was any chance of getting what I wanted, yet used to say in a joking manner after the refusal, — "Mind, there are five pounds to have a good look at Betsy's cunt." I used to say it regularly when the girl had left the room after bringing in the bottled ale. I often gave her the change, but never took the slightest liberty. — One day the Great Eastern said, "I spoke to her mother about your seeing Betsy naked, and told her you were a surgeon, and you wanted to see the girl's virginity out of curiosity, because she was so handsome and fine grown — they are hard up to pay the rent, and I think somehow it can just be managed, if you'll give her five pounds; but the mother must be in the room, and you mustn't talk baudy or touch Betsy." — I replied, "I must open the cunt myself." "Then you must do it like a doctor." — We talked out the matter, and a week or two further on, it was arranged that as a doctor I was to go one day at a particular time, when she hoped the mother would consent to my seeing the girl's pudenda.

On the day, there was I in the room, expectant. The mother came into us, and talked some cock and bull story about wishing to know if any harm had been done to her daughter, it was a mask to hide her intention — to excuse herself. — Miss Great Eastern had said I was a surgeon, so would I look at the child. I indulged in the sham, as if *I* didn't, and as if *she* didn't know it was humbug. Then she fetched the girl, and very deliberately took off her clothing, and I laid her on the bed talking in a soothing tone, imitating a doctor in manner as well as I could. — "Don't be alarmed — I won't hurt you — there, — never mind me," and so on. I had as told passed often in the character before, and having studied female anatomy as far as their cunts go, have a good deal of jargon about it ready to my tongue. — The Great Eastern declared afterwards that I was exactly like a doctor. — Gently I lifted the girl's chemise and opened her thighs, she closed them, but then made no further objection. I asked the mother to hold one leg, the Great Eastern the other, and there they stood holding the girl's legs with one hand, each with a candle in the other. — It was dark at that time at five in the afternoon, of a foggy, early winter day.

Trembling with excitement but controlling myself, I opened the clean, plump, little, slightly fledged cunt lips, and looked till I thought my prick would burst with lust at the sight of the little perforation of the hymen. It was a lovely pink cunt, small and enticing, with little crisp hair just coming on her motte. She was a splendidly well fed, plump, fat arsed young bitch, her thighs round and close, the legs with ample calves — I longed to put my finger thro the little perforated membrane, which nearly closed the prick hole. I nearly licked it, and sniffed hard at the enticing aroma. — The mother got impatient and nudged my arm. — "Can't you see, doctor?" But saying I couldn't, I made the girl kneel with her backside towards me, and looked at her cunt from behind — I stroked gently the red surface of her virginity with my wetted finger, and nearly spent; and then unable with decency to keep up the farce any longer, and resist the request of the mother to be quick, I reluctantly let the chemise drop over her dear little bum. She shook down her clothes, smiled at me, and left the room with her mother—I rushed my prick up the Great Eastern's cunt, almost before the door was closed, spent, pulled it out, pushed it up again, laid on her fat belly, pushing and talking about Betsy's cunt till I spent again.

Then I gave the Great Eastern five sovereigns. How much the mother had of it I don't know, the Great Eastern said all. Then I tipped her some gold extra, thinking what I had seen well worth the money, not however believing her statement. The mother came back shortly after and, "You'll never mention this to any one will you," said she. "Oh, never, my good woman." — She said a lot then about bad times, how glad she was her girl had not gone wrong and so on, I was glad to get rid of her, tho she would have talked ever so long about my investigation of her daughter's cunt, if I had let her — "I don't know what I shall do with her I'm sure," said she. "People who's poor and has daughters, has great trouble with 'em," she whined, "they takes such a lot o looking arter now-a-days, and how is a poor working woman like me to see arter her, but I'm glad she is all right."

In a week or so I went to see the Great Eastern again, and so much does imagination affect me in sexual matters, that I did so largely thro thinking of Betsy's virginity; and whilst up the Great Eastern, in baudy imagination I was up Betsy, and fucked calling out what a lovely little cunt she had. — "I'm fucking Betsy, I'm putting my spunk into Betsy," — and the Great Eastern encouraged me. The desire arose directly after the cunt inspection for which the mother was paid. When I had finished my pleasure, I told the Great Eastern that I should like to see their bums side by side, and of course promised what was quite worth her while to arrange for it, and went a day or two after hoping for the sight. But I found that the mother would not let the girl into the lodger's room since the night I had seen her cunt. — She was not allowed even to bring the bottled ale when men were there — the mother bringing it in herself. I expect she never told her husband.

The Great Eastern at length mentioned a time and day when the mother would be likely to be out, and I then went. She got the girl up, and I promised *her* half a crown. The girl hesitated. "You little fool," said Great Eastern, "he's seen your cunt — who'll know if you don't tell." I showed the half crown and she yielded. — The Great Eastern put the girl on the bed kneeling, and lifted her petticoats up over her waist, then she knelt herself with naked backside by her side. It was a most wonderful sight. The huge arse as big as a horse's but white, and the thick lipped hairy cunt between the thighs, looked as big as a cow's; the other delicate little slit looked nothing by the side of it. But I had but a very short sight of both. The Great Eastern was so frightened of the mother coming home, that letting drop their clothes, she sent the girl off quickly. — I was awfully lewed at the inspection, and shewed the girl my stiff prick as she left the room. — She stood looking at it. — "Feel it," said I, but the Great Eastern pushed her out. — "I'm frightened of the mother, I owe so much rent," said she, — "I don't want her to know you've been here, I'm sure the girl was going to feel it." — Those two backsides side by side I nearly kissed.

This voluptuous sight haunted me so, that one night soon after I frigged myself thinking of the two backsides side by side. Much as I hate self-masturbation I couldn't resist it, so much did the contrast affect me sensuously. — I don't think I have been frigged since little Lizzie did it to me. The contrast between *her* backside and cunt, and Sarah F**z*r's was great, but the huge size of the Great Eastern's rump and split, made this far greater. — Besides that, Betsy had a little short dark hair showing on the lips, and somehow the sight of the two affected me more voluptuously, tho

I was not allowed to touch or open Betsy's little quim for I gave a promise to Great Eastern that I would not attempt that. Again I went and bid so high that the Great Eastern arranged to repeat the spectacle — the girl was not loath, had talked about my prick, and I dare say about every thing else, but both females were in great dread of the parents, the Great Eastern especially. She made me promise again not to touch the girl's flesh if she showed me her rump. If I did, then she said she would at once pull down the girl's clothes, and put her out of the room. — "Honor bright, don't get me into a row, I can't find lodgings which suit me as well." — "Well, let the girl feel my prick, and let her see me fuck you." — I promised still more money for I was mad on my letch, she consented, but the girl wasn't to be forced to do it, or frightened in any way. "Tho she knows a lot, and would like to know more, she's in such dread of her parents."

The mother scarcely ever went out for more than ten minutes excepting on Sundays, and on that day took Betsy with her. — A month elapsed before the Great Eastern, to whom I spoke in the street, and had named a post office where she might write to me, mentioned a day that the mother was going a long way, to visit her sick sister. I was at the lodgings before the time, and after a short chat Betsy was called, and fetched bottled ale, then the knowing lass locked the younger children in their rooms below (she was left in charge), and came to us looking quite modest, yet with a half grin on her face, for she knew what she was to do and get. "Look sharp," said Great Eastern who seemed anxious, "for your mother may come back soon, tho it's not likely." Turning she knelt on the bed, I threw up her clothes and exposed her huge buttocks, which Betsy stared at. — "Show me yours darling," said I. "Get on the bed quick," said Great Eastern. In another minute Betsy did. — Great Eastern pulled her clothes up and *her* tender backside was on view. — How I gloried in the sight of her sweet round bum cheeks, and the little split between them. It certainly was a most unique, libidinous, luscious spectacle to see the two. My prick stood, I pulled it out and thought of frigging but restrained myself, and with difficulty restrained myself from touching Betsy's person as I'd promised, tho nearly mad to look at her virginity again, which I could not see with her legs nearly closed as they were as she knelt, even tho she widened them a little at my request.

I could bear it no longer. "Ain't you seen enough? I can't kneel any longer, the blood's getting in my head," and so saying the Great Eastern got off the bed, the lass following suit. — "I've not looked a minute." "You've been five minutes and more." — I gave the lass money, she kept staring at my prick. — "I'll give you another half crown, Betsy, if you'll feel this," pointing to my erection. She looked at the Great Eastern and burst out laughing. "Shall I," said she. "Yes, I won't tell, and no one will know." — She stood still hesitating by the side of the Great Eastern, I walked up to her, "Feel it my love," and taking hold of her hand I put it round it. Then female curiosity and nature asserted itself, and whilst encouraging her with gentle lascivious words, she felt it to my heart's content and to her evident enjoyment, laughing in a low tone all the time, getting red in the face and excited. — "Ah my darling, you'll have one like that up your sweet little cunt one day, I'd give twenty pounds to do it to you, My God I'm bursting, let us fuck," said I to the Great Eastern. — "All right," said she walking to the bed, she was in her chemise. I called her Mary, but it wasn't her name.

The girl let go my prick and walked quickly to the door, and was going. I stopped her. — "Look at us fucking dear and I'll give you another half crown." — She looked at the Great Eastern. "You may stop this time, but never tell it to any one, will you?" I was now mad for fucking and could think of nothing else, the delight of showing the operation to the girl was intense. The idea of her looking at my prick going up the big one's cunt, of showing myself naked to her, excited me madly, and I stripped rapidly. "Look my darling," and lifting my shirt I showed my tooleywag in its pride. "Come close, you can't see there," and to the Great Eastern, "Come to the side of the bed." "You can't poke there well," she replied.

It was a bitterly cold winter's afternoon, we had but two candles and the room looked dark. I stirred the fire to a blaze and put the candles on a table by the bedside, to throw light on our fucking. The Great Eastern placed herself on the bedside with thighs widish apart, the girl stood far off still. "Come here and look darling." "Come if you want to see," said Great Eastern. — Slowly she came to the bedside. Great Eastern then hoisted up her huge thighs, I pulled apart the thick, dark hedged lips, and slowly as my irritated overflowing ballocks would let me, put my prick up her cunt, the girl looking eagerly, her head bent over us. Somehow the fatness and weight of the thighs and bum prevented me fucking. I had never tried the bedside with her in that attitude before.

"I told you so, come on the bed, and Betsy will see better." Uncunting me, she moved herself with quickness (her agility for her size was really great) on to the bed, and then upon her, my prick plunged up her. — We turned when prick and cunt were well joined, slightly on to one side, and she lifted the thigh high up which was nearest to Betsy. — [Voluptuousness is the joy of life, as much to a whore in her heyday as any one else, and I now feel sure that the Great Eastern enjoyed the idea of the lass looking on.] Clasping her gigantic buttocks I fucked. "Hold the candle and look Betsy," gasped the Eastern. — Her young eyes were good enough without that, nor did she hold the candle, but her head came nearer and nearer to the Great Eastern's backside. Then her dear little virgin notch with the little flood opening for her menses came into my mind and fetched me at once. Plunging my prick deep up the Great Eastern's cunt, "I'm spending, my spunk's coming," I sighed. "Oh — fuck — go on," cried she shaking her huge arse, and as the lewed words sobbed out of our mouths, our soft spendings mingled in her cunt, and we wriggled our genitals slowly in the overwhelming die-away pleasure of the discharge.

"Keep my prick well in you," I said, when my pleasure was over and we kept joined. There stood the girl, her face within a foot of Great Eastern's arse, never moving nor uttering a word, but greedily looking, her eyes staring like those of a waxwork figure, at the side view of the Great Eastern's backside and quim, and my prick stem just showing with its balls hanging outside the cunt; and so she stood till my prick flopped out. Then she drew back. — "What do you think of it, Betsy?" said Great Eastern. — The girl suddenly turned her head and listened. — "Oh my mother's come home," and running to the door, she bolted quickly down stairs. — "There will be a damned fine row if it is," said the Great Eastern, anxiously going on to the landing in her chemise and listening.

It was a false alarm. — The girl came back, I believe hoping to see more, I washed my prick, made her feel it again, gave her money, and Great Eastern sent her away. Baudy questions put to her, she only laughed at and made no reply to.

We couldn't get the girl to come up and stop again, tho she fetched us more ale. — I talked for an hour or so, and then asked the Great Eastern to gamahuche me. She had never done so before. — Now my desire was for her to kneel over me and suck which she did, but being so tall, her big rump was too close to my face to see it well. So she laid along the bed at its side, her head on the edge of the pillow, one foot resting on the under thigh, which opened her gap well to my feel. Then standing, I put my prick in her mouth, and with my right hand clasping the surface of her fresh washed cunt — a complete handful and more it was — I gave her my libation, aiding the movements of her mouth, by myself fucking into it. — It was an expensive afternoon, tho Betsy got so little, — but with the young ones, half crowns go as far as sovereigns.

I could think of nothing else, and went there a day or two afterwards. Betsy gave me a saucy laugh, but the Great Eastern would not permit me any liberties; no money tempted her, she was frightened, for the girl's mother was at home, and Betsy could not stay in the room more than a minute. In that minute I showed her my prick at which she looked lewedly. — "If ever a girl wanted fucking, she does," said Great Eastern, "she'll get it soon from some one."

I wouldn't go to the Great Eastern but met her purposely in the streets, and offered her more to get me the girl naked again. Steadily she refused till one night about a fortnight after, when she told me that the parents were going to the sister's funeral. At the time arranged I was there, and all the spectacle was repeated. Standing with prick nearly bursting, whilst the two backsides were before me — "I must kiss it," said I, and put my lips on Betsy's little buttocks, spite of Great Eastern's objection. "Turn round again, Mary." She did, and there again were the two backsides together nearly touching. Quick as lightning a letch came. Talking to the Great Eastern who, with head on pillow, could not see, and did not anticipate my action, I frigged myself rapidly, put my prick close, and spent over Betsy's bum, some of my sperm hitting her sweet little pouting cunt. As she felt it, the girl turned quickly round, saying, "Oh." — So did Great Eastern, and seeing what I had done, swore great oaths, and pulling Betsy's clothes up again, wiped off my spendings to prevent her dirty little chemise being stained. Soon after I bum-basted the big woman to Betsy's edification, and departed.

Then I became so wild to fuck Betsy, encouraged in the hope by what Great Eastern had said about her getting it done to her soon, that I offered twenty pounds to get her. But it was of no use. I saw the girl once or twice, but the Great Eastern said the mother would not now let her come in when I was there. — The people could not pay the rent, soon after were turned out, and I saw no more of them. A new landlady came, the Great Eastern still lodged there, but I had had enough of *her* and ceased seeing her for a time.

I had a recurrence of desire to see the roly poly big cunt in the huge arse, so called and found she had left, nor could I discover her whereabouts. — As every Paphian knew her well, I asked several, but none knew where she had gone. To one I offered money to take me to her lodgings, she took me to the old lodgings. Some months after I was told she had died of fever in hospital, another said in prison.

I wonder who had that splendid little lass. — She was doomed to be fucked soon. Great Eastern said that the girl had frigged herself, had said she'd like to be fucked, but her father would half murder her if he found it out. — I dare say a lad of her own class did her (and such as *they* get their own opportunities). What waste of beauty and virginity, which might have delighted me.

This treat with Betsy whetted a lustful appetite, and directly I went to Nelly L**l*e who had left Madame S*l*ks, and seemed poorly off. I told her that I wanted a young girl with a hairless cunt, and what I had seen and done (without giving the slightest idea with whom). — I don't think Nelly believed me. — She was now well up in her profession of strumpet, but did not see her way to get me what I wanted, but she was in debt and in want of money, and after two or three interviews, she told me that Martha's husband was again out of work, that she had a niece with her as a servant, and that Martha would persuade the girl to let me do it — at a price.

I had with Nelly continued my custom of always giving gay ladies their fee, when they told me they were poorly, whether I poked them or not. — One day she being in that state she had fetched this Martha — who was a bright eyed, dark, shortish, thinnish woman, of twenty-eight or thereabout, was the wife of a working man, and who dressed like a servant. — She said she had not had any other man since she was married, which I didn't believe — but she was modest in manner and reluctant to let me pull her about — I got angry, and Nelly told her not to be a fool. — "Well then, I won't let him if you stand staring at me along side of him," she burst out. — I sent Nelly out of the room — Martha got more free then, and felt my prick, and then looked lewed, and then we fucked, and a second time. "Have you spent?" said I doubtingly, tho I thought she had. "Yes, but don't tell Nellie will you." A second evening I fucked her, tho Nelly was not then poorly — Martha had had other men since she had me she then admitted, she wasn't going to starve, but directly her husband got work, she'd do no more of the "dirty business."

Nelly said soon afterwards to me that they again were almost starving, and so she'd sell her niece — I thought the girl more than sixteen when I set eyes on her. — "I won't have her if she has any hair on her cunt," I remarked. "She's not a bit," said Nelly. — I satisfied myself with my finger, the girl was then stripped, I sat her on my naked knee, showed her some baudy pictures, then laid her on the bed. — She was very restive and would not let me see her hairless quim, but persuaded by the two women at length did. — She was a virgin, but skinny and bony, very plain, and almost ugly. My prick was in prime order, so I told the women to leave the room, and at once covered the girl, but she cried out, made such a row and baulked me. "Aunt, aunt, come back." — Back came the two women who were listening, there was a little and quite natural scene then, and she declared she would not let me, would rather not have the clothes and money promised. — Partly persuaded, partly bullied by the women, she laid down again, and the business was over in one or two cunt splitting thrusts, during which she howled. — She lay quiet when fully opened and my spunk was flooding her vagina. I kept a long time up her, holding tight to her skinny arse, and then had the satisfaction of finding my prick and fingers well blood stained. — Nelly and Martha both looked on at the whole proceeding at the bedside, each looked at the bleeding cunt and then laughed.

The girl washed — I looked at her lacerated split, and then almost directly fucked her again. — I've no recollection of her having had pleasure, but I was so engrossed with my own, and amused with handling her skinny bum, which seemed ridiculous after Betsy's and the Great Eastern's arses. [Great bums were always my delight, periodically.]

I sent out for spirits (they had already drunk my wine) and we talked. Nelly showed her cunt, Aunt Martha pulled her petticoats up and showed hers. — "I don't mind, now Bess (another Bess) knows what fucking is," said she. "And she won't tell her uncle, I knows." She was sitting on the bedside, and Bess was just beside her. "Show your cunny," said I. Martha pushed the girl back on the bed and pulled up her chemise, and I looked. The girl had had drink and was peevish and had refused. — Nearly two hours had passed since I had last put into the girl, and I was randy again, her freshness caused my excitement. "I'll fuck her," said I. "No, no, no, no, he shan't," she shrieked.

"No," said aunt, "you've done her twice and we must go — it's late and my man will be home, there will be a row if I'm not there." — I said I was not going to pay for nothing. — I had had her firsts and that was enough replied Martha, and the girl was tired. — Nell said that Martha must get home, — I whispered in Nelly's ear an additional tip, she whispered to Martha, who then told the girl not to be foolish. The girl and I again looked at the baudy pictures, I rubbed her clitoris with my finger, taking care not to put it lower down. I must have stirred her senses. "Oh don't, sir," and she put her hands and head right over the baudy pictures on the table, and wriggled her little backside on my thigh. — "Let's look at your dear little cunt." "Let the gentleman," said Martha.

I put her on the bed, opened her legs, her cunt was still slightly bleeding, blood was on my thigh. I laid by her side and frigged her gently, then turned on to her, and with a rapid lunge or two I was up her cunt again. — She howled and wriggled as she felt the thrust, but I held her tight to me by her skinny bum and directly she was quite plugged, she was tranquil — it is always so with them I find. The hammer of the prick against the womb neck stuns the cunt for the moment, or else rouses their lust, and pleasure begins to soothe them.

Then I fucked quietly, controlling myself and she was tranquil. — "Does it hurt now dear?" "A little, sir." — I wriggled rather than stroked. — "Now dear?" "No, sir," — she gasped. Slowly I fucked on, my pleasure increased, my prick got stiffer and stiffer, her cunt tighter still. — "Is that nice dear?" She made no answer, her mouth was wide open, her breathing hard, her eyes were closed, her cunt gripped my prick. — She was spending, and the next minute I spunked in her.

Nelly and Martha had looked on. — "I *must* get home with her or there will be a damned row," said Martha again. — I wouldn't move out, for I was actually stiff up her cunt still, and the girl lay quiet. — "Was it nice?" I whispered. She made no reply. — My prick shrunk out, I turned on my side, and she lay quite still looking up at the ceiling, with thighs wide apart. — "Get up, now do, we must be off," said Martha. — As the girl rose I put my finger to her cunt, there was slight blood on my finger. The girl pissed, I pissed, then Nelly and Martha pissed. — "We've all pissed," said I. The women laughed, the girl washed her cunt, and Martha hurried away with her. — Nelly who had sat nearly naked with folded arms until then, came and sat on a stool at my feet as I sat in an easy chair, and began playing with my cock. — She always felt it unasked when we were together. — She would twiddle it without stopping for hours. — She said she always did so with her friends, she liked the feel of a cock.

We talked about the fucking. — "Do it to me," said she, "looking at you all the evening has made me so randy. — It made Martha randy, didn't you hear her say when you were doing Betsy, that she wished you were doing *her*?" — I certainly had not. "Do me." "I can't if I try." "You can, it's stiff now." "Suck me first." Nelly obeyed, she had well learnt that art — I revelled in her suction and swelled out stiff, but felt that I couldn't spend. — "If you won't do me I must frig myself," said she, and leaving off sucking she laid her head on my thigh, with her mouth against my cock and began frigging herself hard. — "Lay on the bed side," said I. — With alacrity she went there, and laid with wide distended thighs, and gaping cunt. She was beautiful in form then, so plump, so round, so compact, her black motte shewed up between her white thighs and plump, silk clad legs. — I didn't want it but was stiff, so thrust it up her. — In a minute she was spending before I had a sensation. — I fucked on till I fetched her again, and then spent myself. — "I told you you could," said she. It was the first time I ever recollect seeing Nell lewedly frig herself, and chaffed her about it. She was quite lewed and before I left frigged herself right out, after asking me to fuck her again — which I couldn't, and wouldn't even try to do.

Martha and Nelly had tippled with what I had brought them, and what I had sent out for, and now Nell was quietly boozy. She never was noisy, was the quietest of girls, but was now communicative. — She thought the girl was Martha's niece but wasn't sure. She was an impudent young one — Martha couldn't keep her out of the streets, and had caught her with a big boy, a lodger's son, and was being felt by him. — Martha could swear *his* hand was up her clothes and she was nearly sure that she was feeling *his* cock. — She banged her head for it against the wall. — Martha's husband always fucked Martha on Sundays and had said that some ragged arsed young bugger would do it to the girl some night when she fetched the beer, for she was hot arsed like her mother and was safe to be gay.

I arranged to have the girl again. — On the day appointed she never came, tho I went again thinking it strange, for Nell lost money thro it. — A suspicion then kept me from calling there, and I waited for Nell at night in the streets. — She told me it was well I had left that day, for just after, Martha and the girl's father — or some man who said he was — had come to get money out of me, for the girl had told. — Nell had quarrelled with Martha about it. — I never had or saw Martha after, nor the girl until a year had gone, when about midday, I saw her in C*v**t*y Street with another young bitch. I took her to a baudy house and fucked her right off. She had still a perfectly bald cunt, not a hair visible, and was skinnier and uglier than ever. She told me she was sixteen, and did not recognize me at first.

She had now all the manners of a brazen faced little whore. As she washed her cunt, she all at once stopped, looked curious, and said, "You know Nelly L**l*e." "No." Looking at me steadily, "Don't yer — damned if you ain't the man who first fucked me." "No." "You are, and you never gave me any money tho you promised, give it me now." "How long have you been gay?" "Not long, and it's all your fault." — I rang the bell and the baud came. — "This girl's abusive," said I (she became so), "you'd better stop her." — She didn't know her. — "I believe you do, and have put her up to it, and have a good mind to make it hot for your house."

"What for," said the girl. "Because you are threatening and want to rob me." "You lying bugger," said the girl. "You're a gentleman I suppose," said the woman. — I went away without saying another word, only throwing down the money I'd promised the girl. — On leaving, the woman was ballyragging her, and telling her she would not let her into her house again, if she was not square with gentlemen. I saw the girl about the streets afterwards for a year or two, whether she saw me or not I cannot say.

CHAPTER XIV

*Females ready, and male opportunities. — Another adultery. — On the highway. — Costermongers and hucksters. — Mrs. *** met. — Suggestive talk in a quiet street. — The servant sent out. — Myself let in. — On the sofa. — Up the lady. — On the bed. — A flaccid doodle. — A gamahuche. — Penis redivivus. — Alarmed. — At a house soon after. — Fears — tears — feeling — fucking — frigging — and gamahuching. — The lady's history. — A middle-aged husband. — Face, form, and cunt. — My liking for gamahuching. — Sequel.*

[A year or two before this time as already said, I began again to avail myself of opportunities with women who were not gay, but I had many hinderances in these amatory chases. — The chances were many as I saw with clearer eyes than ever, but circumstances, often the risk, prevented my following them up. Most men I expect get such opportunities, for there are plenty of cunts hungry and athirst for a male; yet men for want of time or money let them slip, or else having one female ready at all times to receive their embraces, and empty their sperm reservoirs, are content with that.]

One Saturday night about seven o'clock in early winter of this year, walking through a main thoroughfare leading to the outskirts of London, I had a chance of a woman not gay, and acted upon my intention of not throwing away one whilst my virility remained in force.

It was a wide road with a good through traffic, yet near to a poor neighbourhood on either side of it, and where by ancient custom on Saturday nights, the carriageways next to the kerb stones are filled with costermongers' barrows, hucksters' stalls, and purveyors of goods of all sorts for the poor. — The footways were crowded with purchasers, and were bright with gas at the shops, and petroleum lamps of the hucksters. The shouting of the sellers, the tramp of feet, and the roll of vehicles made almost a deafening noise. — Amused I watched the crowd, and whilst doing so met a fairly well dressed woman, seemingly about twenty-five years old, tallish and stout, and looking in her winter's garb well off, who slowly moving along, seemed to be also watching the busy multitude of poor people.

At a glance I saw she was handsome, had nice soft eyes, dark brown hair, and a sweet, small, red-lipped mouth. She caught my eye and from her look I saw that I pleased her. She stopped to look at a stall, so did I, and standing by the side of her a voluptuous thrill starting either from my brain or ballocks, ran through me. Was she gay, or modest, or game, and what chance had I, flashed through my mind.

I moved close to her till my arm touched her, as one may do in a crowd. As she walked away she looked me full in the face, and stopped soon at another stall where they sold toy windmills — I did the same. — "They are very pretty," said I. "Yes," she replied, looking at me. "I'll buy one for your children." "I haven't any," and she laughed. Then almost trembling as I said it, but my prick was rousing my sexual impudence, "Did you ever try to get any?" "What's that to you," said she, and giving me an astonished stare yet laughing, she walked off. Thought I, that's the manner of a hot cunted one, and I have set her thinking about fucking.

I followed close to her, politely forcing my conversation on her but not on that topic. She willingly entered into it, altho at first quite silent, then looking me full in the face. — But ever and anon she looked round restlessly, anxiously, and on the opposite of the way as well. I began again talking about children. — It was well to avoid having them I remarked "I dare say you have a lot," said she "I know how to get, and how to prevent getting them." She laughed. — We were by that time nearly at the end of the thronged part of the road, and where it was darker I told her how beautiful she was, and asked if I might see her home. "See me home? Oh! no thank you, good night," and she turned down a side street abruptly.

There was something in her manner, which made me fancy that at that moment lust was stinging her cunt, so I followed. "Meet me another night, tell me your name and address." — She hesitated. "Give me a kiss before we part." "What next, sir, you, a perfect stranger, I'm surprized at your impudence." Then she said she was married. — "Ah what a lucky man, what would I not give to be married to you, try another husband for a little time." — Now I had my rutting impudence on and a stiffening prick. She dawdled now, and I guessed by that, that my talk pleased her.

The streets were here narrower, with small but six-roomed houses in them, not well lighted, no shops, scarcely any traffic. I got to lewed hints which without coarse language were yet unmistakable. She laughed suppressing it, and then, "What would your wife say if she heard you?" "What would your husband say if he knew we were talking about fuck — getting children," — stopping short at the word fuck purposely, as if it had escaped me accidentally. — "You're not a gentleman, good night," and she walked on rapidly.

So did I, feeling now reckless, begged her pardon, said that her beauty had made me so long for her directly I had spoken to her, that I could think of nothing else. "Now don't follow me I'm just home, and mustn't be seen talking to a man, my neighbours may see me," and she stopped full under a gas lamp, staring at me full eyed. "My God how handsome you are, do meet me tomorrow, your husband needn't know." "He's abroad," said she, "but I dare not — pray leave me." "I will if you'll kiss me." "I won't sir." — She walked on, stopped between the lamps where it was darker, and directly a pedestrian had passed us I gave her a kiss spite of her sham resistance. — "Oh let me have you, or my prick will burst." — Thinking I should not succeed, I resolved that I might as well indulge in lewed utterances as not. I could but lose a chance, and there is always pleasure in saying words of love or lust to a strange woman. — "Oh! you're disgraceful," said she, in a low tone of voice.

How I wish I could experience a female's cuntal and mental sensations, as desire for a male enters her brain and body. I know that one of the results is a moistening, for I have felt many a cunt when desire was coming on. — Mrs. ***'s cunt I expect was in that state now, for she walked on very slowly, again asked if I was married, then if I lived about there, and at last after a long and seemingly thoughtful silence, "If you come in will you promise never to call again," said she, in an agitated manner. — I promised everything. — "We live over there, wait here, when you see a servant come out, watch till she's turned the corner, then come, I'll leave the door open, but I'm only going to chat with you mind. — No nonsense mind. If the servant doesn't come out, you must go." Her manner was nervous, agitated, hurried; before she had been quite composed.

I thought she was going to bilk me, having been humbugged thus before by more than one, and asked her name which she refused. Saying again that I was dying for her — she crossed the road, entered the house and the door closed. Five minutes passed which seemed to me a quarter of an hour, for I was in a fever of impatience, wild with lust, thinking of my chance of her hidden charms, then that she now was fooling me, and whilst deliberating whether I should risk knocking at her door, it opened, a servant appeared, turned the corner of the street, and in a minute I was in the house with the lady.

She had her bonnet and cloak off, and was a stout comely woman, at a guess twenty-eight years of age. "You mustn't stop long," said she, "my servant's only gone on an errand," — and she sat down on a sofa. The room was comfortable, of the sort which bespoke an income of a few hundreds a year, not a bit of the flash arrangement of a gay woman's rooms. "What did you want to come in here for," said she with that humbugging sham which a woman can put on, as if *she* didn't know what I had come for, and what she had let me in for. — She must have known.

No time was to be lost, so I plugged at once. "My love, to fuck you," and in a second had my hand between the lips of her nick. "Oh don't," she cried loudly, closing a pair of fat thighs on my hand, but not tightly, "you shan't do that." — But my fingers next moment were rubbing her clitoris, now feeling the mouth of the avenue, in another she had hold of my prick in her little hand, and still saying, "Oh don't, you shan't," our lips joined, silently we were handling each other's fucking apparatus, till her thighs moved restlessly, and my prick was at furnace heat. Then gently I pushed her back on the sofa, and in a not very comfortable position, my prick was shedding its pearly libation into her spending cunt. Ah!

what Elysium to grasp the unknown smooth buttocks, to plunge my burning pego up to its balls in the cunt of an untasted beauty, to hear her gentle sighs and murmurs, as the hot spunk throbs out into her hot thirsty vagina; and then to settle down tranquilly with prick in the viscosity of our spendings, thinking of what we had done together and what we had done it with, till the shrinking implement of my pleasure comes out of hers, that cunt so tight, but now loose and surrendering some of its libation, as the delicious conjunction of our bodies is broken. — Such was my pleasure with charming Mrs. *** three nights ago.

Sofas in small houses now are not like those of thirty years ago, on which I have stroked many a woman. — As my prick left her cunt I arose, and she rushed rapidly upstairs. In two minutes she returned. "You've washed that lovely cunt." — She laughed. "Let me see it." "Oh no." — How often I have heard that said, but it availed not the speaker.

She sat on the sofa. "I *will* see it," said I. — She refused. Then kneeling suddenly, I pushed up her petticoats, and buried my mouth between her closed thighs, kissing them upwards till my nose met the crisp hair of a fat soft motte, whilst my hands mounted to her plump buttocks. Then without resistance I pulled her to the sofa's edge. All felt to lips and nose so fresh, so dainty, so moist from the washing, and smelt so sweet whilst my mouth was there, so did the aroma of her healthy cunt rouse me, that distending her thighs, my lips met the clitoris. Out then went my tongue, gliding rapidly to and fro over the slippery gristly projection. "Oh you dirty man," she cried. All women not strumpets say that at the first gamahuche. But she surrendered herself to the luscious exercise, and her voluptuous sensations. I licked, till feeling a gentle quivering of her thighs and backside, I ceased, not wishing to make her spend. With my prick still hanging out I sat down beside her, and guided her hand to it, still sticky as it was with our spendings. She handled it looking at me with humid lustful eyes. — "Let me wash it," said I, wanting to get her to her bedroom.

"I'm so frightened of my servant coming back." "Send her out again if she does." — We went to her bedroom, on the floor was the basin in which she'd rinsed my libation out of her cunt. It was a comfortable room with a large bed, the gaslight burning. I cleared off the evidences of our pleasure from prick and balls, and said we'd do it on the bed. "Oh no — if my servant sees the bed rumpled." "Don't let her — I *will* see your lovely thighs and cunt," so saying I got my hand between her thighs, again standing up as we both were, and she let my fingers take their former place without hindrance.

Mistress M*** was hot cunted and no mistake, I saw it in her great luminous moist eyes, which looked at me in loving manner. I can tell that expression in them still more clearly, now that I write this. The voluptuous expression struck me strongly. — Pressed by me she mounted the bed, saying that I really must not stay long, but when side by side feeling each other's genitals, I found I was not ready for the encounter, having only discharged my semen a few minutes before. This unnerved me for a minute, for her cunt was ready, and she eager for fucking as it seemed to me.

Spending time in praising her beauty, kissing and feeling her cunt, I thought of gamahuching her, tho my letch for that had subsided. So kneeling between her legs, I put my head between her thighs, kissed her motte, and settling my tongue on her little clitoris, began the lingual amourous game, getting my hands under her backside, to lift it up and facilitate it. — "Oh — don't you dirty man," she jerked out, but her cunt in its delight silenced her. The lady liked the lick, her thighs widened out, her cunt rose up involuntarily, nature was on my side, restless her thighs got, her belly and bum gave little jerks, then her cunt pressed up to meet my mouth. — "Ahar — rr — oho — aharr — har —," a tight grasp of the hair of my head, then quietness of thighs and belly, and a salt flush over my tongue, told me she had spent.

Flushed with this victory, inflamed by taste, smell, and feel of her fat full lipped cunt, proudly my prick rose up to duty, and scarcely was her body tranquil after her spend, than dropping on to her belly, my prick was buried up to its root in her, glorying in its power, enjoying the moist soft pressure, but not impatient for exercise it lay enjoying the carnal tingle awhile, and in quiet concupiscence we talked, in the short sentences which alone I can then utter. "Your cunt's lovely, did you like my licking it? — Do you feel my stiff prick in your cunt? — how stiff it is. — It will spend in it soon." "Oh — oh — oh," she murmured at each lewed phrase. But whilst still dallying with my prick, it was getting less in her. "Oh! if my servant should come home." — A sense of this possibility urged me, and thrusting hard, banging my prick tip against her womb, dashing my balls against her buttocks, till responsive her belly heaved up to mine, her thighs clipped mine, and heaving and sighing, "Aha — aha — ahar —ar — ar," whilst I sobbed out my fucking slogan, "fuck — spunk — prick — cunt — c — hunt," I filled her split again with sperm.

She rose hurriedly, excitedly, saying I must go, I really must. "For God's sake don't get me into trouble. — I'm married — Really I am — he's abroad. — Well my name's **** — you'd find it out by asking, but for God's sake never come here again. — If you're a gentleman you won't, will you? I *will* meet you on Thursday next if you'll only go now — go at once. — Do — pray now." — All said so anxiously that I hastily went. She almost pushed me to the door, looked out, saw no servant, and away I went, thinking all the evening I'd been in luck, and that it was one of the quickest bits of fucking I'd ever got with a modest woman in all my life.

Next day I felt proud, yet vexed with adultery, believing her to be really married. It seems my fortune for married women to fall to my arms, tho I object to it and always did. Yet I wrote with feigned hand and false name, time and place for the meeting on Thursday, and went there thinking and half hoping she wouldn't come. I had paid for a room at a house formerly much visited by me, but which I had not entered for some years.

She met me and soon we were in a snug bedroom. — There she lifted her veil and was crying. She had not spoken in the street. "I've come, but I won't let you do anything." "Nonsense, why did you come?" "To beg you never to go near my house again, I've been so frightened ever since. How I came to let you in I don't know. — I'm sure I shall be found out," — and much more was said of the same sort, with much excitement and with tears. At first I was upset, but recovering, argued with her, said that I'd never go near her house, that this should be our last meeting, but now we would do it, no one could possibly know. She refused, I tried to get my hand up her clothes, but she resisted strongly. — "Only to feel it, let me, that's not fucking." But she wouldn't. Then standing up, I pulled out my ruby tipped pego, stiff as a horn, bursting with desire, and poked it towards her face as she sat.

"Let me, let me, dear, only once, let me rub it and only spend between your thighs, I won't put it in your cunt — feel it, and let me only feel that lovely cunt I've fucked —frig me then." — Thus I went on, raising baudy imagery in her mind, kissing her, endearing her, stimulating her senses, sitting by her side, trying every now and then to feel her quim, but without success.

I had brought no wine with me as I usually do on such occasions, but sent for sherry, the finest they could get and not to mind the price. It came, Mrs. M*** took two glasses of it, her tears had dried, her fears subsided as we talked. She told me that her husband was managing clerk to a merchant, and had gone abroad to their agency; she'd never been left alone before. He was fifty-five, she twenty-six, her relatives thought it a good match so she married him, tho he was so old. He was a good man. "He fucks you," said I. "He does what husbands do," she replied, "how I came to let you in I don't know, I've been in fear ever since. — You'll never come near me again will you?" If she said this once she did a dozen times till I was sick of hearing it, and at length not getting a feel of her quim, said, — "Why did you come here if you didn't mean to let me do it?"

An hour had gone in begging, and attempting, and at last I felt her cunt. Then she took her bonnet off, then took another glass of wine. — Then I frigged her a bit, then she handled my tool which settled her; her lust was roused, her cunt craving, sensations of voluptuous delight were coursing thro her body and brain, and she mounted the bed. — Up I threw her petticoats, a lovely pair of white thighs parted, my belly met her, prick and cunt joined, and my libation mingled with her liquids in transports of pleasure.

Never did woman enjoy a fuck more, but her anxiety about getting with child was great. She uncunted me soon. "Oh get off — pray do," and rushed to wash. — She'd never been with child. "But I might — mightn't I?" I couldn't say no when I thought of the many who have ascribed paternity to me; in some cases truly enough. Heavily I have had to pay for that cunt splashing with my sperm, but it was worth paying for. The heaven of life is found between a woman's thighs, women have all the after trouble, we none, and we ought to pay for all the trouble we give, all we beget.

She'd done the deed of darkness with me again, and like all the others under similar circumstances, was ready to let me do it more. For a minute only had I seen her thighs and motte, and now insisted on seeing all in every way. I risked the sheets, induced her to come to bed, and, in chemise and shirt only we laid side by side, limbs interlacing, hands groping and feeling, cock and cunt waiting their next introduction to each other. We talked of fucking, and nothing but fucking and sexual pleasure. Never she declared had she been gamahuched before, knew of it, her sister's husband had done it to her sister, her own husband never to *her*. He was a widower when she married him, a staid man, very fond of her, fucked her once a week, if twice it was on Sundays after church. — I have an intense curiosity about the ways of men with their wives, and never failed to ask about them of the frisky matrons whom I have fucked. — Most of them avoid the subject, this beauty didn't.

She was a fine, soft hazel eyed woman, full, fleshy, and inclining to stoutness, with full breasts, but short ones which didn't hang, with large thighs and buttocks, and thick not very symmetrical calves. — Her belly was large and ample, her cunt had roly-poly lips, yet not the pouters of a skinny woman. The furrow between them was deep, and with a well defined crimson line down half way from a fullish clitoris, and there the red was lost. The nymphæ were small and pretty — if there be such a thing as pretty nymphæ. — Dark brown hair, darker than that on her head covered a very full fat motte, it was a handful, a veritable pincushion. The hair grew less and less and ceased altogether on the lips towards the lower or buttocks end of her cunt, and not a vestige of hair was on her buttocks near her bum hole, for curious, I pulled the cheeks apart to see, which elicited, "What are you doing?" It was in brief a fat, full, well developed cunt, largish in appearance. I praised it and said I'd seen a thousand. — "Oh! what a wicked story," said she.

Then, for I was not ready, and somehow gamahuching a nice woman who is not a strumpet pleases me at times much more than formerly — I gave her a spend by the sole aid of my tongue. — Then I fucked her again. Then in bed we both slept a while, then she had fears and cried a bit. Then after repose, I frigged her as still she lay in bed with me. There is something so exciting to my senses in a nice woman who is a stranger to me, that I essayed my powers again. A long job it was, tho for five days I had kept myself chaste. My cock had had enough at the third, my balls kept back their balsam, and I nearly at one period of the exercise thought of admitting myself a failure. However I succeeded and gave her a fourth fucking, tho the lady I think wetted my cunt rammer more than the rammer wetted her cunt. — But the lady was contented.

Talking with her after I'd frigged her, she said her husband had never done *that* to her. — "Lor — he's quite a quiet man, but he's very good to me." Then I heard that he'd settled a little money on her when they married, to provide for her in case of his early death. "Oh! I'm in such fear of its being found out. — What made me talk to you and let you, I don't know." "You'd not been fucked for a month and wanted it badly." "Oh no, that it wasn't." — She waited with me till quite dark, frightened of being seen going out of an "improper house" as she called it. When she left we had been there some hours, had drunk nearly two bottles of wine, and eaten nothing. I was quite fucked out and tired, not being quite so young now, and she seemed the same.

Of course I never called at the house again, nor did I desire her, tho the temporary connection had been most pleasant. But I drove past the house a couple of years after and out of curiosity enquired at a baker's close by, if any one of the name lived there. I found that they did. But altho that set my cock stiffening a bit, I should have been a blackguard had I sought her, and had no desire to figure in a divorce case.

This was a nice little variety in my amours. How it came about even now astonishes me a little, much as I know of the unexpected consequences of mutual lust on a man and woman thrown together by accident. It must have been that a month's abstinence had left her so full, that meeting me just when a wave of lust heated her cunt, she gave way to opportunity and my incitements. Perhaps curiosity played its part, and she longed to see what another man's prick could do. I hope she hasn't tried a third, for that might bring her to grief. But a second prick they say makes always a woman long for a third. A well known baud once said that to me as her experience.

END OF VOLUME EIGHTH.

[illegible] period of the [illegible]

[illegible] a quiet man, [illegible] I heard that he [illegible] money [illegible]

[illegible] I don't know. [illegible]

[illegible]

[illegible] of the [illegible]

[illegible]

[illegible]

Wordsworth Classic Erotica

ANONYMOUS

The Autobiography of a Flea

Beatrice

Eveline

'Frank' and I

First Training

A Night in a Moorish Harem

My Lustful Adventures

The Pearl

Randiana

The Romance of Lust

Sadopaideia

Suburban Souls

Teleny

Venus in India

The Way of a Man with a Maid

The Whippingham Papers

GUILLAUME APOLLINAIRE

The Amorous Exploits of a Young Rakehell

AUBREY BEARDSLEY & JOHN GLASSCO

The Story of Venus and Tannhauser

GIOVANNI BOCCACCIO

Selections from The Decameron

JOHN CLELAND

Memoirs of a Woman of Pleasure – Fanny Hill

ROBIN DE BEAUMONT ED.

The Pretty Women of Paris

FRANK HARRIS

My Life and Loves

IN FIVE VOLUMES

SHEIKH NEFZAOUI

The Perfumed Garden

TRANSLATED BY SIR RICHARD BURTON

EDWARD SELLON

The New Epicurean

The Ups and Downs of Life

DR C. J. SCHEINER

Essential Guide to Erotic Literature

IN TWO VOLUMES

SMITHERS AND BURTON

Priapaia

VATSYAYANA

The Kama Sutra

TRANSLATED BY SIR RICHARD BURTON & F. F. ARBUTHNOT

'WALTER'

My Secret Life

IN FIVE VOLUMES

LI YU

The Carnal Prayer Mat